Praise for Lynn Kerstan

Dangerous Deceptions

"Dark intrigue and delicious desire . . . come together beautifully in . . . Kerstan's spellbinding new Regency trilogy."　　　　　　　　　　　　　　　*—Booklist*

"Not romance to be lightly skimmed, but to be savored."　　　　　　　　　　　*—Library Journal*

"Kerstan holds you spellbound . . . and has you begging for more."　　　　　　　*—Romantic Times*

"A truly unforgettable story."　　*—The Best Reviews*

"A master storyteller. Riveting and romantic, sensual and suspenseful, passionate and poignant."
　　　　　　　　　　　—Romance Reviews Today

The Silver Lion

"With typical Kerstan flair, this riveting conclusion to the author's stunning trilogy combines electrifying sensuality with strong, passionate protagonists caught in a seemingly impossible situation." *—Library Journal*

"Subtly nuanced characters, exquisitely sensual love scenes, and a plot laced with dangerous suspense and perilous secrets all blend brilliantly together."
　　　　　　　　　　　　　　—Booklist

continued . . .

Heart of the Tiger

The Golden Leopard

"Exquisitely written . . . extraordinarily well-developed characters, stunning sensuality, and a few surprises. A truly exceptional, potentially award-winning romance." —*Library Journal*

"Readers won't be able to put down Kerstan's emotionally captivating and highly dramatic adventure." —*Booklist*

"This is a must read by a marvelous talent." —*Romantic Times*

"An exotic, absolutely riveting tale of suspense, adventure, and a love too strong to be denied. Enthralling from the first page to the last." —*Romance Reviews Today*

"I loved it . . . Delicious . . . An extremely fun book." —*All About Romance*

"A new star in the tradition of Mary Balogh, Lynn Kerstan moves onto my personal shortlist of must-read authors. . . . snappy, fast-paced, entertaining, [and] wonderfully witty." —*The Romance Reader*

continued . . .

Dangerous Passions

Lynn Kerstan

A SIGNET ECLIPSE BOOK

SIGNET ECLIPSE
Published by New American Library, a division of
Penguin Group (USA) Inc., 375 Hudson Street,
New York, New York 10014, USA
Penguin Group (Canada), 90 Eglinton Avenue East, Suite 700, Toronto,
Ontario M4P 2Y3, Canada (a division of Pearson Penguin Canada Inc.)
Penguin Books Ltd., 80 Strand, London WC2R 0RL, England
Penguin Ireland, 25 St. Stephen's Green, Dublin 2,
Ireland (a division of Penguin Books Ltd.)
Penguin Group (Australia), 250 Camberwell Road, Camberwell, Victoria 3124,
Australia (a division of Pearson Australia Group Pty. Ltd.)
Penguin Books India Pvt. Ltd., 11 Community Centre, Panchsheel Park,
New Delhi - 110 017, India
Penguin Group (NZ), cnr Airborne and Rosedale Roads, Albany,
Auckland 1310, New Zealand (a division of Pearson New Zealand Ltd.)
Penguin Books (South Africa) (Pty.) Ltd., 24 Sturdee Avenue,
Rosebank, Johannesburg 2196, South Africa

Penguin Books Ltd., Registered Offices:
80 Strand, London WC2R 0RL, England

First published by Signet Eclipse, an imprint of New American Library,
a division of Penguin Group (USA) Inc.

First Printing, August 2005
10 9 8 7 6 5 4 3 2 1

SIGNET ECLIPSE and logo are trademarks of Penguin Group (USA) Inc.

Printed in the United States of America

PUBLISHER'S NOTE
This is a work of fiction. Names, characters, places, and incidents either are
the product of the author's imagination or are used fictitiously, and any resemblance to actual persons, living or dead, business establishments, events, or
locales is entirely coincidental.

The publisher does not have any control over and does not assume any
responsibility for author or third-party Web sites or their content.

If you purchased this book without a cover you should be aware that this
book is stolen property. It was reported as "unsold and destroyed" to the
publisher and neither the author nor the publisher has received any payment
for this "stripped book."

The scanning, uploading, and distribution of this book via the Internet or via
any other means without the permission of the publisher is illegal and punish-
able by law. Please purchase only authorized electronic editions, and do not
participate in or encourage electronic piracy of copyrighted materials. Your
support of the author's rights is appreciated.

For Trixie (Mary Strand), Kiki (Carol Prescott), and So-fee-ah (Jill Limber). We were born to be wild and are living up to our mission!

—Bunny

Chapter 1

London, June 1817

You are summoned, for your failures, your guilt, and your debts, to undertake a mission that will test your every claim to character and courage. Expect danger to the point of death. . . .
—From a letter to Col. Lord Marcus Cordell, May 1817, Paris

"She's the one." Sir Peregrine Jones gestured with his ribboned quizzing glass. "Over there by the potted palm tree. Your fiancée."

The palm was potted on the other side of the large marquetry floor where couples had begun taking their places for the next set. Col. Lord Marcus Cordell glimpsed four or five females clustered around it like sugared dates, and then a line of dancers blocked his view. "Which one do you mean?"

"Did no one describe her to you?" Sir Peregrine frowned. "I thought you were to be provided a miniature, a biography, and a prepared story to give out."

"I received only a letter of summons and instructions to rendezvous with a gentlemen who would explain the assignment. But when I arrived at the meeting place, his servant delivered a note of apology and directed me to look for you here. And you, it seems, know little more than I."

"At least I know the identity of your partner. Lady Eve will tell you the rest."

Cordell was still chewing on an earlier morsel of information. "You said fiancée. We are already betrothed, then?"

"As I understand it, that was the plan. Which means, my dear, that you ought to be galloping over to your lady fair instead of skulking in this alcove."

"And to which of those ladies should I gallop?" Cordell clasped stiff fingers behind his back, a pose his men would have recognized as the quiet before a lightning strike. "I am signally unimpressed, sir, with this Black Phoenix organization and its way of doing business."

"I can see where you would be." Sir Peregrine withdrew a lacy handkerchief from his sleeve and patted his forehead. "We're generally better prepared at the outset of a mission, but once an endeavor is under way, things are always going amiss. Malefactors cannot be counted on to do the logical thing. If you are uncomfortable with improvisation—"

"Let us get on with it, then. Just point me to the right target."

"I've changed my mind about the galloping," said Sir Peregrine. "Unless you can transform yourself into an eager swain—"

"Good God."

"I gather not. And wearing that expression, you'll frighten the ladies. We had better approach by way of a proper introduction, which I shall now arrange. Later, you can explain that you had chosen to keep your relationship secret for a time. Lady Eve will provide reason for the duplicity."

Not a bad suggestion, Cordell mentally conceded, especially from so astonishing a source. In a world full of odd creatures, Sir Peregrine Jones was odder than most. "By all means," he said. "Set to it."

Shoulders propped against the wall, he watched Sir Peregrine, iridescent as dragonfly wings in his outrageous lavender coat and red waistcoat, flit from group to group. The five women were still in their circle, like witches hovering over a cauldron. He could see them only through the line of dancers, which was rather like watching a play through windblown shutters.

Finally Sir Peregrine alighted near the palm tree and, after flamboyant bows and hand kissing, deftly separated one of the females from the others. Above middle height. Pale hair. Trim figure. Moments later Sir Peregrine took flight again, and Lady Eve returned to her klatch, never once looking in her betrothed's direction.

How the devil had he got himself into this coil? He ought to be selling out his commission—not that ambitious soldiers were lining up to buy commissions these days—and trudging to the family swamp in Norfolk. With the war over, duty had been nagging him to go home, but not to any great effect. It had been almost two years since Waterloo.

Sir Peregrine, easy to pick out even in a crowded ballroom, appeared to be looking for someone. He must be a popular chap, because people kept drawing him over for conversation. Finally he was in motion again, arm in arm with a tall woman who, when she came near enough for measurement, turned out to reach nearly Cordell's own six foot and a bit.

Sir Peregrine released her arm. "Lady Etheridge, may I present Col. Lord Marcus Cordell, newly arrived from France and already enchanted with the second-loveliest lady at the ball. He begs you for an introduction."

"Indeed?" A well-shaped brow went up. "The gentleman does not strike me as a begging man."

"That would be correct, madam." Cordell bowed. "Until tonight."

She was slender, in her forties he would guess, her dark hair streaked with white and gracefully swept back from an attractive face into a chignon. Unfortunately, she was also the wife of Lord Etheridge, master manipulator in the Lords, who had caused no end of trouble for an army desperately short of munitions and supplies.

"Then I must oblige you," she said, smiling. "Lady Eve—Perry confided the identity of your quarry—is something of a protégé, and I am delighted to provide her with a dashing partner for the next dance. That striking ensemble is the uniform of the Thirteenth Light Dragoons, is it not?"

"A good eye, madam."

They began the excursion around the edges of the ballroom to where the ladies were still huddled together, apparently content without male company. With his gaze fixed on Lady Eve, he saw the moment she detached herself from the group and, without ever looking his direction, put herself on an intersecting course.

Neatly done. The four of them came together as if

by accident, and with a smile of pleasure, Lady Eve acknowledged Lady Etheridge and Sir Peregrine. She had well-shaped lips, he couldn't help noticing, and a complexion that put him in mind of Dutch porcelain. Finally she turned to him, her expression all delight . . . unless you were close enough to see her eyes.

A pure, transparent blue, they were colder than a winter storm in the Pyrenees.

He thought, for a moment, that she recognized him. Not impossible . . . she would be expecting a man in a blue uniform. But that wasn't it. She seemed to know him, to have known him for a long time.

Lady Etheridge began the presentation, her words tickling at the edge of his awareness. He managed to bow at the right time, murmured his delight at making Lady Eve's acquaintance, and puzzled at the way she'd looked at him.

The arctic regard had slid underground like an icy stream, and she was all sunshine now—polite, genteel sunshine. But the cold sensation at his spine persisted. And the conviction.

She hated him.

Sir Peregrine was flattering her outrageously, admiring her gown and demanding a length of the blue fabric to create a waistcoat for himself. Sophisticated and at ease, Cordell's companions made ballroom conversation while he stood dumb as a camp stool, trying to fit together his impressions of this formidable young woman.

Supremely confident, that was certain, controlling this encounter without apparent effort. Hair the color of spring wheat, arranged with little artifice. He liked that, and the simplicity of her necklace and ear bobs.

Only the bracelet, breaking the line of an elbow-length kid glove, seemed out of place. It was a strange piece, clearly inexpensive, and the silver inlaid with gold thread reminded him of workmanship he'd seen in Spain.

When his gaze returned to her face, she met it with an expression of amusement. "Are we boring you, Colonel? The waltz has only just begun. Would you care to join the line?"

He blinked. Had she just asked him to dance? Only courtesans did that, at least on the Continent. Nodding to Lady Etheridge and Sir Peregrine, he held out his arm, Lady Eve placed a hand on it, and he led her onto the floor.

"That was forward of me," she said, "but we couldn't keep standing there rabbiting about taffeta. We needn't dance if you don't know the patterns."

"There are ballrooms in Paris," he said, irritated. "Have I at some time offended you, madam? Or did you take me in dislike on a whim?"

"I'm not sure I've ever had a whim, sir. They are so impractical. And how could I dislike you? We have never met."

He had time during the next figure, which required several intricate maneuvers, to analyze her response. Evasion, followed by a return of the ball to his court. "Is it the mission you dislike, then?" he said when they could speak without being overheard. "Why not withdraw? Surely there is someone who can replace you."

"But no one so ideally suited to this mission. It is you who will be difficult to account for, especially if you continue frowning at me. No one will credit that we are madly in love."

"Are we?" Just then, he was required to take her

in his arms and twirl her round and round. Only for a short time, until the promenade resumed, but it left him surprisingly breathless. "Or is there some other rationale for our secret betrothal?"

She looked up at him, a little smile curving her lips. "I am not in a delicate condition, if that is what you mean. But there is no long-standing arrangement, I'm afraid. That part of the plan has collapsed. And in consequence, we shall now have to fall in love at first sight."

He missed a step. Recovered. "Or withdraw. Phoenix seems incapable of the simplest tactical maneuver."

"I wouldn't know about that. But they were in something of a hurry to launch the investigation. Young men are being murdered."

Point to the lady. "That is nearly the only thing I have been told. And that we were betrothed, which it seems we are not."

"All of which you find vexing, and that will serve no one. You prefer being in command, of course. I rather like it myself. But we must begin from where we now stand and plan the next steps together. Unless you really do mean to decamp?"

"No. But we can scarcely plot strategy in these circumstances. Is there a way to be private without drawing attention?"

"Not here. A number of my suitors are glaring daggers at us even now, and when the music ends, more than one will try to separate us."

"In demand, are you?"

"Under siege, since long before my come-out." She dipped under his arm, passed behind his back. "An enormous dowry has that effect. You will occasion a great deal of animosity, sir, by cutting them out."

"For a short time only. When the killer is found, you'll send me packing."

A small frown knitted her forehead. She opened her mouth, seemed to think better of speaking, and then said in a rush, "It is you, sir, who must jilt me."

"Good God. I'll do no such thing."

"Colonel!" She was tugging at his sleeve. "You have come to a full stop."

So he had, and the dancers following the stalled couple were stacking up behind, looking confused. Swallowing an oath, he seized Lady Eve's hand, towed her in the direction of the refreshment table, grabbed a glass of lemonade, and led her through a set of French windows onto a balcony. "Drink this," he said, releasing her hand and putting the glass into it.

The night breeze lifted the curtains and cooled his hot forehead. She was staring into the lemonade, still wearing her little frown, probably wondering if she was alone on a high balcony with a madman.

"Perhaps you don't understand," he said finally. "When a betrothal is ended, no matter the reason, it is the lady calls it off. That is her privilege. Then she need not endure the shame of being"—he could feel himself getting deeper and deeper into hot water—"well, sent back."

"Like returned goods," she said sweetly.

"Precisely." Relieved, he plunged ahead. "A man can survive a rejection in the marriage mart. But he cannot, having given his word to marry, cancel the arrangement. It would be a violation of honor that no reputation could forebear."

"And why, Colonel, is breaking one's word not a violation of honor for a woman?"

This was a trap. He knew it. The logical response,

that a woman did not actually, or at least technically, *give* her word, got cut off at the tip of his tongue. He cast about for something less inflammatory. "It is, of course. But ladies are forgiven such indiscretions."

"Why is that? Generous of you, to be sure, but honor is honor, is it not? You might overlook the incident, but the woman has nonetheless proven herself dishonorable."

"It's . . ." He propped his hands on the wrought-iron railing and looked up at the moon, wishing an answer would write itself there. "You are right, of course. But women are notorious for changing their minds. Men have come to expect it. A quirk of feminine nature, that is all."

"Then, if not in truth and steadfastness, where is it that a woman's honor resides? In her chastity?"

Even a thoroughly befuddled male wouldn't rise to *that* bait. "I expect she must be the judge," he said. "We are speaking of a unique and artificial situation in which no sentiments are involved. This is a matter of business, madam, in which the usual forms should be strictly observed. That you accepted a ragged soldier at all will be put down to youthful folly. Within a short time, our betrothal will be forgotten."

He thought she would strike back. But when he looked over, he saw color on her cheeks, silvered by moonlight, and the frown had returned.

"It is strange," she said, "to speak of the end of an engagement before it has begun. But you ought not to commit yourself to this endeavor without knowing what will be required of you."

"Are you saying my choice is to surrender my honor or to reject the mission?"

"Not . . . exactly. I believe that for your part, more

vanity than honor is at stake here, while I stand to lose a great deal more. To accept a proposal and later turn the gentleman away would have serious, if not destructive consequences to my well-considered, carefully chosen plans for the future. They cannot come to pass if I am thought to be flighty, irresponsible, and, yes, dishonorable."

"Perhaps it is you who should ask Black Phoenix for a replacement."

"But I have given my word."

Damn and blast. He turned to face her directly, to be pinioned again by those blue-ice eyes. "What is a man," he said, "when he loses his honor? What has he left, when his reputation is gone?"

"Just so."

He felt, again, the force of her contempt.

A strategic retreat was in order. "We cannot resolve this now," he said, ignoring the flash of resentment in her eyes. "Perhaps circumstances will direct the choice, or a compromise might be reached. Shall we resume negotiations some other time, and in a less public place? You can, instead, tell me what this mission is all about."

"Tomorrow, I think. As you said, this is not a suitable venue for secrets and.intrigues. At seven, I shall ride in Hyde Park. Perhaps you will join me there."

"As you wish."

After a curt bow he escorted her as far as the ballroom door and left the house, fairly certain war had just been declared. At the least, a gauntlet had been thrown down.

What had Lady Eve's inexplicable enmity to do with the summons from Black Phoenix?

Chapter 2

Portugal, Sept. 1810

> *Exchanged to the Light Division, and the 13th to boot. I've already run afoul of the captain. He don't like it, R says, having relatives serving in the same regiment. Thinks we'll get up to trouble, and likely we will. His name is Cordell. The chaps call him Cannonballs, but he's mostly quiet. Just gives you a look and you hop to it. Bayonets for eyes. I'm on picket duty most times, which is better than I had it with the 3rd Hussars. This is no terrain for cavalry, and I've no patience with sitting around playing cards. I mean to become an exploring officer. But it's the captain directs intelligence and reconnaissance operations, so I must win myself into his good graces. When the dustup about the goat settles, I'll give it a run. R says I need a plan. You could think of one, I'd wager.*
>
> > *Yrs. Etc., J*

A few laggard clouds scuttled across the early-morning sky, following the rainstorm that had swept through London in the hours before dawn. Already the sun was drying the paths, but moisture still gleamed on wet branches, shiny leaves, and the blades of thick grass in Hyde Park.

Eve, wearing her favorite dark blue riding habit and a dashing feathered hat with a scrap of netted lace to conceal her eyes, guided her mare sedately though the Stanhope Gate. Nothing in her demeanor betrayed her tension to the passersby, or to the sharp-witted servant riding beside her.

I will find you, Cordell had said, before leaving her last night.

Unready quite yet to be found, she had come in by a road that he, a stranger to London, would not know. This time, when she encountered him, she must be entirely in control of herself. Nothing must give her away.

Last night, she had been overconfident. Despite her years of social practice and the hours of rehearsal for their first meeting, it had all gone wrong. She had turned. Looked up. And at the sight of him, the ropes of ice twisted inside her had unraveled. She'd felt a blast of fire surge through her, was nearly certain it had reached her eyes. They had burned and burned.

When her vision cleared, when she saw his eyes, something . . . Oh, she was not certain what she had seen. Surprise. Awareness. The swift unsheathing of a saber. For an instant, she was sure he had recognized what she was. What she intended.

But then it was gone, what must have been his instinctive response to a surprise attack. And the flash in his eyes might have been a trick of the light. She hoped that what he had seen in hers, if indeed he had seen anything at all, was being interpreted the same way.

With a tug on the reins, she resolutely turned south

along a path that led to Hyde Park Corner, where he would surely be waiting.

And then she saw him.

Atop a rise about fifty yards from the path stood a single oak. And beneath it, on a steed the color of mahogany, Colonel Cordell sat with the ease of a cavalry officer, at once relaxed and alert. Sunlight, dappling the wet grass beneath the tree, transformed the rainwater to a mist that curled around his horse's hooves and fetlocks. Were she fanciful, she'd have imagined him rising up from a mystical realm.

He was in uniform again, blue and buff with a decorated officer's lace, but less adorned than the formal dress of last night's ballroom. What he might have worn on the Peninsula, she thought, before leading a charge.

She must be on her guard, especially now. Especially with this man. She turned, deliberately, to engage Mrs. Styles in conversation about the fine weather, all the while watching him from the corners of her eyes.

He had looked on guard as well, as if expecting an enemy to ride into view.

And sure enough, one had.

Deciding he should make the approach, she focused her gaze on the puzzled servant and continued by the spot where he was waiting, expecting to hear the sounds of his horse as he moved to join her.

Nothing. A bird flew overhead. Children called to one another not far away. Two horsemen doffed their hats and went single file as they rode past. A woman carrying a basket filled with oranges crossed the path in front of her. A small boy came next, straining at leading strings clutched by a uniformed maid. Eve could no longer contain herself. She looked over her shoulder to the tree.

Cordell was gone.

So much for her tactics. It was the veil, she decided. He hadn't recognized her.

But in that case, he'd still be there, looking out for her.

Outmaneuvered and privately mortified, she went on her way. Damned if she'd chase after the man. Or assume she could so easily bend him to her will, as she had done with so many other overconfident males. A display of apparent compliance when next they met would turn the trick. He wouldn't be expecting that.

Fairly sure she had dashed their plans altogether, she wasn't expecting to see him expertly separate himself from the crowd near Hyde Park Corner and contrive to meet up with her where the traffic was thinnest.

"Lady Eve," he said, nodding in lieu of removing his hat, which he wasn't wearing.

She hadn't noticed that before. But she could not miss the way he was looking at her. Bayonets for eyes.

Putting a bright expression on her face, she advanced her mare a pace. "Why, it's Colonel Cordell. What a surprise. Styles, Lady Etheridge presented this gentleman to me only last night. You won't mind falling back while we renew our acquaintance?"

The tight-lipped woman had minded, of course, and was following all too closely as Eve and Cordell rode side by side off the path and into the heart of the park.

Eve kept expecting him to read her a lecture, or serve her up a coals-of-fire excuse for being late. But he said nothing, and still nothing, until the tense silence began to squeeze at her throat.

Just when words she would likely regret were about

to pop out of her mouth, he slapped a hand against his thigh.

"If that woman gets any closer," he said, "my horse's tail will be brushing her teeth. How are we to converse? Why don't you order her away? Is she not your servant?"

"That's exactly it. My own servants are chosen in great part for their lack of interest in what I do, but this one belongs to Lady Etheridge, who imagines I require more intensive supervision. Whenever I go out, she dispatches Bertha Styles, her longtime maid and companion, to play watchdog."

"What sort of trouble does she expect you to stir up?"

The rebuke singed her ears. "Lady Etheridge fancies I am in danger."

Cordell looked over, frowning. "From me?"

"Not yet. But after Styles delivers a report of this morning's events, you'll probably go on the list."

A swift mental debate then, while Eve calmed her temper and considered how much to tell him. "There have been two incidents, sir, which disturbed Lady Etheridge to the point of concern for my safety. It's all nonsense. They were the merest accidents, and only a bonnet I especially favored has been wounded."

"Did the incidents occur before or after your involvement with our friends?"

"I assure you . . ." A glance at his face gave her warning to change course. "Oh, very well. The first came several days before I received the letter of summons. The other was about a week ago. There can be no connection."

"Later," he said, "you will provide the details. Let us put some distance between us and the hound."

By the first syllable of *distance,* Eve was on her way, the mare responding with enthusiasm. But Cordell must have anticipated her move, because he was with her from the first as they galloped across an open stretch of grass and through a scatter of trees. No one had ventured so early into this section of the park, and when they came out from the decorative woodland, they were alone. Still moving in concert, they ascended a long, sloping hill and reined to a halt.

"Here she comes already," Eve said as Styles approached the trees.

"One must respect dogged determination." Cordell dismounted. "Wave her off."

Styles, unable to pretend she couldn't see Eve making a windmill of herself on the hilltop, finally drew up in the shade and sat glaring at them. Especially when Cordell put his hands on Eve's waist to lift her down.

Eve was a little flummoxed by that as well, if only because he didn't wait to ask permission. It must have been the exhilarating gallop that left her breathless.

When she was on the ground, he took the reins of both horses in one hand and her elbow with the other. "We'll stay visible," he said. "Might Lady Etheridge suspect your involvement with Black Phoenix? Have you told anyone?"

Offended, she snatched her arm away. "Certainly not. I was enjoined to the strictest silence. Only Major Blair and Sir Peregrine are aware of the role I am to play."

"Speaking of which, this betrothal scheme would be more convincing if we followed through with the original plan. Why has it been scuttled?"

"On closer investigation, Phoenix discovered that you and I could not possibly have met before now."

"But in Paris, I encountered Lord and Lady Marbury on several occasions. Do you never travel with your parents?"

"No. I have yet to cross the channel, sir. Scotland is the farthest place I have visited."

"Then why not a secret courtship in England? I returned home to settle the estate after my father's death and remained for three months. Not in London, to be sure, but no one will remember where either of us ventured during that time."

"Probably not, since your father died in the spring of 1806. But we were unlikely to meet and tumble headlong into love, sir. I was eleven years old."

He stopped like a man who'd run into a wall. "The devil you say! That makes you—"

"Two and twenty, as of Wednesday last. Practically on the shelf. People will be unsurprised if I leap at the first eligible man to show an interest in me."

"I doubt it. You told me you'd rejected a score of suitors. But that's not the point. When I agreed to this infernal plan, I assumed the woman chosen to partner me would be more experienced. More . . . worldly. Not so vulnerable to the consequences of our masquerade."

"And older. But then, were you not a boy of fifteen when you bought a commission in the army? So much responsibility, given to so young an officer."

"And a devilish hash I made of it, too. Do you know about that as well?"

"No." That was true, but already she was babbling more information than she ought to have. "In preparation for our work, Major Blair told me a little about your history. That is all."

"Whereas I was told nothing whatsoever about you. And what I have since learned makes it clear you are unsuited for this mission. You will take offense, I presume, if I ask you again to withdraw?"

She looked down to where Styles had begun investigating the tree trunks, one by one, always moving in the direction of the hill. There would be little opportunity to converse while the chaperon was sniffing at their tracks. "I have considerably more experience than my years suggest, sir. And as for worldly, all my adult life has been spent in the heart of the world where we shall do our work. Pray let us close this subject. It is a waste of our time."

"In that case," he said briskly, "we shall proceed. So far I know only that two gentlemen have been murdered, and we are charged to discover the identity of their killer. Sir Peregrine said you would fill me in on the rest."

"There was a third murder last week, although the victim cannot be considered a gentleman. He was employed in the stables at Oatlands by the Duchess of York."

"And Phoenix believes the same killer is responsible for all three crimes? What links them together?"

"The victims were all men in their twenties, no more than five years separating the youngest from the oldest. But it is the manner of their deaths, or, rather, the manner in which they were left for discovery, that indicates a single killer. There appears to be a message of some kind being conveyed, although we have not deciphered it."

They had begun walking again, a relief given what

she had to describe next. "The first victim, Mr. Farley, was found in Lord Gorton's study the morning after Lady Gorton's rout. He was seated in front of the desk with his head immersed in a large tureen of soup."

"He drowned?"

"The coroner determined he had been poisoned and was already dead before the soup. All around the desk were plates of food . . . cakes, nuts, cheeses, biscuits, tarts. I knew him a little. The gentleman was plump and partial to sweets."

"Hardly a reason to kill him. What else?"

"Mr. Harbin, the second son of Lord Besserton, was also slain in London. A passerby found him in the mews. He was without clothing and laid across a wheelbarrow with ankles tied to wrists beneath it. There is more, but Major Blair would not tell me the rest."

She took a deep breath. "The third victim was a stableboy named Jeremy Brown. A groom came upon him in a back stall, half-buried in a pile of mucked straw and manure. He had been struck a single blow to the head with a rake. And his mouth was stuffed with golden guineas."

After a moment, Cordell said, "What in blazes is that woman doing with the trees?"

Eve looked again at Styles, who had nearly reached the foot of the slope. "Inspecting their bark, it seems. But she is about to run out of woodland. We should probably call an end for now."

"Two things first, since you are the only one in contact with Phoenix. I want the reports of the three investigations. Accounts of the inquests, testimony of witnesses, no record or detail is to be omitted."

"Major Blair said you'd ask. Phoenix is having copies inscribed and will deliver them as soon as may be."

"I also want all the information to be had about the three victims. How are they connected?"

"In no way we have yet discovered. Mr. Farley was from Liverpool, and the Besserton estate is in Exeter. So far, little has been discovered about the stablehand. He had been employed at Oatlands for only a short time, and he brought no references with him. The stablemaster said he was good at his job and kept to himself."

"There must be a link. Unless each of them, separately, managed to offend the killer. But if that is the case, it will be nearly impossible to focus our investigation. Let us proceed on the assumption these men knew one another and were involved in something that led the murderer to strike."

"Might they not have been chosen at random? Perhaps they were simply being used to transmit a message."

"That is possible, certainly. But the staging of their bodies seems to me intensely personal. The killer took pains to degrade his victims. We're clearly dealing with—" Halting, he muttered something in Spanish under his breath. "Devil take that female. Here she comes."

"Once we announce our betrothal," Eve said with a strained smile, "there will be more allowance for private time. You'll receive an invitation to dine at Holland House tonight, sir. Can you bring yourself to flirt with me there?"

"I have never been noted for my charm, madam." He laced his fingers, and when she'd placed a half-booted foot in the sling, lifted her onto the sidesaddle.

"Lady Holland is famously an admirer of Bonaparte. Why would she welcome a dour soldier to her home?"

"Because I asked her. Besides, you're fresh from France with all the Continental gossip. Every hostess will send you a card."

"Having doesn't mean sharing." He mounted in a single, swift motion. "Flirt with me as best you can, Lady Eve. And if you manage to persuade anyone I am worth your having, I'll eat my saddle."

Chapter 3

Portugal, May 1811

Jordan Blair finally got rid of his desk at Horseguards. It meant a transfer to the 4th Dragoons, but he'd have gone down to infantry if that's what it took to join the fighting. You never met him, I don't think. He was the friend who sent us the copies of dispatches, the ones you kept pulling out of my hands to read. I'm glad he's come. If there is fun to be had, he's in the middle of it. The chaps call him Prince Jordie because he set up an officers' mess that's almost as good as a club. I was never in a a club myself, so I can't say, but I don't think they have musical nights and theatricals and beetle races. R played Titania in Midsummer Night's Dream. *Couldn't hear his lines, I was laughing so much. Wish I could a take a part in a play m'self, but I'm too much on the move.*

Yrs, J

The hairdresser was weaving a string of pearls through Eve's upswept hair when a servant bearing an engraved card on a silver tray presented himself at the door.

Not long after, Eve made her way to the ground-floor parlor, the leather soles of her slippers sounding overloud against the polished marble stairs and entrance hall. Her parents' town house, fitted out to her mother's austere taste and nearly deserted in their absence, might as well have been a mausoleum. What little color there was seemed garish, like paint on a dead courtesan's lips. Near the front door, a liveried and bewigged footman stood to military attention. In the stark silence, Eve's hushed breathing seemed to reverberate off the walls.

She hated the house nearly as much as the estate where she had spent most of her life.

Entering the parlor, she saw Maj. Lord Jordan Blair standing before a window that looked out onto Grosvenor Square, his back to her, his head a little bowed. Accustomed to seeing him in his hussar uniform, she was surprised at the wilted riding coat and dusty boots.

Quietly retreating into the hall, she beckoned to the footman, sent him to fetch wine, and reentered the parlor with enough of a flourish to catch the major's attention.

He turned, eyes widening at her appearance, and made a low bow. The familiar smile was there, but she could not mistake the lines of weariness around his mouth and at his temples. His tousled light brown hair was powdered with dust.

"My apologies," he said in a strained voice, "for intruding at this hour in all my dirt. I should have waited until morning. You are on your way elsewhere."

"To Holland House, yes. But I can be late. Will you be seated, sir?"

The smile widened to a grin. "After riding halfway across England and back, seated is the last thing I wish to be. Will you mind if I stay on my feet and move around a bit?"

"Not at all." She regarded him closely. "Is something amiss? Has there been another . . . incident?"

"Inci— Ah. No. I went in search of Sir Peregrine, who is out, and because his lodgings are not far from here, I thought to stop by. You do look smashing, Lady Eve. Far too lovely for a dull political supper."

"I am kitted out to impress my new beau," she said, lowering herself onto a white damask-covered chair. "We shall be dull together while the Whigs have at one another over brandy and cigars."

"Then Cordell got himself presented to you last night? That's good news."

But he didn't sound pleased, any more than he'd ever sounded pleased when discussing the mission.

"Our progress will astound you," she said. "This morning we rode in Hyde Park. By tomorrow, the gossips will be chattering like magpies. And by week's end, our betrothal will be accomplished."

"Good." He'd begun to pace. "Good."

It wasn't, she could tell. Jordie Blair, always the gallant officer, seemed distracted and weary beyond the exertions of a long journey. She thought he was trying to tell her something unpleasant and could not bring himself to raise the subject.

The footman arrived, a cut-glass decanter in one hand and a tray of wineglasses in the other. While he arranged them on the sideboard, it occurred to Eve

that Major Blair's agitation might spring from a discovery she had long anticipated. Had he at last discovered her connection with Johnnie Branden?

Amazing, really, that the secret had gone undetected for so long. Blair, serving at Horseguards, was
the friend who had arranged for his friend the purchase of a commission and transportation to Portugal.
Later, when Blair was transferred to the Peninsula,
Johnnie often wrote about him.

She'd always wondered if Johnnie spoke of her to
his friends, in spite of their agreement. But after his
death and Blair's return to England, there was no sign
the major knew of the acquaintance. She was over-
reacting, surely. If he did know about her and Johnnie,
she'd never have been permitted to undertake a mission with Colonel Cordell, of all people. As it was,
she could scarcely believe that any friend of Johnnie's
would acknowledge, let alone associate with, such a
blackguard.

The major had accepted a glass of wine and taken
up a position by the wall. "The thing is, I came to tell
you that I have been separated from this endeavor
and will be departing tomorrow for Cornwall."

"But I thought you were directing the mission. Who
is it did the separating? For what reason?"

"The reasons do not signify. Decisions are made,
and this one is irreversible. Sir Peregrine will replace
me. When I have spoken with him, he'll know everything that I know."

"It is hardly the same. Besides, he doesn't strike me
as an effective conspirator."

"Don't be misled by Perry's eccentricities. He is by
far the best of us. And other assistance is at hand.

Cordell, on our instructions, did not bring his valet to England. We have provided one for him, and you are to have a new maid. Also a dog."

"For protection? None of this has been mentioned before."

"Cordell will protect you. The maid, Mrs. Kipper, will provide you more latitude than a servant who might see or hear something untoward. The dog has its uses as well. Mrs. Kipper will care for it and may, from time to time, offer you some advice. You would do well to heed it."

Uncertainty always roused her temper. "This is because you don't want me involved in the mission. I could tell from the first. Is it truly so dangerous? And why, if I am regarded as fragile and useless, was I summoned in the first place?"

"As window dressing, I suppose. The betrothal game will draw attention from Cordell's real purpose." Color tinged his cheeks. "Take no insult. You simply do not belong in this stew pot. I think there is little danger of a physical kind, but the risk to a young lady of your class is severe. Another woman should take your place, one not so vulnerable to the consequences of a faked betrothal."

"And what, sir, would those be?"

"You know very well." He put down his glass. "All your prospects will be dashed."

"Then I shall find other prospects. I am not without resources, Major Blair. And I'm sorry to say that when directed not to do something, I am seized with an irresistible impulse to leap into the fire."

"No fire-leaping," he said firmly. "If you must continue, I rely on your cool head to keep you from dashing into harm's way. The task itself should not be difficult. Beyond caution and a bit of clever acting, little is demanded of you. Which is why it is so damned unneces . . . Oh, sorry." Splayed fingers combed shakily through his hair. "I mean, there's no reason for you to ruin yourself to so little purpose."

She studied him for a few moments, testing his sincerity. It passed with flying colors. He knew nothing. His sole concern was for her reputation. He didn't realize that Black Phoenix had reached into a hat and pulled out an avenging angel—make that avenging devil—with a purpose that had nothing to do with finding a murderer.

Just as well the major was leaving the battlefield, she decided, reassuring him with a smile. He had once courted her in a desultory way, probably because it was the fashion for young gentlemen to have a go at the resistant Lady Eve, and in truth, she had liked him better than the others. He would learn, eventually, of her treachery, but she'd rather he wasn't there to witness it firsthand.

Meantime, she might as well pluck every feather of information he could provide. "I will not withdraw, sir. And whatever occurs, I shall never regret my decision. But since I must convince even my friends that I have sailed into love with a virtual stranger, I wish you would tell me everything you know of Colonel Cordell. What manner of gentleman is he?"

With a look of resignation, Major Blair picked up his glass, drained it, and made his way back to the decanter. "I cannot say, with any certainty. While the hussars were billeted and passing time waiting for an engagement, Cordell was off gathering intelligence, scouting roads and rivers, plotting transport, and generally making it possible for us to get where Wellington wanted us to fight. When we chanced to find ourselves in the same vicinity, Cordell occasionally joined us in the officers' mess. Never said much. Always seemed to be running calculations in his head."

Blair poured the wine. "He spent so much time alone that I expect he got out of the way of making conversation. The only time I saw him fight was at Waterloo. The Thirteenth was ordered to hold a series of low hills. Time and again, when the Frenchies tried to come up them, he led a charge to drive them back. Nothing to that, except he always knew when and how to rally his men and herd them back into position. No galloping at everything and winding up beyond the turning point like others I could name. Perfect discipline. He kept to the task at hand."

"And that's why he was summoned?"

"I cannot speak to the subject." The major's face had darkened. "But since Wellington chose him for the most difficult assignments, it is no surprise Phoenix would do the same. I'll tell you this much, Lady Eve. You may safely trust Cordell. You may rely on him. But if you are wise, never cross him."

"Why would I?" she said airily, concealing her disappointment. Blair had told her little that she had not already learned from Johnnie's letters. "We will be working together, after all, against a common enemy. Or several, because when my parents learn of the betrothal, they will descend on us like a pair of overbred Furies."

"Are they not away from England? I thought that had been arranged."

At this, Eve shivered. If Black Phoenix could manipulate her parents all the way to the Continent, she saw difficulties ahead for her own plans. "Wherever they are, the news will bring them home in a rush. Cordell isn't of sufficient rank to satisfy their ambitions, so they will devote themselves to prying us apart. Do you see? This will play right into our little drama. When the betrothal is broken off, they will claim credit and free me of being regarded as a jilt."

It wouldn't happen that way, of course, but the major looked relieved by her assessment. He was an awfully kind man, she thought . . . which made him the last man she wanted around her in the immediate future.

After a great struggle, her conscience had been wrestled into a dark corner, bound, gagged, and fed an overdose of laudanum. No gentleman with refined morals must be permitted to rouse the creature hidden there.

When Blair had given her a few instructions, she accompanied him to the door, where he suddenly drew her to one side. Whispering so that the footman would not overhear, he said, "Should this mission turn to ashes for you, remember this. You needn't become an outcast. We'll not permit it. If Cordell does not marry you, I will."

Chapter 4

Portugal, Sept. 1810

*About the goat, then. My first week with the 13th,
R and I hosted a supper for the other officers. R
bought the wine, and I was dispatched for the
goat. Found a good one, not easy when the army's
been in an area for a while, and a pricey fellow
he was. Worth it, though. We roasted the goat on
a spit, and the fellows said they'd not eaten so well
for half a year. Goat tastes like lamb, if you're
wondering, but greasier and gamier. Anyway, next
morning Cordell sends for me, and when I get to
the tent, guess who's there. The farmer who sold
me the goat. And he's claiming I never paid him
for it, but I did, and I said so. Cannonballs told
me to pay him anyway. I didn't have the blunt,
had to borrow from R, had to report back and
hand it over to that scoundrel farmer when all I
wanted was to plant him a facer. Don't know why
the captain didn't believe me. But I'm new, and
he don't know me. I never lie if I can help it. To
save somebody, maybe, or misdirect the enemy,
but I'm not so gone I would lie about a goat!*

Ever, J

A*n alien in my own country,* Cordell was thinking as the hired coach bore him west from London on Kensington Road. Summer daylight was beginning to fade, and he found himself gawping at the parklands on either side, interspersed with plantings of wheat, mustard, and what looked to be lettuces.

No man who had traveled to South Africa, India, Holland, Egypt, Italy, Portugal, Spain, and France, not to mention briefer stays elsewhere, ought to have his head stuck out the window like a hayseed. But for the last twenty years, his memories of England had been of a country altogether different, a dank, flat, dreary landscape that bred midges and mosquitos and discontent. The England where he'd spent his boyhood was not a place he wanted to see again, but this . . . This was a landscape he could come to appreciate.

And he liked that it was near to a thriving city, although he had never imagined himself residing in London. Paris, for all its beauty, had been bad enough. He hadn't belonged there, that was all, had stayed only at the request of Wellington, serving as a decorative soldier in the occupation force so resented by the French.

He was expected to go back after this leave of absence, another round of holding up a wall at state and social functions, but he had resolved to seek a transfer. Inaction always chafed at him. Perhaps he should leave the army altogether. Of what use were his skills in the absence of war?

And in his dreams, perversely, India was beckoning him. Perhaps he belonged with the army of the East India Company, where he'd a chance to advance in

rank and responsibility. In the British army, a great
many generals would have to die before he could be
considered for promotion.

The coach slowed and made a right turn onto Addi-
son Road, according to the map he had studied before
setting out. On either side, oaks and cedars sent long
shadows across the grass. The sky was deepening into
the hues of twilight. He saw a deer walk calmly to an
ornamental pool and begin to drink. A sheep glanced
up, its white fleece tinged gold by the setting sun.

Cordell put away his distractions and prepared for
battle.

Holland House, with its irregular facades, capped
towers, and eclectic ornamentation, looked to have
been assembled by a committee of tipplers. But it
suited its inhabitants, he decided when a servant
showed him into a drawing room the size of a barn.
Guests of varied ages and distinction, most of them
male, clustered in small groups, intensely engaged in
talk. He heard laughter, arguments, a snatch of poetry.

His was the only military uniform there, if you excluded the paunchy admiral snoozing on a wing-back
chair in the corner. He saw no one he recognized.

She was late. Or it was another trick, like pretending not to see him in Hyde Park. Perhaps she
was watching him from beyond one of the open doors
leading into other rooms. He saw servants moving inside one of them, putting the finishing touches on a
table laid out for an elaborate dinner.

A hand closed on his forearm.

Controlling an impulse to shake it off, he looked
down at the hand. Female. Ungloved. Not the hand
of a young woman.

"You are Eve's soldier," said a voice so deep it might have belonged to a man.

He raised his eyes to a face that was no longer lovely but showed the signs of having been so in the past. There were also signs—faint traces, really—of an incipient beard. He guessed the woman to be in her middle forties and had no doubt of her identity.

"Lady Holland," he said, deftly slipping his arm from her grip as he bowed. "You are most kind to have invited me to your home."

"Indeed I am," she said imperiously. "You are a friend of that scoundrel Wellington. But Lady Eve says you are not political, so I cannot feed you to the wolves."

"You dine on Tories here? Perhaps I shall recognize one of the hors d'oeuvres."

A bark of a laugh from his hostess. "Here, Colonel, we savor conversation and arguments more than food. Come sit and regale me with the news from Paris."

For nearly half an hour she quizzed him, insisting they converse in French, while the other guests milled around, casting sideways looks in their direction. It was more of a debriefing than a conversation, with Lady Holland firing pointed questions about matters of substance, not fashion or gossip. He found himself rather liking her.

But all the while, he was annoyed by the continuing absence of Lady Eve and began to suspect she had abandoned him in this nest of Whigs for her own amusement.

He was mistaken. She arrived just as the guests were invited to dine, bringing her own particular light into the room. It reached him, or felt like it did, before he glanced over and saw her standing at the drawing-room door, a self-contained beauty with the poise of a seventeenth-generation aristocrat.

He was third-generation only, a baron whose grand-father had somehow wrung a peerage and a parcel of useless land out of King George II. It was of no consequence, their difference in rank, but this was the second time in one day that seeing her had called it to mind.

"Ah, there she is," said Lady Holland, already on her feet. "Go claim her, Colonel, and escort the naughty gel into the dining room. We don't stand on ceremony here. Not on Tuesday nights, at any rate."

When he'd made his bow to Lady Holland and turned to Lady Eve, she was looking back at him with a distinctive challenge on her face. Or, no. His alarm bells were sounding, but he saw only a lovely young woman wearing a simple gown of the palest blue with a fringed shawl draped around her bare arms.

Circe. Lilith. Every temptress that ever was. But that message came to him silently, borne on the vibrating air. She stood separate from it all, cool and aloof, a mystery beyond his comprehension.

In that moment, he had only one thought. Whatever she had planned for him, she would not be permitted to succeed.

Without words, he cut her free of a would-be dinner partner, led her to a spot near the bottom of the table, and placed her beside the heavy-lidded admiral. Taking the chair to her right, he nodded to the bored-looking man across from him and judged they were isolated enough for his purposes. Curiosity emanated from the upper reaches of the table, but no one in their immediate vicinity paid them any mind. This was the hangers-on sector, and he'd wager Lady Eve had never so much as noticed its existence, let alone found herself there.

She didn't seem to mind, though. Amusement played at the corners of her mouth. "My apologies for being late, sir. I meant to arrive in time to protect you from Lady Holland. Did she pounce the moment you walked through the door? But of course she did. I was detained by a gentleman who stopped by to deliver a message. Major Lord Blair. Do you know him?"

"A little." He gave her a sharp look of warning. "Blair held court over the most popular officers' mess on the Peninsula. But I don't expect you know what that means."

"Messes? No. But he is quite popular here as well. And off to Cornwall, he says. The Cornish ladies will be glad of it."

Another murder? was his first thought. She had a tidbit of news between her teeth and was taunting him with it. Amateur conspirators. How could he be shed of her? But the large-nosed man across the table, formerly intent on Lady Eve's bosom, had lifted his gaze to her mouth. Time for a change of subject.

"I cannot help but notice how few ladies are present," he said, loudly enough to be heard by his neighbors. "Five, by my count, including you, and at least two dozen gentlemen. That must say something about females and their lack of interest in serious conversation."

"It says more, I think, about husbands who will not permit their wives to enter the home of a divorced woman." Her voice remained low, continuing their private skirmish. "Perhaps they believe infidelity is contagious."

"Are they at no risk of catching it themselves?"

"Oh, gentlemen are born with the disease. Only that would explain their behavior from the time they turn, what? Twelve? Thirteen? I have no brothers, so I cannot diagnose the onset. By the time I am introduced to a gentlemen, he is already long gone on the trail of dissipation. At what age, sir, did you know yourself infected?"

"I must be immune." To his relief, a servant reached between them to set down a platter of buttered prawns.

"What thought you of Lady Holland?" said Lady Eve when the servant had moved away.

"She's a despot."

"I should like to hear you say that to her face. She is, of course, and I envy her for it. To have sailed past a great scandal and set up a realm of her own to queen it over is a remarkable achievement, don't you think?"

He glanced at the middle-aged gentleman set apart from the table in a Bath chair, the hairless portion of his scalp gleaming under a chandelier. "More to the point, what does Lord Holland think?"

"Why ever should *that* be the point? But I am certain he approves. Theirs is a love story, you see, if a decidedly unorthodox one. Would you like to hear it?"

He would not, but better that than having her tease him with references to their assignment or, worse, start asking questions about his own history. "I have no objection," he said stiffly.

"Don't worry. I'll be brief. And along the way, I have a point of my own to make. Lady Holland was Elizabeth Vassall, heiress to a wealthy Jamaican planter and quite lovely in her youth. There is a portrait of her in the blue salon you ought to see. At fifteen, she was married to a hunt-mad gentleman from the north and bore him two children, but her destiny caught up with her while she was traveling in Italy. There she met Henry Richard Fox."

Cordell looked again at the rather pudgy gentleman, who bore no resemblance to the traditional hero of a romantic tale. But then, experience had taught him that beauty was a key to passion, not to love. He had no idea how to open that particular lock.

"This happened nearly twenty-five years ago," said Lady Eve, correctly interpreting his thoughts, "and the gentleman has not always suffered from the gout. She remained with her lover, had a child by him, and her husband finally secured a divorce. By then Mr. Fox had become Lord Holland, and a few years after marrying her, he was granted authorization to take the name of Vassall."

"Not uncommon," Cordell said dryly, "when an inheritance is involved."

"I doubt he had anything to gain by it. She was already his wife and chattel. How do you sign letters and documents, sir? What do you write?"

He put down his fork and looked over at her. "Cordell. Sometimes rank and regiment, on military forms and the like. What of it?"

"Henry Richard Vassall Fox, Lord Holland, signs himself Vassall Holland. Is that not a splendid tribute to his wife?"

"I don't know what it is. Having met her, I wouldn't be surprised if she browbeat him into it. Are you suggesting a gentleman, when he marries, ought to take and use his wife's name?"

"Considering that she is expected to surrender her

own name, along with nearly everything else, it would be a nice gesture. Personally, I'd rather retain control of my money and property, along with a number of other rights snatched from me by the men who make the laws that govern how we live."

Good God. He was partnered with a militant reformer. "Is that the point you were trying to make? Men are swine?"

"Necessary swine, though." She was laughing at him. "But no. I simply believe government and the courts would do better if half the citizens of England were not excluded from their deliberations."

"What do you want, then?"

"Access to power for women who can wield it effectively. But that will not come in my lifetime, if ever. For now, we can only bring our small influence to bear wherever possible, as Lady Holland does with her Whig husband and Lady Etheridge with her Tory."

"You must pardon my skepticism. Given that Etheridge led the drive to have the war run from England by a rapacious pack of civilian incompetents, thereby depriving the army of necessary supplies, weapons, and payment for the soldiers, I cannot think his wife a good influence."

"They had not long been married when the worst of his bad ideas were pushed through. Later, she was able to steer him from excessive conservatism to a somewhat moderate stance on many issues, although he will never be so wise a legislator as Lady Etheridge would be in his place. As for Lady Holland, she is a forceful advocate for abolition of the slave trade, which you must admit is a worthy cause."

Her eyes shone with challenge. The Lady Eve, issuing another of her tests for him to pass. "I do admit it," he said. "But your situation is entirely different. How much influence can a young, unmarried female have in the corridors of power? Unless, perhaps, she becomes the mistress of the prime minister."

Her eyes widened. "Do you think he'd have me?"

What red-blooded man would not? was his instant thought. But her brazen question was humbug. She was trying to get a rise out of . . . *Damn.* She'd sent his thoughts down this twisted road, and now every word and phrase was charged with sexual innuendo. She looked untouched, the way a hothouse young female aristocrat ought to look, but her mind was even more intricate and, it seemed, more lascivious, than Talleyrand's.

"I've no doubt he would." Cordell reclaimed his silverware and sliced into a serving of rare roast beef. "Is that your ambition?"

"No. But I should like to marry a prime minister one day, or a member of the cabinet. I do not intend to butterfly my way through ballrooms forever, sir. My passion is for justice." Her voice softened even more, but lost none of its intensity. "That is why I accepted the same invitation issued to you. And my point in telling you about Lord and Lady Holland is this. Whatever becomes of my reputation as a result of what I do now, it cannot be worse than what Lady Holland experienced. Survival is possible. Even triumph."

"There are always rare exceptions to society's rules," he told her, too much in the way he used to instruct young subalterns. "It is naive to imagine you will be one of them."

"You may be right. But I accept the risks that come with my choice of an unconventional life."

"A noble sentiment, but it won't be so simple as you imagine. Not when the artillery takes aim and opens fire."

"Pah! There is no artillery. I stand to lose only the approval of a society that cares nothing for me. At the very worst, I might be compelled to take up luxurious residence abroad. My rank and wealth protect me, Colonel. I cannot fall too far, or too hard."

"You are uncommonly fortunate."

"And how unfair that I should be so. It leaves me, I believe, with an obligation to apply my good fortune to a useful and productive life. If there are sacrifices to be made, I'll worry about them when they appear. You have been useful and productive, sir. No doubt you have sacrificed a great deal for your country. Given the chance, would you make other choices than you did?"

Men never asked that sort of question. "Why speculate on the impossible? I cannot unmake or redo my life. At best, I can learn from my choices and their outfall."

"Yes." A tiny line appeared between her brows. "Might I ask your age, Colonel?"

"Four and thirty."

"There has been time for outfall, then. I seem to have got away with most of my youthful follies, generally because so few people ever found out about them. But instead of learning to control my reckless impulses, I continue to charge straight ahead, wagering that the results will be much as they always have been."

"The odds appear to be with you," he conceded, wondering if she'd ever stop talking long enough to eat her dinner.

The admiral tapped him on the hand with a spoon. "Was you at Waterloo, sir?"

A question he had answered hundreds of times. "Yes. With the—"

"I was at Trafalgar," said the admiral, bent on steering a course to his own great battle.

Cordell, welcoming the escape from Lady Eve's inquisition, kept the admiral talking about his adventures until Lady Holland stood and gazed imperiously down the table. He thought she would depart then, taking with her the other ladies. But everyone began to rise and shuffle toward the door, so he had little choice but to take the arm of his nemesis and lead her from the room.

"Do you wish your politics to be picked at like a bone?" she said. "Or would you prefer a walk in the gardens?"

Where she would pick at *him* like a bone, he had no doubt. But she might also have a message from Blair to convey, so he let her guide him outside.

For a surprising time, she didn't speak. He glanced over at her when he thought she wouldn't notice, watching the play of lanternlight and torchlight on her exposed neck and arms, noting with apprehension the thoughtful expression on her face. The expression of a Borgia deciding which poison to use.

They were walking on a tiled path that led to a large formal garden, but when they reached it, she drew him onto another path, this one curving into a landscape of trees and flowering bushes. There was light here, too, but not so much of it. Now and again they arrived at a clearing that held a fountain, or marble benches, or a fish pond. He heard the rustling of night creatures in the trees and undergrowth.

It was when they came into a circle rimmed with
white-flowering plants of all kinds that she paused and
turned to face him. Light from the half moon washed
over her cheeks, painted her hair with white-gold. She
gazed up at him, eyes glittering like the stars.

He thought of serpents, hooded and venomous, that
rose from round woven baskets and swayed at the command of a fakir playing on a pipe. Swayed to the piper's motion, Cordell had discovered, not to the music.
Like snake and piper, gazes locked, bodies separate
but moving in concert, he looked at Lady Eve and
she looked back at him.

Perfume floated on the night air. His mouth felt dry.
His muscles bunched in the too-confining uniform as
he awaited a pronouncement from the serpent-
goddess.

"Are you adept at subterfuge?" she said.

"Very."

"Then we will likely get away with this, despite my
reputation for being unapproachable. When I came
out three years ago, I very soon became known as the
Frost Queen. It wasn't a compliment, but it suited my
purposes. I dislike being treated as a mindlessly eligible young woman. The conversation inevitably de-
clines when gentleman flirt or condescend."

"Exactly how do you want them to treat you?"

"It depends on my mood, I suppose. When they
don't flirt, I sometimes resent it." She smiled. "In too
many ways, I am everything I do not wish to be."

She was playing with him again. Mocking him. He
didn't like it. "If you intend on making a display of
us, madam, why are we standing here in the
woods?"

"For a blessing. Can you not see that this is a magical circle? And so that I can tell you what to expect in the next few minutes. Should we really decide to get up to something, Colonel, I would take you deep into the wilderness. But as I don't want you to be entirely compromised your first week in England, we shall keep to the civilized paths."

"What, then, am I supposed to be expecting?"

"More people, for one thing. Guests will be wandering in at Holland House for the rest of the evening, and many of them will take the air in the gardens. For us to do the same will raise no eyebrows. I believe we should arrange to be discovered in an embrace. Will that be satisfactory?"

Almost certainly not. The mere prospect of touching her had already set his pulse to hammering. "If you think it necessary. And after that?"

"A discreet separation." She twinkled up at him. "Unless someone calls you out."

"Is someone likely to?"

"Alas, no. But I should love watching you fight a duel. What weapon would you choose?"

Bloodthirsty little witch. Was that her plan? To hook him into a fight, hoping he'd lose? Not much chance that he would. But he could hardly find a killer for Black Phoenix if he had to flee the country. And he didn't want to face a dressing-down from Wellington. He'd rather lose the duel.

"You have drifted from the subject," he said. "The sooner we get this business under way, the sooner it will be done with. Are we waiting here for someone to find us?"

"I have another place in mind. Your arm, sir?"

He offered it, and for the slow walk to her destination, he endured the nearness of a semiclad female body controlled by a devious, dangerous mind.

She chose a vine-covered pergola set at the far end of the formal garden they had earlier passed. The interior lay in shadows, but a golden lantern suspended from an overhanging tree branch illuminated anyone who stood near the entrance. "We'll wait inside," she said, "until a group of people comes into view. Then we'll step forward and provide them a show."

It was rather like entering a cave with a wildcat. He stood in the darkness, hands clasped behind his back, waiting for trouble. But she seemed to have grown bored with her game and with him, because she only looked out at the garden, thinking indecipherable female thoughts.

At long last, voices. He turned to her, but she put a finger to her lips. Then she whispered, "Not yet."

Holding his position, he watched people move through the intricate garden, heard talk and laughter, imagined placing his hands on Lady Eve. Putting his mouth to hers.

It wasn't what she had in mind. She expected a feigned embrace with his arms loosely around her, broken off the moment they were discovered.

But she'd had her own way too long. Tempted him past the limits of his patience, if not his control. Only honor would prevent him from giving her what she'd been asking for all evening, never wanting or expecting to get it.

"Now," she said under her breath, clutching his forearm and drawing him into the light. Even as they reached it, her arms went around him, her body pressed itself against him, her head tilted. . . .

And he was lost. It wasn't the kiss he craved to give her, but no one, not even she, could mistake it for anything less than passion off its leash.

The people for whom this scene was being staged were still some distance away. He'd no choice but to continue as he'd begun, deepening the kiss, enjoying how she instinctively worked her way closer to him. Not experienced, he could tell, but wonderfully enthusiastic. Her hand was on his neck, her fingers moving into his hair. He pulled her nearer still, until her slippers were resting on his boots. . . .

"Lady Eve." A familiar voice.

She was off him in a heartbeat, breathing deeply, straightening her skirts. He saw her swallow, trying to find words.

He found them for her. "Good evening, Lady Etheridge." With military efficiency, he stepped out of the pergola and bowed. There were five or six people with her, but he saw only the look of a woman who had found herself face-to-face with a rodent.

"Colonel Cordell. How unfortunate that I have arrived at Holland House just as you were leaving. Or might we persuade you to join us on our walk? We are discussing the disastrous effects of the Corn Laws on manufacturing."

"A subject that greatly interests me, but I have business in London. Perhaps Lady Eve would like to take a part in the debate."

He put out a hand, Lady Eve stepped forward smartly, laid hers atop it, and allowed him to turn her over to the custody of her mentor.

The young lady's poise, he had to admit as he made his way to the hired carriage, was impressive. She had looked soundly kissed and not in the least concerned what anyone thought of it. But her hand, for the short time it rested on his, had been trembling.

He lifted his own and looked at it. Steady enough. It was the rest of him spinning out of control.

Chapter 5

Portugal, Sept. 1810

> *Cannonballs has got himself another nickname! He was river-bathing when the women doing laundry farther down set to screaming. Hooligans had snatched one up and were carrying her off. We were running from the bivouac camp, but Cordell was closer. He sprang out of the water, grabbed his sword, and charged after the wretches, bare as the day he was born. Caught up with them, too. By the time we got there, he had the villains on the ground, and all the females were gathered around, cheering. In the mess that night, we raised a cup to Captain Gallant (he wasn't there, you may be sure), who exposed himself (ha, ha) to danger for the sake of camp women who sometimes do more than the laundry. Shouldn't have told you this story, now I think on it. But I'd written yesterday's news on this paper already, so it's too late. Paper's in short supply where we are.*

> *Your Bad J*

Eve gently folded the letter and slipped it back into its place among the correspondence from September 1810. There were more than a thousand letters altogether, carefully packeted and filed in a cedar-lined box. She had read them so often that she could immediately put her hands on any one of them.

·The letter she'd just returned had been in and out of the box several times in the last two days. When reading Johnnie's anecdotes, she called up a vivid picture of the incidents in her mind, and this incident was more vivid than most. It struck her that over the years, her perception of the stories—this one in particular—had altered as her own experience grew.

When first she read about Cordell's rescue of a laundry woman, she had thrilled to his gallantry, not recognizing the "Captain Gallant" nickname as a jest. And while she understood that the women were camp followers who entertained the soldiers, she was somewhat vague about what it was they did.

On the first anniversary of Johnnie's death, she had read the letters, in order, one last time before putting them away. For good, she had thought. Dwelling on his last few years of life hurt too much, and her preoccupation with him was making it impossible to let him go.

Then came the summons from Black Phoenix and, shortly after, the revelation of her partner's identity. From that moment, she began once more to relive what had once been her greatest pleasure—sharing Johnnie's adventures through his letters and her imagination.

First she had separated out the ones with references to the man she despised, seeking clues to his character.

Searching, most of all, for his weaknesses. Finding none.

Meeting him, engaging with him, hadn't made a difference. Still no weaknesses that she could detect, although he surely had them. He was human and male, which meant he came flawed from the womb and added to his defects as the years went on. One way or another, she would find out what they were. Then she would exploit them.

Over time, her perspective on the laundry-woman episode had radically altered. Before she turned seventeen, she had discovered a little more about how prostitutes plied their trade, although why men paid for a fleeting contact with a female body eluded her. Research was especially difficult because her parents' library contained no book unsuitable for a rector's wife.

Later came . . . No. She wouldn't think about that. It taught her the how, but not the why.

And then, in a nighttime garden at Holland House, she had been enlightened by a kiss. Passion, dormant in her, had blossomed instantly into a craving that had not left her since he broke their embrace and stepped away. It was with her now, heavy in her breasts, moist between her legs, as if a separate creature had taken possession of her being.

She understood that a separate creature was what her flesh required, a male body joined with hers. A particular male body, supple and powerful, like the one that had held her tightly and joined with her a small distance beyond respectability. She ached to achieve the far boundaries of what she had tasted.

As well that she did. Desire would mask, to his eyes, the darker emotions that swirled beneath.

How strange, she couldn't help thinking, that passion entwined itself with hatred. They ought to be incompatible, but they mated nonetheless. They were coupled now, within her.

She wanted him, and she wanted to hurt him.

With a sigh, she closed the box of letters and returned it to the large safe that held her jewelry. Lady Etheridge was expecting her at two o'clock, an engagement she dreaded but had to keep.

There would be no unpleasantness, for it was not in Lady Etheridge's character, but she could expect a lecture all the more painful for being gentle. And true, for she had made promises, and made them sincerely.

It was becoming difficult to navigate between the expectations of her closest friend and the actions she felt compelled to undertake. No one, not even Johnnie, had ever understood her as Margaret Etheridge did. How had she found herself torn between the friend of her past and the friend now guiding her into the future? She'd only ever had two friends, and it seemed she must let down the one or the other.

But only for a short time. A little damaged, still determined to honor her promises, she would return to Lady Etheridge after the Black Phoenix mission and her vengeance were accomplished.

At the Etheridge town house in Grosvenor Street, Eve was surprised to be escorted upstairs by a footman. Always before, she had been taken directly to the library. And the maidservant who admitted her to the bedchamber wore a grim expression as she curtsied and withdrew.

Lady Etheridge, partly dressed, her hair in disarray,

started to rise from the Grecian sofa and sank down again, her back against a mound of pillows.

Eve moved closer, stomach tightening. Lady Etheridge's face was unusually pale, save for hectic streaks of color on her cheeks. The flesh beneath her eyes seemed almost gray. And against all reason, her russet morning dress had been put on backward. The bodice hooks were open, the collar ribbons loose against her bosom, the skirts tangled around her legs. "You are ill," she said, frightened. "What is it? How can I assist you?"

"By sitting down where I can see you." Lady Etheridge's voice sounded surprisingly firm. "And by not worrying about a gripping headache that has already passed. The better part of it, at any rate. Or should that be the *worst* part? It is nothing, I assure you, except that I just now rose too quickly and went a little dizzy."

What about the gown? Eve wanted to ask. Was she the only one who had noticed? "You must take better care, then. Where is Styles? Shouldn't she be tending to you?"

"Blessedly gone to stay with her cousin. I cannot bear to be cosseted, you know. Strength of body and strength of character are incompatible with self-indulgence."

Eve, taking the pointed hint, tugged over a chair from the dressing table and sat across from her. "Never?" She put shock into her voice. "I must live in an eternal Lent, no champagne, no syllabub, no satin sheets or feather pillows? Then I'd rather not be a Spartan after all."

"Perhaps I overstated. It is because I despise weakness, especially in myself. And lamentably, one always despises the vices one most longs to indulge. This will surprise you, but I have been, in my time, something of a sybarite. Long ago, to be sure. But the demons of temptation have not packed up and moved out. Like everything else that forms my nature, they live inside me still. I must take care they do not cast off their bonds and carry me away."

Eve understood exactly. She was busy untying the bonds of her own demons and had every intention of putting them to work. She also knew that Lady Etheridge had turned the subject to its inevitable destination. "You are leading up, I think, to what you saw last night at Holland House. Am I expected to explain myself?"

A dark brow lifted. "You mean the explanation is not obvious? A balmy night, a perfumed garden, moonlight, and a handsome man. Practically a formula for a bit of experimentation. My concern is the inclination to experiment a little more, and a little more after that. Believe me, the gentleman has it in mind. They all do. It is the lady, if she intends to remain a lady, who must keep hold of the reins."

"I'm a good horsewoman," Eve said, by way of evasion.

"Yes. Styles remarked upon it after your ride in the park."

There was no escape. "With the same gentleman, as you must know. A gentleman new to London, just when the usual men have become an intolerable bore. Is it so astonishing that I seek entertainment? My goal, the one we are working for together, is years and years away. I can hardly attract the man I'll require when the time comes without a little practice."

"Or without your reputation." Chips of ice, not words. "Don't think I merely parrot social restrictions. Let me tell you something in confidence. When I was younger than you, but equally ambitious, my head and all the rest of me were turned by a beautiful man. I thought him an angel come to earth and flung myself into his arms when he opened them. On his account, for he was of insignificant birth, I was prepared to surrender everything. But he abandoned me."

Eve could scarcely believe what she was hearing. Lady Etheridge never spoke of personal matters. "Yet here you are," she said carefully, "wed to a powerful man, engaged in the work you always intended to do. No harm was done."

A tolerant smile from Lady Etheridge. "Indeed, I am where I was meant to be. But there is more to the tale. He did not know it when he left, nor did I, but I was carrying his child. When I realized it, I astonished my parents by suddenly agreeing to marry a gentleman they had long favored. He was a widower, much older than I and without an heir. I did tell him the truth, for in matters of importance, a woman cannot resent the deceptions of men if they themselves deceive. He wished to proceed, and we did, and the child was born seven months later."

Speechless, Eve stared at her in fascination. The tall, willowy, utterly confident woman she looked to as a pattern card for her own future had revealed an unimaginable history. She wondered if the story was even true. Lady Etheridge, so far as everyone knew, had spent her early years as companion to a wealthy relation before coming to London a decade ago. Eve didn't dare ask the questions burning on her tongue. She chose, instead, something innocuous but encouraging . . . as if this expert politician could be fooled by a novice. "And all was well, then?"

"I was content. When my husband died not very long after, I lived alone with my son. But he died as well, far too young, and for a time, I could do nothing but mourn. There was no light in all the world for me, until I thought again of my girlhood dreams and wondered if it was too late for me to seize them. As you have said, no harm was done. I would not exchange any position, however grand, for the years spent with my child, and now I have achieved nearly all I ever hoped for."

"Why, then, do you think I cannot do the same? There is no single path up the mountain you have ascended. It is only right that I find my own way."

"But why should you, if you need not? There are cliffs and traps and dragons on our mountain, Eve. Your beauty and money will take you far, and we'll find legal ways to protect most of your fortune from your eventual husband. But at any time, a misstep can send you tumbling. Society rarely accords women a second chance."

"Well, if it turns out I need a second chance, I shall contrive to wring one out. Memories are short, but status and wealth endure. May I ask what became of the child's father?"

A delicate shrug. "I heard he went out to America. Wherever he may be, I wish him well. He gave me the most precious gift of my life. It seems, however, that my story has not altered your course. I cannot be glad that I told it. But you may be trusted, I am sure, to say nothing of this. Even Etheridge does not know."

"You have my word on it."

"And when will you see your young man again?"

"I cannot say. On Friday I leave to spend a few days with my godmother. Are you coming down for the weekend?"

"Etheridge expects me at his dinner for the American ambassador. Will the colonel join you at Oatlands?"

Eve attempted a laugh that, to her surprise, didn't sound altogether false. "If I said yes, would you change your plans? By all means, come if you can get away. You know that Freddie will find room for you."

"Well done," said Lady Etheridge. "I cannot tell if you plan to meet your soldier there or not. You have a natural talent for misdirection, Eve, but I hope you will not wield it against me. Better if we have honesty between us, even when we are at odds. But never mind, this time. I cannot be spared, so that is that. And now, I think I shall sleep for a while."

Eve rose, concerned again about the weariness in her friend's eyes and the backwardness of her gown. "Is there nothing I can provide for you?"

"Send the maid, if you will. And remember, whatever you get up to this weekend will be reported to me."

"As is everything," said Eve, curtsying.

When Eve came out of Etheridge House, her carriage was waiting at the curb with her new maid standing patiently beside it. Mrs. Kipper, who had reported for work just as Eve was about to keep her appointment, looked rather like an exceptionally neat cook in her fifties, plump and pillowy of bosom, with smoothly coiffed gray-white hair.

On an impulse, Eve had brought her along, intending to show off her mature and responsible chaperon to Lady Etheridge. But there had been no opportunity, once she was taken upstairs, leaving Mrs. Kipper to go the other direction.

"Do you actually perform the duties of a servant?" Eve said when they were settled in the coach, taking up the interrogation she had begun on the way. Most of it had concerned the dog in her sitting room, which erupted into loud barking whenever a man approached. Male servants had been instructed to keep their distance.

"Not to the standards you have come to expect," said Mrs. Kipper in a bland tone. "But I have experience as a dresser, both clothing and hair. Because you wear no cosmetics save a little lip rouge, my chiefest skill will go unused, but in most ways, I can serve you well enough."

"Did you bring instructions for me?"

"If there are any, Colonel Cordell will supply them. My role is to be of practical assistance. I relay messages, help procure whatever you need, and most of all, keep my eyes and ears open. Servants generally know a good deal more than anyone else about what transpires in a household, and I have a knack for eliciting information without appearing to do so."

"Did you learn anything from Lady Etheridge's servants while below stairs?"

"Nothing of consequence to our mission. Of other matters confided to me, I never speak."

Eve laughed. "I hope that applies as well to what you learn of me. Will you tell me what you carry in that tapestry bag? It's even larger than the dog's covered basket. Oh, but I shouldn't have asked. You just cautioned me against wanting information I ought not to have."

"No doubt I'll be reminding you again. But I've no objection to telling you about the contents of my bag. There's my needlework, of course, and always a book to keep myself occupied. Spectacles. A traveling pack of pen, ink, and paper. Sketching materials, because I sometimes need to draw a map or create a likeness. Dried venison for the dog. Later, you shall see how it is used. I have kerchiefs, a wig, and a few cosmetics for crude disguises. Laudanum. A medicament that produces sleep. A kit of tools for lock picking. Binding cord. A knife. A pistol. A garotte."

Eve, realizing her mouth was hanging open, snapped it shut.

"Do you shoot?" Mrs. Kipper's voice seemed always to be calm. Even complacent, as if she'd been through a scene like this one on many occasions.

"No. Do you suppose I'll be required to use a weapon?"

"On this mission? Probably not. But you ought to take it up. I find that women intrepid enough to accept a summons from Black Phoenix are apt to find themselves in trouble at some time or another. You may as well learn a few ways to get yourself out again."

With some relief, Eve felt the carriage slow and draw to a halt. This day had been crammed with surprises, all of them disconcerting, and she had a sudden longing for solitude and tea.

But they would have to wait, she saw as a footman handed her from the coach. Striding along the pavement as if he'd timed his arrival to meet with hers—which he probably had—was Colonel Cordell. Lord

Cordell, she corrected mentally. He was not wearing his uniform.

With a credible display of surprise at encountering her right in front of her family's town house, he swept off his hat and bowed. "Lady Eve. How fortunate. Might we have a few words in private?"

"How ever did you know I'd be arriving here at this very moment?"

"You forget what I've been doing these last twenty years." He took her arm and led her up the stairs, Mrs. Kipper following at a discreet distance. "Or perhaps you don't know of it. Is that your new watchdog?"

"The actual dog is upstairs. And I advise you not to meddle with Mrs. Kipper, who is carrying a small arsenal in her bag."

"My watchdog has arrived as well, you will see by his handiwork. I've spent far too much time being measured and poked by tailors since he took me in hand. Silas Indigo, or so he says. I suspect these faux servants are not using their own names."

When they reached the entrance hall, Cordell drew her to one side. "I haven't much time," he said, dismissing the butler and footman with a wave of his hand. Mrs. Kipper started up the winding staircase. "Sir Peregrine is waiting for me at his club, where I am expected to win enough at hazard and backgammon to pay our expenses during this mission."

"But why? I have more than enough—"

"Apparently we may give our time and risk our lives, but we're not to be out of pocket. That's how they work. We repay anything we do not spend."

"But what if you lose? Are you an accomplished gambler, sir?"

"Games of chance have never interested me, but I can hold my own. And in this case, I needn't worry. The outcome is rigged in my favor."

"But why not simply give you the money?"

"My question as well. According to Sir Peregrine, a double purpose is served. I shall be introduced to many of the people we're likely to encounter during our investigation, and it is important that I be welcomed into their circles. I must also drink to excess and make myself appear somewhat less acute than I like to fancy I am."

"A gamer, a drinker, and an actor. Also a civilian gentleman, not a soldier?"

"All in all, a fish out of water. I am coming to terms with it. And I needn't play the part all the time. As Sir Peregrine puts it, I am to create the impression of pudding under steel. Does that make sense to you?"

"I know exactly what he means." And she doubted that anyone would be misled. This man was steel under steel, with an overlay of steel. But then, everyone thought her to be formed of ice, with harder ice at her core and a frosting of snow on the top for decoration. Perhaps she was wrong about him. Perhaps everyone was wrong about the both of them. "Is this what you came to tell me?"

"No. My apologies. I am come on two small errands. First, you should know that Sir Peregrine brought with him last evening the reports I asked for. After going over them several times, I could find nothing to point us in a promising direction. I still await detailed histories of the three victims, which Phoenix is putting together."

"May I see what you have?"

"To what purpose? They have been combed

through before coming into Sir Peregrine's hands, and he examined them as well. We all arrived at the same conclusions."

"Then there is nothing to lose by passing on the reports to me. Surely the more information I have, the more likely I am to recognize a clue if I chance upon one."

"Your point is well taken. I'll have Indigo bring them by, and if you'll carry them with you to Oatlands, we shall compare notes."

He had capitulated. With grace. Concealing her astonishment, she nodded as if he had not done something altogether unexpected. The way he had in the garden . . . Oh, she mustn't think on that. Seeing him for the first time since she had been in his arms had immediately set her blood to pounding. She only hoped it didn't show on her overly warm cheeks. She'd taken care not to look at his lips, or at his hair, or at anything she had touched, or anything he had touched her with.

There was no sign he had noticed, though, which ought to have pleased her. He appeared unaffected, as if what happened between them was quite ordinary, as if he had kissed a hundred women in a hundred gardens. It probably was, and he probably had. He was very good at kissing.

"You appear taken with my cravat," he said, moving to the door. "Sir Peregrine arranged it when Indigo failed to produce an adequate waterfall, whatever that means. After that experience, I am resolved to keep to uniform whenever possible. By the way, we ride south tomorrow—I'm not entirely sure why—and will not return before you leave for Oatlands."

"Then I'll see you there on Saturday," she said

brightly, welcoming the reprieve. Given his lack of interest in her female charms, seducing him was going to be more difficult than she had thought. And if she was to have any chance of controlling him, she must first retake control of herself.

Chapter 6

Portugal, Nov. 1810

I'm doing everything you said. Even lessons in Portuguese from a local priest, and he's teaching me some Spanish, too. And every minute I'm not on duty, I take my charcoals and sketch pad out to map the area. Seems a waste, we've been here so long. Everyone knows where everything is. I keep telling myself that's not the reason, but I want more than anything to do something useful. Last week we skirmished with a French patrol and got the better of them, but they were four against our seven. Never mind my impatience. I'll keep working on your plan and let you know if I manage to impress Cannonballs.

Yrs., J

Sunlight streamed through the tall windows, lighting the tapestry threads of the cushioned seats and glittering off the blue waters of Broadwater Lake. This was Eve's favorite room at Oatlands Park, the one always given over to her when Lord and Lady Marbury abandoned their nuisance of a daughter to the care of her godmother. They had invariably left precise instructions for her training, which never advanced when she was left at home with the servants. From an early age, she had found it a simple matter to outfox the lot of them.

But she could never bring herself to distress the kindhearted Frederica, Duchess of York, who obliged Eve's parents by providing all the education a young lady seeking accomplishments might require.

The handsome oil-polished harpsichord had survived her mauling of Haydn and Mozart, which usually set the dogs barking and sent the staff in search of tasks at the far end of the house. Her playing instructor persisted year after year, to no avail, but the singing master soon declared himself unable to accept payment in a hopeless cause. The dancing master came to a similar conclusion, but she had been all arms and legs and coltish energy then. Later, faced with the prospect of humiliation at her come-out ball, she buckled down and became quite a good dancer.

The same could not be said for her sketching and painting, although she loved art with a fierce passion. Since first she drew funny faces on the fogged glass in her nursery, she had longed to create something beautiful. Most afternoons at Oatlands had been spent with easel, brushes, and palette, here in this large study or outdoors when the weather was fine, struggling to transfer the perfectly formed images in her mind to canvas.

They never made it there.

She wandered over to the wall most sheltered from the sun, where a bank of pictures hung, among them one of her own. There, amongst the Turners and Constables, the Gainsboroughs and the Reynoldses, her small painting of a midnight thunderstorm in the

Highlands looked as if it had staggered in from a madhouse.

Splotches of clouds painted in bilious gray with streaks of black. Blotches of indeterminate shapes meant to represent something, but she couldn't now imagine what. Rannoch Moor bore a strong resemblance to blood pudding. What she'd intended to be a flash of lightning could as well have been spilt milk.

But her godmother, pronouncing herself delighted with the painting, had insisted on framing and mounting it. And here it still hung, a testament to Lady Eve Halliday's deplorable lack of talent. At least she'd had the good sense not to sign it.

Above her pitiful effort hung a painting that had always been special to her, even before her sole encounter with a live golden eagle. When she was small, she used to drag over a chair and stand on it so she could look into the bird's mesmerizing eye. Only one, because its head was turned as if it had just spotted a mountain hare, and she was it. The experience never failed to terrify and excite her.

The eagle's power had been perfectly captured by the artist. She'd found herself drawn to its beauty, its focus, its impersonal ruthlessness. She always fancied that she could gentle the king of the skies and bring it to rest on her arm.

Then, on her fateful trip into Scotland, she had come face-to-beak with the real thing.

Had she not been utterly downcast and isolated, she might not have dared take herself so close to it. But the night before, the young man on whom she had fixed all her hopes and dreams had galloped off with his cousin to join the army.

While she nursed a broken heart, the two people

escorting her into the Highlands, just married at Gretna Green, were deliriously absorbed with each other. She might not have existed, except as a vessel for misery. Alone in her carriage, buried under heavy blankets, she nursed her aching heart and stared listlessly into an empty future.

Then, as they came through a narrow gorge, she saw a blaze of color against the rocks. An eagle, like the one in her favorite painting, looked down as if it had been waiting for her to pass by.

She pulled on the check strap and erupted from the carriage before it drew to a stop. The eagle, unperturbed by the horses and the driver's shout, remained where it was, perched on a sharp rock jutting from the cliff about twenty yards above the road. She paused for a moment, spotted a path carved out by water from snowmelt, and scrambled up the hillside.

Still the bird waited, unthreatened and aloof. Behind her, the driver had jumped to the ground and was coming after her. But he was too burly, she thought, to navigate the narrow space between the rocks. And it didn't matter. She was almost there, and she knew why the eagle had come.

It was Johnnie, bidding her farewell. Telling her that what had happened was for the best, and that he would return for her.

No one else cared for her as he had done, or understood her, or let her be the strange creature she was without reading her a lecture. And no one so perfectly normal as Johnnie Branden, so steady of purpose, could welcome an ungovernable child into his company if he hadn't loved her.

Of course, he could not have known his own feelings at that time. She was only fourteen, unlovely and unlovable. Even her mother and father kept her out of their way.

But Johnnie would wait for her to grow up, as she had begged him to do. And after the heated encounter at Gretna and the rush of his departure for Portugal, he had sent this emissary to tell her so.

Not in words. She was never so fanciful as to expect an eagle to talk, although her godmother's parrots could do so. But they had been trained, and this was a wild creature, nearly as wild of heart as she had always been.

She stopped when the rocks would let her go no farther, panting with effort and excitement. If she stood on tiptoe and reached out, she might have brushed a fingertip over a long, sharp talon. The eagle gazed down at her from dark pupils set in eyes the color of brandy.

She wasn't afraid. If he plucked her up and carried her off to his aerie, she'd not cry out. He was her fate, the man represented by this great predator. She had willed it to be so.

From behind her, she heard the calls of the driver. The sound of hoofbeats as Lord Nicholas and his new wife rode back to see what had detained the coach.

People always interfered. Meddled with her as if she were an infant. Fourteen was not so young. She had never been young, not really. Impetuous, inept, intransigent, yes. But she had inherited her father's shrewd mind, her mother's iron will, and a fortune that would let her do as she liked when she escaped their legal clutches.

"Seven years," she said to the eagle. "Or sooner, if the war ends. When you return, I will go with you."

"Eve!" That was Lord Nick's commanding voice. "Come down from there!"

The eagle's gaze never left her face. It held her as nothing had ever done, asserting control. Possession. The absolute power to do with her as it wished.

So unlike Johnnie.

Even as the thought popped into her mind, she cast it out again.

• This wasn't a mere bird. Could not be. It would have soared off by now, or flown at her in attack. By heavens, she had needed a messenger and she'd got one!

Never mind that Lord John had always been sunny and single-minded and kind, more like a songbird than a raptor. She alone recognized the warrior in him, the one directing the course of his life since before Evie the gawky girl had been sent to spend summers with his family. Johnnie was born to be a soldier, and when he answered the call of battle, her greatest wish was to be there with him.

"Write to me," she had demanded as he took his leave. "Every day. Make a record of what happens so that I can live it with you."

A letter from Johnnie, she knew, would be a greater miracle than an eagle dispatched to bring a promise she wanted to believe. Continued to believe, even as reason told her that this communion between lonely girl and self-sufficient creature imparted a message she could not yet decipher.

Such a small, calm bird, she was thinking just before it lifted its wings. They reached wider than Johnnie had been tall, six feet at least. And as if an invisible hand lifted it up, the eagle rose without effort into the sky, circled once over her head, and soared from her sight.

She was still in place, motionless and without breath, when Lord Nick's hand closed around her ankle.

"Don't make me drag you down the hill like a sheep."

The insult meant nothing. He had been rightly furious with her since she followed the wedding party all the way from Derbyshire to Scotland. So, cheered by her eagle, she descended the hill without protest and continued to behave herself to a degree that made him suspicious until, a fortnight later, he delivered her back where she belonged.

One day, she had been certain, she would wed his younger brother and become part of the Branden family. But save for the formal exchanges required when acquaintances encountered one another in society, they had never spoken since.

And of course, she had not married Johnnie. Repudiated by his father for joining the army, he remained on the Peninsula until his death four years later.

Nor was he the eagle, she now understood. In the sunlit room at Oatlands, she stared at the painted eye and recognized what she was looking at.

Her supposed emissary, the messenger of promise and comfort, was her sworn enemy.

Cordell's eyes, like the bird's, were the color of brandy flecked with gold. And his hair was the variegated texture of the eagle's feathers, rich brown tinged with copper and bronze. The planes and angles of his face were as beautifully sculpted as the eagle's, and as harsh.

A child might have let imagination carry her off

again, as it had done that morning in Scotland. But in truth, the eagle in which she had placed so much faith was simply a bird in no great hurry to fly off just because a girl had clambered up for a closer look. That Cordell chanced to have similar coloring and, yes, the aloof watchfulness of a predator meant nothing at all.

"Ah, there you are." The small, plain Duchess of York, a dozen dogs curling around her skirts, stepped into the room. "Admiring your painting, my dear? I wish you would do me another."

"It would frighten the dogs," Eve said, approaching to brush a kiss on her godmother's powdered cheek. "Thank you for letting me come with so short a notice."

"And your young man. But I am told you didn't bring him after all."

"Oh, he's not mine. I took pity on a soldier returned to England after many years abroad and thought the relaxed society here would help him settle in. He is to ride down tomorrow morning. Are you expecting many guests?"

"You must ask my steward. But the house will be filled, I expect. It usually is, this time of year." The duchess's English carried the intonations of Prussia, from which she had come sixteen years earlier to wed a royal duke. "I am told you have brought a dog. Might I be introduced?"

"Most certainly." Eve laughed. "But like the colonel, he isn't mine. Nor is he much of a dog, I'm afraid. He belongs to my new maid, who could not bear to part with him. And I knew that here, of all places, a dog is as welcome as an earl."

"More welcome than most of them, you may be

sure. After supper I shall meet the rascal, and then, perhaps, you will read to me?"

"Of course, godmama."

Eve followed Frederica, Duchess of York, from the room and watched her proceed down the passageway, dogs swirling around her old-fashioned skirts and petticoats. She rarely slept, and Eve never minded relieving the servants assigned to read to her throughout the night. The duchess always had the latest and most scandalous novels on her bedside table.

Feeling restless, Eve cut through an empty parlor and used a French window to make her way outside. Her excursion began as a walk alongside the lake, but she soon found herself heading in the direction of the stables, trying not to be obvious about it. The stall would have been thoroughly cleaned by now, but she wanted to see the place where the young man had been found with golden guineas stuffed in his mouth.

Perhaps the stall had been marked in some way, or barricaded. She hoped so, because she couldn't very well ask for a tour of the grisly site. She could, however, make sure her mare was being properly tended to and have a look at the duchess's many pet horses. Something interesting might turn up.

And it did, but not in the way she was expecting.

Chapter 7

Portugal, Nov. 1810

> *R got himself shot tonight. Only a fleabite, but we all ~~took~~ I mean, we all landed in the soup. That's because a French patrol went by us and we never noticed until it was between us and camp. Which was because we were playing cards. R's the one spotted them. He yelled, and we went for our horses. They Frenchies must have figured they'd be trapped, so they made a run for it, firing when they galloped past us. We chased them, R included, but no luck. A real dressing-down from Cannonballs. We deserved it. He confiscated the cards, gave the six of us extra duty, and said I can't go out on picket with R again. I think he wants to transfer one of us. Hope it's not me!*
>
> *Yrs., J*

As Eve aproached the stable block, a stylish and petite young woman on a white mare rode into the yard, flanked by two riders wearing midnight-blue-and-gold livery. There was no mistaking Julia, Duchess of Sarne.

Eve was about to turn back the way she'd come,

hoping she had not been seen, when a light voice called her name. No escape now, but she was surprised the duchess had seen fit to detain her. Like her husband, Julia Sarne kept her distance from the girl who had intruded, all those years ago, on their mad dash to Scotland and a Gretna Green wedding.

Well, someone needed to stop Julia from marrying a young man she had only just met. In such a cause, Eve hadn't minded making a fool of herself. Johnnie was all she had.

So she'd fallen on her knees there in front of Gretna Hall and declared frantic love to a thoroughly astonished gentleman. Johnnie was kind, as always, but clearly he had never regarded her as anything more than an adolescent girl ten years his junior. Within the hour, he rode off unmarried to the wars.

Julia, determined to insinuate herself into the wealthy Branden family, promptly married Nicholas, the brother who was still there. And after a few weeks in Scotland, Eve had returned to London to finish growing up while waiting for Johnnie's return.

It wasn't her fault that Julia and her husband were now estranged. Or mortal enemies, as some gossips swore. Or victims of the family curse. At best, they were getting their just deserts because Lord Nicholas had ignored his duty to marry well and let himself be seduced by a tart.

The tart was proceeding to dismount without assistance. Eve watched her issue orders to her servants and the stablehand who took her horse. Then, a wide smile on her pert face, she crossed to Eve with grace of a faerie traversing a magic circle.

"I thought it was you," she said, the merest trace of uncertainty in her voice. "But if speaking with me makes you uncomfortable, by all means scoot away. I'll not be offended."

Eve cast about for her usual self-assurance, but it remained out of reach. "How can you say that? We have encountered each other a score of times in the last few years, and always it was you who put distance between us."

"But we were in society then, where you would be scorned for acknowledging me. Haven't you heard? I am considered a bad influence."

"I care nothing for that. Indeed, I presumed you were avoiding me for entirely different reasons."

Head tilted, the duchess regarded Eve from wide green eyes. "Not at all. I have longed to talk with you. Shall we do so now, while arrangements are completed for my departure? It was already planned, by the way. I adore Freddie and would not impose myself on her when a horde of visitors is about to descend."

Unaccountably tongue-tied, Eve followed Julia Sarne to her rooms and waited while she disappeared behind a screen to change into a carriage dress. Servants swarmed like bees, helping the duchess arrange her hair, packing her luggage, laying out a tea tray with refreshments in the adjacent sitting room. Accustomed to luxury, Eve realized she had only just dipped her toes into fine living. And she decided all the pampering Julia endured would drive her mad within a week.

Finally they settled on sofas placed across from each other with a low table in between, spread out with tea, biscuits, tiny rolls stuffed with ham and chicken, and Eve's favorite lemon crumbles.

"Why don't you pour," said Julia, "while I set about mending fences? It troubles me that I have caused you distress. Soon after you returned home, I began writing to you. But when you failed to reply, I presumed you wished to sever contact between us. Then—"

"I received no letters." Eve gripped her hands together. "My parents must have got hold of them first. After the Scottish debacle, as Mother called it, Sarne Abbey and its inhabitants were given the cut. Nor, I am sure, would the Sarnes have welcomed me to stay with them again."

"No, indeed. They were furious with the lot of us. I expect your parents did not permit letters from Johnnie to reach you, either. Or did he keep his promise? To skate smoothly over a rough patch, gentlemen often say what young ladies want to hear."

Eve, who had kept the secret for all these years, suddenly wished at least one person to know that Johnnie cared enough for her to do as she'd asked. "It was my good fortune that his first letters arrived while my parents were away. They would certainly have put a stop to our correspondence, so I devised a scheme and laid it out for him in my reply. He then sent his letters to a posthouse not far from Marbury Manor, where a maid collected them and dispatched my own letters. Similar arrangements were made when I went up to London, Your Grace. No one ever suspected."

"I am in awe of your cunning. But please, will you not call me Julia? I'm very little older than you, after all, and we shared a trying experience. To my mind, what happened at Gretna sealed a bond between us, if only because we were both desperate, reckless, and enterprising. I have met few women since who would risk so much, or be so brave, as you."

Eve, who had started to lift her cup to her lips, was forced to put it down again. Her behavior that night had been shameful. The hysterics of an impassioned, unreasonable child. On her return to Marbury Manor, she had resolved to control her emotions on every occasion. And the most effective way to do that, she decided, was to banish her emotions altogether.

Her parents were ideal models—two pillars of ice rooted in a glacier and mounded about with snow. For the next few years she emulated them, cold to the bone and proud of it. On the few occasions they were in company together, she could tell that, for the first time in her life, they were pleased with her deportment. Their approval sharpened her resolve. In future, she would never feel so deeply that she surrendered to her weaknesses, or to a will not her own.

It required only the arrival of Colonel Cordell to stampede her off the straight and narrow path.

"I wasn't brave," she said at length. "Not then. Only stupid. If I'd thought to carry a knife, I'd have plunged it into your heart before allowing you to marry Johnnie. As it was, I made a fool of myself, repented, and am now reformed."

"I am sorry to hear it. Your declaration of love gave me the courage to release from his promise a young gentleman who had agreed to marry me out of compassion. And it helped me to recognize true love when it was offered me by a man from whom I had never expected it. I am, beyond measure, in your debt."

Startled, Eve picked up a thumb-sized lemon-crumble biscuit and popped it in her mouth. It tasted of sawdust and misunderstandings.

"I have been concerned," Julia said, "that you

might be captive to the dreams of your past. Or perhaps to Johnnie's memory, as if loving another would
betray the love you once felt for him."

"Was it love? The attention he paid me was like . . .
like sunlight coaxing open a morning glory. I was
happy in his company, and he put up with mine, which
most young gentlemen would not have done. But half
measures are not in my repertoire. I staked a claim
to him early on, and made him promise not to marry
someone else before I was old enough to be courted."

"I remember you throwing that in his face at
Gretna. You had demanded the promise as a gift on
your tenth birthday and nagged until he gave in. He
could not have taken the promise seriously."

"But I did. And when I turned eighteen, he was
still unwed. We almost had a chance to find out if our
friendship could blossom into love." Bands of invisible
steel were squeezing her chest. "I know he would not
wish me to mourn him forever. One day, I shall marry.
But since we are being frank, it must be a marriage
of my own convenience. I am in no hurry to place
myself under the authority of a husband."

"I quite understand. For position and wealth, I was
prepared to surrender the independence and self-will
I had always valued. You, with position and wealth
wrapped around you at birth, are free to be selective.
Is there no one you favor? No gentleman who has
caught your interest?"

How could she flatly deny it, when her betrothal
would soon be announced? "However does one know
that love has arrived? Does it creep up on you, or
does it strike you in the heart like a bullet?"

"Your metaphors are somewhat ghoulish," Julia
said. "I expect it is different for everyone. In my case,

it was the bullet. But it struck without my realizing it. While I was laying plans to marry Johnnie, my heart was silently bleeding."

Eve regarded her with astonishment. "You loved Lord Nicholas all along? How can it be? You know that I sometimes eavesdropped on your quarrels. He called you an encroaching opportunist, and you called him an overbearing tyrant."

"Both those things were true, and still are. But we tumbled into love nonetheless."

And out again, Eve thought, biting into another lemon crumble.

"Later, though, when the family began to die around us one by one, we could not hold together. I blame myself. I was young and selfish and resentful that our happiness had been snatched away." Julia had gone pale. "Richard had been in such good health that we'd dared to hope his asthma had subsided, as the illness sometimes does. Suddenly, he was gone. Then Johnnie, within the same year, and the disgrace that followed. Did you know that Nicholas went to Spain seeking proof of his innocence?"

"Yes. Robin called on me after his return to England."

"Trust him to remember. Not like the rest of us, who never thought of you and the loss that you, too, had experienced. We nearly lost Robin as well, in the mountain ambush and later, after his recovery, when he vanished for the better part of a year. Wandering alone in grief and despair, he said, because he could not remember what had happened that day. Finally he rejoined his regiment in the Pyrenees, wanting more than a little to die in battle. It was our one stroke of luck that Nicholas was still with the army, conducting his investigation. He ordered Robin to go home, and was obeyed."

"I heard that his grace was in Spain many months before that, when news came of his father's death."

Julia gave a little sigh. "For which he has not stopped punishing himself, although there was nothing he could have done. A bad heart, the coroner said. What lingers, like an unquiet ghost, is the thought of the duke dying alone. The duchess had already removed to London, with his grace intending to follow in time for the opening of Parliament. Sarne Abbey was being closed down for the Season, with only a few caretaker servants in residence. He had been dead for many hours before he was discovered."

Eve remembered how the news had raced through London. Another member of the family struck down. A cousin gone missing. The heir to the dukedom fighting to prove his traitorous younger brother guiltless. When an engraving of Sarne Abbey piled up with bodies began to circulate, its inscription—"The Branden Curse"—caught the public's fancy.

Julia took a sip of her tea, which was surely cold by now, and set down the cup with unsteady hands. "Nicholas returned immediately to Sarne Abbey, for the funeral and all the rest. But as soon as he could escape, he was off to the Peninsula again, determined to clear Johnnie's name. As you know, he failed. Eventually his overdeveloped sense of responsibility brought him back, and while he never wanted the title, he has made himself into the perfect duke. I learned to call him Sarne, on the rare occasions that we speak, and there you have it."

Eve's unhealed wounds split open again. Hearing

the story spoken so briefly, in such a matter-of-fact tone, separated her from Julia Sarne as nothing else could have done. Had the duchess no care for anyone but herself?

And yet, shadows had come over Julia's lovely face. Pain leaped in her eyes. Within a handful of years, she had gone from nobody to wealthy duchess, but her path had carried her over the graves of her husband's family. How must that feel?

The rarely heard from voice, the one Eve tried to ignore when it called her to forgiveness, reached out to Julia. "The dead are not the only victims," she said. "We are, all of us, fallen."

"Casualties of the heart," said Julia, nodding. "My husband lives, but I am dead to him. Your Johnnie is dead, but you cannot let him go. We continue to love, as we must, but do not remember how it is to be happy. We still love, and we still care, and none of it helps."

She had left out anger. The drive to strike down those who had failed. Or perhaps Julia thought Eve too naive, or too well-bred, to harbor rage and thoughts of vengeance.

"I accept that Johnnic is gone," Eve said. "He knew what he was doing. He understood the risks of war and offered his life for his country. What I cannot bear is the injustice. He never agreed to surrender his honor, and did not. It has been stolen from him. This must not stand."

"You and Sarne are riding the same horse, then. But he was obsessively thorough. Everything that can be done *has* been done."

"Not yet. Robin cannot recall the events of that

day. Probably he was struck unconscious at the very
start. But he might have seen something. His memory
might return. Does that ever happen?"

"In novels," Julia said dryly. "And perhaps in life
as well, but who would believe him after all this time?
Johnnie's cousin and closest friend is hardly an impar-
tial witness."

"Robin was willing to lie, but—" Eve clamped her
mouth shut. When the devil got in her, inappropriate
words burst out like grapeshot.

Julia's eyes lit up with interest. "Did he tell you
so?"

No use trying to squeeze the milk back into the
cow. "Only after I demanded to know why he hadn't
already come forward. Johnnie was innocent. We all
know that. If it takes a lie to ensure justice, the lie
should be told."

"I'm afraid I agree with you. But if Robin stood
ready to lie, why didn't he?"

"He was badly injured, and when he'd recovered
well enough for questioning, he could say only that he
recalled riding at the head of the convoy into the pass,
and nothing more until he came awake in the infirmary tent. Later, when he learned that Johnnie was
under suspicion of treason, his protests went un-
heeded. The only hope was that his memory would
return, and that it would disclose exactly what had
occurred. He took leave and traveled alone for the
better part of a year, but while his health was restored,
his memory was not."

Still wishing she had never opened this jar of poi-
sons, Eve slipped by Robin's personal griefs and
jumped to the end of the tale. "Giving up hope, he

rejoined his regiment, which was preparing to enter France, and met up soon after with Lord Nicholas. Well, he was the duke by then, and of course, he had many questions for Robin. It was then that Robin offered to help create a plausible story, based on what Sarne had learned from his investigation, that would serve to clear Johnnie's name."

"I'd wager Sarne told him no," Julia said thoughtfully. "That would be like him. He has an exacting sense of right and wrong, duty and honor, all the starched and pressed virtues. They are something for him to hold to, for he has lost everything else."

"Yes, Sarne forbade Robin to speak, at least until he had exhausted every hope of unearthing a witness or tracing the attackers. Any story he and Robin concocted might later weigh against the new evidence, and at the least, Robin would be charged with presenting false testimony. He must not be put at risk."

"Very true." A bitter tone in Julia's voice. "The Sarnes are running out of heirs."

Before Eve could think how to respond, a knock at the door brought Julia to her feet. "My carriage is ready," she said, looking distracted. "I wish it were otherwise, but tonight I am expected at Penhurst. Pray give my thanks to Freddie and tell her the pavilions for her summer fair will be delivered within a fortnight."

Eve accompanied Julia to the portico, where a lavish coach and six outriders waited. Several houseguests, seeking a view of the scandalous duchess, had found occasion to walk in the adjacent garden, but her grace paid them no heed. She turned instead to Eve and offered her hand.

"May we cry, friends?" she asked, stumbling a little on the last word. "Now that I have found you again, I cannot bear to let you go."

In Julia's voice, Eve heard the echo of her own need for a confidante. For a friend who would not judge her by standards she could never meet. Yet here she was, embarked on a secret mission. Two of them, in fact, one for Black Phoenix and the other in answer to the summons of her own vengeful heart.

"Oh, yes," she said. "But please, whatever may happen in the next several weeks, do not believe everything you hear of me."

Laughing, Julia let a footman hand her into the carriage. "Agreed. And you, Eve Halliday, must not believe everything you have heard about me."

Chapter 8

Spain, April 1811

> *Bad news. I lost my best horse today. We got into
> a skirmish, close fighting, and he took a saber
> across the neck. I jumped clear when he went
> down. After the fight, I had to shoot him. Can-
> nonballs says I'll get used to losing horses that
> way, but I don't think I will. The other two in my
> string are fairly sturdy, so I'll get by. No chance
> of buying another anytime soon, compensation
> being so low, and a bad horse is more trouble to
> care for than it's worth. R and I share two nags
> for servants and baggage, and a mule as well. The
> farrier taught me cold shoeing, and I always carry
> spares and nails. At least the horses I've got won't
> get bad feet. Lots of them do, on this terrain.*
>
> *Yrs., J*

When Cordell rode into the expansive stableyard
at Oatlands Park, the other guests were preparing to ride out. He saw horses being harnessed to
coaches, one after the other, until they formed a long
convoy. Saddle horses stood near the mounting blocks,
their reins held by young boys. More than a dozen

stablemen were hard at work under the direction of an officious head groom.

Spotting the new arrival, one of the younger grooms ran over.

"Is everyone leaving?" Cordell was examining the layout, noting that the map provided him had not done justice to the size of the buildings.

"An excursion, sir, to Windsor. Did you wish to join them, or shall I see to your mount?"

"He has special requirements. Is there stabling apart from the main block?"

"To your left, sir, beyond the carriage house. If you will select a location and secure him there, I'll—"

"Go back to what you were doing," Cordell said. "I'll tend to him myself and make other arrangements when things quiet down."

The chance to get a private look at the stall where the stableman's body had been found had just fallen into his hands. Good fortune stayed with him at the stable itself, from all appearances deserted. He dismounted and led Ghost inside.

Sunlight, dancing with golden motes, streamed through the east-facing windows. Familiar odors hung in the air—straw, oats, leather, oil, horses, a faint scent of manure—and he marveled at the wide center corridor, tall wooden gates, and high ceiling arching over them all. On the Peninsula, he had rarely been billeted in quarters so well fashioned and clean.

At the far end, a wide door marked the saddle room. To its left, according to the sketch in the report, was the murder stall.

He was moving along the corridor, attention focused on his target, when the sound of tuneless whistling caught his attention. Shortly after, he came to an open

stall door and saw a thin youngster on his knees with
a bucket beside him, scrubbing down the concrete
outer wall with a heavy brush.

"Are you alone here?" Cordell said.

The boy dropped the brush into the bucket and
jumped to his feet, his eyes widening when he saw
Cordell's uniform. "You be needin' a groom, sir? I'll
run and fetch one."

"That won't be necessary. Ghost likes a quiet corner. What about one of those stalls at the end?"

Apprehension lined the narrow, expressive face.
"Mebbe not so good, sir. It's been cleaned and
cleaned, but some nags shy at the smell of blood."

"Not this one. Cavalry horses get used to it or
they're no good in a battle. Was there an accident?"

"A man were killed." The boy came to the door
and pointed to the left corner stall. "Right there."

"Ah, yes. I heard about that. Have they caught
the murderer?"

"No, sir. Leastways, I don't think so. The constables
came, and the magistrate, but then they stopped coming. We never heard what happened after that."

There was something in the boy's eyes and the
twitchiness of his hands that suggested he knew more
than he was telling. Cordell guessed him to be thirteen
or fourteen. "What is your name?"

"Tom, sir."

"Well, Tom, come along. Ghost doesn't let just anyone tend to him. Shall we see if you have the knack?"

A glint of excitement gave way to sagging shoulders
and downturned lips. "Mr. Garth, he what be the head
groom, says I needs more training afore he'll let me
work for her grace's guests. If he seen me talking to
you, he'd have me for bacon."

"Would he indeed? I am a colonel, Thirteenth Light Dragoons, in the habit of giving orders and having them obeyed. That applies to you, and to head grooms as well. Do as I say. Mr. Garth will hear from me later."

"But after that, sir, you be gone."

"You needn't worry. My word on it. Let's take the stall at the end on the right, shall we? And while I watch you work, you can tell me what happened across the corridor."

The two stalls at the end were boxes, larger than the other stalls, with plenty of room to let the horse remain untied. Ghost, not in the least temperamental, stood peaceably while Tom removed his saddle and bridle, checked his hooves, and set about brushing him.

Cordell, leaning against the wall by the window with ankles crossed and arms folded, curbed his impatience and let the boy proceed in silence. After a time, he saw the tension in his ruddy neck and face slacken. Tom's movements became smoother, more automatic, until he was working with confidence.

Now was the time. "I've been trying to remember what I heard in London about the killing," he said. "It was a great scandal because of where it took place, but little was made of the victim. Is it true he was employed here?"

"For a little time." The hand wielding the brush faltered, then resumed the smooth, even strokes. "We allus take on extra help for the summer. He come early to ask, and Mr. Garth put him on straightaway a'cause the weather's been fine and we have a full house most weekends. He never talked much, except in his sleep. Didn't make sense, though."

"You shared a room?"

"Lower staff has pallets in the loft over the main stable. He weren't there that night, though. I saw him at supper, and then we were back here, cleaning up after her grace's guests had gone. It were a Monday. He left afore I did. I went to bed mebbe an hour after, but he never came up to the loft."

"And they found him here Tuesday morning? Did you see him?"

Mouth tight, Tom applied himself vigorously to the horse.

"I only ask," Cordell said, "because rumor has it that coins were strewn over his body. I wondered if that was true."

"No, sir. I—" Tom broke off, color high on his cheeks.

"It cannot be a secret. The information will have come out at the inquest. But when I arrived in London a few days ago, the murder was stale news. I'd like to put together the bits and pieces I heard, if only because I'm standing so near to where it happened."

"I weren't supposed to come in here," Tom said in a rush. "The others were to breakfast but Bill Willens, who was doing the inspection like he allus does in the morning afore Mr. Garth gives us jobs for the day. I were late and passing by the stable when Bill come running out like a devil was after him. He yelled at me to stay where I was and kept goin' toward the house."

"So you went into the stable to see what had scared him."

"Yessir. I smelled the blood, so I come down and looked in the stall. Jeremy Brown were on his back on a pile of straw with dung all over him. There was blood all over his head. His eyes were open. Mouth, too, and it had gold coins in it. His cheeks was all fat with coins, like somebody stuffed in as many as could fill it. I ran back outside and stood where I were before. Pretty soon, people came from the house and told me to go away. That's all."

"So no one knew you'd been inside? You were never questioned by the authorities?"

Tom shook his head. "I were scared to tell. Besides, Bill and the others who went in saw the same what I did. I had no cause to speak up. You won't—"

"Of course not. I expect you are trying to forget the whole thing."

"Yessir." Back to the grooming. "Exceptin' I keep seein' him, which sets me to thinkin' about him. And when the others was talkin' later about what they saw, they never said what I were thinkin'. Like why there be dung in the stall when we cleaned it all out on Monday afternoon. Whoever put it there had to bring it in. Wasn't no horses in here after Monday mornin'. We carried in fresh straw, but we'd not be carryin' in dung."

That detail hadn't been in the official report, which indicated that after being struck with a rake, the victim had fallen into a pile of mucky straw. All the attention had been focused on those damn coins in his mouth. "Anything else seem odd to you?"

"They said he was killed with the rake that was on the floor next to him. But we never leaves tools in the stalls. If Mr. Garth did an inspection and found a shovel or a rake layin' around, we'd be thrashed. I were in the saddle room till the sun went down, polishin' brass and oilin' tack. Went by that stall every time I had to go outside and do my business. The door were open. I allus look a last time inside the stalls, every one, afore I call it a day. There were no rake in there when I left."

"Where are the tools stored?"

"Two or three places. Nearest to here is a shed against the wall behind the saddle room."

Easy enough to get to. "And where do you suppose the manure came from?"

"The shi . . . the dung pile. It's away from the buildin's on account of the smell. The farmers come get it in the mornin's and take it to the fields. Bill does a count of equipment on Tuesdays. Done it late that week on account of the constable and the questions, but there were a bucket gone missing. I remember a'cause I'd been wonderin' how the manure got hauled into the stable. Mebbe the others told all this when they was asked questions, but they never said it when I was there to hear."

Small details, and important ones. The killer, carrying out his work at night, must have been familiar with the stable area. He had planned in advance how to stage the scene. Brought in the guineas, found a rake and a bucket, knew where to go for the manure. Chose an area away from where the servants were lodged.

"It had to be a toff," said the boy. "I never seen that much money in m' life, even if you took up all I'd ever see'd and put it in one place."

"Or, perhaps, a toff who hired a killer. Any servants at Oatlands who might take on that kind of work if the pay was right?"

"I been thinkin' about that, too. But most of us has been here a long time. Her grace be an angel on the earth. She treats us right, and we stays loyal. Jeremy were the first new hire for the summer, except for housemaids and a roastin' cook and three laundry maids. Mebbe one of us sold out, but nobody I can point to."

"What about Brown's absence that night? Did anyone explain where he'd gone?"

"Not to me. But the stablemen what aren't married and lives in the stable loft or over the carriage house sometimes go off like that. I seen 'em now and again sneak down to the river after dark and take one of the boats. They call it goin' downriver and laugh, but they won't say what they mean. Not to me."

"You're an observant lad," Cordell said, pulling himself away from the wall. By this time, the vehicle with his valet and baggage should have arrived. He had better make his bows to the duchess, assuming she'd not gone to Windsor with the others. "I'll speak to Mr. Garth about letting you care for Ghost, who seems to approve of you. And I'll not let out you told me anything of what happened that night, if you keep quiet about it as well. I shouldn't like anyone to think I've turned into an old gossip."

"Yessir. I mean, no talk from me. It's over, anyway. The 'thorities pay no mind to what happens to a servant, 'specially one who blew in with the wind. I didn't much like Jeremy Brown, but he ought not to have died like that with nobody to care that he did."

"Agreed." On his way out, Cordell tossed the boy a sovereign. "Ghost is partial to carrots. Also apples and, I'm sorry to say, turnips."

"You don't needs to pay for them, sir."

"I'm not. If you think of anything to add to the story of Jeremy Brown, be sure to let me know. It seems I was mistaken. I *am* an old gossip."

The carriages and riders had departed by the time Cordell returned to the stableyard and located Mr. Garth, who expressed no reservations about a cavalry officer's disposition of his mount. Then it was on to the house, where traps of every sort had probably been laid for him.

To a man who had spent weekends of this sort in lavish French châteaus, there was nothing intimidating about the estate of a royal duke and his duchess. But what waited inside this one had kept his blood pumping and his thoughts spinning all the way from London.

Set a task, he invariably went to it with single-minded precision. But tracking a killer was the least of his concerns right now. That much, at least, he could manage, although success depended on factors beyond his control. But the other struggle, the one he had unwillingly entered and could not escape, still had him flummoxed.

Prescience was what he needed. A better understanding of female peculiarities. A gift for mind reading wouldn't hurt. Meaning his own mind, because damned if he could figure out what was going on in there. His usual good sense had lurched off in a hundred directions, dragging the rest of him with it.

One woman, as single-minded as he, had set herself to bring him down for reasons of her own. That was about the only thing he was sure of.

Lacking evidence. On pure instinct. By the pricking of his thumbs. Even without an open declaration of war—and he had tried to elicit one—they were unmistakably at daggers drawn.

He wanted to know why, of course, but she wasn't

going to give him a straight answer. Not until she had him where she wanted him. Then, if she was in the mood to gloat, he might find out why she hated him.

Most incomprehensible of all . . . he was powerfully drawn to her.

To the darkness in her.

The portico lay ahead, and beneath it, the door he would walk through with anticipation and dread. This was how it felt on the night before a battle.

The Eve of battle.

But more than likely, he would be granted a reprieve. She'd probably gone off to Windsor with the others.

She hadn't. He had scarcely been admitted into the entrance hall when Lady Eve swept out of an adjacent room, the smile of a satisfied cat on her face. "Welcome to Oatlands, Colonel. I hope you had a pleasant journey from London. When your valet arrived ahead of you, we were a trifle concerned."

He handed the footman his hat, gloves, and the walking stick with a concealed blade he'd taken to carrying. "Good morning, Lady Eve. You pounce as effectively as Lady Holland."

"And I'm despotic as well," she said with a laugh. "Her grace has asked me to present you, but it's far too early for her to emerge from her rooms. You'll wish to settle into your own, I am sure. A servant will lead you there. And after, perhaps you will let me show you the gardens."

Bowing to her, and to the inevitable, he followed the footman up several flights of stairs, unsurprised that he'd been relegated to near the attics. But there was no lack of comfort and good taste in the large bedchamber with its adjoining dressing room and, on the other side of that, a comfortable room for his valet.

Silas Indigo, Black Phoenix flunky, was transferring shirts and linens from a portmanteau to the stand of drawers. He was an exceptionally fit man in his mid-fifties with a lean face framed by a shock of graying hair and prominent side-whiskers. "Did you encounter any difficulty on the way, sir?"

"None whatever. I stopped by the murder scene for a little reconnaissance."

Cordell went into the dressing room, removed his jacket, rolled up his sleeves, and washed the dirt of the road from his hands, face, and neck. When he was done, Indigo handed him a towel.

"I learned something that might prove useful," Cordell told him. "Find out precisely what is meant when male servants go downriver. It refers to a brothel, almost certainly, but I want the location favored by the stablehands. Jeremy Brown may have been there the night he was killed."

"I will see to it." Indigo helped him back into his jacket, now freshly brushed, and adjusted his collar. "Formal attire this evening, sir. Will you have dress uniform or—"

"You decide. My next task is, God help me, a public flirtation with Lady Eve. Do whatever it takes to help me look convincing."

Chapter 9

Portugal, Nov. 1810

> *The captain brought me with him to Lisbon. Said
> I needed a break from campaigning, but I'd
> rather be doing that. Here it's all drinking at tav-
> erns and looking for entertainment. The proper
> females are kept away or guarded by their drag-
> ons, but the other kind are everywhere to be
> found. I went to a local assembly with some of
> the fellows, but there were more of them than
> ladies, so I didn't have to dance. All they had
> to drink there was water! We didn't stay long.
> Cannonballs has got himself a widow and a
> house, so I never saw him the whole time we were
> here until tonight. Then he made me go to the
> opera with him and some of the other officers.
> My ears still hurt. We leave for Torres Vedras
> at dawn.*
>
> Yrs., J

"My heavens," Eve said when Colonel Cordell
finished telling her what he had learned at the
stable. "Within a few minutes of arriving, you gath-

ered more information than I have done in twenty-
four hours."

"You could hardly go around interrogating stable-
boys." He gave her a pointed look. "For that matter,
you are not to go around interrogating anyone."

They were strolling along a gravel path that wound
through Oatlands' extensive gardens. "I shall do as I
see fit," she said. "But I know what is proper, sir.
If I cross a boundary, you may be sure the reason
is compelling."

"Fair enough," he said, surprising her. "Did you
find anything of interest in the reports?"

"No." Said with a pang of regret, because she had
read them over and over again, determined to spot a
clue the others had missed. "Like you, I was acutely
aware of what was not there. Then I realized that
unlike Black Phoenix, the investigating authorities had
failed to draw a link between the killings. It probably
requires all three before anyone would notice."

"Phoenix saw the connection before the third murder. But as you say, an exacting study of the victims'
personal histories would not have seemed relevant to
the authorities in the first two cases, if only because
they were rather well known gentlemen. The immediate past was covered fairly well, I thought, but there
was little information dating back more than a year
or two."

"And virtually none in the Jeremy Brown report,"
Eve said. "Was any effort made to locate his family or
discover where he had worked prior to coming here?"

"You'll recall that he had given the stable master
an unspecific accounting of past employment and experience, referring in particular to a Kent estate where

the owner fell on hard times, sold off his horses, and dismissed the servants without pay or references Sir Peregrine thought he'd pinpointed the gentleman in question, so we rode down there on Thursday. The one stablehand remaining in service failed to recognize the name, but he said a young man of Brown's description had worked there for several months."

"Jeremy Brown was using another name, then?"

"We can't be sure. The owner acknowledged dismissing the stable help, but insisted that he had provided references and back wages. And the young man who resembled Brown left a week before the horses were sold. Vanished, in fact, without notice. A maidservant who enjoyed his attentions said he had appeared to take fright of something, although he never said what."

While Eve considered the bits of information just served up, part of her was celebrating. Cordell had spoken to her as a collaborator. No impatience. Not a grain of condescension. She felt as if a light had been ignited inside her. "So we have no idea who Jeremy Brown really was."

"Or how the other two victims are connected, although we'll soon know a good deal more about them. Meantime, I have Indigo tracing where Brown spent his time immediately prior to meeting his fate in a stable stall. Is there more you wish to ask or report?"

"Nothing relating to the crimes. Mrs. Kipper asks that you stop by her room this afternoon and identify yourself to the dog. I'm afraid we encountered some difficulty with him. The servants in this household are well accustomed to dogs and easily passed through the ritual. But we could not subject distinguished gentleman to it, and whenever one of them came along the passageway, the dog made an earsplitting racket. The only solution was for me to relocate from my usual bedchamber to one on the second floor, well away from any rooms containing gentlemen."

"About the ritual. What the blazes does that entail?"

"Oh, it's simple enough. You will use specific words to get the dog's attention, and when he is seated, you will place a piece of dried venison atop his nose. He will leave it there until you speak the code that identifies you as an acceptable male. He then devours the treat and accepts you into his pack, as Mrs. Kipper puts it. From that time on, you may approach without being barked at or attacked."

"Comforting, to be sure. I assume he has been trained to warn and protect, but of what use is he to us?"

"None that I can see, unless one of the gentlemen guests pays an unwelcome call to my bedchamber. Mrs. Kipper is the dog's instructor, and because she foresees a lot of idle time on this mission, she brought him along for further training. We are pretending he's mine, of course. No servant would be permitted to bring a pet into a household other than this one."

"Are we invading other households, madam?"

"I was told to make it possible." She glanced at him sideways. He was walking with his hands clasped behind his back—his ramrod-straight back—looking directly ahead of him. The colonel invariably isolated himself, no matter the circumstances. "Hints were dropped," she said. "Invitations have arrived. Now we await a clue that will send us one direction or another."

"Or for the next murder. This is a race against time,

and the devil of it is, we don't know which way to run. I cannot endure being useless. What, other than ingratiating myself with a dog, am I to do for the rest of the day and the evening?"

"You are to court me, sir. Have you forgotten our impending betrothal?"

"I've been trying to. In my judgment, this charade is needless and frivolous."

Her plan to entice him in the morning, beguile him in the evening, and seduce him in the night was not getting off to an auspicious start. As Major Blair had told her, the man was incessantly running calculations in his head. She must find some way to throw him off balance.

"Perhaps it isn't necessary, after all," she said thoughtfully. "Because you are a virtual stranger in England, the betrothal seemed the only practical way to make sure you could go wherever the investigation led without arousing suspicion. Phoenix, if you haven't noticed, is positively obsessive about secrecy. But should there be reason to call at, say, Wilton or Chatsworth or Knolls, your presence is not essential. Whatever needs to be done, I can undertake it myself."

That got his attention. She felt him looking at her, but kept her own gaze fixed on the path ahead. A little of his own medicine, served cold, and she could tell it wasn't going down smoothly.

"Casting me off, are you?"

"We can't any of us have precisely what we want, sir. I have accepted the summons and will proceed, whatever your decision about the betrothal."

"Not alone, you won't." He'd come to a dead stop and put out his arm to halt her as well.

The physical contact, his wool-clad arm just above

her waist, sent little bursts of heat up and down her body. Since that night at Holland House, she had been anticipating the next time he would touch her. Where would it be? How would it feel?

It felt like an iron bar, quickly removed.

"But I'm not alone," she said in a chipper tone. "I have Mrs. Kipper. And a dog. Truly, sir, if you cannot play the part convincingly, it would be better to call off the betrothal before we start pretending it exists. Don't you think?"

"I'm beginning to wonder," he said, striding forward.

Yes, they were in a race, although not the one he had spoken of. And she knew—more or less—where she was going, if not how she would get there. It had become clear to her that nothing ordinary was going to work with this man. He would only be taken by surprise. And she had a plan for that, already in place, but he was dangerously vigilant. Watchful, like the golden eagle in the picture. Before the surprise, then, a diversion. And for her, a daring gamble.

She caught up with him. "Is that your answer?"

The look of pleasure she'd put on her face had the desired effect. He shot her a black look in return. "You'd like that, wouldn't you? I walk away, the field is yours . . . and then what?"

"I catch the killer. Or I don't. At least I won't be wasting words and breath in a constant battle with you about my respectability and my reputation and my future, none of which are your concern. You were to be a partner, not the protector of my good name. But much of the time, sir, you behave exactly like my *mother*."

"Good God." Another sudden halt. "Is there nothing you will not say?"

"As you see, I am willful to a fault. Another aspect of my character much disliked by my mother."

She'd wanted to provoke him into losing his temper, but no such luck. His gaze, locked with hers, was implacable.

"First, the dog," he said. "Then present me to the duchess, if she is available. For the rest of the day and evening, unless Indigo produces the information I requested, I shall make a show of wooing you. I'll not refer again to your unruly behavior and its probable consequences. In return, when I issue a direct order, you will obey it. Agreed?"

"Oh, yes. Well, all but that last bit. I'll not hop to do your bidding every time you take a notion to order me about."

"I meant orders related to our mission."

"Yes, but what if I have a better idea than the one you came up with?"

"Then lay it on the table. I'm not so lost to common sense that I'd reject a superior plan. I'll not abuse my authority, madam, but you must grant me the little of it I am demanding."

"Very well, sir. Subject to amending your original proposal to include 'related to the mission,' we have a bargain. Shall we head back to the house and present you to the dog and the duchess?"

They walked side by side, Eve taking care to look at anything but the suspiciously agreeable colonel. Her breath was coming too swiftly, so great was her relief. And, yes, her triumph.

She had challenged him and got away with it.

Colonel Cordell, after making friends with the dog, the duchess, and a score of the duchess's dogs, adhered to Eve like a sticking plaster. That was the term he used, an unexpected glint of humor in his eyes, and she warmed to the novelty of his gallant attentions as the day wore on.

Only at dinner, where her status and his required a separation, and later, when he spent an hour in the billiards room, were they apart. She used the time to regather her wits and her detachment, which seemed to dissolve whenever he came within touching distance. She deliberately put a card table between them for several rubbers of whist, where he complimented her on play she knew to be less than her best. But he covered her errors, made up for her mistakes, and when they won, gave her all the credit.

"Slathering it too thick," she told him, laughing, as they left the overheated card room.

"I am besotted. Is this not how a besotted male behaves? You must be familiar with the breed."

She was. But nearly all of them had been besotted with her wealth, her rank, and even her appearance, which had improved considerably after she turned sixteen. Used to thinking of herself as stick-thin and awkward, she had never felt at ease with physical attentions. But now, perversely, she found herself craving them from the most impossible of sources . . . a man she despised. The disconnection between her body and her mind, her passions and her will, continued to mystify her.

They wandered onto the terrace, colorful in the light cast by Japanese lanterns, his arm threaded around hers. Many of the guests were strolling among the knot gardens and miniature trees, enjoying the cool breeze and a three-quarter moon hanging in a field of stars.

"Have we persuaded anyone?" he said after a time.

"In all likelihood. But I'm not certain of *what*. Longtime acquaintances are regarding me as if I've drunk too much champagne or taken a hard blow to the head."

"Because you favor a weathered old soldier?"

"You are hardly that, sir. It is because I have always been regarded as inaccessible. Or, if you will, cold-blooded. To see me fluttering my lashes and hanging on your arm is, in their minds, rather like watching a rabbit dance the ballet. Shall we give them something more intriguing to observe?"

He sliced her a look. "Such as what? Another public kiss?"

"Perhaps. But not here. That would be too déclassé, even for an ensorceled lass. Allow me, sir, to sweep you off to the grotto."

With a shrug, he permitted her to steer him away from the high terrace, down a grassy slope, and onto a path that wound alongside Broadwater Lake.

Scattered all around the lake were torchlit follies, classical temples, gazebos, and clusters of statues. The sky, glorious and radiant, cupped a landscape that must have belonged to faeries in ancient times.

In the silence, Eve found herself sliding into the fantasies of her girlhood. In her favorite daydreams, she had walked these same paths a thousand times, but in the company of another man. Her courtier. Her prince. Her Johnnie.

He had never been to Oatlands, never walked here with her. And she had not come this direction since his death.

Now she felt the strong presence of her antagonist, Johnnie's betrayer, at her side. The same capricious force that had brought them together on this mission must have orchestrated this night as well. Who could have imagined such a bizarre concurrence of events, rare as a comet?

It was meant to be. Planned, she had no doubt, by dark forces in the universe, but nevertheless, a wonder.

On this night, she knew that she must leave behind her forever the child who had imagined a bright, innocent, conventional future. To achieve her purpose, she must now tap into the deepest core of her female nature and transform herself into a seductress, alluring and confident of her powers.

It wasn't how she'd expected her life to turn out. But here she was.

And here he was.

And she would have him.

Directly ahead, perched on a rocky outcrop overlooking a sheltered curve of the lake, stood the famous Oatlands Park grotto. The facade, once that of a classical domed building two stories high, had been transformed not long after its construction into something rich and very, very strange.

"There it is," she said to Cordell, pointing.

"I was expecting a cave."

"Wait till you get inside."

They followed a narrow path up the hill, passing between a tangle of thorny shrubbery and overhanging branches designed to separate the real world from the one that lay beyond.

The Perilous Path, she used to call it, that led to the Lair of the Demon Lord. Curiosity always bade her enter, and, being a foolish and impetuous child, she rushed straight in. Much trouble ensued, depending on the amount of time she had to play out her solitary game, and every game ended with Johnnie riding in on a glorious white steed to rescue her.

The memories came rushing back, vivid and painful, as she led Colonel Cordell through the open door. Everything was different now. She wasn't making up stories in her head. The danger was real. There would be no rescue for either of them. And she was fetching the Demon Lord to the lair.

Inside lay the first chamber of a labyrinth she could have negotiated by touch, were it not dimly lit by concealed lamps. The flames contained within multicolored glass orbs sent flickering lights across the irregular walls, where artfully placed mirrors reflected the light and sent it dancing in every direction.

The impression was much like swimming into an underwater cavern, or so she imagined. The rough surfaces of the walls and ceiling were studded with shells, branches of coral fans, and ornamental rocks, all set within swirling patterns and designs that made one dizzy to look at them overlong.

She glanced over at Cordell, who stood with hands behind his back, gazing up at an inlay of fossils. "What think you, sir?"

"That someone went to a great deal of trouble and expense to create a monstrosity. Is that a stuffed lizard on the ledge?"

There were several, a testament to one of the duchess's passing hobbies. "Much has been added since last I was here. Shall we go deeper?"

They wandered through a chamber lit by chandeliers and adorned with bits salvaged from ships, including a mast, oars, nails, and metal fittings.

Next came the most cavelike chamber, studded with artificial stalactites.

Cordell paused to examine them. "Lathe," he said, "with calcite spars affixed. Clever work, lit as it is. Is this how the duchess entertains herself?"

"She has to do *something*," Eve said. "Not long after their marriage, the duke stashed her at Oatlands and got on about his own pursuits. But the grotto is not her creation. It was here when the estate was purchased about thirty years ago. I have seen the plans for the original construction, sir. They call for ten thousand horses' teeth, ten thousand cows' teeth, and the bones from ten thousand pigs' feet."

"You are making that up."

"No, indeed. The teeth and bones were ground, polished, and used for the ramps and floors."

Now watching his feet, Cordell led the meandering way into another, smaller chamber, this one resembling an overcrowded museum. "A rhinoceros horn?" he said, pointing to a curved shape sticking out of the wall.

"I'm afraid so. Come look at this. It will interest you."

He joined her beside a niche lit from overhead. On it rested the skull of a horse.

"This," she said, "belonged to Eclipse. The racehorse. Have you heard of him?"

"Of course. Good God. They could at least have given him a decent burial."

"They gave most of him a decent burial. People who own and race some of his descendants come here and touch their horses' colors to the skull for luck and a blessing."

"Now *that*," he said, "does not surprise me. Unlike everything else in this freakish place."

"You prefer military order, I suppose. Clean lines, polished and pristine, nothing extraneous or ornamental."

"No one who has seen a cavalry dress uniform ought to say that with a straight face. And in my travels, I have marveled at any number of buildings that would rival this one for overdecoration. But those, most of them, grew from traditional patterns and, often, religious beliefs. Some Hindu temples . . . Well, you wouldn't be permitted to see them."

"Women are not allowed to worship there?"

"That's not what I mean. The nature of the carvings and what they depict is unsuitable for . . . Never mind." A flash of white teeth. "I feel the quicksand sucking at my ankles."

Her heart gave a wild thump. He had smiled. Not a proper social smile. A real one.

Damn the man. She had not brought him here to smile, or to make her pulse race, or to start becoming human in front of her eyes. She was here to arm herself for the upcoming battle. He was here to remind her of what she had to do, and why she had to do it.

And, too, there was the entrapment.

In the cool of a summer night, a few guests always walked to the grotto. Upstairs, in a chamber that had once served as a banquet room, refreshments had earlier been laid out. Two or three footmen would be there now, ready to pour wine and offer sweetmeats.

But first, the guests would follow the trail she had just walked with Cordell, and they must all pass through the largest of the chambers, the one to which she would lead him now.

He had wandered over to a display of stuffed fish, their scales and eyes glittering in the half-light. She used the distraction to put her ear to one of the concealed air vents. Yes. Sounds of voices and laughter from outside, moving closer. The witnesses would be here soon.

This was only practice, really. If he did not respond as she wished, the next step would be all that much more difficult, but at least she would be prepared. And, too, she wanted to seal the betrothal, or make a try at it.

Retribution, she had thought many times, would be so much easier if she could simply plunge a dagger into his heart and be done with it. The idea had tempted her from the beginning. But for one thing, he was considerably stronger than she, a warrior by nature, and not a man to be taken unaware. And for another, Johnnie would disapprove.

In her more rational moments, she had to admit that Johnnie would disapprove any scheme she came up with to punish Cordell. These were plots and plans developed on her own behalf. Johnnie was never so cold and vindictive as she could sometimes be, and for his sake alone, she put aside all stratagems that involved death or mutilation.

But once she ruled out physical harm, vengeance became increasingly complex. How, precisely, could she deprive a man of his reputation without surrendering her own? So far, no coherent plan had materialized, but she'd think of something. She was prepared to accept losses.

And if she survived the wreckage she created, she could gather up the pieces of her reputation again. Perhaps she, like Lady Etheridge and Lady Holland, would end up doing valuable work after a notable fall from grace.

Come what may, she meant to harm Cordell.

She looked over at him. He was studying a large mosaic of shells and polished stones set in the wall. It depicted a mermaid swimming beneath the sea while above her flew a dragon, its fiery breath licking down at the water.

"What will the dragon do," he said when Eve came to stand at his side, "if he catches her?"

"Devour her, I suppose."

"And the moral of the story?"

Surprised by the question, she looked more closely at the mosaic. "That there is always someone larger and meaner than you are, out to get you? But she doesn't appear to be afraid."

"Because she doesn't know the dragon is there?"

"Of course she does. One can hardly miss a great hulking dragon overhead, if only by the shadow it casts. Either she has an escape route near to hand, or she holds power over the dragon."

"That's it exactly," said Cordell. "Beauty controls the beast. He threatens her, he desires her, but he can never master her. There are stories of this kind in every language and every mythology. The ones I am familiar with, anyway."

"Meaning that an ugly mermaid, or even a plain one, is destined to be supper?"

"Physical beauty is only a symbol of the power wielded by a female. In the myths, that is, because I grant that beauty exercises an inordinate control over men in day-to-day life. A reflection of our own weaknesses, to be sure."

She certainly hoped so. And it was time to move

him on to the stage for the next scene in her improvised play. "There is another image of female beauty in the next chamber, sir. The Venus de Medici. Will you come see her?"

He had to stoop a little as they passed through the arched tunnel leading to the chamber known as the bathhouse. A large tiled bath occupied the most of it, the wavy reflection of lights on the water cast back to the walls and ceilings in eerie patterns.

Cordell's attention was immediately caught by a large stuffed alligator set out beside the pool as if sunning itself. Then he looked to the far end of the chamber and the niche on which stood a life-size marble statue of a nude woman preserving an inch or two of modesty with a piece of marble cloth that she appeared about to release from her fingers. "The Venus, I take it," he said, sounding unimpressed.

"The original is a second-century Roman statue, but this is only a copy, recent and, as you see, not very good. That's a little terra-cotta Hercules next to her. He used to be elsewhere, but it appears someone moved him in hopes of sparking a romance."

"I hear voices," said Cordell, looking back toward the tunnel. "We are about to have company."

"Come," she said, extending her hand.

He took it, engulfing most of her hand with his much larger one. They both wore gloves, but it seemed she could feel the blood pulsing through his flesh, beating against hers. She was leading him to a partly hidden nook alongside the statue, her throat burning with nervousness and anticipation.

"More evidence provided to witnesses?" he said softly.

"We'll pretend we didn't hear them. Sound plays

tricks in all the chambers, this one more than the others. And there is a secret way out that we'll take so they cannot quiz us afterward."

"Good. We shall leave people to draw whatever conclusions they will, Lady Eve, but you are to confirm nothing. No private hints or public announcements of a betrothal."

She gazed up at him in dismay. They were standing now where she wanted to be, a spot where mirrors and water and lights would pick up their image and carry it to every part of the chamber. Once inside, the witnesses would be all but surrounded by reflections of Lady Eve and Colonel Cordell locked in an embrace. "But why not?" she said. "We agreed on continuing with the betrothal plan."

"To setting it up, yes, in case we need the masquerade. But anything can happen in the meantime. The murderer might step forward and confess. Someone could catch him in the act. It's one thing to compromise your reputation with a little improper behavior, madam, and quite another to end a betrothal. We'll not resort to that unless we must."

Her plan to humiliate and dishonor him required it. But she nodded, and hoped he sensed none of her frustration. Besides, a rumor could be started. The right sort of hint to the right people. It would spread quickly, growing more outrageous with each telling, especially if fueled by a convincing performance now.

The witnesses were in the tunnel, she could tell, about to emerge. She began to lift her hands, not sure what she would do with them, when Cordell closed the small space between them and wrapped one arm around her back. She looked up into his eyes, brown-gold and shadowed, fixing her with intense purpose.

A leather-gloved finger moved slowly up the side of her neck, to her cheek, across her lips.

The voices, so loud a moment ago, seemed to be coming from a great distance now. There was only his face, very near, his warm breath visible in the damp air, the finger on her lips slipping a little between them and moving inside. Pressing lightly against her teeth until, obedient, she opened them. The tip of her tongue against the tip of his finger, a gentle invasion and withdrawal. When his finger retraced its path across her lips and cheek, she felt the moisture of her own mouth leave a little trail behind.

At that moment, there was nothing she would have denied him. She wondered if he knew it. Looked more intently into his eyes and saw that he did.

The finger moved down her neck to her collarbone, exposed by the low cut of her gown, and from there to the swell of her breasts above her stays. She made a little gasp. He never released his gaze from hers, nor could she look away. She realized that without seeming to, he had adjusted their position to cover all of her but the side of her head and her right shoulder. No one could see where his hand was wandering.

Around the outside curve of her breast now, and then across. Stopping. Through glove and gown and chemise and stays, his fingertip pressed against her nipple, teased at it with a motion like he'd used in her mouth. She knew what it meant. Heat and moisture gathered between her legs. She realized that her lower body was moving against his, restrained only by the pressure of the arm now coiled around her waist.

Sensation tingled over her skin. Inside her, a great emptiness ached to be filled. Burned for it.

His hand settled over her breast, holding her flesh

as if claiming it. Warm breath ghosted against her cheek. Warm lips brushed lightly against her lips. Warmer than the rest, his tongue sought entrance and found it.

The dizzying sensations washed over her like waves on a beach, one after the other, until she was engulfed with pleasure and need. She would have fallen, but he held her just where he wanted her. Her hands were on his back, she didn't know how they came there, her fingers digging into the heavy fabric of his coat. Underneath his clothing, he was hard as sculpted marble.

And still he kissed her, commanding, possessive, purely male. And without thought or resistance, she gave herself over to him.

He was breathing heavily when, after a time, he set her gently, firmly away. Almost arm's distance, except for one hand lightly gripping her shoulder. "They're gone," he said. "Where is the secret way out?"

She looked at him blankly, a sound resonating in her ears as if she were holding seashells up to them.

"Others are on their way in." His hand gripped tighter, shaking her a little. "Let's go."

Partly restored to her senses, she led him behind the niche from which Venus had watched them kissing and opened a narrow door. The shoulder-wide tunnel, barely illuminated with lanterns hung overhead, curved like a child's ringlet until it ended at a narrow door like the first one. They came out of the grotto on the side facing away from the lake, invisible to anyone walking along the main pathway.

The stars and moon seemed unnaturally bright. She looked over at Cordell, who was scanning the area around him. Making calculations, she thought. Getting his bearings.

Silver light dusted his forehead, the slope of his nose, his high cheekbones, the firm outline of his jaw. All else was shadowed. The whites of his eyes gleamed from inside dark caves.

The Demon Lord. She was his captive. And his destroyer.

Chapter 10

Portugal, Oct. 1810

Do you remember the goat I had to pay for twice? That business with the captain got stuck in my throat. Not the money so much, but him thinking I stole the goat and lied about it. So this morning I marched up to him and said the farmer was the liar, not me. "I know," says Cannonballs. "He's always pulling tricks like that on Johnny Newcomes." "Then why," says I, "did you make me pay him again?" "You want to be an exploring officer," he says, "but you didn't trouble to ask for a piece of information easily come by. The neglect cost you a little money. Another time, it could cost lives. Wherever you are, make a point of finding out who can be trusted." "How do I do that?" says I. "If I decide you're worth teaching," he says, "I'll show you." So, I was in the wrong after all. And he didn't think me dishonorable. Just stupid. Now I have to prove him wrong about that!

Yrs., J

Cordell lay on his back, arms folded behind his head, still trying to unriddle the mystery of Lady Eve Halliday. He had been at it for nearly two hours, measured by his interior timepiece, and all he could say for his efforts was that they kept him from thinking about what had transpired in that ridiculous grotto. No more than every three or four minutes, at any rate.

His body had almost returned to his control, which had seemed impossible during the first hour. When they arrived at the house, he'd managed a curt farewell to Lady Eve and all but galloped up three flights of stairs to his bedchamber.

Only to encounter Silas Indigo, brimming over with news of where male servants went when they went downriver. Cordell decided to ride over there directly after breakfast. If Sunday morning was not the usual time to call on a whore, it served to get him out of the house and away from his nemesis for a few hours. The longer the space between their encounters, the better.

He wondered, not for the first time, if she was planning to kill him.

He kept circling back to that idea because of the hostility he sensed every time she came in his vicinity. It was soul-deep, the kind engendered by a long-held, well-nourished grudge. And grudges, unlike rational causes for hatred, could spring up from nowhere. A rumor, a misinterpreted glance, or a little wrong information could set off an explosion.

What had occasioned Lady Eve's contempt he could not fathom. She was too intelligent to have run aground on a mere rumor, and while he had hardly led a blameless life, most of his sins were confined to much younger days. Actions taken in the line of duty sometimes created resentment, or worse, but she had no close male relations who might have served under his command. She was barely out when the war ended, or appeared to have ended. Twenty at the time of Waterloo. If he had run afoul of a soldier she held dear, he could not imagine which one it might be.

Could he have offended one of her female friends? But he had never bedded an Englishwoman, save only the widow of a lieutenant killed at Talavera. She'd no money, nowhere to go, so he established her in his small house and visited her on the rare occasions he found himself in Lisbon. Then she found someone else, someone willing to marry her, and off she went.

Nothing accounted for Lady Eve. He was beginning to think the only way he'd find out what she meant to do was to let her do it. Then, if he wasn't dead, he might find out *why* she'd done it.

The sole candle flickering on the mantelpiece seemed inordinately bright. He let his eyes drift shut, felt around for the discarded sheet, pulled it over his bare torso, and instructed his body to sleep.

Sometime later, a light clicking sound from across the room shot him awake. He put his hand on the pistol alongside his pillow and rolled soundlessly off the bed.

Another faint noise. Hinges. But not from the direction of the door.

The candle was burning low, its golden light outlining the furniture but revealing little else. Crouched on the floor near the foot of the bed, he held the pistol steady and sought for movement where he'd heard the sound.

It came soon after, with the soft rubbing of well-oiled metal on metal. Before his eyes, the wall opened.

A servants' staircase, was his first thought. But from habit, he never stayed anywhere without inspecting the entrances and exits. The servants' stairs in this suite of rooms led to the chamber where Silas Indigo was sleeping.

A secret passage, then, one he had not discovered. And someone was coming in.

He could barely make out the shadow, black against black. His eyes scanned the darkness for signs of an arm lifting, weapon in hand. He raised his own gun.

The figure moved a little forward. Candlelight brushed it around the edges, illuminating a flowing white gown.

He let out the breath he'd been holding and swore aloud.

"Not the welcome I was hoping for," said Lady Eve.

"It's more polite than the bullet I nearly put through your head. Are you mad, coming here like this?"

"I prefer to think of it as impetuous. Are you often attacked after midnight in ducal manors?"

"People have been trying to kill me for twenty years, madam. It's when I presume myself safe that one of them will get to me."

Another step forward. She held out her arms and flexed her hands to show they were empty. Limned by candlelight, she showed a good deal more than that. The almost transparent gown revealed everything that lay beneath it.

He was in more danger than any number of armed men could have visited on him.

Enthralled by curves and shadows, he held in place.

Remembered, finally, to take his finger off the trigger. Remembered to take another breath.

She was here to seduce him. That was as transparent as her gown. But to what purpose? Almost certainly this extraordinary invasion had to do with the message he'd seen in her eyes when first they met, and every time since. Even when he was kissing her, she was hating him.

Did she imagine that if he accepted her offer, she would hold him in her power?

Or did she mean to cry rape? Not many would believe her, given the circumstances, but they would jump to the side of Marbury's daughter and hang the insolent soldier.

"Are you still pointing the gun at me?" she said. "I am afraid to move."

He put the pistol on the floor, started to rise, remembered to grab the bedsheet and wrap it around his waist. "You are safe for the moment. But unless you have a bulletproof explanation for being here, I won't answer for what I'll do after I've heard it."

"There are only three choices, if you think about it. You can shoot me. You can throw me out. Or you can take me into your bed."

That was blunt enough. He wasn't about to shoot her, and because she wanted the bedding, he knew better than to leap at that infernally tempting prospect. Which left him with no choice but to escort her back through the wall and seal off the opening against her.

But he didn't move.

She did, advancing two steps closer. The candlelight shone from behind, creating a halo around her, carving out the indentation of her waist, the swell of her hips, the slope of smooth thighs, the glory of long, perfectly shaped legs.

The thought of surrender tickled at his brain. Why not? What man wouldn't barter his pride for a night with this woman?

But his honor?

"There is only one choice," he said. "Go now, Lady Eve. We shall pretend this never happened."

"Nothing *has* happened. But I want it to. I won't willingly leave, sir. Not until I've made my case." Another step forward. One more and her knees would be touching the bed. "Will you hear me out?"

Only Lady Eve would think of arguing her way into disgrace.

If, like Odysseus, he could be tied to a mast and safely hear the Sirens' song, he might go along for the ride. But there was only a sheet and a night rail between his body and hers. And the width of a bed, too easily crossed. And his own weakness, which he had sworn would never again master him.

And yet, he said nothing.

"This cannot be a surprise," she said at length. "I came here believing you would welcome me. You gave me reason."

"Because I kissed you? That was your plan, not mine."

"Because of *how* you kissed me. It was far more than our deception required."

"But it wasn't an *invitation*. There isn't a red-blooded male on the planet who'd turn down a treat like that. Not when you made it so clear you were willing to participate."

"As I am now."

"This is different. Your reputation—"

"You must not say it! That is a violation of our agreement. No references to my behavior and its consequences. Remember?"

"You lay your traps well, madam. But I am not walking into this one. We spoke of reckless behavior, not social suicide. One day, or so you told me, you intend to make a good marriage. Your husband will have certain expectations." He sounded like a stiff-rumped Methodist preacher. "Look. I know you have a taste for excitement. You are fearless. But this is a boundary you may not cross."

"But I already have. And once the barrier is broken, there is little reason not to cross it again. Don't you think?"

He had stopped thinking just about the time she walked into the light of the candle. Was she lying? During their brief encounters, she hadn't impressed him as having much experience, or any at all. But tonight she had pranced into his bedchamber like a courtesan to the manner born. "I think," he said carefully, "that to get what you want, you stand ready to lie."

"I'll not deny it. But in this case, I am speaking the truth. You will find that out soon enough."

"I am not such a cad, madam, that I would despoil a virgin. Or risk doing so because a lady has decided to play irresponsible games."

"Games are harmless, Colonel Cordell. Why will you not play with me?"

He was fighting a losing battle . . . with himself. "Why do you not fix your sights on a man who would be properly grateful? There must be several right here in this house."

"Because it is you I desire."

The declaration, so unexpected, blanked his mind.

"You are strong, sir, and well made. In your arms, when we really *were* playing a game, I wanted more and still more from you. That is why I am here." She moved around the bed until she was standing within arm's reach of him. "You may turn me away, of course, if you do not desire me. All I ask is that you do not deny us both."

He was drowning. "And should there be a child?"

"If you take care, the chance is small." Her right hand seemed to float across the space between them, her fingertips coming to rest on his bare shoulder. "That is my risk, not yours. I shouldn't mind having a child. It would mean living elsewhere, but I've always been prepared to do that. Have no concerns, I beg you. Nor any expectations. This is what it is. I'll not marry you."

Her hand slid down his chest, stopped over his heart, remained here. Long-fingered, white as cream against his sun-stained body, more threatening than an attack by the Imperial Guard. He could raise no weapons against this woman, and no defenses.

"May I have you, then?" she said.

In submission, he spread his arms.

Her smile carried a hint of triumph, but he'd stopped trying to guess what lay behind her startling conduct, or what she thought she had achieved. If this seduction was prelude to his destruction . . . well, he didn't care.

Her lifted her hand from his chest, kissed it, and went to light another candle on the mantelpiece. And before she could distract him beyond reason, he brought in several towels and a basin of water from the dressing room. Then he returned to Lady Eve, standing patiently where he'd left her, and relieved her of the soft gown. "We won't be needing this."

"Nor this," she said, unwrapping the bedsheet at his waist and letting it drop. Her gaze lowered. He heard her draw in a quick breath. Then she looked up at him, eyes gleaming with fascination and primal awareness.

"Yes," he said. "That is what you are here for."

She smiled as her attention slid back to his engorged cock. She brought a hand near it. "May I?"

"I am yours," he said.

She put one finger on his swollen crest, traced the shape of him, became ever bolder with her exploration.

He tried not to feel the pressure of her hand, the light graze of her fingernails. Tried to distract himself, but he could not make himself stop watching her. White teeth had stolen over her lush bottom lip. Two little lines appeared between her brows as she weighed in her hands the tight globes straining with his erection. He understood her absorption with him. He would feel the same when she offered him access to her body.

At last, her curiosity satisfied, she brought her hands up and up, over his stomach and chest, exploring the lines of his muscles, puzzling at his flat nipples, examining the texture of his skin. There were scars as well, and as she touched the curved mark of a saber wound, she looked a question at him.

"Not now," he said.

She let it be and moved on to his neck. Appraised the feel of whiskers on his jaw.

"I can shave, if you wish."

"No. I want you just as you are. We're nothing alike, are we?"

"Isn't that the point? But we'll fit together well enough."

"It is difficult to see how." Her hand was on his cock again, wrapped around it, trying, he could tell, to imagine it penetrating her. "You had better show me."

"I had better make sure, first, that you are ready. Will you put yourself in my hands?"

"Gladly."

Lifting her, he put his knees on the bed and laid her in the center of it. A large bed, praise Dionysus, because they would need every inch of it before the night was through. On her face, golden in the flickering light, a smile of anticipation welcomed him.

He stretched out beside her, propped himself up on his left forearm, and with his right hand began his own voyage of discovery. Every new destination was claimed with a kiss. Each shoulder and arm and wrist. Her slender waist and the delicate navel below. She began moving restlessly, seeking his touch where he wasn't providing it.

"I need more than this," she said.

"I know. You must allow me time to exert control over my own needs, or you will be disappointed."

"Can you at least kiss me?"

He could, for a long time, while he mapped her legs and sides, slipped his hand beneath her to cradle the swell of her hips and derriere, marveling at the feminine invitation in her every movement. Then, because she could endure no longer, he began to caress her breasts. A little sound, deep in her throat, told him how sensitive they were. How much she enjoyed what he was doing.

Raising himself, he brought his mouth to her nipple, circling it with his tongue, and felt her fingers slide into his hair, urging him to be more insistent. The other breast, then, so lovely, and he sucked on it the way he had sucked on her tongue, letting her enter him the way he would soon enter her.

His right hand went to her soft thigh, moved her legs a little apart, and began to glide up between them. Before he reached his goal, he knew she was prepared to take him. He slipped a finger through the soft, damp curls and lightly pressed the nub, already enlarged, that would receive most of his attention when the time was right.

But he didn't want her to climax yet, not this way. His finger moved down, between the swollen lips and along the sleek flesh to her opening. Later, he wanted to see it. To see all of her. Now he wanted to make sure she would easily adjust to him. He was pacing himself carefully. So long as he concentrated on her without seeing her, his own unruly flesh would remain in check.

A tiny sound when his finger pushed through the tight circle, and then a sigh.

He thought, again, that she might be a virgin after all. The lie would not surprise him. And if it was a lie, they would go no further. He had determined on that before yielding to her will. He pushed deeper, and deeper still.

"I like that," she murmured.

He could tell. His finger was entirely inside, and it had not met a barrier. But no maidenhead was fully intact. Still attending to her breasts with his mouth, he withdrew his finger, pressed another beside it, and sent them both in.

Again, no barrier. He began to think, with elation, that he would be able to finish this.

She was very tight, though. Wonderful for him, but difficult, at first, for her. Her hips began twisting around his fingers, wanting to feel more than they could provide.

"Almost," he said. "Let me stretch you a little more." When three fingers were deep inside her, when he began sucking harder on her breast, she responded like every man's fantasy of a lover. She liked everything, except that it was never enough.

What would she think, he wondered, if he unleashed himself?

Not yet. Not this time. Not, indeed, until she insisted. He rather thought that she would.

He lifted his head to kiss her, doing with his tongue in her mouth what he was doing with his fingers lower down. She writhed under him, altogether lost in the experience. It was perfect. She helped him keep his concentration, which was going to be essential in the next few minutes.

He ended the kiss, removed his hand, used it to spread her legs and lift her knees. Still he couldn't look. He knew his own limits. He looked at her face instead, her eyes a mirror of her unconcealed passion as he placed her where he wanted her. Then he knelt between her legs.

"Be patient," he said. "I mean to come inside you slowly, a little at a time, so that you can feel every sensation. You'll know when I'm fully there. Then you can set the pace. Are you ready?"

"Gracious, yes. Please."

What in the universe could be finer than a woman who gave herself freely, and who freely sought her own pleasure? Demanded it. She hadn't got to that yet, but she would. Lady Eve would not leave this bed unsatisfied. Nor would he permit her to.

Finding her with his hand, and then with the head of his penis, he positioned himself and let her feel the size of him against her.

She looked up at him, eyes wide, and ran her tongue over her upper lip. "You are very beautiful," she said. "Will this hurt?"

"Perhaps a little, at the beginning. I don't know. Tell me if it does."

"Oh, I don't mind. I just wanted to know what to expect."

"There is only one way, really, to find out." He pressed forward, feeling her stretch around him as he sought for entrance. Pulled backed again, long enough to rub himself against her wet cleft. Then he tried again, and got a little farther this time. Brought her knees up higher, moved his own closer, heard himself breathing too heavily.

Steady on, he told himself. *This is for her.*

By small, delicious increments, he pushed deeper. Her flesh accepted him, closed around him little by little as he reached for the core of her. Nearly there. Nearly. He stopped just short, saving for later the fullness of penetration. A woman always knew when she was missing something. A man always enjoyed giving it to her.

"Very well, madam," he said, resting on his elbows, hands stroking her breasts. "What would you like now?"

"For you to hold still," she said, surprising him. "I want to feel you for myself."

More experimentation. He steeled himself to do as she had asked, even as she was pulsing around him, drawing him too swiftly where he didn't yet want to go.

He felt her adjusting to him, contracting herself to squeeze him, grinning when a sound of pleasure escaped him.

"You like that," she said, tightening again around him.

"Very much."

Only a body perfectly disciplined for most of a lifetime could have resisted the primitive need to drive into her. He was close to breaking, and she had scarcely begun. Beads of sweat gathered on his forehead, at the back of his neck. He thought perhaps this had become for her a competition. Or that she had appointed him her plaything. It wasn't that he objected to any of it. But neither did he want to disappoint her.

She began moving her hips from side to side, watching his face, analyzing his responses. Controlling him quite effectively, he thought, and with such small movements of her body.

"And this way," she said, raising and lowering her hips. "It feels good to me, too. I could keep you here forever."

She had discovered the motions that brought her nub to where he could press against it. She raised up on her elbows, looked down to where they joined. "Next time," she said, "let us have more light."

"You are exceedingly bold, my lady."

"And you are too gentle, my lord. On some other occasion, I would like that very well. But on this night, I want everything you have. I want to feel this, to feel you, as I have never felt anything."

"As you wish," he said, blood already racing at the prospect. He pulled out of her, slid his arm beneath her, lifted her hips onto a pillow. "Now you are fully open to me. It will make a difference. If I hurt you, you must say so. Cries of pain and cries of pleasure can sound much alike when the battle rages."

"I can take everything you have, sir."

He knew she wanted him to exert his strength. It was a challenge to her. How else could she strive to overmaster him?

His cock burned as he drove into her, the pleasure intense. She tried to wrap her arms around him, but he placed them flat on the bed at her sides and held them down. "This is what men do," he said. "You should experience it fully."

And as it was with everything else, she threw herself with all her body and will into the game. She met his thrusts with her own twists and turns, intent on her pleasure, knowing he could take care of his own. Driving him nearly mindless, but she wouldn't have known that. He almost didn't realize it either, until after a long bout that sent her into climax once, and again, and again, he almost forgot to pull out at the crucial moment. He managed, grabbed for a towel, and collapsed on the bed beside her.

The room throbbed with the sound of pumping blood and of their breathing, short and fast like champions at the end of a race.

After a while, she rolled onto her stomach beside him and spread her hand across his chest.

Possession. And a show of approval, he thought, the way one would pet a dog to praise it.

She meant no insult. For once bereft of words, she nonetheless could not forebear asserting her will with a gesture both unconscious and telling.

Her game, her rules, her rewards.

He smiled up at the ceiling. What an experience. Altogether worth the trouble she caused him, and the price he would undoubtedly pay for it.

The blessed silence endured a long time. She felt so relaxed against him that he believed she had fallen asleep. Then the hand on his chest stirred. Began to caress him. She snuggled closer, lifted up so that she could see his face. "What shall we do now, sir?"

"What would you like?"

"You are the expert. How about something more unusual? More adventurous. What does a cavalry officer most enjoy after a day of hard riding?"

"A night of hard riding."

"And am I to be ridden, or may I be the rider?"

Wanton creature. He threaded his fingers through her tangled hair. "Why not both?" he said. "If you will put yourself on hands and knees like a dutiful mare, I shall go first."

"And then I can mount you?"

"And then, Lady Eve, you may do anything you like with me."

Chapter 11

I don't know what to say. My dear Ensign, you must not spend your money on me! But I will repay you one day. My word of honor on it. Let me tell you about the horse, then. Cannonballs found him for me, a neat little Spanish bay with perfect footing on rocky terrain, just what I require and fast as well. CB got a good price, too, better than I could have done. Your bank draft covered it and more, so unless I have all three horses shot out from under me, I am well enough supplied for the work I'm doing. And Nick wrote that he and Richard have raised nearly all the blunt for my captaincy, if a place opens up. But I don't want to leave the 13th, not just to advance. I'm useful here. Even CB says so. Did I tell you he's a major now?

Your Grateful J

On Sunday morning, Eve transformed herself from an improper young woman to a fastidiously proper one for as long as it took to attend services at St. James's in the nearby town of Weybridge.

From the time she was seven, her parents had sent her off with her nanny and a few upper servants to the village church near Marbury Manor, joining the party at Easter if they chanced to be in residence. For the rest of the year, Eve sat alone in the family pew as a reminder to the local people that their prosperity depended on the goodwill of Lord and Lady Marbury. She had been instructed to pray fervently for a male heir to join her one day in that pew, and she did for a time. But none ever appeared.

Later, going to church and engaging in charitable works became her only means of escaping virtual imprisonment at the manor house. And later still, she really did pray fervently for Johnnie and the other brave soldiers on the Peninsula. Her prayers had not helped him, though.

But through the years, in fine weather or bad, she continued to attend church for no reason except that she couldn't bring herself to stop. God might notice and visit some wrath upon her, as so many of the preachers said He would. So she sat quietly, observing what people were wearing, watching the play of light through stained-glass windows, and daydreaming.

But it had all been a waste. Good attendance had not made her virtuous.

And while she had previously lacked notable sins to repent, she was practically drowning in them now. Only hours ago, she had left the bed of a man who was not her husband and never would be. She had bathed the traces of their lovemaking from her body, and when dressed, was surprised to see that she looked much as she always did.

Until she drew closer to the mirror and saw the pink abrasions from his whiskers on her neck and chin and cheeks. Her lips were swollen, her eyes over-bright. Standing behind her, placid as always, Mrs. Kipper arranged her hair as if she saw nothing unusual. But she must have known.

A veiled bonnet concealed the visible evidence of her iniquities, but there was no disguising how she felt beneath her clothing. Her body ached, pleasantly, in unusual places. Every movement called to mind those uninhibited, deliriously pleasurable hours in his arms. When the groom helped her onto the sidesaddle and she wrapped her leg around the leaping head, she imagined wrapping her legs around Cordell. Even the rhythmic gait of her mare reminded her of—

Well, this had to stop. If she dwelt on lascivious matters in the house of the Lord, lightning would strike her down.

But it didn't, she discovered when her thoughts kept winging back like homing pigeons to the delights of the flesh. Meantime, the vicar droned on about the wages of sin being death, which seemed to her ridiculous because the wages of virtue were also death, without any of the fun beforehand.

At least she wasn't a hypocrite. She knew she'd done wrong by all traditional standards, and if she could have summoned up a sliver of regret, she might have been able to repent.

Eventually.

But there was a stumbling block on the way to repentance. The Lord had been forgiving of sinners, she knew from hearing thousands of sermons and reading the gospels. But He always added, "Go and sin no more." Whereas she could hardly wait for her next opportunity to sin with Cordell, who had been sleeping the sleep of a man at ease with his conscience when she left his bed.

And, too, there was the small matter of her vengeance, which she would forgo on no account. She preferred to think of her scheme as the restoration of justice, but it felt very much like old-fashioned, cold-hearted retribution. Even vindictiveness, because she would take pleasure in his downfall, and because she would not be satisfied until he suffered for his crime. True bringers of justice would not do evil along the way, nor were they supposed to gloat over their victims.

A woman so lustful and bloody-minded as she ought not to be allowed in a church. Her only hope was that by simply being here, she would absorb virtue passively, the way water absorbed tea.

When the service ended, the groom left his place in a back pew and went to fetch the horses while she complimented the vicar on his sermon and accepted the curtsy of his wife. Several parishioners smiled, but no one spoke to her as she went out into the bright June morning.

Just beyond the graveyard, the groom was waiting with her mare and his own cob. She thought, as they rode away from the town, that she might take a long way round to Oatlands and clear her head. After a sleepless night, she had almost dozed off in the pew, and she wanted to be alert and sparkly when next she saw Cordell. But reminded by the pressure of her saddle that selected parts of her anatomy were a little sore, she chose instead to return the way she'd come.

Drowsiness settled over her like the warm sunshine. The groom was riding a little distance behind her on the winding path that skirted a handful of small farm holdings before entering a stretch of woodland. Beyond it, visible through the trees, lay pastureland and plantings of wheat, rye, and flax.

As she rode beneath green-leafed oak branches, her mind wandering, a sound like the beat of wings startled her. A bird taking flight.

An instant later, her mare bolted.

No sudden fright this time, quickly run out. The horse picked up speed, the way she might if Eve had struck her with a riding crop.

Tree trunks seemed to hurtle past. Then horse and rider were free of the woods. But where the path curved tightly beyond the last of the trees, the mare drove straight ahead.

Eve barely had time to see the low fence before they were soaring over it. On the other side lay a stretch of meadow grass, already mown and harvested. Hooves thundered across the stubble.

She risked a glance behind her. The groom was over the fence as well, but skirting wide to her right. To come up directly behind her would be to press the mare forward. He needed to get parallel to her, she knew. A panicked horse wanted nothing more than the reassuring company of another horse. But the groom would never catch up. Not on his slower mount.

The wind rushing past her whipped at the veiled bonnet, adding to the mare's fright. Eve tried to get hold of the ribbons, but they were windblown as well. And she needed her strength and concentration to stay on the saddle.

Across another low fence lay a field of spring wheat about three feet tall, swaying in the late-morning breeze. Shying, the mare veered left, toward a road that lay about a quarter mile ahead on the other side of a low rise. Traffic and people could turn this mad ride into a catastrophe.

"Juno," she said calmly, again and again. "Juno." But the horse would not be stopped. Easier to turn her. Worth trying. With a firm, deliberate motion, Eve guided her to the left, the direction she had turned to avoid the wheat field. At first, there was no response. Then, gradually, the mare began a wide arcing loop that carried them back to where she'd first jumped the fence.

But she had no liking for the woodland, either. Completing the turn, she galloped alongside the fence for a time. Ahead lay another just like it.

Eve had lost track of the groom, knew he would make no foolish mistakes. The veiling beat at her face and eyelids. Scarcely able to see now, she peered through the windblown fabric and judged that the upcoming field held meadow grass just now being harvested. Near the fence, it had been cut down and left in neat rows of shallow piles with room between each row for the haywain to collect the grass when it dried. Beyond, she could make out workers in the field, methodically wielding their sickles.

Up went the mare, over the fence and straight ahead. The men saw her coming and scattered. Their sudden motion sent Juno into a frenzy. She galloped forward at even greater speed, charging toward the knee-high grass. Eve thought it might slow her a little, or turn her aside, but she held her course and speed.

The mare was beyond any control now. Only exhaustion would stop her, or an accident. She ought to have run out her fears by now. But any change, any movement that caught her eye, was like the crack of a whip.

Another fence ahead, and on the far side, fallow land. Rocky land. Beyond it, a road. The horse refused to turn back in the direction of the creatures that had frightened her.

Eve made her decision. Nothing good waited for her on the other side of that fence, and there was cushioning, a little of it, for the next hundred yards. Better to take a slim chance now than have no chance at all.

She made sure her skirts were untangled, slipped her foot free of the stirrup, lifted her knee above the leaping head, and jumped.

Chapter 12

Portugal, July 1810

I've acquired a Portuguese boy and a donkey. His name is Deniz, meaning the boy, not the donkey, and he used to be with the lieutenant that got killed last week. The one I'll replace, if things go right. Deniz says he's good at foraging, and sure enough, when I got back from a three-day patrol this morning, he'd laid in more food than I've seen since coming to the Penn. That's what we call the Peninsula, but I expect you know that. He stole the food, no doubt, and the provisions for my horses, too. I read him a lecture about Lord Wellington's orders to pay for what we take, but Deniz cares nothing for that. The boys compete to see who can provide the best for their officers. It's a matter of pride, and there's no arguing with that. I'll be eating well tonight.

Yrs., J

With the map Indigo sketched for him, Cordell had no difficulty finding the cottage near Long Ditton where a woman known only as Mary plied her trade. There was another house, better populated with whores, in East Moulsey, and he would call there if necessary.

Curls of smoke rose from near the cottage. He reined in on a little knoll and saw a fire pit with a large metal cauldron propped over it. A few yards away sat a basket piled with linens, and beside it, a woman shaking out what appeared to be a sheet. He watched her hang it on a thin rope suspended between two trees.

Laundry had been done in much the same way on the Peninsula, cauldrons over fire pits, unless the army was on the move. He thought, fleetingly, of charging naked to the rescue of a laundry woman and being needled about it for months afterward.

As he rode up to the whitewashed cottage, admiring the window boxes overflowing with flowers, the woman turned. She looked to be about his own age, with brown hair pulling loose from its pins and a shapeless apron wrapped around a shapeless gray dress.

"Good morning, sir," she said in a pleasant voice. "Begging your pardon, but I do no business on Sundays."

"I am here for another reason," he said, dismounting. "If you will be kind enough to answer a few questions, I'll not trouble you for long."

Crooked teeth nibbled at her lower lip. "Be I in trouble?"

"Not at all. I am inquiring about a young man who may have called on you about two weeks ago. Jeremy Brown. Do you recall meeting him?"

"Nobody by that name, sir. Most times, 'specially with the married ones, names don't be given me. Anyhow, I never talk about the gentlemen what come here."

"Your discretion is commendable, ma'am. But since the young man is dead, there is no need for confidentiality. Will you look at this drawing, which I am told is a fair likeness, and tell me if you have ever seen him?"

Wiping her hands on her apron, she moved closer and examined the paper he held out. "That be a fellow said his name was Jack. He come here three times. What happened to him, sir?"

"Did you hear anything about the murder of a stablehand at Oatlands?"

"They was talking about it for a week after. But Jack said he worked on the canal, loading timber for sending to London."

He held the paper closer. "You are certain this is the same man?"

"Looks like him, except the nose were more bent. But that scar under his eye, like a slice of melon . . . that's spot-on."

"Did he tell you anything else about himself?"

"Didn't talk much at all. Didn't stay long, either. Not the first two times. Last time I saw him, he was jumpy-like. Kept looking out the window. When the cat scratched at the door to be let in, he went under the bed. Said he thought robbers might be in the woods. There's lots of them about, soldiers cut loose with no money and no place to go. I give some of them a toss for free. Seems to me they earned it."

But robbers didn't leave money in their victims' mouths. "Do you recall what time he left?"

"After midnight, I think. He wanted to stay till the sun come up, but I were expecting another client. Jack worked at Oatlands, you say? He's the one with the guineas?"

"It appears so. Can you think of anything that might help us identify him? We're trying to locate his family."

"No, I . . . Well, he did say he didn't like Surrey. Said Wiltshire was the only place he ever lived that suited him."

"Anything about a town? The countryside?"

"That's all. Wiltshire. He were a quiet one."

Cordell folded the drawing. "Thank you for speaking with me. May I ask that you say nothing about my coming here today, nor about the young man, whatever his real name may be?"

In answer, she placed a hand over her mouth. Then she said, "I wouldn't, even if you wasn't an army man like my Henry. He were killed in a bad place. I mean, the name of it were bad, but longer. I got a letter, but I can't read, and the man who read it to me couldn't say the name."

"Badajoz, I expect. We lost many brave men there. Are you doing well, ma'am? Is there something I can provide for you?"

"Things are not so terrible, sir. Henry left me this cottage. But to keep here, I had to go back to my old work. That's how I met Henry, in a Croyden brothel. He took me away from there and married me and said I wouldn't have to work like that again. But, life changes. I don't mind so much. It's all I know how to do. And it makes people happy."

Lost for words, he bowed and vaulted into the saddle. "You have been a great help," he said, thinking she'd probably be insulted if he offered her money. But he could send it later, as if it were an army pension of sorts. England did not do well by the widows of its heroes. "Good day, ma'am."

She waved, smiling, as he rode away, and then turned back to her laundry.

Cordell continued on to East Moulsey and called in at the brothel, in case Brown had done business there as well. But no one recognized the man in the drawing, nor did anyone at the tavern next door, surprisingly crowded on a Sunday morning.

Unable to think of a chore that would reasonably delay his return to Oatlands, he took a meandering route alongside the Thames, not looking forward to another day of playacting with Lady Eve. Not looking forward, either, to the awkwardness of seeing her after the night they had spent together. It mustn't be repeated. But he wasn't at all sure, if she presented herself again to him, that he would have the will to refuse.

She had detected his greatest weakness, the one that long ago had nearly brought him down, and was exploiting his carnal appetites for reasons that had nothing to do with her unmistakably passionate nature. A valuable lesson scratched for his attention. He'd thought the iron control he had exerted over himself for the last fifteen years could not be broken, but one young female had, in the course of a few minutes, penetrated his every defense.

He must arm himself against her.

It was shortly after noon when he reached Oatlands and saw immediately that something was wrong. Guests huddled on the terrace, their faces grim. Servants were gathered in twos and threes in the stableyard, looking worried. Another murder?

When he pulled up in front of the west stable, Tom and a pale young groom came running over.

"Sir!" Tom was panting. "It's Lady Eve. She's been hurt."

Cordell had once been kicked in the chest by a horse. It felt like that now. He stared down at them, trying to catch his breath.

"Charley was with her. She fell off her horse."

"Jumped," Charley said. "I saw her jump. She'd have been thrown anyway, in a worse place."

"How bad is she?"

"Dunno, sir. Farmers brought her here on a hay wagon. She weren't awake. We all be waiting to hear."

Cordell dropped down from his horse and sprinted toward the house.

"Sir," Tom called after him. "Charley has something to show you."

"Later!"

Guests turned to watch him rush past. Three men were standing under the portico. He tried to dodge by, but one of them moved to block his path.

"It's Cordell, isn't it? The duchess was asking after you. I told her we'd seen you in Moulsey." The man laughed. "Didn't tell her you was coming out of a whorehouse."

Cordell gave the man a look that caused him to back away. "See that you don't. In fact, I suggest you say nothing to anyone. My business, which was not what you think, is none of your concern."

Then he was in the house, the object of curious eyes as he tried to figure out where they'd have taken her. He started toward the wide staircase and saw the duchess coming down. She looked sorrowful, but not in distress.

He took his first easy breath since hearing the news.

They spoke alone, not counting the dogs, in the

duchess's private salon. "She appears to have a mild concussion, Lord Cordell. The doctor will stay with her until she is fully conscious. He wishes to assure himself that she has suffered no lasting damage. You may speak directly with him, if you wish."

"Thank you. Yes. Does it appear to have been a riding accident?"

"I cannot say. One of the grooms escorted her this morning, and he will have seen what occurred. Perhaps you will question him and tell me what you learn."

"I spoke to him briefly before coming inside, Your Grace. If there is no immediate urgency regarding Lady Eve's health, I'll take up that conversation now."

"Very well. When you return, a servant will show you where she can be found."

Tom and Charley were waiting where he had left them. Ghost, still saddled and secured nearby, had been provided a bucket of hay and oats.

"Begin at the start," Cordell said to Charley, "and tell me precisely what occurred. Omit no detail. Did you saddle the lady's horse?"

"I did, sir. The mare looked well. I examined her, as I always do, and the saddle. We rode to Weybridge for services at St. James's. I left the horses under the watch of Elton Biggers, who used to be a constable before he got too old. After services I brought the horses around, and we started back to Oatlands."

"The same way you came?"

"Yes, sir. It's the shortest. There's a little stretch of woods not far from Weybridge. We were just about—"

"Stop." Cordell knew by his voice and the look on Tom's face that Charley had reached the moment where the trouble began. "Where were you at this point? By her side? Ahead, or behind?"

"The path won't take two horses, sir, and she never wants me too close. She don't like having somebody with her all the time. I was maybe twenty-five yards back. Clear sight of her, though. She was coming near where the trees end when the mare shot forward like a hornet had stung her."

"Did you observe a nest? A number of insects?"

"The usual number for June, which is a lot. Nothing out of the ordinary. I cut over to one side so as not to be chasing the mare, but I could never get close. She is fast, sir. And just as she was coming out of the woods, it were like she was stung again. She jerked forward, picked up speed, and never slowed after that. Everything frightened her."

"You said Lady Eve jumped. There was no other choice?"

"None I could see. She got the mare to turn away from the road, but we wound up in a pasture that was being harvested for meadow grass. Past that was hard dirt and rocks, and then another public road. She rode like a champion, sir. And she knew just when to give it up and get off. It was the best could be done."

"You saw no one along the way?"

"Only the farmers cutting the grass. They put her on a haywain and brought her here. I went after the mare, who finally ran herself out and let me lead her home. It's when I got her here and set to putting her to rights that I saw . . . Maybe you should come look for yourself, sir."

Cordell followed the boys to the main stable, where Lady Eve's mare, still skittish, fretted in her stall. He entered with Charley and studied the two places on the mare's croup where she had been struck by something. One spot, directly behind where the cantle would have been, showed greater injury than the slight wound near the dock.

"This would have done it," he said. "Shot from above, clearly. Small enough that you wouldn't have noticed the missiles, whatever they were."

He led the way out of the stall, wanting to disturb the mare as little as possible. She'd had a bad time of it as well. "I want you two to go back where this happened and see if you can find the weapons. If you do, leave them where they are. Check the trees as well. There should be signs near the one where the would-be killer concealed himself. Scratches on the bark. An excess of fallen leaves beneath. If you discover anything, one of you keep watch while the other comes for me. Understood?"

"Yes, sir," they said in unison.

"One more thing. Say nothing, except to me. Not one word. The killer could be in this household, as servant or guest. So far as everyone else is concerned, Lady Eve's horse ran away with her and she fell. No more than that."

"But Mr.—"

"I'll speak to Garth, Tom. Do as I say. If he asks difficult questions, just tell him I'm eccentric."

"Yes, sir. Is axcentick a sickness?"

"Of a sort. Go along, now. It's possible the shooter reclaimed the weapons, but if there's anything to be found, I'm counting on you to find it."

They scampered off to saddle their cobs while he returned to the house and was shown to Lady Eve's bedchamber. As he already knew, it lay almost directly beneath his own. The door from the passageway opened to a small sitting room where the doctor, a young man wearing thick spectacles, was seated at a small table eating his lunch from a tray. He rose immediately and bowed.

"Her grace told me to expect you, Colonel. Nothing substantial has altered, except that Lady Eve's unnatural sleep has become restless. She is beginning to feel the aftereffects of her fall, but I hesitate to administer laudanum until we can be certain she has sustained no significant head injury. We will know better when she is able to speak. At present, a slight concussion would be my diagnosis, and she has undergone a considerable shock to her entire body."

"May I see her?"

"I would prefer you did not. The longer she can rest before the pain grows intense, the better it will be. This evening, perhaps? I've agreed to remain for the afternoon, longer if necessary, and will provide you a complete review of her condition and my recommendations. Is that satisfactory?"

No. But Cordell deferred without protest, relieved at the optimistic summary. He looked over at the closed door, imagining Lady Eve on the other side of it, and an overpowering rage welled up in him.

She was suffering. She had barely survived another try at killing her.

Everything had changed.

Chapter 13

Spain, Feb. 1812

> *Four of us on our way back yesterday from meet-
> ing with a troop of Spanish guerrillas when L's
> horse went down. I had to shoot it, and L got
> himself a broken leg in the fall. Cannonballs was
> with us this time. He sent P to find wood for a
> splint and showed me how to pull the bone into
> place and all the rest. L very brave, but I was
> sweating like a pig. We stripped down two
> branches, nailed a blanket to them, and carried
> him twenty-one miles to camp. My spare horse-
> shoe nails came in handy! CB did his share of
> carrying, too. He said I should learn what I could
> from the surgeons, because in this kind of work,
> we're not usually where we can find help. Before
> we left, some locals that heard the shot came to
> see what happened. They wanted the horse for
> meat and gave us some bad wine, which L was
> glad to drink.*
>
> Yrs., J

The pain came on her like the sound of hoofbeats,
soft at first and distant, pounding on dry earth.

Moving closer. Growing louder until it thundered in her ears. Blood drove through her veins like the rush of a galloping horse.

Motionless, she took inventory of herself, thinking she had done that before, on other wakenings. But she couldn't remember what she learned then, so she began at her toes and worked upward. No bindings. A sense that if she tried, she could move her feet and ankles and legs. But she didn't try, because they hurt so much just lying there.

On a bed, she realized. There had been hay, once. And other beds, or perhaps it was the same bed and she kept forgetting. Images flashed across her mind. A boy leaning over her, saying her name. Men lifting her. Sunlight beating down on her closed eyelids. Voices, a great many of them. Mrs. Kipper's face. A man with thick spectacles who poked at her and kept asking her who was king of England and who was prime minister. Didn't he *know*?

She picked up the inventory at her waist and found the pluck to move her arms a little. There was a binding on her left wrist. But nothing else, although her left shoulder hurt more than any other part of her except her head.

She had survived the fall. And relatively intact, which surprised her. She had been expecting punishment, and if the fall wasn't precisely a strike of lightning, it had brought her down hard enough.

Did that mean she was all even with God now?

To think that last night, in another bed, she had felt more wonders of the flesh than she could ever have imagined. Pleasure that made her toes curl just to . . . Ah! No toe curling. Even that hurt. And today, or whatever day it was, she felt nothing but pain and, yes, fear. She might be worse off than she knew. Someone ought to tell her. Someone ought to be here.

Someone was. She sensed another presence. Or perhaps she heard the sound of someone breathing, but it might have been her. She trusted none of her responses to light, sound, or sensation.

What of Juno? Had anyone caught her? Was she hurt as well? Answers were needed. Eve opened her eyes and saw darkness.

She was on her back, looking up. But as her eyes began to adjust, she saw faint golden light fluttering against the ceiling. Saw the moldings and, barely, the gilded oval containing the painted image of two angels blowing on long horns. Her own bedchamber, then. The one just under where Cordell would be sleeping, if it was nighttime. If he was in his own bed.

How could she summon help?

With a groan, she lifted her head from the pillow. And there he was.

The eyes of an eagle, she thought. Steady and relentless. He was seated on a wing-back chair that had been drawn up near the corner of the bed. His feet were propped on something, she couldn't see what, his arms were folded across his chest, and he looked tired. At any rate, he didn't move.

"How do you feel?" he said, not solicitously.

"Peachy. And you?"

A corner of his mouth quirked. "Better than I did five seconds ago. We were afraid your mind had been affected by the fall, although I'm not sure how anyone would be able to tell."

"Because my wits had long since gone missing? Ha, ha. They must have done, though, if I let Juno run away with me. She is high-spirited, but always well

mannered." Her body, coming slowly awake, began to
make its own will known. "Sir, might I trouble you to
send Mrs. Kipper to me?"

He rose instantly. "Do you need the doctor?"

"Something less dramatic, I'm afraid."

With a nod of understanding, he left the room.

Sinking back onto the pillow, she closed her eyes.
He had been watching over her. Nothing, not the mad
flight of her mare or her own deliberate fall or the
pain that made her want to weep from it, had affected
her so greatly as his presence in that chair. What could
be more astonishing than that?

Mrs. Kipper arrived and efficiently saw to her needs
while Eve concentrated on not swooning from the
pain of all the movement required in the process. Finally she was able to sink against the bank of pillows
arranged for her against the headboard. It felt better,
sitting up a little. She thought she might hold this
position for a week or two.

"The colonel tells me you are in good form," said
Mrs. Kipper. "Will you demonstrate that to me?"

"In what way? By naming the king and the prime
minister?"

"Can you? Before now, you could not."

"Truly? I know very well it's George the Third and
Lord Liverpool."

"When last you were asked, you said Richard Lion-
heart and Lady Jersey."

"She only *wants* to be prime minister." Eve watched
a maid enter the room and place a tray on the bedside
table. "Whatever I was babbling before, I appear to
have recovered. Has Juno been found?"

"If you mean your horse, yes. The colonel can tell
you more of that." Mrs. Kipper brought a damp towel

to Eve's face and gently cleansed it. "The doctor said you might have something to ease the pain, so long as there was no sign of permanent damage to your head. I am leaving you a mild draft that will turn the trick. Would you care to take it now?"

"It's difficult to talk," Eve said, bringing a hand to her lips. "Do these look as large as they feel?"

"You are swollen, yes. It will pass."

"Fetch me a mirror, please. I want to see."

Mrs. Kipper went to the dressing table and came back with a silver-handled looking glass. "This is not a good idea, Lady Eve. You should wait."

"No. Hold it where I can—Oh, dear God." The creature staring back at her could not have been human. "I look like . . . like a big round sausage."

"When they brought you in, your face was decidedly green. From making the close acquaintance of some meadow grass, I am told. The abrasions are shallow and unlikely to leave scars, especially with the salve I am having brought from London. The swelling is bad now, but will lessen with time. The bruising, however, will visit upon you a painter's palette of colors before your normal appearance is restored."

"And my wrist?"

"A mild sprain. Nothing appears to be broken. All told, you escaped lightly."

"That's easy for you to say." Not for her, though. Eve's tongue felt swollen behind swollen lips set in a swollen face. It hurt to move her jaw. "Is there more I should know?"

"Do you feel able to eat something? Broth, or a custard? It will help build your strength."

"Perhaps later." She looked once more at her reflection, shuddered, and gave the mirror to Mrs. Kipper. "Excepting the duchess, please keep all visitors away."

"I have placed a little bell on the night table. Use it to summon me. Cordell will be in shortly. He has a few matters to discuss with you."

He had already seen her, of course. But Eve couldn't bear the thought of him looking again at the wreckage of her face. It was too much that she should be both hurt and humiliated. And yet, there was the mission to consider. She couldn't gain entrée for Cordell to fashionable houses when she didn't dare make an appearance herself. What use was she now? He would cut her loose and go on without her. That was best all around.

And hurt worst of all. Tears burned in her eyes.

When he entered, he was carrying a folded serviette, which he laid on the bed beside his chair. Then he settled back in the chair as if he had never left the room.

"I know what you are going to say," Eve told him, watching for disgust in his eyes as he gazed at her.

"I doubt it." Instead of folding his arms, he steepled his hands under his chin. "Do you understand what happened to you this morning?"

"Certainly. I fell off my horse."

"Another attempt was made on your life."

She sucked in a deep breath, started to shake her head, thought better of it. "Nonsense. Juno bolted, that was all. Something gave her a fright. A bird, I think. I heard a sound that might have been wings directly overhead, and then she was off."

"If there was a bird, it happened to be there when someone deliberately sent a missile at the mare's hindquarters. That's what set her running, and she picked up speed when a second missile hit shortly after."

"Whatever makes you think so? Did the groom see this happen?"

"Only the behavior of the mare, not what caused it. But later, he spotted indications on her backside that she had been struck." Cordell reached over, flipped open the napkin, and lifted what appeared to be a dart. "This is light and cleverly designed. The would-be killer was perched on a fairly high tree branch that overhung the path. He threw the first dart from almost directly above you. The second was losing velocity by the time it struck, but on an already panicked horse, it had the desired effect. The mare would not have stopped until winded or injured."

"And he left the darts there to be found?"

"I don't think he intended to. The groom helped me retrace the entire incident. Had the mare stayed on the path when she bolted, you'd soon have been well out of sight. But she jumped the fence instead. Then she went left, which would also have taken you away from the woodland and to a trafficked road. But you turned the horse and sent her back the way she'd come. Not long after, the mowers in the adjacent field were looking in your direction. They'd have seen someone coming out of the trees to search for the second dart. Even the first dart would be hard to find quickly in the undergrowth. He did try."

She began to wonder if she was dreaming. "How can you possibly know that?"

"I'm an experienced tracker. The boys—I had two of them looking—couldn't pinpoint the tree, but it was simple enough when I started from the fresh footprints and worked back. An easy tree to climb and descend, by the way. Some leaves and grasses were slightly flattened in the area where he was searching before he realized there was no time, not if he was to escape undetected. The moment you jumped off the horse, one of the mowers ran toward that woodland path on his way to fetch a doctor in Weybridge."

Cordell placed the dart on the napkin and folded it again. "Perhaps the killer meant to return when the hubbub had died down, but there was a good chance no one would find the darts or connect them to the accident. They are brown and green, like the terrain. And we only went looking for a weapon because the groom noticed the marks on your horse's backside. It's remarkable she did not injure herself on that frantic run. Had there been an accident, the small dart wounds would have gone unnoticed."

"May I see the darts?"

"When the light is better. I'm surprised you can see at all, with so much swelling around your eyes."

"You needn't point it out." She sounded plaintive without really trying. "Can you not spare me a little pity?"

"You'd hate that."

"Yes." She liked that he knew it. "But I'd have enjoyed watching you pretend to be sympathetic."

He was looking at her hands lying atop the sheet. She looked down at them as well. They were shaking.

"If you are frightened," he said, still in that neutral tone, "I am glad of it. This is a serious business, and you must treat it as such."

"But what am I to do? Keep myself locked up in fear? That is much the same as dying."

"You needn't be afraid. Only cautious. I will protect you, and these attacks will be stopped."

I will protect you.

Before today, she'd have bridled at that pompous statement. Thrown it back in his face. She required no protection. She could take care of herself. But she had never imagined becoming prey to a murderer, and whatever else Cordell might be, he knew a great deal about slaughter. Phoenix had summoned him all the way from Paris to find a killer.

"Do not forget, sir, that we have another murderer to track. Unless you think the same man has also targeted me?"

"I see no reason to draw that conclusion, unless you or someone else connected with Black Phoenix has been talking out of turn. In any case, that mission is no longer my concern. Nor yours. We'll leave it to Sir Peregrine and the others."

"You mean, dishonor our promise? Just walk away?"

"I doubt you'll be walking anywhere for a while. Accident or murder attempt, the outcome would be the same. Our investigation has been effectively halted."

"Why not proceed on your own for a time? I'm very strong. I'll soon be able to rejoin the hunt."

He lifted a warning finger. "This isn't a negotiation. Let me tell you what is going to happen next. Tomorrow morning, our betrothal will be made public. The guests will take the news to London, and I shall arrange for an announcement in the *Times*."

"I don't understand. What is the purpose of that now?"

"When you are able to think more clearly, the reasons will be obvious. It is one thing to attack a helpless female, madam, and quite another to reckon with me. I expect the betrothal and my constant presence to deter the killer long enough for me to put my hands on him."

She made herself ignore "helpless," because at the moment, she was. "At which time, we'll explain that the betrothal was a ruse to protect me and entrap him?"

"My apologies. You are thinking more clearly than I realized. That story would harm you less than a jilting, it is true, but reputation is the least of our concerns. I may even decide to make public our suspicions about this incident, and the others as well. Later, you will provide me a complete accounting of them."

"Another deterrent?"

"The killer has been careful. He knows that the accidental death of a young woman is an occasion for private sorrow, but the deliberate murder of Lord Marbury's daughter would capture the public's attention and provoke a thorough investigation. If we make it impossible for him to stage a credible accident, he might abandon his plans altogether."

"Then why not put out the information straightaway? Oh, of course. Because you want to *catch* him."

"How else can I kill him?"

"You should let me do that."

He gazed at her for a considerable time, his expression unreadable. Then he shrugged. "If you wish."

He *meant* it. She was nearly sure. He might have been humoring her, but there had been something in his eyes. An acknowledgment. A tip of the hat. He thought her capable of doing it.

About that, she wasn't so sure. If she could kill a man, Cordell would be the one. She didn't care that he'd appointed himself her guardian angel. He should have done the same for Johnnie, who admired him above all others. Cordell had long since proven himself faithless. Look how easily he cast off his commitment to Black Phoenix.

Likely he would stick with her for a time, though. So long as their purposes marched together, she could count on him just as he could count on her. But the parting would come soon enough. She had taken his measure.

"Do you need to rest now?" he said. "I have questions for you, but they can wait until morning."

The last thing she wanted was to be alone with pain and fear coiling around her. "I am well enough. Let us begin, and if I start to babble like a baboon, you can take yourself away."

Another hint of a smile, swift as a blink. "I wouldn't want to miss that. But first, tell me who has a reason to want you dead."

She didn't have to think about her answer. "No one. You'll find it hard to believe, but I am not generally offensive. My indiscretions have been many, it is true, but nearly all of them took place in my girlhood. They were certainly annoying, especially to my parents, but they did no harm and made me no enemies. At worst, I was a great nuisance."

"There are people who take offense where none was intended. Can you think of anyone you may have slighted? Anyone who might have resolved to pay you back?"

"In all likelihood, sir, I would have grown into a rude, self-serving, and insufferably arrogant woman. It is in the blood. But three years ago, Lady Etheridge took me in hand, and with her help, I have mastered my unruly temperament. I have developed patience. And while I am not adept at making friends, most people welcome me into their company."

"Try to see this from another point of view," he said. "You have every quality and privilege that matters in society. That makes you welcome, but it also makes you the object of envy."

"I know. I cannot help it, sir."

"What about your time in school? Was there an occurrence that turned someone against you?"

She felt suddenly cold. "I never attended school. According to my parents, there are no schools for young females that can be guaranteed to exclude riff-raff. I was instructed at home by a succession of governesses. Some were quite nice, others were martinets or fools, and none of them lasted very long."

"Did you spend all your time at Marbury Manor, then?"

"Most of it. But if my parents were to be absent for several months, they sometimes farmed me out to another household. I was a child, sir. How many life-long enemies can a child make?"

"We'll leave this for now. But I want you to think hard about people you have dealt with in the recent past. Say, within five years. Make a list of those who merit a closer look."

"So that you can badger them?"

"If need be. I'll try not to antagonize everyone you know." His face hardened. "We are seeking a motive, Lady Eve. Short of catching the killer in the act, a motive is our only guide to his identity. You say that you are wealthy in your own right. Who stands to profit from your death?"

"The charities included in my will. But they don't know who they are. The solicitors recommended the information be withheld, for if the charities knew of the bequest, they might overextend themselves or borrow against expectations. That could be ruinous, should I later change the will. In truth, the solicitors are persuaded that I will marry, have children, and leave the money to them. I was thinking more of spending the fortune, a large part of it, on myself."

Cordell gave her a look of mild surprise. "Your parents have no control over your funds?"

"My grandmother, who was determined they should not, placed the legacy in trust until I came of age. At that time I made certain changes, extended the trust, and built in every possible barrier between my fortune and the claims of a husband. Lady Etheridge advised me."

"That woman, I must say, exercises an uncommon degree of influence over your affairs."

"Not all of them. For example, she unreservedly disapproves of you. Her sole investment is in my future, sir. I am meant to continue her work. And I doubt you'd find her ascending a tree and throwing a dart at a horse."

"As a matter of fact, the murderer almost certainly employs someone else to take the risks while making sure of an alibi for himself. Or herself. Which leads me, with difficulty, to ask about your family. Do you stand to inherit anything from either of your parents?"

"It has never been discussed, but I doubt it. They know I am provided for, and Marbury is fixed on preserving the family name and estate. Probably they will leave everything to the heir, William Halliday, who breeds exotic fish and collects butterflies. Dull as dirt, Cousin Will, but goodhearted.''

He leaned forward, hands locked together. "Then we come to your lovers, Lady Eve. Or possibly to their wives. Can a motive be found with any or all of them?"

The question robbed her of breath. She could not betray Robin. Like all the Brandens, he had troubles enough. But she must tell the colonel *something,* if only to prevent him from mounting a search of his own. That would lead, inevitably, to her connection with Johnnie and shut the door on her vengeance.

"There has been only one lover before you, sir." She looked directly at him, kept her voice level. "He is unmarried. We were together for one night, and it was a long time ago."

Cordell's expression did not change. "You are not an easy woman to forget, madam. Had he reason to believe you would marry him?"

"It was nothing like that. We had been acquainted for many years, although we rarely saw each other. And then he suffered a great loss—several, really— and I, too, had lost someone I held dear. While both of us were deep in mourning, we chanced to meet. I can hardly explain it to myself, let alone to you. We sought consolation and gave it one to the other, but our embrace led us further than we ever intended. Perhaps we sought to extinguish a fire by creating another. I cannot speak for him. I know only that I needed someone who understood my sorrow and would not make light of it. Perhaps he needed the same."

She lowered her head. "Afterward, he naturally did

the honorable thing and proposed that we marry. But grief is a poor foundation for a marriage, nor are we suited. When I declined, he was, I think, greatly relieved."

"Despite the fortune you would bring to the marriage?"

"Even so. I have seen him on occasion since that sad night and the difficult morning that followed. We are as we always were, as if what happened between us never took place."

"It is never that simple, Lady Eve."

"I wouldn't know. But the circumstances were unique, as is the gentleman."

"Does he live in London?"

"No. Do not importune me, sir. I will say nothing more of this."

"One more set of questions, then, and we will be finished for tonight. Who would have known about your ride into Weybridge?"

"A number of people, if they gave it any thought. Wherever I am, I always attend Sunday services."

"You astonish me."

"I expect the Lord is equally surprised. But it is my lifelong habit, and here at Oatlands, most of the servants and many of the guests would be aware of it. Quite often the duchess attends as well, but in that event, we take a carriage and another route." A shiver ran down her back. "I hadn't thought of it until now, but the first accident also occurred on a Sunday morning, when I was walking to services at St. George's."

"Proving that virtue is its own punishment." He stood and pulled his footrest—a leather ottoman— next to the table beside her bed. "You must take some broth. Can you move your hands and arms?"

"Probably. But I don't want to. And I'm not hungry."

"Once again, this isn't a negotiation." He took a serviette from the tray and draped it over her night rail. "If you wish to be useful, try to recall whom you saw this morning before you left for Weybridge."

"Almost no one. Sir Basil Leonard and Mr. Arledge were on their way to the lake to fish. I heard voices from the breakfast room, but didn't go in." She watched him pour broth from a pitcher into a cup. "And where were *you* this morning, sir?"

He sat on the ottoman, putting his head on a level with hers, the cup in one hand and a spoon in the other. "As it happens, I was in a brothel."

"I shouldn't have thought you'd be needing one so soon."

A sound that was almost a laugh. "No, indeed. I was making inquiries about Jeremy Brown, who called on one of the ladies the night he was slain."

She waved away the spoonful of broth he was lifting in her direction. "Well? What did you learn?"

"It doesn't matter now. I shall provide Sir Peregrine the few twigs of information I've gathered, along with my suspicions, and wash my hands of the business. Lady Eve, I am perfectly capable of forcing this soup down your throat."

"But you wouldn't. I will try to drink some, though, if you answer my question."

"Extortion." He put the spoon to her lips. "First a show of good faith."

She swallowed three or four sips of the lukewarm chicken broth before he spoke again.

"There's little enough to tell. Brown saw the woman three times, giving his name as Jack and claiming to work at loading barges on the canal. The night of his death, he seemed fearful. Robbers, he said, and asked to stay the night. But she could not accommodate him, so he left a little after midnight. He also mentioned having lived in Wiltshire and liking it there."

"That's all?" she said, when she could find space to talk between relentless spoonfuls of broth.

"I'm afraid so. But that doesn't mean you can stop eating. More soup, or will you try the custard?"

"Of all the nannies I have had, sir, you are by far the oddest. But consider this. What if Jeremy Brown knew the killer was after him? That would explain why he suddenly left his place of employment in Kent without collecting his pay. Why he lied about his name, which we still do not know, and about where he worked."

Cordell returned cup and spoon to the tray. "That was my conclusion. But it gets us nowhere."

"Except that it suggests a link between at least two of the victims. The first of them, Mr. Farley, was from Liverpool and came to London for the Season. But the reports you gave me to read mentioned an uncle with an estate in Kent."

"It's a large county, madam. But I'll suggest that Sir Peregrine find out if the estate is near where Brown was working. Perhaps the uncle knows something. There was no mention of him being questioned."

While he dished custard onto a saucer, she watched his face, shadowed as it had been in the grotto, lightly whiskered as it had been in his bed. An odd nanny to be sure, gentle with the spoon against her sore and puffy lips, issuing orders like a commanding officer.

Her plan called for enticing him, and it had succeeded. Briefly. But there was little hope of resuming their affair, not while she looked like this, and it would be a considerable time before her looks improved.

She would have to come at him from another direction. Instead of his male passion, she was now the object of his male protective instincts. But how could she use that to discredit him? He failed only if she died.

"Custard," he said, extending a spoon.

Last night, she had been his lover. Tonight, she was his *project*.

She wanted to curl up and weep. But she ate the custard, for the strength she would be needing, and even swallowed the draft Mrs. Kipper had prepared for her. All of them, medicine and custard and broth, tasted bitter. She slumped back against the pillows, drained and aching in ways that had nothing to do with her injuries.

From beneath lowered lashes, she watched Cordell carry the ottoman to a shadowed corner of the room. He pulled the heavy wing-back chair to join it, placed the napkin with the darts on a table, and took the glass that had held the sleeping draft and set it on the floor by the wall. She started to ask why and realized that the door to the secret passage opened at that spot. He lit a second candle from the first and seemed to take care where he placed them both. Then he retrieved something from a leather case on the floor, sat himself in the chair, lifted booted feet onto the ottoman, and settled back.

"What are you doing?" she said.

"Standing the watch. Until the threat is eliminated, you will not be left alone."

"You can't mean to sit there looking at me all night long."

"I would enjoy doing that, of course, but you are out of the light. There's no reason to feel uncomfortable. You'll soon be asleep."

"Do you really think anyone would try to kill me here, in this house?"

"Let's say I'm taking no chances. When I am away, Silas Indigo or Mrs. Kipper will be in your company. You are to eat or drink nothing given you by anyone else."

"The *duchess* isn't going to poison me. Besides, how do you know those two can be trusted? The draft Mrs. Kipper brewed could have contained anything at all."

"Which is why I made her drink half of it. As for Indigo, it's simple enough. We need him, and at the end of the day, we have to trust someone. I intend also to confide in Sir Peregrine. For the rest, they will hear only the story we'll be putting together when I return from London."

She didn't want him in this room, but she very much wanted him within call. "You are leaving?"

"When you awaken, I'll be gone. There are arrangements to be made. I can't say how long my business will keep me there, but you'll not be well enough to leave this room any time soon. Indigo and Mrs. Kipper have a full list of instructions. You are to obey them without question. For now, do you want help lowering yourself onto the bed?"

"It's easier to breathe, sitting up a little."

"Then close your eyes and your mouth and try to sleep. I am beginning to regret that you drank only half of that sleeping draft."

"Sir, is that your pistol on the arm of the chair?"

A theatrical sigh. "I always have it within reach. Loose women keep showing up in my bedchamber."

"And tyrannical gentlemen in mine," she said.

Chapter 14

Portugal, April 1811

*You won't believe what my father has done. He
ordered my uncle to keep R on a strict allowance
so he won't have extra funds to loan me. As if I
would keep picking my cousin's pocket in any
case! Even from far away, Sarne must control
everyone in the family. At least, he tries to. I told
R that maybe if he transferred to another regiment, he wouldn't find his allowance pared. He
says he'll go if a captaincy opens up in another
cavalry regiment or if CB boots him out, which-
ever comes first. I said I might be the one booted
out. CB don't care which of us leaves, so long as
one of us does. There's no reason. We don't get
up to trouble. There isn't time now. Besides, I'm
always off gathering information, so we hardly
ever see each other. It makes me angry that he is
punished by Sarne on my account, and CB is
nearly as bad. I think he's just worried we'll both
get killed at the same time, and he'll have to write
the family. But nobody ever knows what CB is
thinking, not for sure. Beg your pardon. I*

*shouldn't write when I'm in bad humor. But you
made me promise a letter every day, so you'll
have to put up with this one. Don't send money,
E. I mean it. The trouble is with my father, not
with my purse.*

Yr. ill-tempered J

"I'm not sure why I bothered to come here," Cordell
said. "You have heard the news already."

"A good part of it, I'm sure." Sir Peregrine stirred
honey into his tea. "White's was abuzz last night about
the accident and the announcement of your betrothal
to the unfortunate victim. By other means, I learned
you have withdrawn from the mission, taking Indigo
and Mrs. Kipper with you."

"I am here to ask for your help as well."
shall have it. Do try the coddled eggs, my dear. Without food and the sleep you look to have missed, what
use can you be?"

They were in Sir Peregrine's sunlit breakfast room,
the unshaven host wearing a russet dressing gown over
a loose shirt and trousers, in reasonably good humor
despite being dragged from his bed at the uncivilized
hour of ten o'clock. Cordell, who had done no more
than knock on the front door of the London town
house, was provided coffee by a servant and waited
only five minutes before a decidedly unflamboyant Sir
Peregrine came down to join him.

"I expected an argument," Cordell said, "about
the mission."

"We have no hold on you. And it happens that last
year, a gentleman summoned as you were summoned
objected most vigorously when we failed to assist his
partner, who required our help. We took the lesson

to heart. Never again will we neglect those who have served, however briefly, in our company. Even when they demand, as I expect you will, to give the orders. I don't suppose you have a plan?"

"Beyond finding and killing Lady Eve's attacker, none whatsoever. I don't even know where to start looking for him. By her account, she has accumulated no enemies. No one stands to gain by her death. Even so, this was the third attack within five weeks, all of them disguised as accidents."

Sir Peregrine put down the slice of toast he had been buttering. "I have heard nothing of prior attacks. You say five weeks. They began before we summoned her?"

"So she said. But I haven't ruled out a connection to the Black Phoenix mission. Lady Eve will provide details of the first two incidents when she is recovered. Meantime, I am looking for anyone who might have a reason, real or imagined, to do her harm. You have known her a long time?"

"Since . . . let me see. The spring of 1813, I believe. She was just turned eighteen, practicing her company manners at teas and musicales before her come-out ball. Everyone wanted to take her measure. The eligible gentlemen wanted to take her fortune. Hers was the most anticipated debut I can remember, and her parents guarded her like a pair of fire-breathing dragons. The unsuitable males were speedily driven off."

"We might be dealing with a rejected suitor," Cordell said.

"They are thick on the ground. For a time, it was all the thing to woo Lady Eve. A rite of passage, if you will, followed by a drinking party after the inevitable rejection. I don't know that any of the fellows took it seriously. Everyone knew Marbury was holding out for a duke or marquess, and if a lesser creature had the temerity to formally ask for her hand, I never heard about it."

"She is of age now. Free to accept or reject as she will."

"I have seen her show no partiality to any gentleman. Of late, she has devoted herself to politics and good works."

"And made enemies?"

"She has garnered the usual resentment from men who believe she should keep to her place, and from women who also believe she should keep to her place. But she has nearly always behaved with discretion. At worst, a few people consider her eccentric. The others assume she will get over this political nonsense, marry well, and host elegant parties."

Cordell rubbed the bridge of his nose. "Then you have nothing to tell me? I need a direction. A place to start."

Sir Peregrine frowned. "The one time her demeanor seemed out of the ordinary was the night of her ball. Devonshire had been persuaded to give over his London house for the event, and we all reckoned Marbury was trying to match his daughter with the duke. Not much chance of that, Devonshire not being the marrying kind. But it was the party of the year, and throughout the evening, Lady Eve fizzed like champagne. Unless you came near enough to look into her eyes. They were . . . How can I describe what I saw? Death. Ghosts. A pain I have never forgotten."

"Do you know the reason?"

"Not then, nor later. She vanished for more than a week, and when she finally appeared at Almack's, she looked pale and too thin. She had been ill, she said, but was fully recovered. And sure enough, she attended every important social event until the Season ended. I thought there must be more to it, because no survivable illness could have accounted for the despair I had seen in her eyes. But that was four years ago. Whatever happened to overset her, how could it be relevant now?"

"Hard to say." Cordell had already decided to follow up on what he had just learned. Perhaps the Duchess of York knew something. "Let us turn," he said, "to practical matters. Lady Eve must be kept out of harm's way until the threat is eliminated. I want a safe location, entirely secret and easily defended."

"Simple enough. Black Phoenix maintains two properties in London fitting those requirements."

"No. Too many people know about them."

"But surely, my dear fellow, you don't suspect anyone associated with Phoenix?"

"Why not? I don't even know how many of you there are. One incident has already caught my attention. Why is it that Jordan Blair was coordinating the mission one day and off to Cornwall the next?"

"There is nothing to that. He had been setting up a complex endeavor in Cornwall when the murders of young men began, and of the senior members of our fellowship, he was the only one available to launch this investigation. When I returned to London, he went back to what he had been doing."

Smooth as fine cognac. Cordell was impressed. "Why don't I believe you?"

"I am offended. The explanation is both plausible and true." Sir Peregrine leaned back, looked up at the ceiling, and sighed. "Perhaps there's a trifle more to add. From the beginning, Jordie objected in the fiercest terms to Lady Eve's recruitment. He considered her too young, too refined, and in danger of losing her reputation as a consequence of the feigned betrothal. When he was overruled, he immediately asked to be removed from the mission. On my return, he got his wish. And that, truly, is the entire story. You knew him, did you not, on the Peninsula? Can you not attest to his character?"

"I'd bet my life on it, yes. But not Lady Eve's." A too-familiar sickness gripped his stomach. "It is impossible to be absolutely certain of another man's character, or of one's own judgment. I know what it is to be disastrously wrong. If I accept you, Mrs. Kipper, and Silas Indigo into my confidence, it is only because I must. No one else can know that yesterday's attack was other than an accident."

"But if I cannot explain to Phoenix what we are doing, how am I to account for the lot of us walking away from the murder investigation? Might we take action if an opportunity arises, at least until replacements are found? You, I understand, are adhering to the false betrothal. Or do you actually mean to wed the lady?"

"I do not. I'm putting the killer on notice that she is no longer an easy target. In fact, if you will direct me, I'll see to having an announcement published in the *Times*."

"Oh, I shouldn't do that. A written declaration will make it all the more difficult to extricate Lady Eve when this is over. Besides, word is already circulating at a rate that would astonish you."

"Very well, then. What is to be done about the hiding place?"

"I'll see to it."

"I want bodyguards for her."

"My auxiliary valet will do, and he has a brother nearly as large. You may safely leave this to me, Colonel. But if you are to come and go from the bolt-hole without drawing attention, you'll need to leave off that uniform and alter your appearance. Pardon me for a moment."

Sir Peregrine went out of the room and soon returned with a fussy little man carrying a measuring tape, paper, and a pencil. "Donald here will take your dimensions and purchase what is required."

Cordell rose and subjected himself to the measurements while answering a slew of questions from Sir Peregrine. Then Donald took himself off, fresh coffee was provided, and the questioning continued.

"What are your plans for today, my dear? Will you return to Oatlands?"

"Not directly. I mean to call at Marbury House and inform the servants that Lady Eve will remain with her godmother until she is able to travel, after which she'll recuperate . . . I don't know where. By the sea?"

"Brighton. Give the killer somewhere crowded to go while we figure out how to identify him. But speaking of Marbury House reminds me. Last night, a chap fresh in from Paris mentioned seeing Lord and Lady Marbury at the embassy. Apparently they mean to return to London within a fortnight."

"Just what we need." Cordell scowled at his coffee cup. "We can't tell them where she is. They'd insist on seeing her."

"Perhaps not. A pair of cold fish, those two. They scarcely acknowledge their daughter, even when they're in the same room. But you may be sure they will descend on her fiancé with all guns blazing. Prepare for threats, bribery, and public scorn."

"The least of my concerns. I'd like to move Lady Eve as soon as she is able to travel. When will the house be ready?"

"By Wednesday." Sir Peregrine slathered marmalade on a slice of toast. "Meantime, I require a summary of everything you have learned or concluded about our original mission. May I point out that I have undertaken a job you expected to be handling? In return, why not use the time to pursue any leads you have developed?"

"There is only one," Cordell said. "Lady Eve noticed that the first victim has an uncle living in Kent, where the third victim resided before coming to Oatlands. A slim thread at best, but he might be worth talking to. His name is Walter Burford."

"I'll provide you his direction. Tonight, come dine with me at the club. As the man who bagged the golden goose, you will naturally be the center of attention. There might be something—or someone—worth observing. Rumors to be squelched. False trails to lay."

"You'll have to excuse me. I want to assure myself—"

"Of the lady's well-being. Of course you do. But there's no use trotting back and forth between London and Oatlands. We fly pigeons, my dear fellow, and have more people in place there than you know. I'll have the latest word for you this evening. Will you reside at Stephen's in Bond Street again?"

"I expect so." Cordell wondered why he felt so driven to attend to Lady Eve in person. He should be detaching himself, as Sir Peregrine was proposing, in order to remain clearheaded. The events of the last two days had rocked him more than he wanted to admit.

He resolved to keep in mind that she was a responsibility he had accepted, an assignment like any other. His duty was to protect her. And his greatest obstacle, he foresaw with dread, would be the lady herself.

Dinner at White's in company with the irrepressible Sir Peregrine was about what Cordell had expected. He got himself talked into calling on Walter Burford in Kent the next morning, fended off intrusive questions from gentlemen he didn't know, and refused to apologize for spoiling the Lady Eve stakes. White's betting book, he learned, was chock-full of wagers regarding whom she would marry and when, so when a dark horse entered the race and won it practically overnight, every bettor found himself a loser.

No one pointed out that Colonel Cordell was a most unsuitable suitor, nor did they express astonishment that Lady Eve had accepted him. Given the free and insulting way so many of the men bandied about her name, he was surprised at their restraint with him and mentioned it to Sir Peregrine in a rare moment of quiet.

"They are afraid of you, my dear Colonel. You are a most intimidating fellow. Lud, if I weren't an accomplished swordsman and shot, not to mention a fast runner, I'd be shivering in my silver-buckled slippers."

Cordell gave him a sour look. "I've done nothing remotely menacing, although a few of those louts could use a good thrashing. Are all the ladies treated with such disrespect?"

"The chaps are showing off to one another, that is

all. And really, sir, unless one of them goes completely off his head, you haven't the time to fight a duel. Laugh it off. Or at the least, refrain from glaring at them with blood in your eyes."

"I can't help it. This is my natural expression."

"Dear me," said Sir Peregrine, raising his quizzing glass. "You are sorely in need of gentling. I shall present you with a kitten."

"For a stew?" Cordell took a drink of claret. As if he didn't already have a hellcat on his hands.

"I say, sir. It's Colonel Lord Cordell, isn't it?"

Cordell glanced up to see an earnest young lieutenant of Horse Guards, a nervous smile on his smooth face, making a formal bow.

"We've been looking for you, sir," the lieutenant said. "Or rather, trying to deliver correspondence. Someone said you were at Stephen's Hotel, but when we inquired, they said you had gone to Oatlands. So we sent a courier this morning, but were informed by the steward that you had returned to London."

"And will be here for several days. Forward the correspondence to the hotel."

"I'll see to it, sir. But you might wish to make preparations for Wednesday. The packet includes several invitations related to the opening of Waterloo Bridge and the social events to follow. There is also a letter from His Grace, the Duke of Wellington." That bit of information was served with a touch of awe. "We included a map with all locations marked, along with your schedule."

"My *what*? Am I under orders, Lieutenant?"

"As near as one can come without anyone saying so. His Highness the Regent is anxious that officers who fought at Waterloo be present, and some have been selected to accompany him during the dedication ceremony. I believe you are among them."

Cordell managed not to swear aloud. "Thank you for the information. I shall expect the materials to be delivered tomorrow morning."

Flushing, the youngster bowed and returned to a group of uniformed friends, all equally young. They kept casting glances at Cordell over their shoulders.

"An unfortunate development," Sir Peregrine said, studying his manicured nails.

"More of a nuisance." *What next?* Cordell was thinking. "I might require to make a brief appearance. But should it become necessary to go absent without leave, I doubt that I shall be missed."

Chapter 15

Portugal, Jan. 1812

> *I can scarcely write, my hand is trembling so. To-night I dined with Lord Wellington! There were a dozen officers, twice that many local authorities, and even some Portuguese ladies. Wellington sat near to the prettiest of them, and there was much laughter from that quarter. I spoke only when I was presented to him by Cannonballs, and then I stumbled over Leicestershire when he asked where my home was. CB said I turned red as fresh meat, but not to worry because Wellington is used to that. He sat very close to Wellington, and I even saw him laugh a time or two. That was a bigger wonder, even, than me being in the presence of the greatest man I have ever met. Someone said the food wasn't very good, but I can't remember anything we ate. We were bivouacked not far from winter headquarters, and on the way back, CB said Lord Wellington had invited me to join his hunt the next morning. Guess he thought that with me being from Leicestershire, I'd be used to hunting. But you know,*

*I only went out for the riding. Didn't care a fig
for the fox or the hounds. I told CB that, and he
said, "Just don't fall off your horse." Not much
help!*

Yrs., J

Cordell, half hoping he would be late, arrived at
Whitehall steps shortly before the Prince Regent.
It was the uniform got him through the packed streets,
he supposed, and all the medals, but primarily the
laurel on his shako identifying him as a Waterloo vet-
eran. The crowds parted like the Red Sea to let him
pass, cheering him on his way. Sometimes he was
forced to smile and wave back at them.

Last year, on the first anniversary of the battle, he'd
found a quiet spot on the banks of the Seine, drunk
cognac until he was dizzy, and let the memories take
control of him for the night. Then he put them away,
best as he could, figuring they'd be back the following
year. And so they were, chanting in his ears like a
Greek chorus while banners flew and artillery fired a
salute of two hundred and two ungodly blasts.

He joined the other veterans invited to participate
in the ceremony and watched the Regent board the
Royal Barge in company with the dukes of York
and Wellington.

"You could walk across the Thames without getting
your feet wet," said Colquhoun Grant as they took
their places near the rear of the barge.

There were so many vessels of every sort clogging
the river, from ships of the admiralty to private yachts
and dinghies, that one could barely see the water.
Flowers, tossed from adjacent boats and from the riv-
erbanks, landed on their shoulders and at their feet.

Cordell looked up at the Waterloo Bridge, where subscribers to the construction of it mingled with the Horse Guards and the artillerymen shooting off those damn guns. He should have held back, made sure to arrive after the barge had launched. For one thing, he didn't want to find himself in company with Wellington, however briefly. And Grant, now commanding a brigade of cavalry in France that included the 13th Light Dragoons, might expect him to attend the regimental reunion supper that evening.

Nothing must be allowed to delay him. Tonight, while London celebrated, he would be spiriting Lady Eve into the city.

He almost made a clean escape. The Regent's party, of which Colonel Cordell was the lowliest member, ascended the steps to the bridge on the Surrey side, watched His Royal Highness pay the toll while everyone cheered, and tagged along with the military procession. Bands played. Flags of the allied countries fluttered in the wind. Flowers and ribboned laurels pelted the officials. Flanked by Wellington and the Duke of York, the Regent walked the length of the bridge, graciously acknowledging the accolades. Then he descended to the barge, now tied up for him on the north side, and the party was transported back to Whitehall Gate.

Cordell stayed aboard as long as he could, waiting for the dignitaries to climb into their carriages and depart. But when he stepped onto land, the Duke of Wellington—failing to altogether conceal his famous self under a large, open umbrella—was waiting for him.

"What is this I hear?" said the duke, drawing him

under the shelter of a tree. "You are to wed the Marbury heiress?"

"It surprises me as well," Cordell said between his teeth. "How did you learn of it?"

"The Regent is a dedicated gossip. Told me about it while we were walking on the bridge."

"In this case, gossip outpaces reality. No arrangement will be formalized until I have spoken with the lady's father."

"If you are angling for Marbury's permission, you bloody well won't get it."

"I know. This may come to nothing, sir. Indeed, I have been in discussions at Leadenhall about an assignment in India."

"What has got into you?" Even in the late-afternoon shadow cast by the tree, Wellington's blue eyes were sharp with disapproval. "A fortnight ago, none of this was in your head."

"I don't tell you everything." Cordell gave him back eye for eye. "Duty with the occupation army has not suited me. I cannot bear to be idle, and I must begin to consider my future. There is nothing for me in the regular army. That I am looking elsewhere cannot surprise you."

"No. But I would expect you to seek my advice. And now you shall have it. India is bad for you. Do not return."

"I am not the same man I was, sir."

"Far from it. What occurred is long in the past. It is the waste that concerns me. There is little you can accomplish in India that could not be managed by a lesser man. Today England celebrates, but the consequences of Bonaparte's ambition will be with us for years to come. Your experience and judgment are needed in the government."

"Politics?" Cordell couldn't help laughing. "You are mistaking me for someone else. I am not tactful, sir. Not diplomatic. Not patient with fools."

"I am none of those things, either," said Wellington. "But sooner rather than later, I shall find myself at Whitehall, and I insist you be there to support me. We have served together for more than twenty years, Marcus. Are we not, the both of us, retained for life?"

And how did one resist an order, disguised as a plea, from this man?

Whatever he had become that was good, Cordell owed in large part to Wellington. But he need make no commitment now, nor could he. For the present, his life was not his own. "You may be right," he said. "But what if I look into my political heart and discover a reform-minded Whig?"

"Then I shall put you on the India Trader myself. Ah, well. I must be off. Walk me to my carriage, will you? It is the curse of greatness that I require protection, mostly from importunate women."

Eve, who had rebelled at inaction and complained of boredom since Cordell's departure, discovered on Wednesday afternoon that she felt perfectly fine only when motionless in bed. She felt tolerably fine when walking slowly around her bedchamber for a minute or two. But when she was levered in and out of a bathing tub, every inch of her protested. Being dressed in a servant's spare uniform by Mrs. Kipper was no walk in the park, either. She declared herself unready to leave the comfort of Oatlands.

"But there will be no better occasion," Mrs. Kipper

advised her with the calm demeanor that had begun to grate on Eve's last nerve. "Everything has been arranged for tonight. Are you certain you cannot manage?"

There was no arguing with logic. Nearly all the servants had been given leave to attend the ceremony at the bridge, followed by the Waterloo Fair on the banks of the Thames. And it was her godmother who had the worst of it, being compelled to join her husband at the social events following the dedication. Eve knew what an ordeal it would be for her, but like a dutiful Prussian princess, the Duchess of York accepted the responsibilities that came with her dynastic marriage.

With Oatlands practically deserted, Eve's departure would not be noticed. Nonetheless, she was disguised, veiled, and bundled down the servants' stairs well after dark. The carriage, which she shared with Mrs. Kipper and a young stable boy, headed southwest, away from London.

She hurt too much to give the arrangements much thought. "Imagine yourself a parcel," Mrs. Kipper had suggested. "You need do nothing but let yourself be delivered."

Taking the advice to heart, Eve was paying little attention when the carriage turned into a posthouse stable yard, where she was transferred to what looked like a hackney coach that had seen better days a half century earlier. A man who reminded her of Silas Indigo was on the driver's bench, along with a rough-looking fellow half again his size. The stableboy clambered onto one of the horses.

Just before the coach door closed, she saw a man on horseback gesture to the driver. His face was obscured by a floppy-brimmed hat, but something about him seemed familiar. The horse was nothing special, though, and he wore a battered cloth jacket over a homespun tunic and trousers. With all the talk about killers, she had grown suspicious of everyone, even a common laborer.

Traffic and crowds forced a number of detours along the way. Inside the poorly sprung coach, Eve bounced around like a marble in a box. Every two or three minutes, she thought of asking Mrs. Kipper for laudanum, but that very morning she had resolved to leave it off for good. The laudanum gave her ease from pain and an odd sort of mental clarity that later dwindled into befuddlement, making her crave another dose to get back where she had been. Better the pain, she had decided. But that was while she lay comfortably in bed, before the bath and this miserable journey.

It ended, a long time later, in a stable. Limp as a wrung-out handkerchief, Eve leaned on Mrs. Kipper's arm as they walked a little way down an alley, through a gate in a high stone wall, and past a small patch of garden to the rear entrance of a narrow house. Her new home.

Through the kitchen, then, and along a dim passageway to a tiny foyer, where a woman wearing voluminous gray skirts and a mobcap curtsied gracefully. "Welcome," she said in a scratchy voice. "I am Mrs. Marsh. You seem a bit fagged, my dear. Let us take you directly to your bedchamber. Time enough when you are settled to ask your questions."

Eve's only question, as she looked up the long, steep staircase, was how she would make it to the top.

"I'll take her."

It was Cordell's voice, from directly behind. Before she could react, he had swept her into his arms and started up the stairs.

The man in the floppy hat. He had been with her all along. Lying painfully in his rock-hard embrace, she felt relieved and angry at the same time. Being a parcel had been well and good, until she ended up as *his* parcel. Pride boiled up inside her.

Without another word, he delivered her into a bed-chamber not much larger than her dressing room at Marbury House, set her on her feet, and departed.

While Mrs. Kipper helped her into a night rail and dressing gown, Eve scraped up her wandering wits and lashed them together. People efficiently tended to her needs, for which she was grateful, but she could hardly spend the rest of her life hiding out in this clean but dreary room. She didn't think she could tolerate it for a week, if that long. As soon as she could get about without too much difficulty, she'd be on her way.

When she was seated on the bed with her back against the padded headboard, Mrs. Marsh bustled in with Cordell a little behind her.

"Ah, my dear girl." With a swish of her skirts, Mrs. Marsh sat on the edge of the bed near Eve's waist. "How are you feeling?"

The light was dim, only a few candles on a side table, but Eve thought she must have met this woman before. The shape of the nose, and especially the un-usual curl of the lips, put her in mind of—

She leaned forward, looked more closely. "Sir Peregrine!"

"Fiddle!" he said with a laugh. "I know a disguise cannot conceal my identity from friends and acquaintances, but I'd hoped to fool you a little longer."

"You are wearing that costume to *entertain* me?"

"No, indeed. Our neighbors are certain to be curious about the new residents, and the surest way to satisfy them is with a good story. I am a widow who provides fine piecework to mantua makers, as does my daughter. That would be you. I don't suppose you make lace or are skilled at embroidery? It doesn't matter. Your hands are swollen, I see. I'll buy good work and resell it."

"You must actually *do* what you say you do?"

"It's much less trouble, in the long run, to be convincing in every detail. Cordell there is John, my son and your husband. Poor fellow. Used to be a soldier, but got hit on the head at Waterloo and all but died. The large chap you may have noticed earlier dragged him from the battlefield, thereby saving his life. In gratitude, we provide a home for him and his brother. Your husband's injuries, alas, have left him slow-witted and hot-tempered."

"Perfect casting," Eve said.

"We don't want people trying to chat him up. You, by the way, are carrying a child. But you lost another not long ago, and the midwife advises you to remain quietly in your room. Tom, the lad who came with you from Oatlands, is my nephew. Mrs. Kipper, now known as Mrs. Crick, is my sister, and Silas Indigo is Mr. Crick. You needn't memorize all this, as you'll not be speaking with anyone. But the rest of us, who will be buying food and other supplies from local merchants, will play our roles whenever we leave this house."

"And am I, sir, to lie here like a bolster pillow for the indefinite future?"

"Yours is, I expect, the most difficult part. We'll

supply what we can for your entertainment. I've brought books, cards, trick-track, a chess set, stationery. . . . You must tell us what you'd like. But until your attacker has been apprehended, you will not leave this house."

"And you have a plan to find him? Some notion of his identity? I certainly don't."

"You must think harder on this, Lady Eve. Cordell told me that no one came to your mind when first you considered the question, so you need to cast your net wider. Anyone can be despised without knowing it, because we all give offense. Often we don't mean to, or we don't realize we have done so. It needn't be a direct offense to the attacker. Perhaps you did injury to someone he cares about. Do you understand what I am trying to explain?"

Perfectly. She managed to not look at Cordell, although she sensed his gaze focused on her. She had despised him long before they met, because he had done harm to someone she loved. But his offense was great and public. If she had done anything half so terrible, she would surely remember it.

"I do understand," she said. "And since the colonel questioned me, I have thought and thought and thought about it. Because you ask, I will think some more. But I suspect the only way we shall find the villain is to set me up as a target and catch him in the act. Preferably before he succeeds."

"Out of the question," said Cordell.

"In the end, that will be my decision." She saw his lips set in a rigid line. "How different this is—have you noticed?—from the Phoenix murders. I'd wager the victims knew precisely what they had done wrong. And the killer made sure of it by creating little set pieces to illustrate their offenses. Certainly Jeremy Brown understood what was happening. Knowing the killer would come for him, he changed his identity, fled his employment, and lied to everyone about who he was and where he worked."

Cordell, who had been leaning against the wall, pulled himself upright. "You are changing the subject. But let us not argue about this tonight. It has been a long day, you are weary, and Sir Peregrine has another engagement."

"So I do." Fluttering off the bed, he curtsied to Eve. "Not wearing this lovely gown, I assure you. We regret the accommodations are less than what you are accustomed to, but try to endure them."

"I don't mind discomfort," she said. "I do mind being forced by Colonel Cordell to abandon the Black Phoenix mission."

"Oh, he's not given up on it altogether. Yesterday he rode to Kent, on your suggestion, to interview Mr. Harbin's uncle. Not much came of it, as has been the case with all our inquiries thus far, but we continue to gather pieces of the puzzle. Perhaps you can fit them together for us." Sir Peregrine gave her a warm smile. "Good night, Lady Eve."

Cordell, without a pleasantry, followed him out. But shortly after, he was back, filling the doorway. "Mrs. Kipper will be here in a moment," he said. "Have her attend to whatever you need. I'm here to warn you. The house is small, so we're forced to bunk up together. I'll be sharing your quarters."

Chapter 16

An astonishing thing has happened. One of Lord Wellington's aides-de-camp is returning to England, and I have been invited to replace him! CB brought the news, and said it the way he'd tell me to go out on picket, as if a chance to serve with the commander was everyday fare. Told me to think it over and let him know my reply. I expect I'll say yes. I might not have done, if CB had said he would be sorry to lose me, or something of the kind. But it's neither here nor there to him if I go, so probably I will. First I'll do some reconnaissance, speak with a couple of the fellows I've got to know on the hunts, and see what sort of duty it would be. There's no great compliment in being asked, you should know. CB says Lord Wellington likes to have young gentlemen from good families around him, so I expect I was chosen because the father who isn't speaking to me happens to be a duke. I never thought being a Branden would turn up useful!

Yrs., etc., J

When Cordell returned, hatless, he was carrying a bottle in one hand and a glass in the other. The glance he shot her was not friendly. "You should lie down," he said in his commanding officer voice. "Go to sleep."

Like a good little girl. Instead, Eve asked the question that had preoccupied her since he left the room. "Are you to sleep with me on this bed?"

"There's a pallet underneath, which I can pull out if I want it. Tonight, I'll make do with the chair."

Leather-covered and wing-backed, the chair looked to be reasonably comfortable. He dropped onto it, pulled the cork from the already opened bottle with his teeth, and filled the glass with amber liquid.

"What is that, sir?"

"Cognac. French. I brought it with me."

"May I have some?"

He shrugged. "Maybe it will keep you quiet. What's in that glass on your night table?"

"A sleeping draft, but I don't intend to take it. You could empty it into the chamber pot and—"

"I'll get you a clean one." The bottle and glass went on the floor, and he went out.

He seemed different, as if his thoughts were somewhere else entirely. A good time, then, to learn more about him, to probe for the weaknesses that must be there. Since she was not permitted to hunt for the Black Phoenix killer or even for the killer who had his sights on her, she might as well concentrate on her own revenge. Closing her eyes, she thought of Johnnie refusing Wellington's invitation in favor of serving with Cordell. Had he chosen otherwise, he might still be alive. At the least, he'd not have been caught in that ambush. His honor would be intact.

She wouldn't be plotting to do harm.

Cordell returned with a glass, into which he poured a meager amount of cognac before giving it to her.

She took a sip. "Oh. It tastes like brandy. You may as well give me more of it before rooting yourself in the chair."

He obliged, a look of indifference on his face. "Do you mean to get drunk? Try not to be sick, because I've no intention of cleaning up after you. I plan to be stinking drunk myself, and useful for nothing."

She tried to keep the surprise off her face. "You had better close the door, then, so we don't disturb the others when we start singing scurrilous songs. Isn't that what gentlemen do when they drink?"

"Sometimes. I just mope."

"That seems quite out of character, sir."

"And what would you know of my character? No, don't answer that. I'm not up to being dissected this evening."

"A pity. I had all my instruments laid out. But you can understand my concern. As my self-appointed protector, you will be fairly worthless while desolately drunk."

"For one night only. It happens to be this night. You shouldn't have to witness it, which is why you ought to take the sleeping draft instead of the cognac. But I know better than to try talking sense into you. And I won't misbehave, in case you were hoping otherwise."

"Well, of course you wouldn't. Not with me looking like—what is it the Corinthians say?—like I've gone ten rounds with Gentleman Jackson. I'm surprised you haven't turned the chair to face something else, like the wall."

"I wasn't referring to carnal matters, Lady Eve. Only the sort of rowdiness you might find amusing. As for your appearance, you look pretty much as anyone would after a bad fall. I have seen many wounds in my time. Yours will heal."

"Even so, it makes me uncomfortable to be the object of attention. I wish for no one to see me until the shape of my face is normal again, and the colors somewhat less . . . vivid."

"I'll turn the chair, if you wish. But what you describe is not what I see when I look at you."

"You don't see distorted features and splotches of brown, yellow, purple, and blue?"

"All of that is undeniably there. But I see Lady Eve Halliday. Proud. Obstinate. Clever. Manipulative. Witty. Brave. Graceful. Idealistic. Devious. A score of other qualities I suspect but cannot prove to be there. Your injuries are no more significant than your clothing, madam. I see *you*."

To cover her confusion, Eve took a large swallow of cognac and all but choked on it. What an astonishing thing for him to say. They had been, briefly, colleagues and lovers, but he'd never seemed to really notice her. Except for the night he bedded her, she'd have guessed that whenever they happened to be together, he was wishing her somewhere else.

"You needn't turn away," she said, mainly to silence her own thoughts. "Unless you'd rather. But will you explain why this is the one night for drinking? Has it to do with the anniversary of Waterloo?"

"I told you. No dissection." He had already emptied

his glass and was refilling it. "I am, in fact, honoring and deploring the battle that brought an end to one brilliant man's attempt to rule Europe and any other place he could get his hands on. I have been a soldier for twenty years, and for nearly than long, he directed the course of millions of lives. Was responsible for millions of deaths."

"Shouldn't you celebrate, then, our victory and his defeat?"

"So I do. But the pursuit of adventure and glory was not his alone. I believe every soldier has the responsibility to seal in his heart and mind the price of war, and there is no better—or worse—image to hold than the battlefield at Waterloo. I hope never to see its like again."

"I wish you would tell me a little about what happened there. When we were coming into the city, I heard what sounded like cannon fire. It was far away, but I was thinking how deafening it must be to hear it close to hand."

"What you heard tonight was fireworks being shot off. Artillery sounds much like that. A battlefield is all noise. Artillery fire, gunfire, drums beating out orders, horses, the shouts of men, the screams of men. And smoke everywhere."

He leaned his head against the chair. "At Waterloo I was, for much of the time, on the crest of a hill, so I had good view of the immediate area. And I was fairly distant from the cannons and smoke as well. My orders were to prevent the French from using the hill to get to a place Wellington didn't want them to go, and on that day, as on so many others, the Thirteenth performed with distinction. It was, I must say, one of the rare times I felt like a true cavalry officer. My duties on the Peninsula involved me in a great many skirmishes, but I saw action in few important battles."

She thought he was finished, but after a few moments, he began speaking again. "Late in the day, Wellington summoned me. Because so many officers had been killed or wounded, I was to carry orders—in their names—to regiments in disarray. That gave me a good look at places where the battle was especially furious. I'd find the troops I sought, identify myself as Captain This or Major That, and rally them into order. Some recognized me, others responded to the names I gave. They all sought direction, even from a ghost. That's the name they've given a man assigned, as I was, to represent the dead."

She realized that she was leaning forward, captivated by his story, and immediately lowered her gaze.

"That duty," he said, "brought me a souvenir of the battle. My horse was shot out from under me, the second I'd lost that day, but very soon a riderless French mount came by and I managed to snag him. He's an easygoing fellow, spirited but disciplined, and has served me well ever since. Not knowing his name, I gave him a new one in honor of all the men, on both sides, who had fallen that day."

Cordell took another swig of cognac. "When the battle was over," he said at length, "and twilight lowering over the field, Ghost and I wandered among the dead, searching for any poor sod clinging to his life. We were still there when the sun rose, although I can tell you I was sick beyond words. There was no stopping the looters or preventing the atrocities that occurred. I remained quartered near the field for several days, helping to coordinate what must be done in the aftermath of such a catastrophe. There was little time for sleeping, none at all for drinking, and all I could think of was how to achieve, for a few hours, the release of oblivion. I promised myself that I would parcel it out, once a year, on the anniversary of the battle. And you have now heard, Lady Eve, all I intend to say about Waterloo."

Questions swarmed to her lips and died there. She could not intrude on his memories, nor dared she betray her fascination, since childhood, with soldiering, and the knowledge of it she had acquired over the years. For four of those years she had been with Johnnie and, yes, with Cordell, in Spain and Portugal. What she didn't learn from Johnnie's letters she picked up in conversations with soldiers taking leave in London, and from the soldiers she helped care for in the infirmaries sponsored by Lady Etheridge's relief organization.

She hungered to hear, directly from this man, about military life, starting the day he arrived in Portugal. But Cordell wasn't the sort to talk about his experiences, except in the most general terms. She was amazed that he had, for a few minutes, confided so much to her. A measure, she was sure, of his bleak mood.

On a night like this one, exhausted and already a little blurry from the cognac, she could so easily grow careless and drive a greater wedge between them. She must watch what she said. But she wasn't yet ready to abandon what he had called the dissection of his character. Perhaps she would even be doing him a service by urging him to talk. It had to be better than reliving the nightmare of Waterloo.

"Mrs. Kipper told me you participated in the bridge ceremony today," she said, a little too airily.

"What?" He looked up, ran his fingers through his hair. "The bridge. Yes. Not willingly. I daresay you'd have enjoyed it, and the grand ball at Windsor taking place right now."

"Yes, indeed. I am a frippery female, partial to light diversions. Probably I should relish them less, while you should relish them more. What do you do to entertain yourself, sir?"

"I play bodyguard to frippery females, which is sufficient diversion for a jaded old soldier. If I give you more cognac, madam, will you drink it and promptly fall asleep?"

In reply, she held out her glass and watched him rise with the natural athletic grace she couldn't help admiring.

"Only this much," he said, giving her perhaps two fingers' worth of cognac. "Any more and you'll be ill. Besides, I want all the rest."

She wouldn't have described him as mellowed by the drink. More like resigned to enduring her presence and her conversation while his thoughts wandered far from this room. She found herself longing to be with him, wherever he was going, and not only for the purpose of discovering something that might be used against him. After all that had transpired since they met, they were too entangled with each other for her to think dispassionately about this man. Or perhaps the cognac was affecting her more than she realized.

He was back in the chair, head against the padded leather, eyes closed. For a short time, she watched the play of candlelight on the planes and angles of his face, an altogether masculine face that was somehow beautiful as well.

He must not be left to go alone, she decided, into

his own dark world. She drew in a long breath. "What of Wellington, sir? I met his grace two or three times during the Victory Celebrations of 1814, and he seemed quite amiable. He appears to have relied on you. Do you know him well?"

"I suppose so. And he can be amiable, although that is not the term that comes first to mind." Cordell had opened his eyes, candlelight reflecting off them, giving him the somewhat demonic look she'd observed the night she took him to the grotto. "We have served together for nearly all the years I have been in the army. In fact, excepting only the two men who delivered me to the ship, he was the first soldier I ever met. I was fifteen years of age and callow as a puppy."

"Ship?"

"It is odd," he said, staring into his glass, "how a coincidence can turn out to be the most significant event of one's life. He was Arthur Wesley then, twenty-seven and already a full colonel with the Thirty-third. They had been assigned to the West Indies, but after storms and other difficulties prevented their departure, they were dispatched instead to India. Wesley, down with a fever, had not sailed with them. And as it happened, I was trying to secure a commission at just the time he got well enough to head out on a fast ship, meaning to catch his regiment up in Capetown. I was rushed through the paperwork, carted to Portsmouth, and sent along with him."

Cordell took another drink, and she noticed the bottle was more than half empty now. But his voice, while husky, wasn't slurred, and he appeared his usual incisive self. Except, of course, that he was talking to her of personal matters.

"It was the pair of us, along with Wesley's servants,

and I tried not to be too much underfoot. His boredom during the long voyage was my good fortune. He undertook to educate me, primarily by requiring me to read from the large number of books he had brought with him. My only schooling until then had been with the local vicar, and once I got used to the discipline of study, a new world opened up. He was also learning Hindi and Arabic, to prepare for the languages we'd be dealing with, and ordered me to master them as well. His lessons in map reading have proven invaluable. We arrived, finally, in Madras and journeyed to Calcutta in the spring of 'ninety-seven. When he returned to England in 1805, I was still with him. We have, more or less, served in tandem ever since."

"You were in India a long time, sir. Did you like it there?"

"Sometimes."

She knew she was close to losing him. Thank heavens for a superb memory, at least where he was concerned. "You told me, I think when we were riding in Hyde Park, that you had made—how did you put it?—a hash of your early years in the army. But it seems otherwise, or surely Wellington would have put you at a distance."

"He should have done." Cordell fixed her with a stern look. "You won't let this alone, will you? Won't let *me* alone until you have wrenched off a pound of flesh to chew on. I don't mind. You cannot have a lower opinion of me than you already do, and I have long since stopped caring what anyone thinks of me."

He was too near the truth. She scrambled for a way to deal with this now, before he sealed himself off from her for good. "You have said something of the

kind before, sir. I don't know why you imagine I dislike you. Did I not demonstrate otherwise on a night
you appear to have forgotten?"

She thought the direct challenge would spark a reaction, but his expression did not change. "Whatever
you think you perceive," she said, "consider that the
circumstances are unusual. I am unaccustomed to
seeking out a killer or being sought out by one. My
conduct is not always what I would wish. I beg you,
sir, to have patience with me."

"I am being the soul of patience, Lady Eve. And I
am sure that when you are ready, you will disclose
the truth. I'm equally certain that I won't like it.
Meantime, if you seek even more proof I am a rotter,
here it is."

He stretched out his long legs and crossed them at
the ankles. In the loose garments, homespun and the
color of oatmeal, he looked as if he'd wandered in
from the hayfields. "What I will say first is not meant
to excuse my behavior. From the moment I set foot
there, India was, to me, a land of wonders. I had
grown up in a quite different place, isolated and generally unpleasant, from which I emerged green as grass.
Suddenly I was in company with young men my own
age, all of us determined to enjoy ourselves before
any serious fighting got under way."

"This was in Calcutta?"

"For the most part. The English community carried
on much like London society, except that the men
drank prodigiously, day and night. To fend off the
sickness borne in the air, they said, and we newcomers
welcomed any excuse to indulge ourselves. There were
women, too, exotic women who cost very little and
were extremely obliging. The shock of discovering my-

self to be a creature of extreme passions quickly evaporated in the heat and the pleasure. For the better part of a year, we young rakehells gave ourselves over to dissipation."

As if inspired by the thought, he put aside his empty glass and took a swig of cognac directly from the bottle. "This went on until we paid for it. One night, six of us were riding back to Calcutta from a nearby town, where we had been about our usual pursuits. We were drunk, of course. Three had also developed a taste for opium. I'd have done so eventually, I suppose, if not for what happened when we were in the middle of nowhere under a moonless sky. I was dozing in the saddle when the attackers jumped us, some from the trees, others from the bushes."

He had the nearly empty bottle between his palms, moving it around and around. "I recall very little. There was a cry, probably the order to attack. Guns went off, and I felt a bullet graze the side of my head. I grabbed for my pistol, but the fellow riding alongside struck me a blow that all but knocked me to the ground. I was out of the saddle, hanging off the side of the panicked horse. More gunfire. He bolted, taking me with him. Next I knew, he'd thrown me. I hit the ground and went rolling down a ravine. The horse kept going."

"You were ambushed?"

"Picked off by robbers like the sitting ducks we'd let ourselves become. Between the bullet that grazed my head and the fall, I was unconscious before I hit the bottom of the ravine. It was daylight when I awoke and made my way back to where we had been assaulted. The others had been slaughtered, including the native servant who rode ahead of us with a lantern. They had been stripped of everything, including their clothes. Small animals were . . . Never mind that. I ran nearly all the way to Calcutta, hired the first wagon and driver I encountered, and reported the incident to Government House. The robbers were never caught."

He was staring directly ahead, but Eve could tell he was seeing only what he had seen that morning. "I don't even know," he said, "which fellow it was who saved my life."

"None of what happened was your fault."

His head swung up. His eyes blazed at her. "Do you think I don't know that? But if there had been something I could have done, I was in no condition to do it. As on most other nights, I was careless. Unready. A stupid boy intoxicated by pleasure. I had sold myself cheap, madam. It seemed absurd that I had survived, when my existence was of so little value."

He made a vague gesture with his hand. "I thought I would be cashiered. Sent home. But nothing occurred, leaving me threadbare with worry. After a fortnight, Wesley—no, he was Wellesley by then, I lose track—called me in. 'Do you want to stay in the army?' He snapped the words like a whip. 'Do you want to be a soldier?'

"I was downy enough to recognize they were two quite different questions. 'A soldier,' I told him, realizing I meant it. 'Then you must put aside everything that stands in your way,' he said. And he went on to tell me about his decision, taken firmly in 'ninety-three, to make his own future in the military. He had, before then, taken much pleasure in playing the violin, as his father had done. He allowed as how it had been his only distinguishing skill from boyhood. But it wasn't soldierly, nor conducive to the formation of a military career. That summer, with his own hands, he burned the violin. He put away other things as well, but the image of the burning violin remains with me even now."

Cordell looked up at her. "Having no talents or skills of any kind, I could make no such sacrificial gesture. But my life as it is today can be dated from that afternoon. The decisions I made then are reaffirmed every day, as they must be, for my nature has not changed. I thought it would, over the years, but for my sins, I remain in tenuous control of my wayward emotions and desires. We are, immutably, what we are."

He put the bottle on the floor, rose, and extinguished all but one of the candles. Its light didn't reach the chair. She heard the creak of leather when he sat again, the rustle as he arranged his long body into a comfortable position.

"What I am," he said softly, "is drunk. At last. I ask that you go to sleep, Lady Eve. Or sing, or dance a jig. But ask me no more questions, for I am done with you now."

Chapter 17

I decided not to be an aide-de-camp after all. It seems they mostly run errands and make a good show in front of important people. They do a great deal more, of course. The fellows wouldn't boast about important or dangerous assignments. But I like to be busy, and where I am, I'm busy nearly all the time. Nobody seems to care one way or the other where I go. CB conveyed my decision, and three days later, I was invited to join another hunt. Lord Wellington treated me the same as always, which is to say, I was one of the pack. Later I did something I shouldn't have done. I asked CB if Wellington was put out with me because I'd rejected the honor of serving with him. "He didn't mind," said CB. "Not after I told him you were a rotten dancer." Any mule can dance better than I, so it's just as well I won't be doing the pretty in front of the commander of the army!

Yr. clumsy J

Eve spent the next afternoon penning brief replies to letters from well-wishers. Most had been sent up from Oatlands by her godmother, but Cordell had retrieved a number of them from Marbury House. The servants ought not to have admitted him to the house, let alone handed over letters directed to her, but he was a difficult man to oppose.

She had not seen him since he extinguished the candles and their conversation. It was Sir Peregrine, frumpy in his Mrs. Marsh disguise, who brought the post late that morning, along with a nuncheon of steak-and-mushroom pie from a nearby shop. She was learning how people who lacked ovens and cooks managed to feed themselves, except, of course, they didn't have a baronet to do the shopping and lay out the meals.

"And where is the colonel today?" she had asked with the indifferent tone she had been practicing.

"Out giving the impression there is no reason for concern about your health. Taking note of anyone who betrays inordinate interest in you. Generally trying to stay busy. The lack of a direct purpose or an identified target is onerous to him."

"I wish I could help, Sir Peregrine. Who, after all, wants this over with more than I do?"

"Cordell, for one. He requires a dragon to slay. For myself, I am accustomed to slow and twisted paths, for they are where Black Phoenix missions invariably take me."

He had departed not long after, promising to supply her with more stationery, and by two o'clock, a tall stack of letters waited on a table to be posted. Only three messages remained unanswered, all of them sent her by the same person. She paced her cramped bed-chamber, building her strength and steeling herself for the upcoming negotiation with Cordell.

When he finally arrived, she saw little evidence he'd swallowed nearly an entire bottle of cognac the night before. But she could tell, instantly, that he had erected new barriers between them.

She wasn't surprised. He would naturally regret having spoken to her of personal matters, never mind that the events in question took place twenty years ago. Almost her entire lifetime ago.

"Thank you for retrieving my letters and cards," she said, easing her way into what was sure to be a difficult conversation.

He bowed stiffly. "Most of the cards came attached to flowers. The house is full of them. I'd have brought you a sample, but the displays were too conspicuous."

They were both standing, and in the small room, he seemed taller and even more formidable than usual. "Will you be seated, sir? There is something we must discuss, and I expect this will turn into a quarrel."

"Standard fare, then." He clasped his hands behind his back. "Take your first shot."

Against a wall of steel, she thought, wishing she didn't look like she'd been dragged backward through a hedge. Before the fall, she had not realized how much of her self-confidence was tied to knowing she made a good appearance. "It's a simple matter, really. There is someone I must see, and I wish you to help me arrange it."

"No."

"You haven't even heard who it is."

"I can guess. Lady Etheridge has already invaded

Marbury House and terrorized the servants. Fortunately, they're even more terrified of me. She didn't make it past the vestibule."

"She has been to Oatlands as well," Eve said. "And only the fact that a royal duchess blocked the way prevented her from searching every room. I have three letters from her, each more insistent than the last. She wishes to see for herself that I am unharmed."

"Then she will be disappointed. No one must know about this house, and for you to leave it is out of the question. Was there anything else?"

"You underestimate her, Colonel. The next time she calls at Marbury House and Oatlands, she will get in. And if she doesn't find me, she will raise a hue and cry. Hire Bow Street Runners. Call in magistrates. Petition judges."

"And make herself look ridiculous? I doubt it. Write to her, madam. Say that you are well and preparing to depart for the seaside."

"If you knew her better, you'd recognize that proposal as a waste of time."

"How is it you defer to this woman? Are you her creature?" He passed a hand wearily across his forehead. "Who the devil does she think she is?"

"My friend. Consider, sir, that I am injured and under threat of death. And yet, excepting only Sir Peregrine, I am surrounded by people I have known for little more than a week. You must allow me *one* friend."

"Would you settle for a kitten?" he said.

"Don't be ridiculous. You are trying to protect me, and I am grateful. But we cannot guard against everything and everyone. For all your efforts, the outcome may be unpleasant."

"You've never minced words before. Let us be straightforward. If we fail, you will die."

"I *know* that. But if the worst happens, you will not be responsible. You needn't feel guilty—"

"My feelings are nothing to the point." His eyes locked on her face. "You would be not be in this world. And the world has few enough treasures, Lady Eve. It cannot afford to lose you."

Disconcerted, she gazed back at him. The steel wall she could deal with. But no one had ever spoken to her like this.

A treasure? Not so far. Her life had always been reserved for the future. For when Johnnie came home from war to marry her. For when she had prepared herself to be the influential wife of an influential politician or diplomat. She had never thought herself of value in the present. She was always becoming something better, on her way to earning the good fortune accorded her by birth. Until she succeeded, she would continue to feel attached to her position and wealth like a parasite.

Quelling the warm pleasure conjured by his words, she charged back into the battle. "Do you forget that Lady Etheridge recognized my first two accidents as deliberate attacks? She will think the same of this one and spread the word . . . unless I persuade her otherwise. Either bid farewell to our deception, sir, or arrange for me to call on her."

"While you and I keep to our story, no one will credit what she says. And have you asked yourself how she so quickly leaped to the truth about the first two incidents? From what you told me of them, I'd have drawn no such conclusion."

"There is no reason I can think of, except that she

is overly protective. I'll try to learn more when I speak with her. Perhaps she is aware of someone who has taken a strong dislike to me, or someone who fancies I have given offense. We *need* this information, sir. Is it not worth a small risk to secure it?"

"Possibly. But under no circumstance will you concede that the attacks, any of them, were other than accidents."

"Then you'll let me call on her?" Eve tried not to crow, but he must have seen the satisfaction in her eyes.

His own eyes narrowed with displeasure. "I haven't the stamina, madam, to endure a long campaign with you as my adversary. Invite her to call on you at Marbury House tomorrow morning. I'll have one of your servants deliver the letter. If Lady Etheridge confirms the engagement, I shall make the necessary arrangements."

"Oh, my dear child!" Admitted to the flower-filled sitting room by a footman, Lady Etheridge sped to the sofa where Eve was sitting and looked down at her with sharp, evaluating eyes.

Wearing a high-necked, long-sleeved gown and soft gloves, Eve showed nothing of herself below the neck. She had wanted to veil her face, still a patchwork of ugly colors, but recalled the last time she had seen her friend. Lady Etheridge had been wearing her dress backward. After that, to stand on ceremony would be insulting.

Lady Etheridge settled on a chair directly across from her. "Did the horse gallop over your face?"

Eve grinned, which, like every move she made, hurt. "You see why I am in hiding. It will be several weeks,

I am told, before my appearance stops frightening puppies and children. But I took no great hurt, except to my pride."

"Her grace told me your mare bolted."

"Just so. We were coming through a woodland when a bird suddenly lifted from a branch directly overhead. It startled Juno, and off she went. After that, no matter which direction she turned, there was something else to spook her."

"And why is it, I wonder, that you are so remarkably prone to accidents these days?"

"An infection of clumsiness, I expect. Or a cluster of coincidences. My groom was witness to the latest embarrassment, and he can testify no one else was in the vicinity at the time. What I wonder, Lady Etheridge, is why you imagine someone might be out to do me harm. I've no enemies I know of, and if I have offended someone, it was entirely inadvertent. Are you aware of any such possibility? I would gladly make amends. Or take greater care, if there is reason for concern."

Eve looked up to see Lady Etheridge gazing into the middle distance from tear-filled brown eyes. The notion of this woman weeping, especially for no cause, shook her to the core. Whatever could be wrong?

But no tears fell. And when Lady Etheridge turned to her again, it was with the aloof poise Eve had always tried to emulate. "My dear," she said, "how can we ever be sure that we are safe? Consider poor Spencer Perceval, shot down in the lobby of the House of Commons by a merchant who had nursed a grievance for many years. Perceval was not the offender, but in declining to prosecute the case, he became the imagined source of all his murderer's ills. Likely the man was insane. He went to the gallows maintaining his right to take justice into his own hands when the authorities failed to act."

Not sure what to make of all that, Eve nodded.

"Directly after, my husband, who has accumulated enemies the way some men collect snuffboxes, hired a large man to accompany him everywhere. That lasted only a few weeks, primarily because his colleagues made a jest of it. But he has lived in fear ever since."

Lady Etheridge smiled, but to Eve, she appeared distracted. "I did not mean to frighten you regarding the accidents. The older one gets, the more cautious one becomes, at least on behalf of others. While I take myself freely wherever I want to go, it troubles me to think you sometimes do the same. But I shall say no more on the subject."

When Lady Etheridge's lips tightened into a line, Eve knew she had come to what was really on her mind.

"As for your betrothal, I am frankly shocked. It is quite other than what you intended for yourself, or what we have planned for all these years."

Mentally crossing her fingers, Eve plunged into the icy water. "But I have always intended to marry, if not so soon as this. And there was never any guarantee I'd find, as you did, a spouse willing to open political doors for his wife. Cordell is good raw material, don't you think? Between the two of us, I believe we can shape him into the husband my ambitions require."

Lady Etheridge leaned forward in her chair. "If you believe that, you can know nothing of this man. It would be easier to shape a moon of Jupiter than the

despotic colonel. And he is a nobody, Eve. He can
never rise to prominence."

"I know he's only a baron," she said, wishing she
had better prepared herself for this conversation. "But
he is a soldier of excellent repute, a Waterloo hero.
Beyond that, my own status will elevate him."

"He's a Norfolk baron," Lady Etheridge said with
disgust. "A fen farmer. There's no money in the family, nor any connections by marriage or friendship with
important families. The land is meager and of poor
quality. My dear, the man grows *turnips*!"

Taken aback, Eve fumbled for a response. "It cannot be. He hasn't been home more than once in
twenty years."

"I don't mean he plows the fields himself. He's left
the farm to the care of his stepmother and the two
children she brought to the marriage. Commoners, all
of them. She is the daughter of a shopkeeper, the widow
of a tailor. Can you imagine the embarrassment when
they descend on you in London, as they surely will?"

If she had really been going to marry Cordell, Eve
would have been appalled. But under the circumstances, she was pleased to have such ascendancy over
him. His presence too often raised in her feelings of
inadequacy. Unworthiness. This information would
give her more confidence as her plans unfolded. "It is
true," she said, "that we have never discussed his family. How is it you know so much about them?"

"I undertook an investigation of Colonel Cordell
the first evening you showed interest in him. He is a
handsome young man, to be sure. I can quite understand how you came to be infatuated. But make no
mistake. He is not malleable. If you marry him, you
will find yourself entirely in his power. He will breed

an heir on you, stash you in Norfolk, and spend your money."

It was maddening to defend the man she hated, almost as maddening as the times she found herself not hating him quite so much. "Can you give him no credit at all?" she said. "He has at least one powerful friend, the Duke of Wellington, and that must count for something. He is abrupt, I grant you, but I enjoy wrangling with him. It is good practice. If I cannot learn to bend him, on occasion, to my will, I'll be ineffective in the world I hope to enter."

Lady Etheridge gave her a penetrating look. "Do you love him?"

"I . . ." Flustered, Eve stared down at her gloved hands. "No. At least, I don't think so. How would I know?"

"My very thought. It has occurred to me that the rigid circumstances of your upbringing have bred in you a longing for affection. It is all too easy, when one seeks love, to see it where it does not exist. This is what troubles me. I fear that marriage to him will leave you disillusioned, wounded, and entrapped."

Lady Etheridge leaned across the space between them and put her hand on Eve's tightly clasped hands. "You may imagine I wish to separate you from Cordell in order to keep you to myself. But I would never take you, Eve, where you do not wish to go. I offer counsel, no more than that. And whatever you decide, I will always stand your friend."

Tears sprang to Eve's eyes. She looked up at Lady Etheridge's face, saw in it the sincerity of true affection. "I know," she said. "In all the world, I have no greater comfort. But I am sorry to prove such a disappointment."

"You are nothing of the kind. Plans are always subject to change, and what man proposes, the devil disposes. Only remember that while there is no decision that cannot be unmade, our actions hang on us like shackles. From them, and from their consequences, we can never escape."

As so often in the last few minutes, Eve sensed that Lady Etheridge was carrying on two conversations, one of them with herself. The brown eyes, so warm just a moment ago, had darkened, as if she had wandered into shadows of her own creation.

But then she smiled, patted Eve's hands, and rose. "I don't want to tire you, my dear. May I call again tomorrow?"

Eve stood as well. "I won't be here. My doctor has prescribed a regimen of sea air and sea bathing, so I am leaving for the south coast."

"Where will you reside? The Regent intends to go down to Brighton, and Etheridge has leased a house there for the summer. Would you like to stay with us?"

"Oh, no. Thank you, but I mean to find a quiet, out-of-the way spot where my injuries will go unremarked. An agent is arranging for me to examine several properties. When I have settled on one, I shall write you immediately."

"Make sure that you do. For now, you needn't accompany me downstairs. My carriage is only a short distance away. Take very good care of yourself, my dear, and when you are mended, come join us in Brighton."

Eve returned to the sofa when Lady Etheridge was gone, relieved that she hadn't been expected to show her face to the servants. And glad, too, that she had escaped a hard journey up and down the stairs. She kept forgetting how weak she still was. It had been only five days since the attack, although being incarcerated made the time pass with excruciating slowness. And while she always exaggerated the speed of her recovery, especially to Cordell, the preparations for today's meeting and a good deal of fretting about it had drained her last bit of energy.

She was leaning back with her eyes closed when a knock at the door forced them open. Assuming it to be Cordell, she said, "Come in," and watched with horror as a footman stepped inside. At the sight of her face, he blanched.

"It's all right," she said. "What is your message?"

"M-my lady, your guest appears to be . . . that is, she doesn't leave. Her carriage is in the street, and I offered to escort her out, but she doesn't seem to understand what I say. And she is talking to herself."

Eve held steady as a rush of fear swept through her. "I'll be there in a moment. Go make sure no other servants come into the entrance hall. Then wait by the front door."

Moments later, gripping the balustrade, she began to make her slow way down the great arc of the staircase. Not far from the door, Lady Etheridge was standing in front of a large gilt-framed mirror. Her hands, both of them gripping her netted reticule, twisted it the way one might wring out a washcloth. She seemed to be speaking to her reflection.

By the time Eve arrived at her side, Lady Etheridge was motionless, gazing silently into the mirror. "Are you feeling unwell, Lady Etheridge?"

"I have greeted her politely. I have conversed with her. But she will not reply. Not aloud. I see her lips moving. Can you see them? They are moving now, and yet, I cannot hear her. Is she very rude? Do you know her?"

Eve's heart began pumping wildly. What was happening? Ought she to send for a doctor? "I do, yes," she said. "I'm sure she doesn't mean to give offense. Will you wait here a moment?"

"If you like. I am expecting my carriage, but it hasn't arrived."

Eve went to the footman and directed him to fetch Mrs. Kipper. Then she crossed back to Lady Etheridge, who was twisting her reticule again.

"I am glad you got rid of that young man," she said. "He kept trying to take me somewhere. I told him I must wait here for the carriage. He said it was just outside, but why would it be there instead of coming in here to collect me? How I am to go to it? I thought perhaps I could pass through the wall this way"—she pointed to the mirror—"but it won't open. And that woman is blocking my path."

Cordell could handle this, Eve was thinking as she took Lady Etheridge's restless arm and led her away from the mirror. But she had no idea how to proceed. More than the attack that had nearly killed her, she was frightened by what was happening now. "The woman ought not to do that," she said gently. "We shall find another path to your carriage. I have summoned a guide to escort you home."

"But why must I go to my carriage? Why will it not come to me?"

"Because it is larger and finer than my poor house can accommodate. Lady Etheridge, have you another of your headaches?"

"Why, yes, I do. How did you know?" She looked down at Eve, who was still holding her arm. "They

cause me, sometimes, to behave foolishly. Am I behaving foolishly now?"

"You are, perhaps, a little disoriented. Will you permit my companion to escort you home? Or I will come
with you, if you prefer."

"No, no, my dear. You have been injured. And I
am quite well now."

Indeed, her brown eyes had cleared. Her reticule
hung properly from her wrist. Eve could detect, because she was looking so closely, the small signs of
Lady Etheridge gathering herself and retaking control
of her behavior.

How could this be? Eve wanted to drop to her
knees and weep for what she had just seen. Her mentor, the person she most admired in the world, was ill.
No mere headache could account for this. She tried
to still the trembling of her arm, the one wrapped
around Lady Etheridge's arm. Inside, she was cold
with fear and misery. If she lost her friend, she would
be entirely alone.

And how selfish, to think first of herself. She hadn't
meant to. The thought had popped into her head, and
she was sick to the heart that it had done so.

Mrs. Kipper arrived then, and Eve spoke privately
to her before presenting her to Lady Etheridge.

As if the past few minutes had never occurred,
Lady Etheridge greeted Mrs. Kipper politely,
thanked her for accompanying her in the carriage,
and pressed a kiss on Eve's cheek. "Do not worry,"
she said softly. "It's only a bad headache. They don't
happen often, and after a good sleep, I shall be perfectly fine."

Eve knew that song. She had been singing one much
like it since her fall. But she smiled, walked with Lady

Etheridge to the door, and watched from the window until the carriage had disappeared. She didn't realize, until she heard Cordell's voice, that tears were streaming down her face.

Chapter 18

Portugal, Nov. 1811

I am billeted for the month in a very small house with a very large family. Senora Jacome has two daughters and wants me to marry one of them. The young Portuguese ladies are generally kept apart from soldiers, so I thought I was safe. But she is determined I shall take the hook. At first she was dangling the older one, and when I didn't bite, she brought out the other. They're pretty girls, with big dark eyes and rosy lips, and they giggle a lot at my bad Portuguese. When I told CB I was under siege and asked for a new billet, he said I was old enough to manage aggressive women. Maybe, but that doesn't mean I know how! Finally I lied and said I was betrothed to a girl back in England. Now it's Senora Jacome trying to get me a new billet. Said I kept flirting with her daughters. Word is out to half the regiment about all my women, and the fellows are making my life miserable. So if you hear I'm engaged to be married, don't believe it. That's a bad thing to lie about, I am finding out.

Yrs., J

Cordell, surprised to see Lady Eve with her face uncovered, gazed down at her from the top of the staircase. She was looking out a window to the street, her head a little bowed and her shoulders slumped. The conversation with Lady Etheridge must have gone badly.

With a wave of his hand, he ordered the footman to disappear. Then, starting down the stairs, he spoke her name in a soft voice.

At first, he wasn't sure she heard him. But after a moment she turned, and he saw that she was weeping.

If Lady Etheridge ever came within his reach, he'd wring her neck like a chicken's. What in Satan's name had she said to this girl?

Lady Eve stood in place, waiting for him, trying to dry her eyes with her sleeved forearm. He withdrew his handkerchief and held it out to her. "Will you tell me what has happened?"

"Thank you." She took the handkerchief and blotted her cheeks. "I will, but I mustn't stand here like a watering pot for the servants to see." She glanced over at the staircase, winced, and began to walk slowly toward it.

He fell in by her side. "Let me take you up."

She appeared to think it over. But when they reached the stairs, she shook her head. "I need to do this. It may take awhile, though. You should go on ahead."

"I'm in no hurry. And if you stumble, I will have the pleasure of catching you."

As they began the ascent, she clutching the polished oak balustrade with her right hand, he matching her pace close beside, Cordell ran a mental count of the stairs. Forty, in a great sweeping arc that was more dramatic than practical. Especially now, with Lady Eve struggling to raise herself one foot after the other, using the balustrade like a crutch.

Early on, she made reasonably good progress. But as they neared the halfway point, she was breathing heavily. Perspiration bloomed on her forehead and cheeks. The look on her mottled face was one of dogged determination.

After restraining himself as long as he could, he chose a time when she had paused to catch her breath and said, "Whatever you are trying to prove, you have proven it. The rest is mule-headed stubbornness."

She gave a small shrug, pulled herself up another two steps, and stopped again. "I will never be strong if I do not make myself strong," she said, panting. "But I wish there were not so many steps."

"You can test yourself another day, when you've had more sleep than you did last night. When you have eaten properly, as you failed to do at breakfast."

A choked laugh. "Good heavens, sir. You sound like a prissy old nanny. Leave me be."

Mastering a strong impulse to override her wishes, he let her be for the several minutes it took to mount the next five steps. Six to go. Her hair, damp from her exertion, was pulling free of its pins. She had both hands on the balustrade now. Her knees were bent, as if on the verge of buckling. He watched her closely, poised to seize her no matter which way she tumbled.

And then she said, as if forcing out each word, "Might I have your arm, sir?"

He had rarely been so glad to hear anything in his life. She looked over at him, and he could see in her eyes how much it had cost her to ask for his help. Saying nothing, he lifted his right arm, not sure how she wished to make use of it.

With care, she laid her left arm along his forearm and laced her fingers through his fingers, gripping his palm for leverage. Using her two crutches, his arm and the balustrade, she dragged herself up, and up, and up again.

Another pause. She leaned for nearly a minute against his shoulder. Then she raised herself and achieved another stair. Only two remained. Seen through her eyes, they must look like a pair of Alps stacked atop each other.

Of all the journeys he had ever taken, this had been the most arduous. Watching her suffer, and persist, and suffer even more had become unbearable to him. Remarkable, ungovernerable woman, valiant as any medaled soldier and more foolhardy than the rawest recruit. Had he not arrived when he did, she would have attempted the climb on her own.

She whispered something that sounded like "excelsior." He didn't know what it meant, but it carried her onto the next-to-last step.

Eight more inches, he silently urged, waiting for the pressure on his arm that would tell him she was ready.

She glanced over at him then, a little smile curving her still-swollen lips. It wasn't a smile of thanks or of triumph. It was the smile one gave a comrade in arms when they had survived a hard battle. Using his arm for leverage and the newel post to pull herself up, she planted two feet on the first floor landing and sagged a little, still clutching his hand.

He thought she might let him carry her the rest of the way to her bedchamber, but no such thing. When her breathing had steadied, she used him for support long enough to walk to the sitting room where she had met with Lady Etheridge. He helped her to a sofa and watched her slump onto it with a rasping sigh.

"I'll summon Mrs. Kipper," he said.

"She's escorting Lady Etheridge home. I should very much like some tea, sir. Might you request it?"

He did, along with a thick, creamy soup, soft bread, cheese, and custard. Lady Eve was still having trouble chewing, he had noticed. She invariably denied having trouble with anything at all, but he had learned to read past her deceptions.

Some of them.

While the servants were setting out her meal in the room next door, he carried in a basin and some towels for her to wash up. Her look of gratitude surprised him. But then, with the barbed humor he had come to enjoy, she pointed out that he was now serving as a lady's maid, which was a decided step up from nanny.

"At least when I leave the army," he said, "I will be able to find employment. You said that you would tell me what occurred to overset you."

"Yes, and we must get it out of the way before I launch into another river of tears. Lady Etheridge is ill, sir. So much so that it frightens me. I saw evidence of it last week, when I called on her, and again this morning. She says the affliction is no more than an occasional and exceptionally acute headache, but I don't believe her. Nor do I feel at liberty to disclose to you what I have witnessed. She is entitled to her privacy."

"You are persuaded she has a serious illness?"

"Her behavior was, to me, incomprehensible. I fear the worst for her. That is my greatest sorrow. And I fear for myself as well, which is my deepest shame. She is my friend, the only one I have, and I cannot imagine my life without her."

He couldn't begin to understand why this independent young female felt so attached to a woman more than twice her age, one who seemed bent on directing her behavior and her choices. Nor could he discount her grief, which was digging its talons into him as well. "It won't help to assume the worst. At present, you've little information to go by."

"It doesn't matter. She is in great difficulty. I can't explain how it is, but I *know*." Lady Eve looked up at him. "I wonder what else is to be taken from me."

Nothing, if he could prevent it. But there was no mistaking what she meant, and what she feared, and why she had needed to climb those stairs.

A knock told him the servants had finished their work. "Come, now," he said, offering his arm to help lift her to her feet. "There's food next door."

"I'm not hungry."

"After you've eaten, I recommend a nap. And if you accomplish both to my satisfaction, I will give you something you want."

She perked up noticeably. "What is it?"

"You'll find out only when you've earned the right. Come along, Lady Eve. And you are not to refer to me as nanny, lady's maid, or serving wench."

"Oh, I should very much like to see you as a serving wench."

He did, in fact, serve her, dishing out the soup and fixing her tea the way she liked it. While he was stirring in an exorbitant helping of sugar, Mrs. Kipper returned and, from the doorway, asked to speak with him. But when he joined her in the passageway, he thought how Lady Eve would react to being excluded. They both trooped back into the room.

"Lady Etheridge was silent throughout the drive," Mrs. Kipper said, "and it would have been improper for me to address her. But there was nothing unusual about her behavior. I went with her into the house, hoping for an opportunity to speak with some of the servants, but she thanked me graciously and asked the butler to see me returned to Marbury House in her carriage. While we were in the vestibule, a large, dark woman joined us. Her companion, perhaps, addressed as Styles. She appeared worried, searching Lady Etheridge's face in a manner not like that of a servant."

"They have been together for many years," said Lady Eve. "Whatever is wrong, I am sure she knows about it. But none of us can ask her. Nor would she reply."

"Your bonnet is damp," Cordell said to Mrs. Kipper.

"As you foresaw, the rain is coming. I shall complete our preparations."

When the door closed behind Mrs. Kipper, Eve leveled her spoon at him. "What are you up to now?"

"Only a little misdirection, in case the house is being watched. A maid about your size and wearing your clothes will set out in the Marbury coach for Oatlands. A great deal of luggage will be loaded aboard, giving the impression you are leaving the city for a considerable time."

"Are these theatrics necessary? They seem excessive, like Sir Peregrine's disguise. Why did he have to be a female?"

"A simple disguise would have done as well, but

I think he enjoys being outrageous. As for today's subterfuge, we have nothing to lose by it. I'm taking advantage of the rain, is all. You will be winkled back to our hideaway after midnight."

"May I take some luggage of my own?"

"Whatever you like." He cut off a slice of cheddar from the wedge. "You haven't told me about your conversation with Lady Etheridge, the one before she began behaving oddly."

"You didn't hear it? I assumed you were eavesdropping from next door."

"You mistake my character, madam."

"Only if one disapproves of eavesdropping. I cannot, having done so much of it myself. In a nutshell, sir, Lady Etheridge is opposed to our marriage."

"That's the general consensus," he said. "When your parents return and express their own sentiments, the verdict will be unanimous."

"Her objections are entirely practical and centered around my own ambitions. Indeed, they are the same objections I would raise against you as a husband, were this anything more than playacting."

"Let me guess. Inferior status. Inferior fortune. Advanced age. Off-putting temperament."

"She did not mention your age, which is hardly advanced. Although I must say, you often behave in the manner of a much older gentleman. But then, I have carried on as an adult since I was twelve. Most of the time. Oh, and she allowed as how you are exceedingly handsome, but I expect you care nothing for that."

"You would be right. Is she likely to mount an active campaign against the marriage? Under the circumstances, that could prove a nuisance."

"In fact, I thought she would oppose us with every

resource she could call upon." Lady Eve gazed into her barely touched soup. "But she doesn't mean to stand against us. She only advised me to remember that a canceled betrothal would cause me less trouble than an autocratic husband. I expect that when the time comes for me to cast you off, she will help me navigate the rough waters."

He was glad to hear it. Above all things, he wanted no harm to come to her on his account. Well, on any account. But he saw in her eyes what she wasn't saying. When most needed, Lady Etheridge might not be there to help her.

"Have you known her long?" he said, directing the conversation onto a less rocky path.

"We became acquainted when I was invited to a meeting of women assembled for the purpose of supplying necessities to soldiers fighting on the Penn. The government wouldn't see to it, as you know, and we could do very little, compared to the greatness of the need. But we worked together until peace was declared in 1814, and we still provide assistance to families that lost their breadwinners in the war."

"What sort of necessities? Mittens and neck scarves? That sort of thing?"

She gave him the sort of pitying look usually reserved for a child who had tripped over his own feet. "As a matter of fact, we sometimes knitted or paid wives and widows to knit. But when Lady Etheridge pronounced my own mittens so bad that we ought to send them to the enemy, I devoted myself to providing oilcloth capes. I was responsible for raising the money, choosing the manufacturer, and arranging the shipping and delivery."

"*You* sent the cloaks?" He regarded her with astonishment. "The Thirteenth received a supply. We had been requesting something of the sort for years. When they were distributed, the men cheered."

"Oh, did they?" She glowed with pleasure.

The cloaks had arrived in the winter of 1813, when Lady Eve would have been about eighteen years old. It came as a revelation to him. Officers of that age routinely led men into battle, but he had always assumed that young females from good families preoccupied themselves with gowns and parties. "How did you acquire the funds?" he said, still bemused by her accomplishments. "From your own wealth?"

"If only it had been that easy. My trustees at the time required Marbury's permission to disburse even a tiny amount, which he naturally refused to give. So I was forced to be inventive, which never failed to mortify my parents. A side benefit of doing good works," she added, grinning. "One time I had a sample cloak made up and wore it to a rout at Somerset House. That got attention, as you may imagine. I went around pleading with everyone I met to please buy a cloak, only one cloak, for a cold, wet English soldier. The next day, money enough arrived to finance a considerable order. The day after that, Father sent me to rusticate in the country until I learned proper behavior."

"And did you?"

"Can't you tell?" She gave him an impertinent look. "I was released after a fortnight, but only because so many people asked what had become of me. For the rest of the season, I behaved fairly well. Making a spectacle of myself had been shockingly effective, but no one wanted me to make a habit of it. I was soon up to less controversial ventures. And about then, Lady

Etheridge disappeared for several months. It turned out she went north to sell a property she owned. The proceeds from that sale kept us going a considerable time."

Her bright eyes, her eagerness, her pleasure in what she had achieved, reminded him of a young officer who had turned up one afternoon with just such an expression on his face. The lieutenant, who had made an important discovery, was on fire with his message. And having delivered it, rather like the fabled runner bringing the news from Marathon to Athens, he collapsed at Cordell's feet. Only the consequences of a slight wound and loss of blood, as it later proved, but Cordell had swept him up and carried him on a run to the infirmary tent set up nearly a mile away.

"The cloaks were of great use," he said, putting aside memories better forgotten. "Thank you for what you did. But now you must stop talking and start eating."

"Honestly, sir, eating causes more pain than it's worth. When I fell, the inside of my mouth got rather too well acquainted with my teeth."

"A strong infusion of salt in water or ale will help that. Hold it in your mouth for several minutes."

She nodded unhappily. "That's what Mrs. Kipper advised. And I did try, but it hurt so much that I spit it out."

"Try again. In the long run, you'll be glad of it."

"Perhaps. But why is everything good reserved for the long run? When you leave the nursery, Eve. When you are presented in society. When you come of age. When you go to heaven, not that I'm holding out for that possibility." Leaning forward, she gazed at him from purposeful eyes. "I can tell you, sir, that an attack on one's life produces a great appreciation for the short run. Why concern myself with a future that might never be? From now on, when I want something, I shall immediately take steps to get it."

"Start by fulfilling my wish, then. Finish your soup and the custard."

She wrinkled her nose. "Very well, Colonel Tyrant. But you must distract me with conversation. Lady Etheridge tells me you are from Norfolk."

"There is little to be said about Norfolk." He reached across the table, picked up her spoon, and put it in her hand. "The Cordell estate is in the west. It is small and unproductive."

"But good for turnips?"

"If you know all about it, why ask? I presume Lady Etheridge has parsed my family down to the marrow."

"She conducted an investigation, but details were few. I have never been to that part of England. What exactly is a fen?"

"Marshland. Flat, watery, grassy. In my area, peaty. The house sits on a small mound of elevated land, but the rest of the Cordell heritage is, to put it plainly, a swamp. The estate has no name, but I think of it as the King's Revenge."

She sat up, pert with curiosity. "How is that?"

He pointed to her soup, and with a resigned shrug, she took a spoonful. "Remember, Lady Eve, that if you stop eating, I stop talking. So. My grandfather, a functionary in the court of George the Second, must have unearthed something unpleasant that the monarch wished to conceal. Nothing but extortion could account for Mr. John Cordell's elevation to Lord Cordell, but the king made sure the family would not prosper by awarding him a tub of bathwater."

When she opened her mouth to ask another question, he looked meaningfully at the soup bowl. "The first baron, my grandfather, took his wife and infant son to his new property, set them down, and promptly returned to London. I'm not sure he ever came back. With the little money she inherited from her own parents, my grandmother bought turnip seed, hired a few laborers, and managed to sustain the household. I never knew her, but I'm told she was a remarkable woman. My father said I inherited her eyes and the color of her hair. There is little more to say of Norfolk. I've been there only once in the last twenty years."

"Will you return home when you leave the army?"

Home? The word startled him. To hide his discomfort, he filled his cup with tea that had long since cooled. "That would require me to displace my father's second wife, who raises geese. Since I dislike her even more than I dislike geese, I shall leave them to continue as they are."

"And do what?"

"You were born to be an Inquisitor." With effort, he chased back into its cobwebbed corner the guilt that whispered, *Finish it*, whenever he thought of the land that had killed his father. "I am considering India," he said, rewarding her for taking up the dish of custard.

"There is money to be made there, I am told. But have you no wish to live in your native country, for which you have fought all these years? And while the land belonging to your family is poor, can it not be improved?"

Lifting his teacup, he thought of the years spent attempting to drain the land. The musky smell of dank vegetation. The squish of mud under the soles of his boots. Midges swarming around his head, clouding his eyes. The wetness stealing through his clothes as he carved out ditches to carry off water, built dykes to hold it at bay, chopped through reeds and sedges, shoveled until his muscles burned.

The work had shaped his body and given it strength. He had never minded laboring at his father's side, and every evening they would catch pike or roach or bream to carry home for supper. There was beauty at the end of the day, with the red and purple sunset sky reflecting off the water, the twilight birdsongs, the small creatures scrabbling about in search of their own suppers.

It wasn't the work he had resented. It was the failure. The downright futility. The land was an enemy they could never defeat.

"Sir?"

He looked up at Lady Eve's worried eyes. "As a matter of fact," he said, "the property is suitable only for raising geese and a few root crops. It cannot be drained."

"Why? I've seen extensive areas transformed. Only a few years ago, a large section of the Marbury estate was reclaimed for pasture."

"The devil lives in the fens, madam. My father battled him with every resource he had. And for a short time, it appeared that he had won. The land was freed of water. But as the soil dried out, it began to shrink at an alarming rate. And as it shrank, it cracked, opening up new pathways for water to seep in. Worst of all, the level of the land dropped below the neighboring rivers. Water from rain and overflow from the rivers could not be drained back into those rivers. Our initial success led to catastrophic failure."

He drank the tea from the cup he was still holding, careful not to look again at Lady Eve. He ought never to have begun this, but more than likely, she would have squeezed the whole story out of him. He had met few people, male or female, so incorrigibly relentless.

"When I turned fifteen," he said in an even voice, "Father told me he intended to give it one last try. But because the risk would be great, he wanted me free and clear. He had set apart enough money for my schooling or a military commission, and as you know, I chose the army. After I was gone, he borrowed funds and invested them in two windmills, hoping they could pump water into the rivers fast enough to sustain the reclaimed land. But they could not keep up with the flooding. Father lost everything he had, including his health, and amassed significant debts. When I returned from India about seven months after his death, I used the prize money I'd accumulated to sort things out. Then I left."

"But *never* to return? I have grown up with the tradition that an English peer is custodian of his land, and just as it belongs to him, he belongs to it."

"A pleasant ideal for some. Not for me."

"Where, then, do you belong?"

He blinked. "Nowhere I know of. On the move, perhaps. When I transferred to the cavalry, I felt more at home than anywhere I had ever resided. But as you have not finished your custard, madam, I shall stop regaling you with my tedious history."

She quickly scooped up the rest of the custard before sitting back with a contented smile. "I have earned your surprise, don't you think?"

"After the nap."

"Before it. First I must decide what to take with

me when we return to the prison. Then I'll be too wide awake for a nap, and unable to sleep in any case from wondering what it is you had promised and withheld."

He could not, unfortunately, compel her to nap. Or, for that matter, to do anything at all. He raised his hands in a gesture of surrender.

She looked smug. "Do you find me difficult, sir?"

"I find you impossible, madam." Rising, he glanced at the mantelpiece clock. "See to your packing, if you will. I'll join you in a few minutes, surprise in hand."

When Cordell, a leather satchel in his right hand, arrived at Lady Eve's bedchamber, the door was open. He stopped a little distance away and looked inside.

On the canopied bed, three portmanteaus lay open and nearly overflowing with clothing and other items. Mrs. Kipper was holding up two garments for inspection.

"The blue one," Lady Eve said. She was leaning rather heavily against a side table, one hand planted on it for support. Where it was not marked with bruises and scrapes, her skin seemed to him overly pale.

He took a backward step, and another, putting himself out of view. The satchel felt as if it were filled with bricks. He had hoped to provide a diversion, but if he gave it to her now, she'd not get the rest she needed. Then again, the more he coddled her, the more she rebelled.

Before he could change his mind, he marched to the door and knocked on the casement. "I have something for you, madam."

"Come in, sir." Her eyes were fixed on the satchel. "What is it?"

"The papers from Black Phoenix we have been waiting for. They were delivered yesterday to Sir Peregrine, who passed them on to me."

"Oh! The information about the victims. Did you find anything helpful?"

"I've not looked at them, nor has Sir Peregrine. There are a great many papers containing biographical information, interviews with family and acquaintances, that sort of thing. If there is information of value buried in those pages, I've no doubt you will recognize it."

From the look on her face, he might have presented her with the crown jewels. "I will go over them thoroughly," she said, eyes shining.

"You needn't feel obliged to hurry your evaluation," he began, but it was too late. She snatched the case from his hand, took it to her writing desk, and unbuckled the closures.

With a resigned shrug, he beckoned Mrs. Kipper into the passageway. "The carriage for Oatlands will depart at three o'clock. Have the maid ready. I'll ride along for a time. Don't look for me again until late tonight. And make sure Lady Eve gets some rest."

"I do not," said Mrs. Kipper blandly, "work miracles."

Chapter 19

Portugal, Oct. 1810

> *I hope you can read this. I'm writing with my left hand because I got shot in my right shoulder. Only a fleabite, but I was chased a long way and lost a good deal of blood before reaching camp. It was the best day ever in my life. I found a track through some mountains used by the French that we'd been looking for this past month. Too bad they saw me, but no real harm done. I made it as far as Captain Cordell's quarters, told him the news, gave him the map I'd sketched, and then I ruined everything. Fainted dead away at his feet. I'm back in my hut now. He came to see me this morning and wanted to know when I'd be ready to go out with a patrol. No rest for the wicked! It's hard to tell with him, but I think he's pleased with the news I brought. And maybe even, a little, with me.*
>
> *Yrs., J*

When Mrs. Kipper's voice shot her awake, Eve sat up on the bed and looked around her in bewildered dismay. The counterpane was littered with papers, some in stacks, some helter-skelter. For a few moments, she tried to think what they were. Then, with a warm glow, came the memory of what she had discovered.

She glanced over at Mrs. Kipper, who was igniting a colza lamp, and thought better of telling her. Cordell must hear it first, must hear it from her, and she must be watching his face when it all transpired.

Swiftly she gathered up the papers and returned them to the satchel. There would be time later to sort them out. She was still dressed in the gown, now sadly wrinkled, that she'd worn to speak with Lady Etheridge that morning. There was a soup stain on the bodice. "I must change my dress," she said, fumbling around on the floor beside the bed for her discarded shoes.

"There isn't time," said Cordell from the door. He was wearing his workman's clothes, with the floppy hat that concealed his hair and most of his face. "The neighbors will notice a hackney drawn up in the alley."

"I found it," she blurted out. "I found what links the victims together."

"Later." He crossed the room, located her shoes, and dropped to one knee to slip them on her feet.

She realized, as the exhilaration seeped out of her, how weak she felt. Not enough food, not enough sleep, too many stairs climbed that morning. She managed to stand, thanks to the arm Cordell extended, and looked up at him. "I suppose we'll have to descend the stairs to get to the street?"

"Unless you can fly, madam."

Pride, when swallowed, tasted lumpish going down. "Should I be offered a ride," she said haltingly, "I believe I would accept it."

A small quirk at one corner of his mouth, like a

smile that wouldn't let itself be seen. "You are most welcome." He bent his knees a little. "Put your arms around my neck."

She did, and a moment later, she was lifted up. Secure in his arms, she considered what to do with her own arms, now clasped loosely around his neck, and left them where they were. "I agreed to this for the sake of the horses," she said as he carried her into the passageway. "They mustn't be left to stand."

"Just so."

"Wait!" She tried to free herself. "I forgot the satchel."

"Calm yourself. Mrs. Kipper will bring it. Your luggage is already aboard." After a beat, he added, "There's a devilish lot of it."

"With nothing else to occupy me, I thought I would change clothes several times a day. It will be good exercise."

Only one candle was lit on the ground floor, and they soon left its light behind them. Navigating in darkness, he got her to the alley and deposited her inside the battered coach. Mrs. Kipper arrived soon after, and then they were off.

Disgruntled, Eve folded her arms and stared out into the drizzly night. Cordell had failed to join them in the coach, so once again, her news would have to wait.

"Oh, good," said Sir Peregrine, looking up from the maps spread out on the trestle table. "I couldn't have waited much longer. There's been another killing."

Eve, who was first to enter the kitchen, thought his usually impeccable disguise seemed decidedly haphazard. Then his words sank in.

Cordell, following her with a portmanteau in each hand, let them drop. "Another young man?"

"I'm afraid so. The news came by pigeon, so the message was necessarily short. His name is Peter Yarborough, son of a Berkshire squire, found this afternoon tied to a standing stone in a remote field south of White Horse Hill. Someone taking a shortcut spotted him. He appears to have been dead at least twenty-four hours, perhaps longer. He was strangled."

They were all in the kitchen by now, Eve and Cordell, Mrs. Kipper and Silas Indigo, who had driven the hackney, and the two bodyguards. The stableboy, Tom, was sitting cross-legged in the corner with his hands wrapped around an earthenware mug.

"The message didn't say where they took him." Sir Peregrine said. "I'm trying to decide where to base myself while I investigate. Marlborough, perhaps."

"That's in Wiltshire," said Lady Eve.

"But near the Berkshire boundary, and it boasts an inn where I like to stay. The Unicorn. Send any messages you may have to me there."

"I mean," she said, "Wiltshire is what connects the first three victims."

"The lady," said Cordell, "found something in the papers you gave me."

"Indeed?" Sir Peregrine gestured the bodyguard and Tom to leave the room. "Cordell mentioned that our Oatlands victim had spent time in Wiltshire. Come. Sit here and tell me what you have discovered."

Glad of the invitation to sit, she chose a spot across from him with Mrs. Kipper at her side. Indigo sat next to Sir Peregrine, and Cordell predictably remained standing, one hand clasping his other wrist behind his back.

"It's little enough," she said, "but it is a link. And now, the fourth victim has been discovered not too far away. There is a school, Stanton St. Bernard's, a little northeast of Devizes. Mr. Farley and Mr. Harbin were students there, and while not of an age, they were both in residence during 1805 and 1806."

"My, my." Sir Peregrine gave a delicate shudder. "There is nothing like an English boarding school for turning young boys into monsters. Do you recall how old they were at the time?"

"In 1806, Mr. Farley was fourteen and Mr. Harbin two years older. A note mentioned that he was a prefect, which I presume is an honor."

"It's supposed to be a position of responsibility. But with some chaps, it becomes a license to bully. I shouldn't leap to conclusions, but my own experiences at Eton taught me a good deal about the beasts lurking inside fresh-faced choirboys. You may have found, not only a link, but a motive."

"The killer is taking revenge against students who bullied him? But why would he wait so long?"

"Perhaps there is more than one killer. Perhaps the victims got together and decided a little injustice was due. As for waiting, you know what they say about vengeance being served up cold."

"You are both speculating," Cordell said. "We must find out if the latest victim attended the school around the same time."

"I will do that, of course, and let you know the answer."

Eve, watching the two men begin to make decisions

as if she didn't exist, lost no time reminding them. "You cannot, Sir Peregrine, conduct a thorough investigation on your own. Not with dispatch. Even as we bat around theories in a kitchen, the murderer may be planning his next crime."

"I have already asked Phoenix for help. Cordell, can you spare me Indigo? Truth be told, I could use you both. Lady Eve should be safe enough here with the Bremer brothers and Mrs. Kipper."

Cordell looked at Eve, frowning. "Unless I'm on hand to keep watch, the lady might decide not to stay in place."

"You may be sure of it," she said. "Even if you don't go."

Sir Peregrine and Cordell communicated silently over her head.

"Both of you remain here," Sir Peregrine said. "I'll ask Phoenix to handle inquiries at the school. Someone will be sent."

"Have I been replaced?" Eve said. "Has my summons been revoked? All of us in this room were assigned to the mission. And all of us are needed. No one will waltz into Stanton St. Bernard's and trip over conclusive evidence. If the motive for the killing originated there, the events took place more than a decade ago. I never attended a school, Sir Peregrine, but I imagine those in charge of this one will do everything possible to guard its reputation."

"I daresay. But they'll not let a female conduct an interrogation, Lady Eve. You'll be of no use to us."

"We'll see." She looked over at Cordell, his feet planted apart, his shoulders square. Yielding not an inch, as usual. "I know you want to protect me, and because I was afraid, I have done as I was told. I am still afraid, sir. But I will no longer hide. If I have only a short time left to me, I will spend it trying to prevent another murder."

"I am sworn to keep you safe, madam."

"Sworn to whom? To me? Then I release you." She forced her lips into a smile. "But if you are going in the direction of Wiltshire, I would be glad of your company."

After a long moment, he turned to Sir Peregrine. "Perhaps she is right. What can we accomplish in hiding? We've done nothing to find the killer and nothing to find Lady Eve's attacker, but only because we had no idea where to look. Now we do. Let it be a full assault, then, by all of us."

"Excellent!" Sir Peregrine rose, sorted through his maps, and plucked out two of them. "For the present, I'll need Berkshire and Wiltshire. Come directly to the Unicorn, north from the market square. Rooms will be arranged for you there. I'll try to have more information by the time you arrive."

Eve's heart pounded with excitement and relief. They had come around. *Cordell* had come around. She could hardly believe it. The two men were bent over the table, studying the maps and making plans for a deceptive exit from London. Her second in one day, although this time, it would not be a disguised maid-servant in the coach. She herself would be the parcel on its merry way to Wiltshire.

One thing, at least, was certain. No one would come looking for her there.

Chapter 20

This morning I nearly ran straight into a pack of deserters. There were five of them and one of me, so a good thing I heard them coming and slipped behind some rocks. I didn't know who they were when I hid, but it pays to be careful where I am operating. They were all wearing tattered uniforms, two English, two French, and one Portuguese. Sometimes they get together in a sort of outlaw regiment, robbing the local people and lying in wait for small convoys. They're after the ones carrying money or gold, and if a transfer is planned, my job is to find out if a band of deserters is in the territory. When they set up camp, they take a goat or pig to every village in the area and slit its throat in front of the people. They say that's what they'll do to anyone who betrays them, but they leave the animal as a token of their generosity. Mostly I get information from the guerrillas and have made friends with some of them. I'm almost never with my own regiment now. Even my reports are delivered by someone else, as this

*letter will be, soon as I rendevous with a patrol.
I'm alone so much that when I'm planning what
to write, it feels like my Ensign is here with me.
You are good company!*

Yrs., J

"That explains the traffic, anyway," Eve said to
Silas Indigo, who had watched for their coach on
the outskirts of Marlborough and escorted them to the
inn. "I have taken the Great Western Road many
times, but never when I might have walked it faster
than the coach was traveling."

In the overwarm room, Indigo's bald pate gleamed
with perspiration. "Sir Peregrine forgot that Marlborough has a Saturday market, and this weekend of the
summer solstice, the town decided to hold a Longest
Day Fair as well. I'm afraid we can expect noise,
crowds, poor service, and even poorer accommodations."

"Is that why we've been shuffled into this parlor
instead of our bedchambers?" Cordell was standing by
the room's sole window, looking outside. "Are there
bedchambers to be had?"

"One," Indigo said in a mournful voice. "Sir Peregrine secured it, and this parlor, by dint of a considerable bribe to the patrons who had reserved the space.
The Unicorn's proprietor attempted to find lodgings for
us at another inn or in a private residence, but had no
success. He has offered a room in his own home, probably the one belonging to himself and his wife."

Eve, sipping from the glass of iced lemonade provided her when they arrived, looked around the neat
little parlor with its half-timbered walls and polished

oak furnishings. The Unicorn, centuries old and set on a quiet street far from the market square, seemed to her an ideal place to stay, especially when compared to setting out again in the coach. It had taken more than eight hours in hot weather to make the fifty-mile journey from London.

Cordell, who had been in the saddle for those same eight hours, began to pace the short distance between window and door. "It will be too late, I suppose, to speak with anyone at the school today."

"A letter requesting an interview has been sent to the headmaster. This morning Sir Peregrine encountered a friend, the lord lieutenant of Wiltshire, who added a message of his own, so there is reason to expect our request will be granted. But as yet, no reply has come."

Cordell made a sound of impatience. "Well, then. Do we know anything more about the killing?"

"Very little. Tom, who accompanied Sir Peregrine to the site, returned about an hour ago with this." He handed Cordell a thick letter. "Sir Peregrine was intending to speak with the victim's father, if possible, before going on to Reading. The body has been taken there for the autopsy and inquest."

"And what have you been doing all this while?"

"Waiting here, for the most part. We thought you'd arrive by noon at the latest, giving us time to drive out to the school and impose ourselves on the headmaster. I rode that direction this morning to sketch you a map. Stanton St. Bernard's lies six miles southeast from here, with Devizes not far beyond. Shall I attempt to secure better lodgings there?"

"We'll stay here for tonight," Cordell said. "Come show me around."

Eve couldn't restrain herself. "You haven't read the letter, sir. And I'd like to be shown around, too."

"In good time. Here." He placed the letter in front of her. "When I return, we shall read it together."

The men were gone before she could object. She looked over at Mrs. Kipper, who had pulled out her sewing and begun to darn a stocking. Curled up in his basket at her feet, Malvolio emitted a little snore.

On the table, the letter burned like a coal. Eve doubted that it contained anything of great importance, but its very existence rubbed at her frustration. So many delays, just when they were beginning to make some progress.

"What is to prevent the dog from barking at the guests?" she said, to distract herself from the letter.

"In these circumstances, Malvolio can be something of a nuisance. We'll know better what to do when the colonel has completed his arrangements."

Silence fell. Eve went to the window where Cordell had stood, but there was nothing of interest to be seen in the fields behind the inn. Another day spent enclosed in a small room. Or in a small carriage on a hot day, where she had to conceal her face with a veil or lower the window shades.

To give him credit, Cordell had come alongside the coach to let her know when it was safe to raise them. And while the occasions had been few and brief, it still surprised her that he had thought of her comfort. She wished he would not. A considerate enemy was difficult to hate, and with all that had occurred in the last week, she was finding it increasingly hard to stoke the fires of her revenge.

But a few admirable qualities did not make up for a black soul. She looked down at the simple damascened bracelet Johnnie had bought for her in a Spanish shop. He had liked Cordell, as she sometimes did, but he'd trusted him as well. That was something she would never do. The bracelet, which she now wore every day, reminded her of her purpose.

Her time would come, and her chance.

To Eve's disappointment, Sir Peregrine's letter added little to their store of knowledge. Although rain had washed away most of the evidence, there was some indication that two people had dragged Mr. Yarborough from the road to the standing stone where he had been tied. A constable who had seen the body reported that the victim had been strangled with a garotte made of braided horsehair. It was still around his neck when he was found, and the same material had been used to secure him to the stone.

"What would that signify?" Eve said. "Assuming the murderer is again sending a message. Why horsehair?"

Cordell, standing by the window, looked up from the letter. "On the Penn," he said, "we used braided horsehair to make fishing lines. But the message, if there is one, must surely be connected to the standing stone."

"There are any number of them," Indigo said, "not very far from here." He unfolded the map of Wiltshire that Sir Peregrine had enclosed in his letter and pointed to a spot a little distance northwest of Marlborough. "Avebury. Too public, I suppose, for stringing up a body and getting away unseen."

Cordell moved to the table where Eve, Mrs. Kipper, and Indigo were seated and, with his fingertip, traced a path from Avebury to the X that marked the village of Stanton St. Bernard, where the school was located. "Close enough to be of interest to schoolboys. Speaking of which, I don't think I told you about my conversation with Walter Burford, the uncle of the first victim."

"The one who lives in Kent." Eve sat straighter. "You haven't mentioned him at all."

"He had not seen his nephew for ten years or more and knew nothing of a stablehand with a scar under his eye. But he did say one thing, rather offhandedly, that seemed irrelevant until now. The last time Master Farley was there, he brought half a dozen schoolmates to spend a week's holiday. According to Mr. Burford, they were a pack of rabid hounds who bounced around the neighborhood pulling pranks and getting up to no good. Before the week was out, he banished the lot of them. I wish I'd thought to ask their names."

"None of us would have thought of it," Eve said. "But we must ask if he remembers the names after all this time. If Mr. Harbin and Mr. Yarborough are among them, the others who were there might be marked for death as well."

Indigo rose and moved to the door. "I will send word to have it done."

Eve had noticed several cages tied to the boot of their coach. Pigeons. She turned to Cordell, who'd gone back to the window. "Is there more, sir? You must read it all to us."

"The rest concerns Mr. Hamish Dolburn, the headmaster. He took up his position more than a year after Farley and Harbin were there, and by all reports, has transformed Stanton St. Bernard's into a well-regarded school for young gentlemen."

"That's too bad. He won't know what happened to

trigger these murders, nor will he be glad to have us rummaging around in the school's unpleasant history. What story can we give him to win his cooperation?"

"I expect that dropping the lord lieutenant's name will accomplish that. We should find out what it is." Cordell gave her one of his colonel looks. "And keep in mind, Lady Eve, that we've no evidence that whatever transpired at Stanton St. Bernard's ten years ago has anything to do with the killings."

"Well, I hope we find some," she said cheerfully. "Otherwise, we'll be back where we started. What else did Sir Peregrine write?"

"Before Mr. Dolburn took it over, the school was foundering. Enrollment had declined, and according to local residents, the boys—some of them—were worse than hooligans. Within a year of his arrival he had dismissed all the teachers, most of the staff, and many of the servants. It's unlikely we'll find anyone there who knew Mr. Farley, Mr. Harbin, or anything about conditions at the school when they were students."

"Dismissed employees have to go somewhere. Some of them must have been pensioned."

"I expect I'll be able to pry a name or two out of Mr. Dolburn." Cordell folded the letter and slipped it into his jacket pocket. "Shall I show you upstairs, madam?"

"Thank you." She understood he wished to speak privately with her, and had a fairly good idea what he wanted to say.

The Unicorn was small, with narrow staircases and crooked passageways. Cordell led her to a room at the far end of the third floor, knocked on the door, and waited until Tom opened it. Without speaking, the boy slipped by them.

"There are no locks," said Cordell, moving aside to let her pass. "The door can be latched from the inside, but if someone wanted in, it wouldn't hold very long."

The room's location provided for a window on each of three walls. Sunlight streamed into the small bed-chamber, brushing the simple furnishings with a patina of gold. Lacy curtains billowed in the warm breeze. A canopied bed dominated the space, its drapes tied back against the posts with tasseled cords. She saw a well-appointed dressing table, a privacy screen against one wall, a washing stand, an armoire, and several portmanteaus. Two of them belonged to Cordell.

She shot him a glance.

"Did you think I would leave you here alone?" he said.

"But Mrs. Kipper—"

"Her lodgings have been satisfactorily arranged."

"But how? Is she to displace the proprietor in his own home? And what of Mr. Indigo?"

Cordell hesitated. "Indigo and Mrs. Kipper have worked together on several Black Phoenix missions."

"Ahhhh. I see." She chuckled. "Good for them. And you will sleep here with me? My, oh, my. We Phoenixes are a veritable hotbed of . . . of hot beds."

"You shock me, Lady Eve."

"And not for the first time, I'd wager."

"Quite right." He picked up one of his portman-teaus. "I'll send Mrs. Kipper and the dog. Have a meal and a nap, why don't you?"

"While you slink off to Stanton St. Bernard's on your own? I think not, sir."

"You heard Sir Peregrine. You'll not be admitted there. I mean only to ride over and have a look at the place. Speak with the headmaster, if he's there. Since we haven't heard from him, more than likely he's right here in Marlborough for the market and fair."

"I should like to wash up and change clothing," she said as if he hadn't spoken. "Shall we leave in half an hour?"

"Now I know," the colonel muttered as he went out the door, "how Bonaparte felt after Waterloo."

The headmaster's invitation to call at their convenience arrived shortly before Eve and Cordell left the Unicorn, but it was clear when they entered the office of Mr. Hamish Dolburn that he had not been expecting a female.

Before Mr. Dolburn could speak, Cordell claimed the center of the room. "Col. Lord Marcus Cordell," he said in the quiet tones of absolute authority. "Thank you for seeing us on short notice. We'll try not to take up much of your time."

The headmaster, a short, stocky man with graying red hair, freckles, and suspicious blue eyes, made a polite bow. But his gaze was focused on Eve when he said, "I had been expecting Sir Peregrine Jones."

"He was called away. This is Lady Eve." A short pause. "My wife."

If not for her veiled bonnet, both men would have seen her jaw drop. She managed to incline her head gracefully.

As Sir Peregrine had advised, Cordell was wearing his dress uniform. "Not being sure how much Lord Winfred told you about our inquiries," he said, stirring the lord lieutenant's name into the mix, "let me sum up our requirements. There is reason to believe that criminal acts committed within the last few months are related to incidents that took place at Stanton St. Bernard's some ten years ago. We are here to examine records from the years 1804 through 1808. Can you provide them to us this afternoon?"

Mr. Dolburn, his lips pursed, glanced at the longcase clock. "Pardon my manners, Lord Cordell. Lady Eve. Will you be seated while we discuss this matter? I am at somewhat of a loss."

When they were settled across the desk from him, he fumbled with some papers for a moment before deliberately stilling his hands. "Are you familiar with the history of the school? It will surprise you that I know little of it, except in the most general way. When I was brought in by the directors in 1810, it was to clean house, and that is precisely what I did. What happened prior to that did not concern me, although I could not help but hear the local gossip. And I could see for myself the sad condition of the property, the poor attitude of the staff, and the incompetence of the instructors. Only sixty young men were enrolled at that time, down from two hundred a year earlier. Within three months during the Michaelmas term of 1806, more than half the students withdrew."

"Do you know why? Did something occur to drive them off?"

"From what I understand, the school was well regarded until after the turn of the century, at which time it began to decline. A decision by the headmaster, now deceased, was likely a factor. He chose to accept, even to recruit, young men from wealthy families whose behavior at other establishments had caused them to be sent down. By the time I arrived, discipline had flown out the window. Fagging was rampant—begging your pardon, Lady Eve—and the younger boys lived in fear. Although I expelled the worst offenders, disorder had taken root. With no help but to start afresh, we did precisely that. Highborn lads can no longer bribe their way into Stanton St. Bernard's. Now we educate only the sons of decent families whose boys could not gain admittance to the more elite establishments. Discipline is strictly enforced. The quality of our instructors is high. The school is flourishing."

"And you don't want anyone raking up the old stories," Cordell said. "Nonetheless, we are here on a matter of the utmost importance. For the moment, it remains a private inquiry, and those involved will do everything possible to keep it that way. But without your assistance, we will be forced to turn the matter over to the authorities, who do not always act with discretion or finesse."

"You cannot, surely, expect me to release private school records into your custody?"

"If you prefer, we'll examine them here and make a few notes. I'd like to do that this afternoon, returning tomorrow if it proves necessary. Your cooperation, Mr. Dolburn, will go a long way toward preserving the school's reputation."

"I am a practical man, sir. With nearly everyone gone to Marlborough for the fair, you may work undisturbed in the room adjoining this one. I'll fetch the ledgers to you. As for Lady Eve, perhaps your coachman can return her to the inn? Or if you prefer, she may wait in the parlor used by visiting relatives."

"I am unwilling for Lady Eve to travel unescorted,

and she cannot wait alone while I work. The business may take several hours. She'll remain with me."

"But females are not permitted beyond the entrance hall and parlor. I made an exception, bringing you to the office, because no one was here to notice. But they'll soon be filtering back. You understand, Lord Cordell, that I cannot enforce rules if I am seen to disobey them myself."

Eve, watching the encounter with growing unease, recognized a telling blow. Cordell was a stickler for regulations. But she had come prepared for this eventuality.

"Mr. Dolburn," she said in an artificially meek voice, "Lord Cordell does not like to speak of this, but I feel you should know why I was brought here today. At Waterloo, he happened to be close by when a cannon misbehaved. Exploded, I suppose. He refuses me the details. Unlike the two men standing near him, he was not killed. But he took an injury that has affected his vision, and he is no longer able to read for any length of time." She opened her reticule and pulled out a pair of thick-glassed spectacles. "Even when he uses these. Do not think of me as a female, sir. Think of me as my husband's eyes."

Mr. Dolburn's expression was one of sympathy mingled with suspicion. Cordell looked uncomfortable, but that had been accounted for by her story. She waited, head bowed, for a ruling.

"Under those circumstances," Mr. Dolburn said at last, "I must make another exception. You'll not object, I trust, if the curtains and the door remain closed?"

"Better all around," Cordell said crisply. "We don't wish to draw attention. Shall we proceed?"

*   *   *

"Wife?" Eve said when they were finally enclosed in the room with a stack of dusty ledgers and files.

"Exploding cannon? And where the devil did you come by those eyeglasses?"

"Mrs. Kipper. She carries all sorts of things around. Keep them nearby, in case Mr. Dolburn pays a call."

They settled across from each other at a large table, surrounded by the extra lamps and tall candle stands supplied by Mr. Dolburn. There was paper as well, along with inkpots, pens, a sharpening knife, and blotters. Once he'd accepted the inevitable, the headmaster even gave them a pot of tea, a decanter of wine, and directions to his own privy room.

Cordell took up the records from 1805, while she started in on 1806 and immediately found Peter Yarborough's name listed as a fifth-form student. Later, she saw it again on a housing list that included James Farley and Roger Harbin. Three victims, sharing a dormitory called Kennet House with twenty-seven other boys. Or, perhaps, twenty-six. One line had been blacked out.

When she showed the records to Cordell, he quickly found similar listings from 1805.

They went to the 1804 ledger. Yarborough and Farley were there, but not Harbin. The first-term list for Kennet House showed a full complement of thirty boys. But starting with the second term, one name was blacked out. Further exploration showed that after the first term, one boy had left both the school and Kennet House. A new boy had come in, easy to find because every place his name appeared, it was covered by a heavy coat of ink.

By no means could they read through it. The paper

was thick, and Cordell's efforts with a pencil and a sheet of paper failed to disclose so much as a single letter. The boy's identity had been efficiently stricken from the record.

Eve began making notes. All the names recorded in Kennet House over a period of four years. The year each boy came to the school, what form he was in, and when he left. She wrote the names of the instructors, observing that different tutors had been assigned to the victims. No link there.

Cordell was making notes as well, most of them questions for his own use. How were the dormitories supervised? Why were boys from the first through sixth forms living together? Were there reports on the students' progress? Disciplinary files? Records of the parents and where they lived?

"We got what we asked for," Cordell observed, pulling out his pocket watch. "But it's too late now to ask for more. We'll have to come back tomorrow."

"Don't tell him what else we want," she said. "He might accidentally lose the records. Just tell him we aren't finished going over these ledgers."

"Very well. However, we need the names of instructors and staff so that Indigo and Mrs. Kipper can start tracking them down."

"You found what you were looking for?" said Mr. Dolburn.

"We're not finished." Cordell was holding open the 1805 ledger. "Can you explain why a name would be blacked out, as you see here? And here?"

Donning his own spectacles, Mr. Dolburn looked more closely. "I cannot. A simple error would have been lined through."

"We'd like to know who this boy is, and what became of him. Also, we want names and directions of anyone who worked here, in any capacity, from 1804 through 1806. Is that information contained in files we have not seen?"

"Yes." Dolburn studied Cordell's face and seemed to come to a decision. "This is a most serious matter, is it not? One that could do significant damage to the school if it becomes a scandal. I will help you any way I can, Lord Cordell, but I implore you to be discreet."

"Insofar as possible, I will."

"Then tonight, I will search the records for the information you need and send what I find to the Unicorn. You may, of course, return and examine the material yourself. But I think you'll be disappointed. Nearly all the instructors and staff were of fairly advanced age when I took up my post, which may explain in part how the boys came to run wild. Some will have died by now. Most, I know, have long since moved away."

"Do what you can. Even a small bit of information may be significant." Cordell turned to Eve, who stood a little distance away with an armful of papers. "Madam, give the Kennet House lists to Mr. Dolburn."

Her protest died on her lips. Cordell had decided to trust the headmaster, and she had no good reason to quarrel about it. While she separated the requested pages from the others, Mr. Dolburn was explaining how the system of "houses" had been organized.

"In theory, the younger boys were to learn from those above them, while the older boys developed a sense of responsibility by providing a good example. In fact, without intense supervision, such a plan never works. The fifth and sixth formers virtually enslaved the younger boys, exploiting them in ways I should not care to describe. My first major decision was to eliminate the house system, but I did not investigate specific incidents that had occurred beforehand."

"Mr. Dolburn," said Cordell, "we have reason to believe the students on these lists are in danger. Some of them, at any rate, probably the older boys. Provide us, as soon as may be, information about their families, where they live, anything at all that will direct us to where they can be found."

"I am thinking that . . ." Mr. Dolburn rubbed his chin. "But no. She is past helping now."

"She?" Eve, stepping forward, gave him the sheaf of papers.

"The matron. Mrs. Fenbow was the only staff member I retained, observing that she genuinely cared for the boys and they for her. She retired several years ago and must still be alive, because her pension continues to be paid. I used to visit her now and then. Unfortunately, her memory was growing uncertain when she retired and deteriorated rapidly after that. I doubt she will have anything to tell you. But if you wish, I'll provide directions to her cottage. It is in Devizes, not far from St. John the Baptist church."

Cordell nodded. "Might I have that now? We'll call on her first thing tomorrow."

Chapter 21

Portugal, June 1812

*Tonight, CB let some of us go into Oporto for
the festival of St. John the Baptist, only they call
him Sao Joao. I don't think CB knew the celebra-
tion is mostly about finding true love. Boys and
girls of marrying age strip a pine tree, cover it
with flowers, and have a parade. Then it's put in
the middle of a bonfire and they dance around it.
Some of the couples hold hands and leap over
the flames, and some of our fellows wanted to try
it. Good thing they didn't. I saw CB watching the
fire, and they would have caught the devil from
him. The people made us welcome. We bought
garlic sausages and maize cakes, which were very
good. When a boy wants a girl to notice him, he
gives her a pot of spices. And if a girl wants to
be courted, she gives the young man a leek. It's
a token of good luck, and he's supposed to keep
it for a year. After the fire dancing, a girl came
up to me and put a leek in my hand. R said my
face went red as a pomegranate. When she asked
my name, I told her John, and then she went*

around pointing at me and saying, "Joao, Joao."
The girls must have thought it a good omen to
court me on Sao Joao's Day, because pretty soon
I had an armful of leeks! I guess I'll have Deniz
make a soup with them. Can't keep all those leeks
for a whole year, even if eating them brings me
bad luck.

Yr. popular J

Twilight, dusted with the faint gleam of stars, was settling over Marlborough when Cordell and Eve returned to the inn. They could hear the crowds before they saw them, spilling out into the fields where the bonfire would be lit at midnight, into courtyards where morris dancers and jugglers and magicians cavorted, into the market square and the narrow side streets. Spilling, too, from the Unicorn's packed taproom into the stableyard, forcing Tom to clear the way for the coach.

Cordell foresaw a sleepless night and little luck securing a decent supper. Lady Eve must be even hungrier than he was, which was saying a good deal. He could eat a roast pig about now and then sleep the clock around. Even on a hard wooden floor, which was where he would be spending the rest of the night.

At the stable, he turned Ghost over to Tom, lowered the carriage steps, and offered Lady Eve his arm. The moment she touched it, her barely contained excitement sizzled through him like an electric shock. She practically leaped down the steps, all energy and fire.

"Do you understand what we have done?" she said, her head tilted up at him.

He couldn't see her face under the veil, but he knew her eyes were shining with triumph.

Even a wary realist like himself would not dash cold water over her high spirits now. Let her enjoy their success, although in truth, they were little closer to the murderer than when they started. All they had acquired was a list of potential victims, a suspicion the killer was among them, and a possible motive. "Progress indeed, madam," he said, mustering a smile that she probably couldn't see.

As it had done when he made his way through London for the Waterloo Bridge ceremony, his medaled uniform opened a path for him. All he could think about was the pleasure of latching the bedchamber door, stripping off his sword belt and tunic, and sliding down onto the floor. How long had it been since he'd slept more than an hour or two?

But before the stripping and the sliding, he had better tie Lady Eve to the bed. She did not appear, this night of the solstice, to be eager for a peaceful night's rest.

An hour later, after yet another skirmish, Cordell escorted Lady Eve back into the streets of Marlborough. He was wearing his workman's clothes, and with the skilled assistance of Mrs. Kipper, Lady Eve might pass for a workman's wife if one didn't look too closely.

"I cannot bear another moment under that veil," she had declared roundly. "And it will draw too much attention."

So would her battered face, of course, but on that subject he had kept his mouth shut. He was learning.

With theater cosmetics disguising the worst bruises and something she called a poke-brimmed bonnet shadowing the rest, she sailed through the crowded streets while he endeavored to keep up with her. As ever, he had come prepared for trouble with a sheathed knife at his belt, a smaller blade secured in his boot, and a pistol in his pocket. Now and again he spotted one or the other of the Bremer brothers, and Tom, the least conspicuous of her protectors, was somewhere nearby. Lady Eve declared the precautions unnecessary, for how could anyone guess to find her at a country fair in Wiltshire? He didn't know, but he would be ready nonetheless.

They went first to the noisy market square and harvested a makeshift supper from the stalls. While Lady Eve nibbled on a sausage, he wolfed three of them. Then came cheese pies washed down with ale. Chunks of roast pork threaded on a stick. Cold chicken legs. They shared a paper cone full of toasted walnuts, a basket of strawberries, and a packet of spice cake.

Children squealed. Across the square, a brass band was playing. Street sellers cried their wares. "Buy my gingerbread. It's all hot, nice smoking hot." "Buy my sweet oranges. Fine, juicy oranges."

"How do they *do* that?" she said as they stood watching a sword swallower and a fire-eater. Before he could respond, she was off to a pig race. He pounded after her, dodging a man selling kites, and caught her up as she was placing a bet on a weaner named Prinnie. It lost.

Later they found themselves outside a tavern where the proprietor had set up a table to sell mulled wine in large souvenir tankards made especially for the fair. "I must have one," she said, "to remember this wonderful night."

He bought two, thinking it safe enough to have a drink while they made their way back to the Unicorn. It was coming on to midnight now, and a procession was forming, led by the brass band and a platoon of boys wearing medieval tabards and carrying torches. The fairgoers strung out behind them, laughing and dancing through the streets. Ahead, in the center of an open field, people were staking out spots near the mammoth bonfire.

"No," he said.

But Lady Eve took his hand and towed him into the field. "Just for a little while, sir."

Once again, he found himself unable to deny her. But damned if he'd wade into that crowd, where anyone might slip a knife into her back and vanish before she fell. He led her instead to a sloping hill some distance away from the bonfire and sat on the grass beside her. "One would think you'd never been to a fair," he said when she kept pointing out to him a Maid Marion—of which there were several—a Robin Hood, a horned satyr, a shepherdess leading a miniature horse.

"Oh, I've attended a great many fairs. My godmother has a large one every summer at Oatlands, and country house parties often coincide with local festivals. But always, I have been expected to play my role as a proper society lady. The ritual never changes. First, with a maid to hold a frilly parasol over my delicate head, I stroll in company with other proper ladies, commenting politely on the exhibits and the decorations."

She took a long drink of mulled wine. "Sometimes I am expected to help judge a competition, like the arrangement of flowers or the best strawberry preserves or the finest summer squash. If the event is for charity, I pour tea and distribute pastries in a pavilion set up with crisp linen and elegant chinaware. And just when the common folk are starting to have a good time, when games are being played and the music and dancing have begun, we proper ladies steal quietly back to the manor house and play cards or take up our embroidery. So you see, this is the first fair where I am permitted to set decorum aside and enjoy myself like ordinary people."

"You will never be ordinary, madam." He looked down at the boys dancing with their torches around the pile of logs and kindling. Hundreds of people had already assembled in the field, and more were coming in. The nearest, who had discovered the excellent view from the hill, were settling down within a few yards of where he was sitting with Lady Eve. A low vibration hummed up and down his spine. Something was there, something he ought to notice.

Or perhaps it was nothing. More likely he had tuned to the excitement of the young woman seated beside him, her legs curled under her, the ceramic tankard cradled between her palms. Fascinated by the smallest detail, she was trying to see everything at once.

"It is strange," she said. "The world should be open to me, but it lies beyond a wall I am not permitted to cross. I have many privileges, but they are thorned with the expectations of others. How odd that my good fortune, which ought to make me free, enchains me. These people can go where they like, do as they wish. How I envy them."

"You imagine they are free? How much of the world would you experience while laboring to keep a roof over your head? Does a female in service have license to wander off when she pleases? Without your family and fortune, you would be working in a shop, or taking in laundry, or bearing children to a tenant farmer. These people enjoy a holiday because they have so few of them, while you are spoiled for luxury and entertainment. Of this I am sure, madam. You would hate being common and poor."

She took another drink and sat for a time, staring down into the tankard. "That is true. I ought never to complain. You must think me very poor stuff indeed, pampered and selfish and willful."

"Willful, certainly."

"If you go to India," she said, "you should take me with you."

Good God. What next? "That is the wine talking. The only place I will take you, before you are unable to walk, is back to the Unicorn."

When he started to rise, she put a hand on his knee. "They're about to light the bonfire. And you are wrong about the wine. It may have given me the rashness to speak up, but the idea has been in my head since you told me the riding accident was an attempt on my life. How better to keep myself out of harm's way than to put an ocean between me and the killer? Besides, I wish to travel to exotic places, and you happen to be going that direction. Is it so bad a proposition?"

For a few seconds, he thought of how it would be to show her the Yellow Fort, the Taj Mahal, the Vale of Kashmir. He imagined keeping company with her, watching her experience with fresh eyes what he had first experienced in a drunken stupor. But he could not do over what had happened there, nor would he entangle her in his own uncertain future.

"Sir?"

A few seconds had stretched to considerably more. "I beg your pardon. The day has been long, and my thoughts are muddled. There is no question of your going out to India, as I am sure you know, nor would I consider taking you there. If I leave the army, I must make my own way best as I can. I don't mean to do it as a tour guide."

She gave him a wine-befuddled smile. "I would pay very well, sir. And there would be fringe benefits. Or have you forgotten what we were doing this time a week ago?"

Had it been only a week since she had come through the secret door into his bedchamber? It seemed months had passed since that night. And he still couldn't believe she'd actually done it. Or stop thinking about the other things she'd done in the hours that followed.

"When you have had more sleep and less wine," he said, picking out his words with care, "you will remember how difficult it is going to be when our sham betrothal is broken off. There would be no saving you from the consequences of running off with a lover."

"All in all, my dear Colonel, I should rather face the consequences of a scandal than confront the alternative. A fatal attack would leave me quite beyond salvaging."

"Then find yourself a husband, madam, and persuade him to take you traveling."

"But once I become his chattel, there is no guarantee that he will. And I'd have lost my freedom. Although I suspect Major Blair would deal honorably with me. He . . . Oh! They're lighting the fire."

Silence fell. The audience seemed to be holding its breath. Then the boys, forming a neat circle around the construction, put their torches to the kindling. For a time, the fire lay hidden beneath the square of logs and the slender tree trunks coned over it. Then, with a whoosh, sparks shot into the air and flames began licking up the edifice of wood. The crowd oohed and ahhed. The band struck up a lively tune and the people nearest the fire joined hands and began to dance.

Cordell watched, only vaguely aware of what he saw. She was considering a marriage to Jordan Blair? There were no suspects, not yet, but Blair had raised a number of questions in Cordell's mind, questions that Sir Peregrine's glib accountings had not satisfactorily answered. He still thought, without plausible reason for it, that someone connected with Black Phoenix was involved in the attack on Lady Eve. That's what kept him on edge, made him watch ever more closely over her. Phoenix knew where she was.

"Sir?"

The low voice came from behind him and near the ground. Without turning, Cordell leaned back on his elbows and forearms, gazing up at the star-strewn sky. "What is it, Tom?"

"You said to tell you if I seen anyone paying too much interest in the lady. There's a man was outside the inn when we come back from the school, and I seen him again four times, allus in the square or the street where you was. He's down by the fire now."

"Pretend it's a clock. What time is he at?"

"About ten, sir. He looks like a country man, but browner than most, and there's something odd about his nose. The bottom of it looks funny. I didn't get close enough to see what's wrong with it. He's wearing a brown shirt and trousers with a coat that has no sleeves. And a hat, with the brim wider in front than in back."

"Does he seem to be alone?"

"He didn't talk to nobody, except when he bought ale at a stall. Nate Bremer is watchin' him now."

"Very well. Take up a position opposite Bremer and try to get a better view of his face. But don't give yourself away. And if he leaves, follow without being seen."

When Tom left, Cordell waited for a while before sitting up again. Lady Eve, swaying a little to the music, was still watching the bonfire. His gaze went to the position where the man was reported to be and easily found him. Above middle height and broad in the shoulders, he wore a hat that, like Lady Eve's bonnet, obscured much of his face. Firelight burnished a strong jaw and chin, but only the lower portion of his nose could be seen. He looked familiar.

Cordell couldn't think where he might have seen him before, although he was sure it wasn't in England. Perhaps a soldier who had known him on the Peninsula, one who recognized him and his uniform at the inn and thought he spotted him later in the streets, wearing homespun garments. The man might be curious, as was Cordell, the both of them wondering about the other's identity. No point reading anything sinister into this. Curiosity or coincidence more than accounted for his actions.

In any case, it was time to get Lady Eve away before the crowd started to disperse. He reached over, gently detached her hand from the now-empty tankard, and helped her to her feet. She was still swaying, and he suspected it wasn't because of the music.

"My head feels lighter than the rest of me." She looked from her empty hand to the ground. "Where's my cup? Ah. By your foot. Those are exceedingly large feet, sir." Bending to retrieve the cup, she nearly toppled over.

Cordell caught her, wrapped an arm around her waist, and held on while he picked up the tankards. His own still held wine, which he poured onto the ground.

"You shouldn't have thrown away my wine," she said in a chiding tone. "I wanted that."

"Come along, madam." He risked a glance in the direction of the Nose. The man was still there, watching the dancers. When they shortcut through the field to the inn, the only one following them was Bert Bremer.

Cordell turned Lady Eve over to Mrs. Kipper, who was found in the parlor with a book, and checked with the proprietor to see if any messages had come for him. Nothing yet from the headmaster, but Indigo had received word that Sir Peregrine would return the following evening.

"Tomorrow morning," he told Indigo as they sat in the parlor with the Wiltshire map spread out between them, "you and Mrs. Kipper are to trace and interview the people on the list Mr. Dolburn will supply. I suggest you hire transportation tonight. Lady Eve and I will take the coach into Devizes, with Nate Bremer driving. Tom can ride Ghost. I want him to show the sketch of our stablehand victim around the area and see if anyone recognizes the face."

"And Bert Bremer?"

"He'll shadow us on horseback. See that he has a mount up to his size. A firearm as well. When—"

A knock, followed by Tom, his face red and streaked with sweat. "The man with the nose left not long after you did, sir. He went back into the town and picked up a horse at the posthouse. I saw him turn onto the Bath road, but after that . . ." He gave a disappointed shrug.

"Did you get a better look at his face?"

"Not to speak of. Except when he came out of the stable with the horse and said something to the ostler. He was passing through the light from a window, and two of his teeth flashed."

"Gold?"

"Might have been. Hard to tell. I thought more like silver. One was a bottom tooth, and the other a top tooth right above it. Oh, and when he turned his head, it looked like this part of his nose"—Tom put thumb and forefinger on the cartilage between the nares—"had been cut off. From where I was looking, I saw just one hole into his nose."

"Good God." Cordell rubbed his forehead. "A sergeant with just such an injury deserted in . . . let me see . . . 1811 or the spring of 1812. I knew about him because he was sighted a time or two after that by exploring officers. What was his name? Not that it matters. He wouldn't be using it here."

"Had he a quarrel with you?" Indigo said.

"I don't recall any contact with him at all. He wasn't in the Light Division. The question is, why would a deserter with an uncommon appearance risk showing himself in England?" Cordell could not restrain a yawn. "But that's hardly our concern at the moment. When we return to London, I'll report the sighting to Horseguards. They can deal with him."

Shortly after, Mrs. Kipper arrived in the parlor. "Lady Eve is tucked away, but not, I fear, quietly."

"You shouldn't have left her alone."

"Nor did I. Bert Bremer is stationed by the door. She is excessively thirsty. If I procure some light ale, will you fetch it to her?"

"I'll come with you to the taproom, making my apology for doubting you on the way. Good night, gentlemen, and sleep well. We've a busy day tomorrow."

The current day wasn't yet over for him, Cordell discovered when he dismissed Bremer and entered the room with a pitcher of ale and two glasses.

Lady Eve, from her sitting position in the middle of the bed, started chattering the moment he appeared. She chattered between swallows of ale, and while he was brushing his teeth, and while he arranged his weapons where he could swiftly reach them.

She stopped only when he unrolled a pallet and spread it in front of the door. "You will not sleep on that," she said in a tone he might have used. "It is too short and too hard."

"When necessary, madam, I can sleep in the saddle."

"And when behaving intelligently, you sleep in a bed that has plenty of room for you. Do not be concerned for your virtue. Whatever my own wishes, I know very well no man could desire me, looking as I do."

He went to the bed, sat near her waist, and put a finger under her chin to turn it this way and that. "The swelling is all but gone. You look much as you always did, if a little more colorful. It doesn't signify. Beauty draws a man's attention and will generally arouse him, but that has little to do with desire. Not as you should experience it, or receive it."

"Do you desire me, then?"

"*Then*, yes," he said, stroking her cheek with his forefinger. "And now. But you have been injured. I will not chance hurting you. Tomorrow, we have important work to do. This is not the time."

Her eyes were filled with longing. "But there might never be another time."

His finger went to her lips, sealing them. "From the day we are born, we begin our dying. Each moment is a miracle. We must not tarnish it with anxiety, nor demand from a moment anything more than it can give us. If we are again to be lovers, Lady Eve, we will be. But not on this night."

Which was, he thought, returning to his pallet, the most difficult thing he had ever forced himself to say. His heart was beating out a double-time march, as it had been since he learned that she'd been injured. No matter what else he was doing, or what was going on around him, he simmered with apprehension. And so he lectured her about how to feel and behave, as if he had the smallest right to admonish her. All the while, he kept himself in check with a constant and punishing act of will, which left him exhausted and surly.

He extinguished all the candles but one, moved his firearm nearer the pallet, and prepared to stretch out on top of it. She had been right about the length. This bedding had been intended for a maidservant, and a short one at that.

"Colonel Cordell," came a drowsy voice from the bed. "If you insist on sleeping like a hearth hound, you give me no choice but to join you on the floor."

He bit back an oath. "Don't be absurd."

"How can I be otherwise, with your example to inspire me?" A pillow caught him on the head. "I'm next," she said.

He heard the rustle of sheets. She would do it, he knew. Surrender her comfort because he refused to claim his own. Obstinate, maddening woman. "Stay as you are," he said, taking the pillow she'd thrown with him to the bed.

She had slid over to one side, leaving him a wide expanse of territory to occupy. They could pass the entire night without touching, and in the heat of June, that was just as well. As for self-control, he had no fear of losing it. Wine, weariness, and worry had scraped him down to the bone. He lifted the sheet that was the only covering, lowered himself onto a surprisingly good mattress, and stuffed the pillow under his head.

Before he had drawn two breaths, she was snuggled up next to him with her head against his shoulder and one arm curled over his chest.

"That's better," she murmured. "Thank you. I so dreaded being alone."

He felt suddenly cold. Invariably alone, even when in company, he'd got used to solitude. Had come to prefer it, really. And now she had forced him to surrender to her his last defense.

But this felt nothing like surrender. As she lay soft and still by his side, her warmth stole into him like cognac, smooth and intoxicating. She asked nothing of him but his presence.

He was thinking, as sleep came over him, that if he took her to India, she would find it easy to kill him there.

Chapter 22

Spain, July 1812

A sad day. Five brave men killed and seven wounded in a skirmish. I came upon them just as the fit soldiers were preparing to carry the injured where help might be found. The Spaniards will not permit heretics to be buried in consecrated ground, and though I begged the priest to make an exception for good Protestant Christians, he would hear none of it. "Some of my flock," he said, "would dig them up and leave them for the crows." He wasn't happy about it, but what could he do? I told the priest to take Fitzroy, at least, him being Irish. The Spaniards think all Irish are Catholic, and not for me to straighten them out! But now I wish I'd said all the dead chaps were Irish. The priest helped me and my batman to dig graves for the others. The ground was so hard and rocky that it was nightfall before we were done, so he invited me to sleep at his rectory. And he gave me extra paper, because I was almost out and it will be a week before I return to camp.

Now I can still write you every day, but with better news, I hope.

Yrs., J

"Do you think," said Lady Eve, taking Cordell's arm, "that wanting to do something forbidden is as bad as actually doing it?"

They were walking from St. John the Baptist church in Devizes to the cottage where Mrs. Fenbow, former matron of Stanton St. Bernard's, had agreed to welcome them. The message from Mr. Dolburn had arrived early that morning, along with the lists Cordell had requested, and now all the Phoenixes were on the wing.

"In whose eyes?" Cordell said. "If I wanted to pound a man into sausage, I presume he'd rather I didn't."

"I mean, in the eyes of God. When the rector was speaking of sin and the final judgment, I was wondering if what I wanted to do last night was as wicked as what I actually did last week."

"Lady Eve, I cannot fathom, at any time, what is going on in your head. Do not expect me to decipher the mind of the deity. Come. This is where we turn."

They were drawing as much attention on the quiet Sunday streets as they had in the high box pew at the church. Cordell wore the unadorned clothing of a gentleman, but his bearing never failed to distinguish him. And nearly everyone paused to steal a second look at her widow's weeds, heavy and grim on this bright summer morning.

"It's that one," he said as they approached a two-story graystone cottage with its door and window casements painted bright red.

In the front garden, a woman who appeared younger than Eve had expected was snipping roses and laying them in a basket. Seeing her guests, she put down her scissors, brushed her hands over a billowy apron, and smiled.

"Mrs. Fenbow?" Cordell bowed. "Thank you for agreeing to speak with us."

"You are both welcome here, Lord Cordell. I am Mrs. Hannity, Mrs. Fenbow's daughter. With my children now grown and gone, I live here and tend to her."

"Will our questions cause her distress, ma'am?"

Still smiling, Mrs. Hannity picked up her basket. "You mean, is there any point to asking them? She could not tell you, my lord, what she ate for breakfast, but the distant past—some of it—remains vivid to her. If she speaks with confidence, you may safely believe what she says. Shall we go in?"

The small parlor, airy and sunlit, was cheerful with vases of flowers and colorful tied rugs on the polished floor. Three orange cats were curled on the sofa next to Mrs. Fenbow, who looked to be in her late seventies despite a remarkably smooth complexion.

When Eve stepped across the threshold, the old woman gave a small cry and tried to pull herself erect. Her daughter hurried over, helped her rise, and stayed by her side as she tottered across the room with outstretched arms.

"It is you," she said to Eve. "It is you. I had not thought to see you today. I am so sorry, so sorry. He was a lovely boy."

Eve took the wrinkled hands into her own. Mrs. Fenbow had mistaken her for someone else, probably a woman in mourning for a dead son. Unsure what to do next, she glanced over at Mrs. Hannity and got a helpless shrug in reply.

"I was hoping you would speak of him with me," Eve said. "Do you mind?"

"Oh, no, my dear. I would be glad of it." Mrs. Fenbow looked up at Cordell, now standing beside Eve. "Is this your husband? But no, he cannot be. You told me he had died."

"He did, yes. This gentleman is my brother."

"How nice. Will you come sit with me? My knees shake if I stand too long. I don't know why. They didn't used to."

Eve let go her hands, took her arm, and led her to the sofa. When they were settled with an entwinement of cats between them, she said, "I am pleased that you remember my son with affection."

"How could I not? He was the most beautiful child, hair the color of sunlight, and so gentle. Books were his greatest love, after the birds. He kept them safe, his doves, from the terrible boys who would have killed them for amusement. But I must say my apologies, for I cannot recall your name. Nor his, except . . . Oh, my." Her hands began to tremble. "He was named for an angel. I remember that now. The golden one. What is the golden angel's name, Mary?"

Mrs. Hannity drew a chair closer to them and sat, leaving Cordell to loom over them all. The ceiling was so low that his hair nearly brushed against it. "I'm not sure, Mother. Was it Raphael? Or perhaps Gabriel?"

"That is it. Gabriel. The one who brought news of the baby. He said, 'Be not afraid.' I used to say that to the sweet boy, and sometimes he would say it to me."

Eve, perspiring under the heavy veil, didn't dare raise it now. "Will you tell me, please, about the terrible boys? Was Peter Yarborough one of them? James Farley? Roger Harbin?"

"Oh, all of them." Mrs. Fenbow shuddered. "Others as well. The Stone Circle."

Eve glanced up at Cordell, who was watching Mrs. Fenbow with sharp-eyed attention. "What does that mean?" she asked. "Is it a game?"

"It is what they called themselves. There were seven. Everyone feared them, even the teachers, and if a boy tried to keep out of their way, it only made them punish him the more. That's why they killed Sebastian."

"They *killed* someone?"

"Not someone," Mrs. Hannity said. "The boy's canary. Mother told me about him."

"Oh, yes." Eve's heart raced. "I didn't realize he'd given the bird a name."

"His father's name," said Mrs. Fenbow. "The gentleman died when he was a small lad. But of course, you know that. After the bird died, he found a dovecote that was closed up. When you sent him spending money, he would hide it there so the Circle didn't take it. And after a time, when he had cleaned the dovecote and unboarded the cupola, he bought some birds at the market. But the dovecote was close to the school, where the Circle might find it, so he later took his doves to some other place. I think it was Avebury. He gave them to an estate there and asked to visit them, which he sometimes did. Not long after, the Circle burned the dovecote he had restored. But he had saved his birds, which made him happy."

At first, when listening to her, Eve had begun to think it was the boy's father killing the members of the Stone Circle. But since he had died before Gabriel entered the school, she began to consider the mother. The woman she had been mistaken for.

Mrs. Fenbow gave a long sigh. "I have always wondered what to tell you. The last time you came to the school, I thought it better not to say what I thought had happened. There was no proof. There is no proof. I didn't even tell Mary, because she would insist again that I leave Stanton St. Bernard's. But I finally did leave. Why did I leave, Mary?"

"Because the nice man came, and the boys did well after that, so you didn't have to worry about them so much."

"Oh, yes. I remember now. It must not have been long ago," Mrs. Fenbow said to Eve, "because you are still in mourning."

"I expect I always will be. But I am stronger now. Will you tell me what you believe occurred?"

"I don't know. I don't know." Mrs. Fenbow stroked a cat with a hand that was shaking in earnest now. "I thought I did. But I can't remember."

She was overset and becoming more so, Eve could tell. Mrs. Hannity was regarding her with concern on her face. If they were to learn more, it would not be today.

Rising, Eve thanked Mrs. Fenbow, who kept petting the cat and appeared not to hear her. Cordell looked as if he wanted to pursue the inquiry, but she shook her head and drew him out the door.

Mrs. Hannity, who followed them into the garden, gave her a reassuring smile. "Please don't be concerned. What happened years ago seems, in her mind, to have happened yesterday. And what happened yesterday didn't happen at all. She won't remember you were here, or that you spoke of horrible events at that horrible school."

"Can you tell me the woman's last name, or what happened to the boy?"

"I was living in Salisbury back then and know nothing of Gabriel or his family. But I heard rumors, when I came to fetch Mother to stay with us at Easter, about a child who had fallen from the bell tower. That would have been in late 1806, or thereabouts."

"Might he have been pushed?"

"I cannot say. It was months after the event when I came to Devizes, and to be honest, I tried not to speak to Mother about the school. It usually led to a quarrel. She was so unhappy there, and I wanted to give her a respite during the holiday."

"It may be necessary," Cordell said, "to speak with her again. Will you permit it?"

"If you must. It is possible she has shut the darkest part of the story from her mind, but she might remember at another time. There is no telling if, or when."

"Thank you, Mrs. Hannity," Eve said. "We shall try our best to find the truth another way."

In silence, she walked with Cordell the short distance to where the coach was waiting with Nate Bremer on the driver's box.

"We have the entire afternoon," she said. "What shall we do with it?"

"Try to locate the justice of the peace, or whoever it was looked into the death of the boy. The school may have covered it up entirely, of course, the way they wiped out Gabriel's presence at Stanton St. Bernard's. But I suspect there was an inquiry, if not a serious one, and it would certainly record the family name."

He handed her into the coach, where she threw back her veil and began fanning herself with vigor. "The lord lieutenant could direct us," she said. "But how are we to find him?"

"He was in Marlborough yesterday morning. We can look for him there, but the crowds will make it difficult. Shall we go by way of Avebury and find a place to eat?"

"I was going to ask you to stop there. We'll inquire about the dovecote."

When they turned onto the country road, she removed her bonnet and let the breeze from the window cool her face. "It is like a prison under there," she said. "I could hardly breathe in the cottage, it was so warm."

"Even so, you were quite splendid. I know few people who would have understood what Mrs. Fenbow must be thinking or have the wits to play along."

The rare compliment sent a rush of pleasure through her. "I had no idea what to say or do," she admitted, "but it all worked out for the best. And we are, perhaps, another step closer to finding the killer. Might Gabriel's mother hold the Stone Circle responsible for his death? Although . . . if she is behind these crimes, why would she wait so long to take her revenge? Gabriel died more than ten years ago."

"Who can say? If the other persecuted boys are guilty, they have waited the same amount of time."

"Yes, but they'd some growing up to do. Oh, I don't know. Is it possible for a woman to undertake such elaborate and brutal murders?"

"I have seen remarkable examples of brutality in my time, not a few of them perpetrated by females. But the boy's mother could not have subdued healthy young men without help. Perhaps she joined forces with other Circle victims." He folded his arms behind his head. "Let us not rush our fences, Lady Eve. We may be on the wrong track entirely."

He was the sort to be cautious, she supposed, although he'd been quick enough to jump to the wrong conclusions about Johnnie. But she felt, deep in her bones, that they were poised at the heart of the mystery. All they needed was the mother's name and where she could be found.

"I just realized," she said, leaning back against the squabs, "that within minutes of leaving the church this morning, I was lying through my teeth to a sweet old woman. Is there any hope for me, do you think?"

"None whatever," he said.

A few hundred yards back, riding parallel to the road behind a screen of trees, a lone horseman kept pace with his quarry.

He had been waiting outside Devizes, reasonably sure they would take the back way round to Marlborough. He had also pinpointed the bearlike man following the coach at a distance. Watching out for someone like him, he thought, amused.

Today might be his best opportunity, but as with other opportunities that had come and gone, he would be taking no chances. It didn't matter greatly when he accomplished his task. Only that he did. Failure meant certain death for him. He'd few illusions about his employer, and none at all about his determination.

For his own part, it was the danger he most valued,

the spice that peppered his days and nights. That, and the challenge of defeating a worthy opponent. His prey had managed to elude him for a week, thanks to the formidable colonel, and he'd had to learn from his employer where they could be found. That smarted a little.

Never mind. This was to be his last job, for which he would be paid exceptionally well. Not that he was doing it for the money. He'd enough stashed away to finance a lifetime of self-indulgence. This was a debt he owed, a tip of his hat to a soul even darker than his own.

And besides, he was more than willing to kill the girl for the sport of it.

Chapter 23

Spain, July 1813

> *We're on our way to France now. After all these years! But the Pyrenees come first, and we won't be let to cross them without a fight. I've been exploring the territory for several months now and have a good idea what we face. There are many places a detachment can get lost, and the landscape is made for ambushes. I trotted into a trap only yesterday, set by four locals hoping to pick off a French soldier and rob him. They know the English army is on the march, so they weren't out to get themselves into trouble with us. Not yet. But if it looks like the French are going to trounce us, they'll cut us down like weeds. That's what happens when you live between two alien armies. You play both sides and hope to land with the winner. I can't blame them. They were kind enough to me, and fed me a good supper of mutton stew. Better than the stale rations I was carrying in my haversack!*
>
> *Yrs., J*

The only dovecote in the area, Cordell and Lady Eve discovered, was located at Avebury Manor. But according to the shopkeeper selling them a packet of cheese, ham, bread, and a jar of lemonade, it had been damaged in a fire.

"A man was killed," he added, wide-eyed. "Nobody knows who he was."

Cordell's interest in the dovecote shot up. "Who lives at the manor?"

"Not the owners, since more than thirty years. You'll find only caretaker servants there now, and the sheepmen, and the farmers. Mr. Hammett is the steward. If he's not at the fair like most folks, he'll show you around."

Nate Bremer, for whom Cordell had bought the lunch, had found a shady spot for the horses and carriage not far from a deep, circular ditch that surrounded a grassy plateau about a hundred meters in diameter. On it, like the aftermath of a ninepins game played by giants, they saw the remnants of a large stone circle. Sheep grazed around the few sarsen stones that remained upright. Others lay where they had fallen. According to the pamphlet Lady Eve had asked him to purchase at the shop, many stones that once stood there had been buried years earlier by religious zealots. Even more of them were broken up and used for building.

She was reading aloud to him about ancient quarries and megaliths and primitive rituals as they walked, her veil thrown back, her voice bubbling with excitement. "The manor is this direction," she said as they left the heart of the village, "and very near."

They walked between a double row of aging lime trees and soon found themselves at an open set of tall wrought-iron gates leading into the stableyard. Cordell saw a young boy scrubbing out a horse trough and sent him off to fetch the steward.

"That must be the dovecote," she said, pointing to a circular stone building with a conical roof topped by a lantern-shaped entrance for the birds. From the outside, the building seemed unmarked by the fire.

The inside was a different story, they learned when Mr. Hammett arrived and led them through an entrance designed to prevent anyone from barging straight in and frightening the birds.

There were none there now. The interior smelled of smoke, burned timber, and scorched flesh. The nest holes were dark caves set in smoke-blackened walls. The hard-packed dirt floor was gray with excrement and ash.

"The body was found just there, in the center," Mr. Hammett said. "According to the authorities, the man had set a fire to cook his supper, more than likely a few eggs or squabs pilfered from the nests. But the charred wood they found surely belonged to the potence, which stood in the center with beams atop it to support the ladders. Those burned as well. It seemed to me the fire was not great enough, nor sustained enough, to reduce the body to the state in which it was found. Had it been so, the roof would have been consumed."

"I'm told the victim could not be identified," Cordell said.

"Handbills were put out, and notices placed in the newspapers, but no one came forward to report a missing person. While the inquest remains open, the authorities are persuaded a vagrant took shelter here and lit what became his funeral pyre."

"And you believe otherwise?"

"Oh, it might be true. We're not far from the London-to-Bath road, and travelers have been known to spend the night in our barns or stables. Former soldiers without jobs or money, most of them. If they make no trouble, we let them be. But none have stayed in the pigeon house before. Why would anyone wish to sleep on a bed of bird droppings?"

It was hot inside the dovecote. Cordell helped Lady Eve through the low-set door that required them to bend double and seized a long breath of clean air. "Then what do you think happened, Mr. Hammett?"

"You will probably think me mad, but I believe the man—they could tell that much by the height and the pelvis—was dead and burned before he was brought in. The fire set here was an attempt to disguise the murder. And yes, I testified to that effect, but the constable's theory prevailed. What I had not seen at the time of the inquest was discovered later by the boy you met when you arrived. And even had I known, I don't suppose I'd have included them in my testimony."

A garrulous man, Mr. Hammett. About sixty-five, Cordell would guess, with sharp intelligence mostly wasted at this underdeveloped estate. Containing his impatience, he said, "What did the boy find?"

"Feathers." Mr. Hammett waved a hand, as if he continued to be surprised by what he had seen. "Yellow feathers, scattered around the outside of the dovecote. We didn't at first notice them because they were darkened with ash and trampled into the ground. But some had been carried onto the grass and shrubs.

When we saw those, we understood the yellowish tinge under our feet."

"Sebastian," Lady Eve murmured.

Cordell had already recognized the message. The unidentified victim was a member of the Stone Circle, brought to the dovecote where Gabriel had brought his birds for safety and enclosed in a symbolic circle of yellow canary feathers. The fire was not a subterfuge. It represented the burning of Gabriel's dovecote.

No question about it now. The murderer they sought knew the significance of the child's love for his birds, especially the canary named for his father. And while a woman would require allies for the killing and the staging of theatrical scenes, Gabriel's mother stood at the center of these crimes.

Lady Eve, vibrating at his side like a tuning fork, realized it as well. She looked up at him, and while he couldn't see her face through the veil, he could always picture it in his mind's eye. Her face had become as familiar to him as his own face in the shaving mirror. He nodded, and knew she understood.

It had been a simple matter to kill the watchdog. He'd approached the mound from behind a line of hawthorn trees, tethered his horse, and located the man silhouetted against the sky. Then, using the shallow ditch that surrounded the hill, he crept to the opposite side and began his ascent.

He was in a hurry. The girl and her protector might return to the coach at any time, and he wanted the watchdog out of the way before then. But he was cautious. He was always cautious.

In Spain he had scaled any number of rocky slopes without giving himself away. This one was covered with turf, and he made no sound as he climbed on hands and knees, his body slung low. Just below the lip of the hill, he dropped to his belly and slithered the rest of the way. Stopped to listen. Caught the faint sound of an off-key drinking song.

The fool was whistling. What luck. With his target's location identified, he checked quickly to make sure the fellow's back was to him. Yes. Looking through a spyglass in the direction of the village.

Gripping his knife between his teeth, he came over the hill with the stealth of a predator and was within arm's reach before the man sensed his presence.

Too late. The blade sliced across his throat before he could make a move. The spyglass dropped from his hand as he rocked back and forth a time or two. Then he fell with a thud, blood pumping from his neck onto the green grass.

It was a quality field glass, finer than his own and not to be left behind. It might even belong to Colonel Cordell, which would make owning it all the more gratifying. In fact, he would put it to use while executing the rest of his plan.

He had decided to waylay the coach at a spot picked out early that morning, where the road to Marlborough made a tight loop around a copse. He'd conceal himself within a few feet of where the coach would pass, send two shots through the window, and make a quick exit.

As he descended the hill, he saw the dead man's horse tethered loosely to a nearby bush. He didn't want it calling attention to the hill and the body, but he didn't want it running loose, either. At the end, he left it where it was and took a roundabout way to the point of ambush.

By the time the coach left the village, he would be in position and waiting.

Sitting opposite Mr. Hammett, who had invited them for tea inside the Elizabethan manor house, Eve had raised the veil of her bonnet, explained her bruised face, and was now waiting her chance to ask the questions Cordell kept skirting around.

He was an adept inquisitor, she had to admit. They learned the Stone Circle had used several locations in and around Avebury for what they described as initiation rites, although Mr. Hammett refused to say, in the presence of a lady, what he knew of them. Everyone in the village had dreaded the boys' arrival. Some closed their shops and shuttered their windows.

"Nasty pieces of work," said Mr. Hammett. "The older lads came in on horseback, and the younger ones stumbled along behind them with ropes tied around their arms. Mostly they confined themselves to the barrows or Silbury Hill, but sometimes at the full moon, they played their disgusting games at the circles."

"I am told," Eve said, "that a boy from the school once brought his doves to live here, and that someone agreed to let him return for visits."

"Ah. A dear wee lad with the palest skin you ever saw. I remember the first time he came, carrying handmade wooden cages that must have weighed as much as he did. I thought those were the only birds he meant to leave, but two days later, he returned with another load and said there would be several more trips before he was done. It is four miles to where he had been keeping the doves, so I took a wagon and went with him to fetch the others. After that he would, from time to time, pay them a call."

Mr. Hammett, his expression sorrowful, took a drink of tea. "Those birds look much alike, but he knew each of his own by name. Then he stopped coming, and I heard that he had died. An accident at the school, I was told, but I didn't believe it until I read the accounts of witnesses."

"You thought someone might have harmed him?" Cordell said.

"I was sure of it. But many people saw him fall from the clock tower. And the door that is the only entrance to the tower was latched from within."

Eve put down her cup before she spilled its contents. He had not been pushed? Until this moment, she had been quite sure the Stone Circle engineered his death.

Cordell leaned back in his chair. "Was anyone in the tower with him when he fell?"

"Two gardeners broke down the door and found no one inside. That's according to the report published after the inquest, but I place little reliance on those who worked at the school or those who investigated them. My opinions are clouded, I must admit, by my fondness for the child. Sometimes when he came to see his birds, he would ask me to tell him about the sarsen stones and the legends of this place. And more than once, we invited him to stay with us instead of remaining at the school during a winter holiday. He lived in the north, and could not always make the journey home."

"Do you know where?" Eve asked.

Mr. Hammett's brow furrowed. "Not precisely. In

the area of Harrowgate, I believe, but I cannot be sure. He rarely spoke of himself. I didn't even know his surname until after his death. Whenever I questioned him about personal matters, he would fold up like a letter that one dared not unseal. But otherwise, his unbounded curiosity made him engaging company. He always carried with him a pencil and a book of blank pages. I once asked what he wrote in it, and thought he would not answer. But he said, 'What I see, what I hear, what I feel, what I learn.'"

Eve and Cordell left not long after, both of them silent as they walked back to where the coach was waiting. Finally, just before they came into the village, Eve said, "Was it suicide, do you think?"

"More than likely. The school would have done everything possible to conceal it, and I expect the authorities bent a little in their evaluation. Hard enough to deal with a grieving mother without laying on her an additional burden. A suicide cannot be given rites or buried in consecrated ground."

"We have lost our motive, then, for the Phoenix murders."

"Not necessarily. It depends on what she learned from other sources. Mrs. Fenbow must have suspected the suicide, but she did not speak of it. That was, I am sure, what overset her this morning. She was still trying to protect the mother from the truth. Others being interviewed today may have been more forthcoming to her with their suspicions. We'll see what Indigo, Mrs. Kipper, and Tom have to say."

"Sir, why didn't you ask Mr. Hammett about the boy's family name?"

"Because we can easily find it by other means." He glanced over at her. "You didn't ask, either."

"It seemed too much like using him to betray Gabriel's mother. I know that's foolish, but it's what I felt."

"And I," he said. "The gentleman stood friend to a boy who desperately needed one. I shouldn't like to make him sorry for speaking with us today."

Cordell was being considerate again. It cost him nothing, of course, but it sent the price of her vengeance ever higher. She had even begun to wonder if, when she came to the edge of no return, she would give it up altogether.

"Must we go back immediately?" To distract herself, she pulled out the map. "The others won't be finished so early. I was hoping we could explore a little."

Cordell agreed, without enthusiasm, and stopped at the coach to speak briefly with Nate Bremer. She still found it hard to imagine the large driver with muscles swelling on every part of his visible body was one of Sir Peregrine's valets. Probably a joke, but she didn't want to insult the man by asking.

Cordell was inquiring about Bert, who had not been seen all afternoon.

"He came by mcbbc half an hour ago, said he meant to climb up Silbury Hill and watch through the spyglass." Nate pointed to a patently artificial mound rising on the flat plain about a mile away. "That's where he be."

It was a hazy afternoon, and nothing the size of a man, even a large one, could be seen from this distance. "We'll go by there on our way back," she said, "after we've investigated the barrows."

"You want me to drive you to the barrows?"

"That's not necessary." She smiled at him. "I wish

to walk. And besides, the horses are enjoying the shade.''

He'd been waiting in the copse more than an hour. Had he been wrong? Had they returned to Devizes after all?

He'd planned to be heading north by this time. It never paid to remain long in the vicinity of a man you had killed. And soon, the traffic on this road would start to pick up. The fair closed at six o'clock, but not everyone would stay until the end.

He gave it another few minutes before starting back the way he had come, keeping himself out of sight of the road while watching it through his new field glass. No sign of the coach. It looked more and more like he'd have to give it up for the day.

Swearing a series of Spanish and Portuguese oaths, he considered what to do next. Damn that stupid watchdog. By killing him, he had alerted Cordell to the threat.

Not that he was unaware of it before. Why else would he have taken the girl into hiding? Cordell was a lot of things he despised, but not stupid. Never stupid.

Hugging the Kennet River, he came near the tree-crowned East Kennet Barrow, shaped like a long bread loaf and a good place from which to have a look around. He dismounted, led his horse up the steep mound, and turned his spyglass on the village.

By Satan, the coach was where it had been. He still had a chance to finish the job.

But the original plan was out. Too much traffic, too many witnesses and obstacles. If an opportunity presented itself, he must strike here.

Turning the glass to Silbury Hill, he saw no one on it or near it. He slid his field of view then to the left, to another barrow the size of this one, but lacking the heavy cover of trees.

West Kennet Barrow, shaped like the picture of a whale he had once seen, started low in the west and rose to a goodly height at its eastern point. There, scattered in disarray, were perhaps a dozen sarsen slabs lying athwart one another like toppled dominoes.

He was about to swing the glass again when a motion caught his eye. He adjusted the focus, looked more closely at the unshaped sarsen stones.

Yes. Someone was there. Only one person that he could see, coming up from behind the stones to the overhanging crest of the barrow. He recognized the lean physique and athletic stride.

Cordell. And unlikely to be there alone.

Another sweep of the barrow with his glass disclosed no other movement, no sign of the girl.

He calculated his options and their hazards. With little cover between where he was and the other barrow, he risked being seen if he rode or walked in that direction. He might gamble on where they'd go next. If they came this direction, he could easily take them both down. But if they went northeast to Silbury Hill, or due north to the village and their coach, he would have difficulty isolating them.

Think. Think. From a distance, he looked harmless enough. A chap, perhaps a bit worse for too much ale, meandering home after the fair. Cordell hadn't identified him, probably wouldn't recognize him from the Penn. And he had a light wig in his saddlepack. That, and the matching mustache attached with thin fishing line to conceal his distinctive nose, would turn the trick. He could limp as well. By the time he got close enough for anyone to mark the trappings of his disguise, it would be too late.

Swiftly he donned the costume, chose a brimless cap to make it appear he wasn't hiding anything, and proceeded to conceal a host of weapons on his person. A knife and a pistol threaded under his belt. A knife sheathed under his armpit, another strapped around his forearm. A pistol in one jacket pocket, a cudgel in the other. Inside his blackthorn walking stick was a short, sharp blade.

Leaving his horse where it was, he descended the barrow on the opposite side, cut north to walk along the river, swigged imaginary ale from a canteen, and when he got near the West Kennet Barrow, began to wander a bit aimlessly in its direction.

Cordell was not to be seen, nor was the girl. For all he knew, they had gone down the opposite side of the barrow and were merrily on their way back to the coach. But this was the hand he had chosen, so he might as well play it out.

Taking a cue from the dead watchdog, he whistled an improvised tune. Remembered to limp. Tried to be invisible by making himself obvious.

And caught another glimpse of Cordell. Only his head, and he wasn't moving. It appeared the colonel was sitting on one of the stones, looking out across the fields of barley and pastures thick with grazing sheep.

Elated, confident of success, he continued his meandering path. He'd require to come around from nearer the whale's tale. The front was too high and too jagged. Or maybe he should pass by the front and . . . No. The more clever he tried to be, the more likely he'd trip up. Veering left and out of Cordell's sight, he kept whistling for a time, starting loud and letting the sound grow fainter until it faded off.

Then he waited, hidden in the shadows of the barrow as the sun lowered behind him. He had chosen a path carved out by rainwater, and when he saw nothing and heard nothing from above him, he began the climb to the top. If he had judged correctly, he would come out not far from the disordered sarsens, which would block Cordell's view of him while he crept closer.

Cordell wasn't his target, but he stood in the way of the girl, who would be defenseless without him. First the guardian, then the guarded.

He drew out one of his two pistols, checked again that it was ready to fire, and moved silently in the concealment of the stones.

Chapter 24

I know I oughtn't to tell you this, but yesterday I killed a man. Three, actually, but I didn't know until later about the other two. They weren't enemies. CB says it happens in a war, that civilians die for no reason except they were there, and I've seen it happen more than ever I wanted to. But I was never part of it until now. Our patrol was passing through a village when we were attacked by renegades, and when we fired back, the blackguards used the local people as shields. But they were inside huts, so we didn't see them. The man beside me went down, and CB took a bullet to the shoulder. I fired where the shots were coming from. Now I keep asking myself what I could have done to make this not happen. Worst of all, we took some of the renegades alive. They are locked in a stone chapel under guard, and all I can think is how much I want to batter down the door and shoot the lot of them. This is not how I usually am. But I don't know myself anymore.

J, not yrs. today. You wouldn't want me.

The peace of a quiet Sunday settled over him like the warmth of the afternoon sun, now making its slow journey across the blue western sky. About three o'clock, Cordell estimated. They could spare a little more time here.

He had chosen for his chair a fallen stone that provided a good view on three sides while letting him keep his feet solidly planted on the ground. To his left and a foot or two lower, Lady Eve reclined on a flat sarsen slab like a virgin sacrifice. She had removed her veiled bonnet, and tendrils of soft hair come loose from their pins stirred in the light breeze.

Not uncommonly, the two of them were quarreling.

"I don't know why you keep asking about him," she said. "Jordan Blair has no reason to harm me, nor would he. Not every gentleman who has asked me to dance or flirted a little can be described as a rejected suitor."

"You implied, strongly, that he had proposed marriage."

"He said he would marry me if necessary. That is a quite different thing."

Cordell's hands tightened. *Necessary?* Was it Blair who had been her first lover? That man, she had said, offered marriage in the event of a child, as any decent gentleman would. And like any fortune hunter would do, Blair might have seduced her in the expectation she would feel obliged to accept his offer.

Without moving his head, Cordell looked over at the man he'd been watching for several minutes. Why would a fellow with a walking stick and a limp choose a path on soft ground alongside a river, especially with a practically deserted road only a few yards away? "Perhaps Blair did not take your refusal kindly."

"I expect he took it gratefully. His concern was for my reputation after the Phoenix mission is completed and you have gone on your way. He said, rather like a man throwing himself into the path of a bullet, that if you declined to wed me, he would do so."

"Hardly the stuff of martyrdom, given the rewards. Will you accept him?"

A pause. Then she said, "I sometimes wish it were possible. In many ways, we are ideally suited. Not by my parents' standards, to be sure, but dukes and marquesses aren't exactly queuing up for my hand."

It was none of his concern whom she married. And his suspicions about Blair had little foundation. But he couldn't seem to let go the subject. "Then what is preventing you?"

"You wouldn't think so, but Lord Blair is a romantic of the deepest stripe. He will marry for love."

The man with the walking stick had turned away from the river, and his course, if unchanged, would take him parallel to the barrow some fifty yards distant from it. Without haste, Cordell slipped one of the small pistols from his pocket. "You are right. I wouldn't think that of him. Don't sit up. Have you a mirror?"

"What?" Her eyes, which had been closed, flew open. "Yes, but—"

"Pass it to me. Someone is approaching a little closer than I would like, that is all. I want you to keep out of his view." He watched her remove a small gilt-framed looking glass from her reticule and said, in a voice louder than he had been using, "Are you saying he doesn't love you? How can that be?"

"You should know better than anyone, sir. Am I supposed to raise my voice as well?"

"No." He took the mirror. "Keep talking."

"Lord Blair told me several years ago that when he saw the woman meant to be his, he would know her instantly."

"Hogwash."

"It surprised me as well, him saying such a thing. Perhaps he feared I was developing a tendre for him and was making sure I did not. He had seen me, conversed with me, even flirted with me, but I was not the woman he would love for all of his life. I told him I understood, and we have since been at perfect ease with each other."

The man's direction had subtly altered, bringing him by slow increments nearer the barrow. He appeared to be drinking, which helped explain his meandering course, and except for a notably muscular upper body, seemed to pose little threat. Both his hands were occupied, one with the walking stick and the other with his canteen. He was not within accurate firing range.

Even so, Cordell palmed the mirror in his left hand, which made it possible to keep the man in view while his own head was turned away. Almost directly across from them now, the man had not once looked their direction. In an otherwise deserted landscape, a well-dressed gentleman was perched atop a crown of stones on a barrow like a captain on the prow of his ship. That ought to merit at least one glance. Even a friendly wave.

"If you are going to take a nap," Cordell said, sounding irritated, "let me have the Avebury guidebook. I may as well know what it is I am looking at."

Then, in a whisper, "I am going to slip you a knife. Cut off the bottom half of your skirts. Do it quickly."

"Is the man closer?" she whispered back.

The exchange of map and knife accomplished, he opened the map and held it up, leaving clear the mirror view behind him and to his right. The man was drawing subtly nearer the barrow, but not so much as to indicate he meant to climb it. He was whistling now, which reminded Cordell of Bert Bremer. Was he still up there on Silbury mound, watching the stranger through Cordell's field glass? It didn't matter. The barrow would soon hide the man from sight, Bert's and his own.

Lady Eve was sawing through her skirts and ripping them with her hands, never questioning his orders. Good trooper.

He checked the mirror again. The stranger was still moving, his whistle growing fainter. But the short hairs on the back of Cordell's neck were standing on end. All appearances the man was harmless to the contrary, he was sticking with his instincts.

Midway along the barrow, the side of it bulged out like the torso of an overweight animal. Without standing or climbing onto a higher stone, Cordell would lose sight of him within a minute or so.

But the sun was his friend. The late-afternoon shadows were casting from the rear of the barrow and a little to the side. The man could be tracked that way for a time. And even if he mounted the barrow from the lowest slope and came up that way, some part of his shadow might be visible on the ground.

If not, Cordell would use the shelter provided by the stones to change position and determine the man's location. Meantime, what to do about Lady Eve? He had two vague contingencies in mind, was providing for them, had no idea if either would be of use.

Just then she wriggled free of the torn-off fabric, leaving her clothed in only a thin chemise from her lower thighs down to her half boots. "What shall I do with the skirt, sir?"

"First, without showing yourself, try to determine if there's a place beneath the fallen stones where you can hide."

She turned onto her belly and pulled herself over to the edge of her chosen bed stone for a look around. For a time, she was practically dangling from the pile of sarsens. Then she swung back to where she had been. "I can see cavities between stones, but I'm too large to make my way through the openings to reach them." Her whisper was a little breathless.

"All right. If it comes down to it, you'll have to take a runner. Back along the barrow, then cut toward those trees alongside Silbury Hill. You'll be in the open a considerable time, but I'll keep our visitor occupied."

"You think he's after us?"

"Not necessarily. He may be drunk and wandering around. He might be out to rob us. He might even be gone. I can't see him now. Choose one of those hiding places you found and arrange the fabric and your bonnet to make it appear you are under there. Not too subtle, not too obvious. Visible from this flat area in front of me. If there is to be a dispute, it will likely happen here."

Again without questioning, she did as she was told and created a small masterpiece of deceit. She even tore off a tiny fragment of skirt and snagged it on a stone, as if it had ripped loose while she was threading herself through the narrow opening.

Despite everything, he couldn't help smiling.

But he was all business when she came close enough to hear his next order. The man, he had detected from the barest hint of a shadow, was climbing onto the barrow. Still a distance away, however, and they were well concealed until he came around to the right or over the sarsens. There was no path, Cordell already knew, between the stones and the sheer edge of the barrow on his left side, where Lady Eve would descend.

"Good work," he said soundlessly when she was looking directly at him. Even a whisper might carry now. "There won't be a chance to run along the barrow to where you can easily get down. You'll have to go over the side. Is that possible?"

"It is if I have no other choice. I'll hold on to a stone and lower myself over it. That should put me no more than six feet off the ground."

"Take this." He held out the small pistol.

"I cannot shoot," she said. "Or hold it while I'm going off the barrow."

"Come closer." He untied his cravat, unwrapped it from his neck, and secured the gun inside a loose knot in the middle. Then he wound the neckcloth around Lady Eve's waist. "This will hold until you are down."

"I hope it doesn't go off," she said.

"It wouldn't dare." He gave her a small knife. "Drop this over the side near where you'll be landing. You can sever the knot with it, if need be. Otherwise, just run like a harried fox. Go. Get into position. I'll signal you when to take your leave."

She held his gaze for a long moment, silent and indecipherable messages passing between them. Then, with the fist-to-chest salute of a Roman soldier, she pulled away and climbed down the stones as far as she could go.

He could see only her head and shoulders. She was studying the stone that was to be her platform, selecting her handholds. Then she knelt, facing him with her shins and feet over the side, prepared to move when he directed her. She was still affected, he knew, by the injuries she had taken a week earlier. But she would do what she must. There was no choice for either of them now.

He turned his attention, all of it, to the man creeping slowly along the barrow. He was more than halfway its length, bent nearly double, but the top of his head was visible as a moving shadow imposed on the shadow of the barrow.

Cordell raised the open map, deliberately marking his location for the man to see, and withdrew the other pistol from his pocket. He had a second knife as well, which he set on the stone within reach. He took up the mirror again, but considered that the sun might reflect off it. He'd use it only if the shadow disappeared, leaving him to locate the man by other means.

Time to move. He lowered himself to the stone Lady Eve had abandoned and propped up the map in such a way that a little of it would be visible to the man moving in from behind. Then he cut off the end of his jacket sleeve and fixed it to protrude near the map. He'd rather have used the entire jacket as decoy, but his white shirt would make it impossible to avoid notice even for the short time he required.

Taking knife and pistol with him, he slipped behind a nearly upright sarsen. Lady Eve, to his left and a few feet lower, would be able to clearly see his signal from where he stood. He hoped she could go down quietly. When the moment came, he'd make as much noise as he could to cover her. It was all in the timing now, and that depended on what action the man chose for himself.

Lady Eve wisely kept still, allowing him to tune his ears to the natural sounds around him, and the unnatural ones of the man's approach. The slight afternoon wind made an eerie noise, like the faint echo of a ghost's passing, as it blew between the stones. A crackle of paper when the map fluttered, but he'd anchored it well enough to hold. The occasional whir of an insect's wings.

He felt the presence of the dead.

Like other mounds distributed across the landscape, this one had probably been erected as a burial chamber. He hoped the spirits were benign. He hoped Lady Eve and a man who had failed to protect her wouldn't be joining them.

A tiny sound, like a pebble dislodged. Close now. Cordell stopped breathing. Listened for the man's breathing, for the rustle of his clothes, the pad of his feet.

He was good. Careful. Experienced. Had Cordell not been suspicious from the first, been watching and listening for his arrival, his presence would have gone undetected until too late. But at the last moment, the last second before he appeared, he'd have to betray himself. Cordell was waiting for that moment.

It came almost immediately, the gathering of muscles, the poise before the leap.

Cordell signaled Lady Eve, put her from his mind just as the man sprang onto the flat clearing and fired a shot at the map. The bullet hit the stone. Ricocheted off with a whine.

Cordell was already in motion, out from behind the sarsen, gun held steady at the man's chest.

They were perhaps five feet apart, legs bent slightly, each man's eyes taking the other's measure.

The man spat on the ground. "Where's the girl?"

"Where you can't reach her." Cordell risked a glance to where she'd supposedly hidden herself, meaning to draw the man's gaze. It worked.

The man said nothing, but there was satisfaction in his eyes. He thought her safely stowed away until he could get to her.

"Why do you want the lady?" said Cordell. "What's she to you?"

"Money. What else? And don't ask who's paying me. He'd kill me more surely, and more painfully, than you'll try to do."

"Have you failed to notice? I hold the loaded gun."

"I see it. You won't use it. Not fatally. You want to know who hired me, because if I die, another will come in my place, and another."

"I can fire into your belly. You know what that means. In exchange for a lethal shot, you'll tell me anything I want to know."

A short, mocking laugh. "I'd use that tactic. Most men would. But not you. A gentleman's honor, and all that rot."

"Honor requires me to protect the lady. But I concede a distaste for torture. And you haven't killed anyone yet. One name, the truth, and I'll do everything in my power to help you get clear of this."

"I think you might. The problem is, I already slit the throat of your oversize watchdog up on Silbury Hill."

Cordell bit back an oath, stilled his racing heart. Kept talking, futile though it might be, to give Lady

Eve more time to escape. "That's unfortunate. But I could pretend I didn't hear you confess to it."

"Then they'd hang me for half a hundred other crimes, including desertion. If I took off this wig and face hair, you might recognize me."

"I do. I've seen you before, but I don't know your name."

"Well, if ever you find the man that sent me, you can ask him."

This was going nowhere. And the man was right. With Lady Eve safely gone, a shot in the gut was beyond Cordell's power to inflict. He was more than willing, though, to turn this killer over to someone with a less exacting conscience. "If you've nothing to lose," he said, making one last try, "why not tell me what I want to know? I can, at the least, provide you with comforts while the lawyers wrangle."

"You're wasting your time. I've a grudge against the army, and you are everything about it that I hate. More than twenty years a sergeant major, and what did I get?" He spat again. "The army didn't take kindly to some of my methods. It never did right by me. But my employer used me well after I deserted, and even a bloody rascal like myself can scratch up a little loyalty."

"Loyalty to a man who would kill an innocent girl? Why does he want her dead?"

"I dunno. Spoiled bitch. Maybe she wouldn't dance with him. She'll dance with me, though, before I cut her."

With the last word, the man threw his empty gun at Cordell and flung himself after it, a knife materializing in each of his hands.

Chapter 25

We're back at camp, and the surgeon pulled the ball from Cordell's shoulder without doing too much damage. The trouble is what the bullet might carry in with it, like a bit of fabric picked up when it was passing through the clothes. CB said not to worry, because his shirts are always clean. But they're not. No exploring officer has much time for laundry. We wear the same one or two shirts for days and days, even longer if the rivers are dried up. But I expect he was joking. This means the reconnaissance we were about to undertake together now falls to me. It's important business, Ensign, and I'll be in the mountains a considerable time. Don't worry if you don't hear from me for a while. I'm taking lots of paper and will write as always, but I'll have no means of posting the letters until I report back to Cordell. One day you'll receive a great many of them in a batch!

Yrs., J

P.S. Yes, I am in better spirits now. It's good to be entrusted with a difficult job. But I suspect the ghosts of the civilians I killed will follow me into the mountains.

At Cordell's signal, Eve planted her hands on the sarsen, lowered herself over the side, and hung there for an endless moment before making herself let go.

She hit the ground hard on both feet, no damage. Worst fear done with. Grabbing the knife she'd tossed down, she sped alongside the barrow nearly to the end before veering in the direction of the trees near Silbury Hill. At every moment she wanted to look back, knew better, kept her eyes on the ground ahead of her. Three quarters of a mile, she guessed, to the hill, more than a mile from there to the village.

The remnants of her skirt slapped against her thighs. The chemise kept tangling between her legs. She paused long enough to tie a knot in the thin muslin and risked a glance over her shoulder. No one running her direction. She could see nothing at the high east end of the barrow except the outline of the sarsens.

Already she was out of breath. Too much time lazing after her fall from the horse last week. *Watch your feet.* It became a chorus repeated over and over in her head. The ground was pocked with rabbit holes.

A small knot of sheep scattered as she blazed by them. She'd given up on the trees. They were out of her way. The afternoon sun beat at her face and arms. Sweat streamed down her forehead, salting her eyes. She kept going, legs driving up and down. The chalk mound with its cover of grass loomed larger and larger.

A stitch in her side now. Hard to breathe. It hurt.

She seized shallow breaths every few steps, knowing she couldn't keep up the pace much longer.

She came to a wide ditch, not deep, that circled the hill, and took herself down it. A little shelter, in case the man had overpowered Cordell and was hard on her trail. In case he had an accomplice. It was a chance to slow a little, pull air into her burning lungs.

When she came around the other side of Silbury Hill, a miracle was waiting for her. A horse, tethered to a shrub, saddled. Bert Bremer's? Then where was he? Why hadn't he seen what was going on?

She didn't hesitate. Grabbing the reins, she dragged herself onto the horse and drove it to a gallop.

The distance to Avebury went by in a blur of barley and grass and sheep. She met up with the road and turned right, dodging the sparse traffic coming from the direction of Marlborough. Then the turn into Avebury proper. She clattered into the village and to the place where Nate Bremer waited with the carriage.

He was at the front, giving water in a bucket to the horses. She reined in.

"West Kennet Barrow." Barely a sound huffing out, but he was attending her closely. "Cordell attacked. Fighting. Where the stones are. I'll get help."

As she finished, he was already taking himself to the driver's box. She sent the horse forward again, this time to Avebury Manor.

When she came through the gates, she saw Mr. Hammett and the boy near the stables. They looked up, saw her, broke into a run.

Her side felt like a hot poker had been stuck through it. The words she'd said to Nate Bremer came out again to Mr. Hammett, disjointed and faint. Her ears had begun to ring. She leaned over in the saddle, rested her forehead on the horse's mane, ordered her head to clear. *Breathe. Breathe. Breathe.*

Distantly, she heard Mr. Hammett giving orders. He'd understood. She could go back now. Head swimming, she pulled herself upright and tried to turn the horse around.

Mr. Hammett had hold of the reins.

"Let me go!" It sounded pitiful, like the whine of a gnat.

"I'll take you," he said. "Workmen are fetching weapons and getting under way. Come down, Lady Eve."

When she struggled for control of the horse, Mr. Hammett put his hands on her waist and swung her to the ground. "I humbly beg your pardon," he said, leading her to a bale of hay and sitting her on it. "I have sent for something to replace your skirts. The gig is being readied. We'll set out as soon as may be."

Cordell was ready for the attack, had been expecting it. Even the weapon, but not two of them.

He spun, sent a sideways kick to the man's elbow, heard a yelp of pain. One knife went flying. The maneuver bent him over long enough to set his pistol on the stone and retrieve his knife. Even at this range, a shot intended to wound might turn out to be fatal. He must not—*must not*—kill this man.

Just as he regained his footing, the man leaped again. Cordell planted his feet, taking the assault by grabbing the man's right forearm. The man did the same to him, both knives held in check while they wrestled for leverage and control.

The man was strong, kept pushing him backward. He hadn't far to go before his calves met the stone he'd been sitting on earlier. The man pressed and pressed harder until he was bent back over the stone. That weakened his grip on the man's knife arm.

He abruptly sat on the stone and simultaneously brought a foot hard to the man's groin. It was blocked with a thigh, but the defensive action gave Cordell a chance to let go of one arm, duck under the man's extended knife arm, and wrench it behind his back.

He couldn't hold it long, nor could he keep hold of his own knife. He dropped it and kicked the back of the man's left knee. It buckled. The man dropped, let go of Cordell, and rolled over in a neat somersault. They were both free now, Cordell unarmed, the man chuckling as he passed his remaining knife back and forth between his hands.

He meant to throw it. Cordell saw that much in his eyes. Watched them instead of the knife, and when it flew at him, he was already spinning out of the way. Bad luck that it caught him where he'd ripped off his jacket sleeve. Blood rose to stain his shirt where the blade had sliced through his left arm just above the elbow.

Both his weapons were behind him. He had to keep the man clear of them, disable him long enough to have a chance of reaching his knife. The gun had fallen from the stone and was somewhere at his feet, but he couldn't see it. Dared not look away from the man, even for a heartbeat.

A laugh from his adversary. "Not bad. I underestimated you. Didn't think a toff colonel could fight like a real soldier."

Cordell wasn't about to waste breath. He had a surprise of his own. When he was escaping the attempt to force him down onto the stone, he'd managed to put his hand on Lady Eve's mirror. It was in his palm now. Good for nothing more than a distraction, but that was what he needed. Anything that prolonged the fight, gave her more time to escape, more time to find help. Gave the help more time to arrive.

Blast. The man had got a cudgel into his hand. He was a damned walking weapons depot.

Cordell calculated the angle of the sun. Aligned the hand holding the mirror.

"I'm thinking I'll beat you nearly senseless," the man said. "Then you can watch what I do to the girl before I kill you both."

Trying to provoke him into doing something rash, Cordell knew. He sent a glance to where Lady Eve was supposedly hiding. The man's gaze flicked over, just long enough for Cordell to open his fingers, make a small adjustment, and send a ray of reflected sunlight from the mirror to the man's eyes.

He blinked, jerked his head aside. Cordell was instantly on him with a blow to the stomach and another to the jaw.

But in the struggle that followed, the cudgel hit the side of Cordell's head. The blow sent him reeling. His vision blurred. Not for long, but the man had his opening. He lunged for the knife on the stone.

Cordell blocked him by lurching across his path and ending up on his knees. Another blow with the cudgel, glancing off as he ducked and rolled onto the stone where Lady Eve had reclined.

The man followed. It was a battle among the fallen stones now, and the sarsens themselves became weapons. Cordell was thrown against them and again. And so was the man, who lost his cudgel along the way but got hold of someone's knife and nearly managed a killing strike to Cordell's chest. It went into his shoulder instead, not very deep.

Cordell eluded the man and dove for where he thought his pistol had gone. The devil was right on him, though, clinging to his back. He slammed his elbows up into the man's ribs. Threw him off.

They were both in the small clearing again, unarmed and with weapons all around them, none easy to hand. Cordell bled from shoulder, arm, and head. It felt like he'd been cut on the side as well, or he'd got a cracked rib or two. Couldn't remember.

He was weakening faster than his opponent. Trying to keep the man alive had put him at a disadvantage. He ought to have sent a bullet into him when he had the chance.

His own last chance was on him now. The last strike, with what remained of his strength and cunning, that would end this one way or the other. He staggered a little, made as if to go limp even as he gathered his muscles for the attack.

The man was three feet away, poised in the center of the clearing with his back to the easternmost point of the barrow. He, too, was poised for a leap.

"One thing," said Cordell in a conversational tone. "It's only a bonnet and a bit of skirt under that stone. The Lady Eve is gone."

Again the man shot a glance to where he thought she'd been hiding.

Head down, arms extended. Cordell drove straight at him.

The man returned his attention just in time, but he was caught off balance. Cordell's rush carried him a little way back before he could dig in. Like wrestlers, the two men grappled with each other, Cordell always pushing his adversary toward the edge, the man beating at him with rock-hard fists.

It wasn't going to work. Cordell was down to the last reserve of strength. Not even that much. Just enough to crouch as if succumbing to his wounds and follow the diversion with a swift knee to the man's privates.

This time he hit the target. The man let go his grip of Cordell's wounded shoulder. Flailed with the hand that had been beating at his head. Cordell pushed and pushed.

The man clung to his shirt and jacket, trying to pull Cordell over with him. He nearly did. With a final effort, Cordell brought both arms up and out, breaking the man's grip and sending him over the side.

A loud cry and a thud as the man hit the ground below.

Silence, as if each fighter were holding his breath. As if the world had stopped breathing. Then a bird passed overhead, the sound of its wings like thunder in the hushed air.

Cordell sank down where he was, onto his knees, panting like a dying animal. He leaned over just enough to see his enemy lying on his back with one leg bent at an unnatural angle. The man's eyes were open, staring up.

He might be dead. He might be badly hurt. He might be faking.

Cordell couldn't see him well enough to judge. Black spots danced in front of his eyes. Blood roared in his ears. He crawled back to the stones, fumbled around until his hand met with his pistol.

Still on his knees, he shuffled back to the edge of the barrow and sat where he could keep his eyes on the man who had come close to murdering Lady Eve. If he could be absolutely sure the bastard was already dead, he'd put a bullet in him just for the hell of it.

He had a few other thoughts, wispy as ghosts, as his vision began to cloud. And regrets, sharp as Lady Eve's inexplicable contempt for him.

Formerly inexplicable. There was reason enough for it now. He had failed her.

Chapter 26

Spain, Jan. 1813

R is back from leave. It took him a long time to cross from England to Lisbon, what with the weather, and he was seasick the whole time. While he was home, he saw my father. All is not forgiven. There's nobody so stubborn as a Branden, including me. I'm here in spite of him, and I'll never be sorry for it. Nick and Richard send me the news from home, and they say the duke asks about what I write in my letters to them. Maybe he'll speak to me when the war ends. R says I could go to England on leave and not call at Sarne Abbey, but I'd rather be doing my duty. And if I do come, it will be you I want to see. I wager you've changed a lot, Ensign, since we conquered the world together. So have I. For one thing, I've got twice as many freckles!

Yrs., J

Cordell opened his eyes to a fuzzy wooden canopy draped with fuzzy fringed velvet. When his vision cleared, he tried to raise his head. Bad idea. It felt as if a carpenter had got himself stuck in there and was hammering to get out.

After a while, he made another attempt. Enough light slanted in from between closed window curtains to illuminate the large room, which looked not to have been inhabited for a considerable time. He had never seen it before. The furnishings, solid, ornate, and ugly, belonged in someone's attic.

"Lord Cordell." Silas Indigo rose from a chair in the corner. "What may I do for you?"

"Tell me what the hell is going on. Where is Lady Eve? Is the man who attacked her dead?"

"She is here and well. We finally persuaded her to take some rest. You have slept the clock around, my lord. This is Monday, and it is nearing six o'clock in the evening. Will you excuse me for a few moments? Sir Peregrine asked to be informed directly when you woke up."

"Is the man dead?" Cordell repeated, without much hope it wasn't true.

"I'm afraid so. Sir Peregrine can tell you more."

While he waited, Cordell took stock of his condition. He was clothed only in bandages, around his head, around his forearm, around his shoulder, and very tightly around his chest. An ice pick was lodged on his left side between his ribs, or so he would have wagered.

"Ah, there you are." Sir Peregrine bustled in, a vision in pale blue satin, and began flinging open the curtains. "The physician expressed no concern about your eventual recovery, but you have been sleeping a devilish long time. Are you up to a conversation?"

"I insist on it. Why are you dressed like a macaroni?"

"Lud, but these curtains are dusty. As for the costume, a little too much shine for Wiltshire, but helpful with my interrogations. People give straighter answers when they think I don't know the significance of what I'm asking. And I shouldn't want to get a reputation for being clever. That would serve Phoenix not at all."

"Where are we?"

"Avebury Manor." Sir Peregrine, arms folded, propped his shoulder against one of the canopy posts at the foot of the bed. "Mr. Hammett has been most accommodating. Shall I first tell you what has occurred, or would you rather ask the questions most on your mind?"

"You first." It hurt to talk. "Except, did you find Bert Bremer?"

A look of sorrow passed over Sir Peregrine's unlined face. "On Silbury Hill, with his throat cut. I presume the fellow you dispatched was responsible?"

Cordell started to nod, raised a hand instead.

"Nate has gone to arrange services and burial, but means to return as one of Lady Eve's bodyguards for as long as need be. He was the one reached you first, after she made her run to the village. The killer broke his neck in the fall. We are trying to identify him. He looks to be hired help."

"He is. I couldn't get anything out of him. He said he didn't know why his employer wanted Lady Eve dead, but was sure he wouldn't stop until she was. He'll send another, and another. Those were the man's words."

"So we are where we were before. You're sure the employer is male?"

"It was 'he' this and 'he' that. No slips. The rogue was an army deserter, but I don't know his name. Tom spotted him hanging around at the fair on Saturday. He has a distinctive face. They should know him at Horseguards."

"I'll look into it." Sir Peregrine hesitated, like a man about to step into a raging river. "There is new information regarding the Black Phoenix mission. The reports from Lady Eve and the others, combined with my own investigations, have led us to the identity of Gabriel Haskins's mother."

"That's the name? Haskins?"

"It was at the time. She has since remarried." Sir Peregrine pulled himself away from the bedpost and went to the window, where he stood looking out. "This is difficult to speak of. It was the lord lieutenant who pointed me to her. When the boy died, Winfred played a role in the official inquiry and became acquainted with Mrs. Haskins. She refused to accept the verdict of accidental death from a fall and badgered the authorities to look into rumors of trouble at the school. When they declined, she pursued the matter on her own. You know enough of conditions at Stanton St. Bernard's to imagine how difficult they made it for her. After several months, she gave up and returned to her home in Yorkshire."

"Do you know where she is now?"

"Winfred usually keeps away from London, but he went up for the Victory Celebrations in 1814 and saw her there." Sir Peregrine turned, his lips set in a hard line. "I have not told this to the others. Gabriel's mother is Lady Etheridge."

"God in heaven." None of the blows Cordell had taken in the fight struck him so hard as this one. For Lady Eve, the pain would be unendurable. "Has she been arrested?"

"We'll not take that step until incontrovertible evidence has been pieced together. It shouldn't take long."

"She is ill. Did you know that? By her own account, Lady Etheridge suffers headaches, but Lady Eve believes the affliction may be worse. There are signs her mind is affected. She talks to herself, cannot recall where she is, and minutes later, appears her usual self."

"That could explain a great deal. There seems no mistake about her involvement, but we must also trace her accomplices before they strike again. All the members of the Stone Circle have been identified. One died in the war. Phoenix has sent emissaries to warn the others and stand watch in case of an attack."

Phoenix, it seemed, had a great many resources at its disposal. "What of the stableboy? How does he fit in?"

"Witnesses remember him working in the Stanton St. Bernard's stables around the time of Gabriel's death. His connection to the Circle has not been determined." Sir Peregrine drew nearer the bed. "Lady Eve will have to be told. Shall I do it, or would you rather?"

"I'll tell her." A cramp gripped his stomach to think of it. "Send her in, will you?"

"It will have to wait. She spent all of last night and most of the day hovering in the passageway outside this room. Some fear of permanent damage from your head injuries, I take it. You seem well enough to me. But she requires to sleep, and I expect you should have a meal." Sir Peregrine ambled to the door, his expression uncharacteristically somber. "Indigo will see to your needs, and I'll let you know when the lady is stirring."

Eve felt better after her nap, and better still when Sir Peregrine told her that Cordell showed no sign of damage to his wits. She had paced outside his room for hours, thinking about the cautions given after the injury to her own head. There was reason to worry. His injuries were far worse than hers had been, and he had remained unconscious for a long time.

She did wonder about Sir Peregrine's reserved mood, quite unlike his usual irrepressible humor. But of course, he would have a great deal on his mind. He had accomplished wonders in the last twenty-four hours, all the while giving the impression of a man who never lifted a finger except to sugar his tea.

About the man Cordell had slain, she refused to give him a single thought. She refused also to think about the man who had hired him. The next ordeal would come when it came. For now, she was on her way to see Cordell. A flutter of anticipation quickened her walk.

Mr. Indigo admitted her to the bedchamber and departed with a tray, closing the door behind him. She smelled chicken broth, chocolate, and basilicum ointment.

Cordell, half reclined against a bank of pillows on a high-platformed bed, regarded her with the unblinking eagle's gaze that never failed to unnerve her. "I hope you are not here to play nursemaid," he said.

"I'll leave that to you." She realized she'd been holding her breath for his first words. They were purely Cordell, dry and ironic, putting her at once on guard and at ease. He had treated his soldiers in the same manner, she knew. It was his habit. She ought not to feel singled out because he'd quoted one of her remarks back at her. "Is it forbidden to ask how you feel?"

"Peachy," he said. "And you?"

This time she laughed, as he'd meant her to do. How astonishing that he would remember so many things she had said and done in his company.

But there was nothing of amusement in his eyes. Nor of implacable command, which was the only message she'd ever been able to read with certainty. Now she saw, or thought she saw, a deep sadness there, and she remembered Sir Peregrine's quiet evasiveness.

Something was profoundly wrong.

Putting her hands behind her at her waist, a stance so like his distinctive one that it felt almost natural to her, she looked into the face of the dragon. "What is it, sir, that you do not want to tell me?"

"As you have realized, something you will not wish to hear. Nor will you want to believe it, although there can be no doubt it is true."

His uncompromising tone steadied her. "Go on, then."

"Sir Peregrine has located the woman responsible for the Black Phoenix murders."

"Mrs. Haskins?" But this was *good* news. "Has she been taken into custody?"

"A year after her son died at Stanton St. Bernard's, Mrs. Haskins, a widow from the time Gabriel was an infant, came down from Yorkshire to London. Sir Peregrine has just received confirmation of what he had already learned by other means. In 1808, she was married at St. George's Hanover Square to Lord Etheridge."

The air deadened. Her eyes locked on his face. Searched it for doubt. Error. Hope.

But truth, like a knife in her heart, twisted and held fast.

Lady Etheridge had been married before. And before that, she had loved a man she called her angel and conceived a child with him. Her son, Gabriel, named for an angel.

She felt suddenly weak. Light-headed.

"Sit down!" Cordell said sharply.

She was near the bed and dropped onto it, wrapping an arm around a bedpost for support.

"What do we do now?" she finally said.

He gazed at her in silence, one of those assessing looks he'd given her when she was recovering from her fall. She took long breaths, willing the strength in her body to return. With effort, she straightened her back and lifted her head.

"Watchers have been sent to make sure she doesn't scarper," he said. "Tomorrow, Sir Peregrine and I will go up to London and make whatever arrangements are appropriate."

"You will speak to her first? Give her a chance to defend herself?"

"No decisions will be made until all the evidence is considered and weighed. Do you want to come with us?"

"You know that I must."

But how was she to bear it? Already she was splintering. Flying apart. An icy wind blasted in her ears.

"Very well," he said. "We will leave before dawn.

Two questions, if you don't mind. Have you the name of her physician?"

"No. She once recommended someone with offices in Harley Street to Lady Holland, but I cannot recall his name."

"That may help. If it comes down to it, we'll ask her directly. I know this will be guesswork, but have you any idea who might have helped her carry out the murders?"

Murders. She knew it was true, and yet she did not *believe* it. Since she had known her, since long before that, Lady Etheridge had done nothing but good.

Eve shook her head. "Sir," she managed in a weak voice, "I think I am going to be sick."

Rising up off the pillows, he grabbed the bellpull, gave it a hard tug, and sank back with a wince. "Stay there," he said. "Don't try to walk."

Silas Indigo came into the bedchamber. "My lord?"

"Assist Lady Eve to her room. Carry her if need be. And fetch Mrs. Kipper to her."

Mr. Indigo moved to where she was sitting and held out his arm.

She looked at Cordell. "Do not try to shield me from this," she said. "I *must* go with you."

"I know. You will." His gaze held hers for a last, long moment. "I am sorry."

Nothing could still her pain, but his words lent her the strength to stand and walk, with Mr. Indigo's help, from the room.

Later, alone, she would weep. And when she was done, she would banish tears and make no place for them ever again.

Chapter 27

I've been staying with a Basque shepherd while mapping passes and roads in this area. He lives in a hut with two skinny dogs and one of his sons. The rest of the family lives in a village down the mountain, and this morning he asked me to take his son for a visit. I got there just in time for church. Sometimes, like today, I creep in at the back of a church and try not to be noticed. It's the Catholic Mass, which is something like our service except it's in Latin and there's more incense. I like it, the ritual and the way people put everything else aside when they are there. And I am in need of prayers, even my own. After church, the family invited me for Sunday dinner. Roast chicken! Then all the neighbors came over to look at me, and I ended up giving rides on my horse to the children. One day I should like to have some of my own. I'm disinherited, though, and a captain doesn't make enough money to keep a wife. I must become a general!

Yrs., J

*S*he is my friend, the only one I have, Lady Eve had told him the afternoon she saw Lady Etheridge talking to herself and knew her to be ill.

As the coach made its way into London, Cordell was thinking of that afternoon, and of how she had climbed the long staircase to prove herself strong enough to deal with any adversity. She could not have guessed how many others she would have to endure.

Or perhaps she had. *I wonder,* she later said, *what else is to be taken from me.*

They weren't traveling together. She was in a smaller carriage with Mrs. Kipper and Sir Peregrine, while he rode in an antique vehicle from Avebury Manor large enough for him to semirecline on the squabs. Indigo sat directly across, prepared to push him back if he started to roll off.

He felt worse today than he had done yesterday, weak as the kitten Sir Peregrine kept threatening to foist on him. Every part of him ached, throbbed, or felt as if a hot knife had been driven into it. But his head was relatively clear, except that it could think of nothing but Lady Eve.

He had seen her at breakfast around three o'clock that morning, neatly dressed in clothes sent over to them from the Unicorn. Her demeanor was calm, quiet, and contained. To him it appeared that she had withdrawn into herself, shutting all the doors and windows behind her. No trace of feeling showed on her face or reached her eyes.

They had come into Mayfair now, with its trim town houses and wrought-iron fences and swept streets. Last night, he and Sir Peregrine had agreed on a course of action for the meeting with Lady Etheridge, and for what would come afterward. Always they had to consider the safety of Lady Eve, especially with Bert Bremer gone and Cordell unable to swat down a housefly. No plan to successfully manage the choleric Lord Etheridge had materialized.

The other carriage had arrived in front of the house ahead of his, and Lady Eve was standing beside Sir Peregrine on the pavement while he spoke with two of the men who'd been watching the house. Cordell stumbled down the coach steps and joined them in time to hear that Lord Etheridge was in Brighton and Lady Etheridge inside the house.

Then Sir Peregrine led the way to the front door and got all of them admitted with a combination of charm and implied threats. Inside, the servants appeared unsettled, as if strange occurrences in the household had become daily fare. The butler didn't even object when they insisted on seeing Lady Etheridge immediately.

While Sir Peregrine, Indigo, and Mrs. Kipper set about interrogating the staff, Cordell and Lady Eve followed the taut-lipped butler up the stairs. Collected and distant, she put Cordell in mind of an aristocrat ascending the guillotine. Her hair was bound up and concealed under a simple bonnet that did nothing to hide the bruises on her face. Her dark blue dress, high-necked and unadorned, made him appear gaudy by contrast in his uniform. She had not once looked at him since he emerged from the coach.

When they reached the bedchamber, Cordell moved the butler out of the way and, without knocking, opened the door.

Across the large, airy room with its light-colored carpets and graceful furniture, Lady Etheridge was sitting at her dressing table while a servant pinned up her hair. She looked back at them from the large mirror, her face expressionless. Then, with a wave, she dismissed the servant, sat for a moment as if gathering her thoughts, and turned to face them.

She knows, he thought. *Or she has guessed.*

"Are you alone?" she said.

"No." He stepped aside to admit Lady Eve. "The others are waiting downstairs."

Lady Etheridge rose. "For a moment I hoped you were here to announce your wedding. That would be tragedy indeed for Lady Eve, but a windfall for you, of course. What has occurred, then, to cause you to break into my home?"

"We are here," he said, "about the Stone Circle."

"Ah." Her gaze went to Lady Eve. "Do you know of this, my dear?"

"I'm afraid so." Lady Eve's voice was cool and steady. "Are you going to deny what you have done? If so, I will try to believe you."

"You needn't. I never expected to get away with it. I only hoped I would stay free long enough to complete the eradication of the Circle. How many are left now?"

"Two," said Cordell, somewhat awed by her sangfroid. They might have been discussing how many biscuits remained on a saucer. "Both are under guard."

"Unfortunate. But we did fairly well, all things considered. Will you carry me off to Newgate now? May I gather a few things first?"

"What becomes of you, Lady Etheridge, depends in great part on your cooperation in the next few minutes."

A dark, imperious brow lifted quizzically. "But surely I must hang. It was always the price of my retribution, and I was always willing to pay it. Are you saying there is room for negotiation? If possible, I should like Etheridge to be kept clear of this. He isn't a very nice man, but he does not merit the scandal that is sure to crash down on him."

"Are you exonerating him?"

"Oh, entirely. No one will be more shocked than he when the truth comes out. I'd rather it didn't, but not altogether for his sake. He's done his share of harm in the government, and almost no one in government ever gets the punishment he deserves."

She looked around her, a little distracted. "If we are to talk, shall we be seated? The two of you look much the worse for wear. Am I responsible? If so, you have my regrets."

"You are not." Lady Eve went to a Grecian couch and perched herself on its edge, gloved hands folded in her lap. "As you once suspected, I am the object of attacks by someone as yet unidentified. Cordell was injured protecting me."

After a moment, Lady Etheridge sat in a chair angled near the couch. "Then I am indebted to him. You are the last good thing in my life, Eve, and perhaps the last good offering I can make to the world. Nothing I have done should cause you to abandon the principles we share. It is my greatest wish that you continue to pursue justice and the welfare of those less fortunate. They have so few advocates, and even those of us who care for them may, in the end, let them down. As I have done."

She was growing agitated, plucking at her skirts,

rubbing her hands together. "What is it you want to know? I . . . sometimes I do not think so clearly as I used to. Tell me the questions."

"Who helped you do the killings?" said Cordell.

Eve shot him a look of warning.

"You will find them, I have no doubt. But do not ask me to betray them. Strange as it will seem to you, they have acted from affection and loyalty."

"Then tell me which victim they mean to strike next."

"I don't know. My part was confined to naming my son's tormentors and choosing the manner of their deaths."

It was becoming difficult for Cordell to stay on his feet. He had decided the woman posed no threat, and this seemed a good time for Lady Eve to take over the questioning. He went to a bay window overlooking the street and sat on the window bench.

Lady Eve picked up the cue. "Will you tell me, Lady Etheridge, why you set out to punish these young men so many years after their offenses?"

"I wonder at it myself," said Lady Etheridge reflectively. "After Gabriel's death, I returned home and mourned the greater part of two years. But as time passed, I understood that he would not want me to bury myself with him. So I began laying plans for the rest of my life. I wished, first, to honor my son by doing good works. And I wished to claim the power and influence I lacked in my search for justice at the school. I determined that no one would again treat me as a common female unworthy of attention and respect."

She had achieved that much, Cordell thought, drawn against his inclination into her story.

"I closed up part of the house in Yorkshire, the portion holding Gabriel's rooms, and leased the rest of it along with the farmland. From the time I came to London and married Etheridge, my life was very much as you have seen it. Do you remember when I went north to sell a property, meaning to be gone only a few weeks?"

"Yes," said Lady Eve. "You stayed nearly five months. I assumed you'd had difficulty finding a buyer."

"Not at all. But I had left Gabriel's things as they were, and the time had come to pack them away. When I was doing so, I came upon a trunk with a false bottom. In it, concealed for all those years, were the journals he kept during his residency at Stanton St. Bernard's."

Her hands twisted on her lap. "He wrote every day, and to read his observations, you would think him far older than he was. But there were sections, more and more of them as his time at the school went on, that were written in a code of his own devising. It took me three months to decipher it." She looked up. "I wish I had never succeeded."

"You needn't speak of this," Lady Eve said quietly. "It is not material to the investigation. I simply wanted to understand."

"I think you will not, even when I have finished. But you needn't fear raising memories I had put down. Gabriel's words, once read, never left me. He told of what the other boys were doing to him. How they stole his money, his possessions, even his food. How they poached the woodland and the rivers and blamed the crimes on him. How they killed his pets. How they raped him."

Cordell looked at Lady Etheridge, who appeared to have forgotten anyone else was in the room. She was speaking to Lady Eve, but her mind was elsewhere, in a hell created by the young men she had killed.

"Gabriel had asked me to let him leave the school. I knew he was unhappy there, but I thought it was because I was, except for a few servants, alone in the house for most of the year. Our farm was remote. There were no neighbors. It was one of the reasons I sent him away to study. He was so bright, and so wise. He needed friends. He never told me what was happening there. Not in words. I should have heard it in his voice, seen it on his face."

"Stanton St. Bernard's is a long way from Yorkshire," Lady Eve said. "Was there not a school for him nearer by?"

"Oh, yes. I made poor decisions from the start. I knew someone who had attended the school and recommended it. He could not have known how greatly it had changed since he was there. And, too, I sent Gabriel south because his health was never robust. Our winters were difficult. Ah, but what use to think of this now?"

Lady Eve leaned forward, put her hand on Lady Etheridge's knee. "You have one of your headaches?"

"It doesn't signify. They come two or three a day now, more if I am overset. Let me finish while I can. He killed himself, you know."

"I suspected it. Why are you certain?"

"The last entry in his journal was written the day before he left for Michaelmas term. I remember the words exactly. 'I wish I could be free, like the birds not caged. Perhaps all will be different this time. I cannot bear it otherwise. If they do again what they

have done before, I shall go to a high place where
they cannot reach me. And then the bell will ring, and
I will fly.' "

Tears had come into her eyes, were flowing down
her face. "That's how it happened. He went to the
top of the bell tower, rang the bell, and . . . and . . ."

Lady Eve was on one knee beside her, offering a
handkerchief, speaking softly.

Cordell held still, giving them what privacy he
could. Thinking he wouldn't mind killing the other
two members of the Stone Circle himself.

The dramatic staging of the killings was explained,
and the reasons for them. He'd wager Lady Eve knew,
or could guess, who had carried out the murders on
behalf of Lady Etheridge. Whether she'd tell him or
not remained an open question.

After a long time, with Lady Etheridge and Lady
Eve now side by side on the couch, Lady Etheridge
spoke again. She was looking at him. "In spite of what
I learned four years ago, I did not seek revenge. Nor
did I think the testimony contained in a child's journal
would stand as evidence if I tried to bring the boys to
justice. I returned to London and my projects, and to
Lady Eve, who had become my joy. On a few occasions, one or another of the young men crossed my
path, but I turned away from confronting them."

"Then why?" he said. "What happened to trigger
the killings?"

"I cannot be sure. I can tell you a little of what led
up to the decision, although I never consciously made
one. It began a few months ago, when I began having
headaches unlike any I had ever experienced. They
occurred when I woke up, endured a few hours, and
went away. About the same time, words and phrases

from Gabriel's journal began replaying in my mind. I knew them by heart, but had forced myself to never think of them. Suddenly I could not stop myself. They spun around and around in my head, leaving room for nothing else. I became obsessed with each image, like the boy who tied him with fishing line to one of the stones at Avebury, or the night he found his canary roasting on a spit over the fire."

Cordell glanced at Lady Eve, remembering the burned man in the dovecote and the yellow feathers. If she was remembering them as well, she gave no sign of it.

"One evening, I saw the worst of the lot, the leader of the Circle, at a party. Roger Harbin, laughing and drinking. It was a crime against nature, that demon free to enjoy himself while my son lay in the ground. When I returned home, I made a list of each man I wished dead, and what I would do to them if I could. That, sir, is all I can or will tell you. They deserved to die. I deserve to die for slaying them. It is not true justice, but it may be as close as we will come in this world."

Lady Eve was gazing over at him, defying him to condemn Lady Etheridge.

He stood, waited for the light-headed sensation to pass, and came nearer the ladies. "May I have the name of your physician, Lady Etheridge?"

"He is Mr. MacClyde, in Harley Street. My butler can provide his direction."

"I will leave you, then, with Lady Eve, while I make inquiries." He bowed, careful not to catch Lady Eve's eye, and let himself out.

To his surprise, Lady Eve followed him down the passageway. "You mean to question the doctor?"

"I'll give Sir Peregrine his name, yes, along with a summary of what Lady Etheridge had to say."

"Tell him this as well. The actual killer is almost certainly Lady Etheridge's companion. You recall that she accompanied me the morning we rendezvoused in Hyde Park. The only name I know for her is Styles, and she worked for the family when Lady Etheridge was a girl. She had a brother worked there, too. They both went with Lady Etheridge when she married the first time and have been with her since, although I believe the brother lives and works now at the Etheridge estate in Hereford."

"Thank you. That gives us a better chance of catching them before they do another killing."

"There is one more thing you and Sir Peregrine should know. I do not want Lady Etheridge turned over to the authorities."

"We have no choice, madam. She is a confessed murderer."

"Of course we have a choice. We are not officers of the law. We are engaged in a private endeavor. If the authorities connect her with these crimes on their own, I suppose we cannot prevent them from taking her. But there is no reason we must put her in their hands."

"Her accomplices will do that when they are captured. We cannot protect her, even if some justification could be made for doing so."

"Mercy? Compassion? The scandal that will stain her family, her associates in any number of charities, and the government itself?"

"You think her crimes should go unpunished? Even Lady Etheridge acknowledges otherwise."

"She was punished, sir, before the crimes. And during the crimes, and after them. Can you not see that she is desperately ill? That she will be dead before much more time has passed? What sort of justice compels us to make her die at the end of a rope?"

"The law of the land. The preservation of order. It is not enough to secure justice. Justice must be *seen* to be done. In any case, it is not my decision."

"Oh, but it is. Sir Peregrine told me so. You are in charge of this mission, and while Phoenix can overrule you at any time, they rarely interfere."

Her strong convictions could not be misunderstood, but she spoke in the same ashen tones she had used since he told her the identity of Mrs. Haskins. Her face showed little expression. Earnest, excitable Lady Eve, who could argue a snake back into its tree, had dissolved into this snowy creature with dispassionate eyes.

"What do you expect me to do?" he said, impatience fraying his voice. "Let her walk away scot-free?"

"At one time, we pretended I was taking a cottage by the sea to recover from my injuries. I propose to do exactly that and keep Lady Etheridge there with me. She will have the best care I can provide, and I'll employ guards to make sure she can do no harm. It is the best solution, Colonel. Can you not let go your rigid, authoritarian, by-the-book self-righteousness long enough to accept it?"

He'd no answer for that, nor did she wait for one. With a sick feeling in the pit of his stomach, he watched her return without hurry to Lady Etheridge's bedchamber and close the door.

Chapter 28

Spain, April 1813

> *Deniz was killed last night. He's the Portuguese boy who took care of the mules and foraged for me and the horses. I usually can't take him where I go, so I haven't written much about him. No one will tell me what happened, not for sure, but in this place, you cannot turn your back without someone throwing a knife at it. He had just got himself a lady admirer, and I even caught him picking a bouquet of wildflowers to give her. He used to say he wanted to be like me, but I told him he could do much better. Now he can do nothing at all. Do you remember how I thought war to be glorious? A testing ground, where men proved themselves worthy of respect? I was a fool. War is where boys get killed, and if they are lucky, someone finds them and buries them. Where's the glory in that?*

> *Yrs., J*

The Black Phoenix mission was finished, Eve kept reminding herself as two days went by without a word from Sir Peregrine or Cordell. It seemed nothing could be decided until Styles and her brother were caught, although she couldn't think why. Perhaps she wasn't so sure about the brother, but Styles would say nothing against the woman she had served for nearly forty years.

Eve spent most of her time with Lady Etheridge, returning at night to the house where Phoenix continued to hide and protect her. She had become one of their causes, like the murder victims, and no longer played a part in their decisions and actions.

It was just as well. She had been sleepwalking through the hours, keeping silent company with her friend, holding at bay every emotion that battered at her defenses. To feel, she knew, would be to lose herself entirely.

I am all that I have, she had realized for the second time in her life. Twice she had dared to love, had found herself depending on another person, and both had been taken from her.

But to dwell on her misfortune, as she had done the first time, led to unbecoming bouts of self-pity. She had grown up now. Helped solve a terrible crime. Found within herself a little courage and a great store of determination. They would carry her past these terrible events, and when her mind and heart were clear of them, she would seek ways to be useful.

On this Thursday morning, she had come to remove most of her possessions from Marbury House. Her parents were due at any time, and she lacked the will to confront them. If they hadn't yet heard about her betrothal to Cordell, they soon would, and one way or another, there would be the devil to pay. A continuing betrothal or a broken one would make them equally furious.

She was sorting through her wardrobe, choosing

what to keep and what to box up for charity, when the steward knocked at the open bedchamber door. "I beg your pardon, milady. Colonel Cordell has arrived. Do you wish to speak with him?"

Her heart gave a thump of apprehension. If he had come to the wrong decision about Lady Etheridge, she didn't know what she would do. Threaten him with something? What? She ought to have made a plan.

Her hands went to the ties on her dusty smock, lingered, and fell away. She cared nothing for how she looked.

He was standing in the entrance hall, too near the gilded mirror where Lady Etheridge had seen a stranger instead of her own reflection. A smaller bandage had replaced the bulky one around his head, and the bruises on his face looked worse than her own. He wasn't wearing his uniform.

When he rose from his bow, she searched his eyes for answers. But as usual, he gave nothing away. She would learn only what he chose to tell her.

"Bertha Styles has been taken," he said, "but her brother was shot and killed while trying to escape. They are holding her at Shrewsbury, where she has confessed to five murders. Our news is by pigeon, so I have few details to give you. So far, she has not implicated Lady Etheridge."

"Nor will she. Loyalty is not solely the province of honorable men."

"So I was informed by the man I killed at Avebury," he said. "But in this case, I am glad of it. The crimes themselves were brutal enough without having them played out in the London news rags. And according to her physician, Lady Etheridge is unlikely to survive long enough to stand trial."

"He would not talk to me," Eve said. "What did he tell you?"

"She has a growth in her head," he said with obvious reluctance. "In her brain. Her symptoms are worsening at a rapid rate and will probably overtake her within a month. Two at the most."

Cordell's chest rose and fell as he took a long breath. "Look. It isn't going to be pretty. Mrs. Kipper has offered to supervise her care. You needn't put yourself through this ordeal. Starting very soon, she probably won't even know you are there."

"But I will be," Eve said. "And she will know it in her spirit, if not in her wounded brain."

"I knew it was futile, but I had to say it. Sir Peregrine has found a suitable property for rent near Sidmouth. It sits on a promontory overlooking the ocean and can be easily defended. You should be safe there. Indigo, Tom, Nate Bremer, and Mrs. Kipper have all asked to stay with you until this is done."

She swallowed past a lump in her throat, touched against her will by their kindness. "Not you?" she said after a moment.

"I'd be of little use in a fight," he said with a self-mocking smile. "My task—the last I'll perform for Black Phoenix—is to remain in London and let the gossips and critics have at me for breaking off our betrothal. You still want me to do that? Or would you rather handle the jilting yourself?"

"I no longer care who does it. But why must you put yourself in the line of fire? Leave the city. Leave the country. You mean to do that anyway."

"It's a long shot, but I'm hoping the scandal and my own expressed grievances will lure out your attacker. I shall be complaining about the legal knots you have tied so tightly around your property and fortune that I might as well marry a church mouse. And the mouse would be a lot less trouble to manage than Lady Nose-in-the-Air Eve Halliday."

She stared at him, astonished. "That will do nothing good for your reputation, sir."

"Nor yours. But you'll survive the reproach, and I'll soon be off to India. It seems to me we should both take any reasonable means, however harsh, to expose the man bent on doing you harm. However, it will be your decision. If you prefer, I shall say only that we ended the betrothal by mutual agreement, and that I was never good enough for you in the first place. That has the virtue, at least, of being true."

"Do that," she said. "Except for the last part, which is unnecessary. Will you not visit your home before leaving England?"

"There is no reason."

"But—"

"I do have a little personal business I'd hoped to complete," he said, firmly changing the subject. "Long overdue, to be sure, but it must be handled personally and with discretion. And as you know, I've not been in England for many years. The matter concerns an officer who once served with me. After his death, we discovered a packet of letters he had no opportunity to post, and I should like to see them delivered into the right hands. But I have just come from the post-house to which they were directed, and the new proprietor could not tell me the real identity of the recipient. The officer was apparently writing to someone whose name had to be kept secret. His own as well, because he signed only with an initial."

Eve's pulse had sped up at the mention of letters

going to a posthouse. By the end, she could hardly draw breath. Could it be? She had resolved, after much inner debate, to let her revenge against Cordell die unborn. What was the use of it? And even if her foolish plan of seduction and heartbreak had not been scuttled by her injuries, he would never have responded as she'd intended. Yet here he was, standing before her, unknowingly opening a door she had closed.

It was destiny, like the destiny that had brought them together on the mission. She could not turn away from it again.

"Can't you just send the letters to the officer's family?" she said, wondering why he hadn't done that years ago.

A slight flush on his cheekbones. "It hasn't seemed advisable. They weren't sealed, and I read them hoping for a clue to the recipient. The tone is rather unusual. Not intimate, precisely, but with a level of affection that implies a close relationship. They are written to a young man."

"Are you sure? I thought you said the recipient was unnamed."

"After a fashion. I'm thinking they met on the Penn, because the recipient seems also to have been a soldier. One who must have returned to England before late spring of 1813, when the letters were written. Next I mean to try at Horseguards. They might be able to pinpoint the man by rank and initial. The name given is Ensign H."

Retribution fell into her cupped hands like rain. Not a great punishment, no harm at all to Cordell. But it would give her a little satisfaction. And at least he would know what she thought of his character, and how she loathed him for what he had done.

"I know who that is," she said.

His brows flew up. "God in heaven. Then I'm glad I mentioned it, although I shouldn't have."

"Come," she said, turning toward the staircase. "There is something I want you to see."

Eve took him to her bedchamber, which was spread out with piles of clothing, and directed him to sit at her oversize writing table. He looked puzzled. And wary, as if he had picked up a warning from her mood.

She took the cedar box with its store of letters from the safe and laid it in front of Cordell. "As he promised when he went into the army, Johnnie Branden wrote me every day. You should read the letters, Colonel. Read them and ask yourself how such a man could betray his fellows and his country. The answer will be as clear to you as it has always been to me."

A muscle was jumping at the curve of his jaw. His breathing had picked up. His gaze locked onto her face. "This is why, from the beginning, you have hated me?"

"You were right all along, sir. I tried hard not to show it, but my contempt was too sharp to contain itself. Read! And then explain to me why you branded him a traitor."

She was shaking as she walked from the room, back straight, head high, unsure where she was going. Eventually she wound up in her father's study, where his stern face looked down on her from the portrait with disapproval. She sat at his desk, gazing into nothingness, cold to the bone.

* * *

Later, an hour or two, she didn't know, Eve left the study and made her way back up the stairs. It would take him a long time to read all those letters. He might not have read any of them. He might have waited until she was out of sight and left the house.

But he was still there at the writing table, holding an open letter, his face austere as he read. She stopped in the passageway, watching him carefully fold the letter, put it away, and remove another. He was marking the place in the cedar box with a quill pen.

She almost left him to it, but hadn't the strength to endure more waiting. It had to end now. This had to be the last time she saw him, spoke to him, spent time in his company.

He looked up when she entered the room, and as she drew closer, she couldn't help seeing that his eyes were suspiciously bright. She saw, too, the faint traces of salt on his cheeks where tears had dried.

She didn't care. Ice clogged her veins, slowed her heartbeat, crackled in her voice when she spoke. "Well, Colonel? Is that the officer who led twenty-six men into an ambush? Watched as they were slaughtered? And was slaughtered in turn, because he had been stupid enough to trust a band of rogues and deserters?"

He put down the letter he was holding and came slowly to his feet. "Reading the letters was like hearing his voice again. You must have been a child when he wrote them."

"Fourteen when the first arrived, just turned eighteen when I received the last. I spent those years living his adventures with him and trying to make myself into the woman he would want to marry when he returned. He did promise, on my tenth birthday, to wait for me to grow up. But when I got older, I understood he could not be held to it. I even came to think of you as my ally. You kept him so busy, gave him so much work to do, that he'd little time for courting."

"He was the most dedicated young officer I ever served with. How did you know him?"

"When my parents traveled for any length of time, they farmed me out to anyone who would take me. After the first visit, few were willing to accept me for another. But I was always permitted to stay at Sarne Abbey, which is large enough for the family to keep out of my way. Only Johnnie welcomed me there. He was lonely, too. The first time I came, he was eighteen and a self-appointed general. I was nine and promptly commissioned an ensign. We studied the history of warfare, played with his armies of tin soldiers, and refought every important battle from the past. He turned me from an indifferent rider into a good one. And I loved him."

"I understand why you resent me," Cordell said after a long silence. "Even why you hate me. I can tell you only this. I was the last man on the Peninsula to believe him capable of what he did. I welcomed the assignment to lead the investigation, certain that what I found would prove him guiltless. You may be sure I investigated the incident thoroughly, sought other explanations for what had occurred, traced every hint of a lead. And when I was called to testify, I spoke only the truth. All the evidence pointed to Captain Branden."

"Except the evidence of character. The evidence of devoted service." She calmed her voice. "Do they count for nothing? How could the young man you knew, the one who wrote those letters, do what he was accused of? What motive would he have?"

"I asked myself those questions a thousand times." His hands, usually controlled, clenched and unclenched. "Lady Eve, I don't know the answers. Men turn, especially under duress. Most especially in war. They endure hardship and deprivation, they are never valued at their worth, they watch their fellows die around them. They grow bitter and cynical."

There wasn't a grain of bitterness or cynicism in those letters, and he knew it. Sometimes sadness, sometimes discouragement, but Johnnie always rallied. He was an optimist to his heart's core. It was she who had turned bitter, who had cut down her optimism and planted cynicism in its place. Who had shriveled in her own darkness until Lady Etheridge pulled her into the light.

"You know very well," she said, "that Johnnie was never like that."

"I thought, at the end, it was the money that tempted him. He was always short of it. Couldn't buy the horses he needed, or replace worn equipment, or join the other officers at any recreation that required funds. I'm told he was disinherited. He ought to have advanced more quickly in the ranks, but he couldn't afford to buy the commissions when they came available. Lesser men rose to positions of authority over him."

"I know about the money. His brothers sent what they could, and even I saved enough to buy him a mount. But the real reason he did not purchase a higher rank when he might have done is that he didn't want to leave his regiment. He had to wait for an opening there, and to be the one with enough seniority to claim it."

"I wouldn't have thought him so foolish as that. Men seize opportunities wherever they arise."

"It is because he didn't want to leave *you*, Colonel. You were the model soldier. He admired you. He wanted to learn from you, and to be like you. Ironic, isn't it, that you are the one who turned. When most he needed your trust and your support, you turned against him."

"Not willingly. I had no choice. Was I to fabricate evidence to clear his name? Was I to lie during an official inquiry?"

"In the name of a greater truth, yes. Sometimes what appear to be facts are the greatest lies of all. If you are so poor a judge of character, sir, you ought not to be in command of men."

His jaw tightened. "That is, I think, more than enough. There is nothing I can say that will alter your mind, and nothing you can say will change what I have done." For a moment, he put the fingers of one hand on the cedar box, his gaze lowered. "We end now, Lady Eve, as we began. I bid you good day."

She had to step aside as he strode swiftly past her, not looking her direction as he went by.

Frozen in place, stunned by the abrupt close of what she had scarcely begun, she heard only the pounding of blood in her ears. He wouldn't even listen to her. Wouldn't hear her out. Yielded not a paper's thickness of his inflexible will. His *facts* were the only truth he understood, but what were they, after all, when measured against Johnnie's decency? His integrity?

She tore from the room and reached the top of the staircase just as Cordell was opening the front door.

"Do you know," she called to him, "that I tried to find a way to punish you? That I accepted the summons from Black Phoenix only because it was you I would be partnered with?"

It wasn't true, but what had truth to do with him? Let him find *facts* to disprove what she said.

He had removed his hand from the doorknob and turned, straight-backed and unblinking, to face her.

"I could not harm you physically," she said. "Nor financially. And I could not bring myself to assault your reputation, because our false betrothal would do that all by itself. It was part of the mission, and what I sought was personal retribution. I wanted to *hurt* you, and by my own hand."

Solid and unmovable as a sarsen stone, he gazed up at her.

She might have been a kitten spitting at him, for all he cared of her vengeance. But she couldn't stop her words any more than she could hold back a waterfall. "So I seduced you, Colonel Lord Cordell. I came to your bedchamber and pretended you were what I wanted. But my intention was to make you want me. I thought, being naive and overbuttered with flattery, that you would desire me, and from there would fall helplessly in love with me. Does that amuse you?"

"No," he said.

"You lie. Only silly females imagine a fall from grace is a tumble into love. Men laugh at them for it. But I didn't give up. If I couldn't properly reject you because you wouldn't even notice, I might parlay a few repeat engagements in your bed into making myself a habit you enjoyed. Then I could deprive you of me. But I fell off my horse, became a creature no man could desire, and all my nonsensical plans turned to ashes."

She thought he would patronize her. Assure her she was overset because of Lady Etheridge and her childhood playmate. If he were standing closer, he might pat her on the head.

But he said only, "Why are you telling me this?"

She didn't know. She didn't know.

Because she was bleeding and could not stanch the wounds.

Because she was the hysterical female of her own nightmares.

Because she had once feared she was falling in love with her enemy, and was certain that if she did, he would reject her.

"Just *go!*" She was shivering from cold and misery. *"Go!"*

He turned. His hand was on the doorknob again. He stood for a few moments, head bowed. Finally, he cast a look at her over his shoulder.

"If it matters," he said in a low voice she had to strain to hear, "you have succeeded. I did fall in love with you. How could I not?"

Her breath caught in her throat. Tears burned in her eyes. He had turned her knife back on her.

"You shouldn't have told me," she said. "You should have walked away. I would never have known, never have guessed."

"Isn't it what you wanted?"

"Yes. I said so. And I told you why. I meant to use love to hurt you. How could you give me the power to hurt you?"

"Because I love you," he said. And opened the door, and left her.

Chapter 29

Spain, May 1813

Thank you for the invitation to your ball! How I would like to see you lead out the first dance, or is that the way it works? I've never been to a come-out ball, let alone one at Devonshire House. You will be the loveliest creature in all London, I am sure. On that night, I will think of you and wish on a star that you find everything you want in the world laid out at your feet. Think of me, too, a little. I am still in the mountains, alone, awaiting my orders. And by the time you are waltzing, the most important task I have ever been assigned will be completed. Successfully, I hope! I don't expect to be there when it happens, though. That's how it is with exploring officers. With the advance into French territory, everything is more and more urgent now. Otherwise I'd have taken leave and come to London for your ball. I'd even have asked you to dance. But I haven't improved any. Perhaps you should be glad I am over the hills and far away!

Yr. admiring J

When Lord Etheridge, missing throughout his wife's illness, appeared at the house near Sidmouth to carry off her remains for burial, Eve left him to it and took her first long walk on the cliff above the ocean.

It was over, five all-consuming weeks that had seemed to last forever. She had rarely ventured from her friend's side, and would have slept in Lady Etheridge's bedchamber if Mrs. Kipper had permitted it.

At first Lady Etheridge was often herself, witty, a little imperious, determined to cram Eve's head with as much knowledge as would fit in there about politicians and how to manipulate them. Then the headaches became more frequent and debilitating. Her mind wandered into the past, until, like the matron of Stanton St. Bernard's, she recalled only events that had occurred many years before. Eve learned about her early life, about her first marriage and her son, about Bertha Styles, the servant who became her friend and eventually her accomplice in murder.

Nausea stripped half the weight from Lady Etheridge, and Eve lost weight as well. She couldn't make herself force down more than a few bites of anything, and now the simple dresses she'd brought with her hung loose as curtains on her body.

The last fortnight was the worst. The seizures grew more violent. Lady Etheridge became incoherent, except when a few words or a phrase fixed in her mind. Then she would repeat it over and over again, like the beat of a drum. "Don't do it. Don't do it. Don't do it." For nearly all of one day and night, she kept saying, "I am sorry. I am sorry."

The last time she spoke words that could be understood, Eve was leaning over the bed, applying damp cloths to her forehead. Suddenly her hand, usually limp and weak, clutched at Eve's shoulder. The dark, fevered eyes looked at her intently. "I will fly!" she said clearly. "I will fly!"

"Yes," Eve had replied. "You will fly."

And she believed it even now, as the wagon carrying Lady Etheridge's coffin bore her down the winding road and toward her grave.

The road stretching out before Eve was long and winding as well, but without a destination. She had come onto the cliffs to breathe clean air, and feel the sun, and make a plan for the weeks and months directly ahead. For however long a time remained until her killer put an end to her. She could not hide forever.

She could not hide for another day without going mad with it.

The wind off the ocean whipped at her skirts and her hair, loose and unwashed for longer than she could remember. Sunlight glinted on the water like diamonds set afire, blinding her.

There was no reason to be here after all. She already knew what she was going to do.

"My dear girl!" Sir Peregrine bustled into the room with a flurry of skirts. "What have you done with the rest of you?"

He was Mrs. Marsh again, in sad need of a shave. "Thank you for coming," Eve said. "And as you see by this table spread out for our tea, Mrs. Kipper is determined to fatten me up like a Christmas pig. I am sure to recover my appetite soon. Have a bun."

He broke off a piece and popped it in his mouth while his sharp gaze scrutinized her. "I'll not ask you how it was," he said after a time. "I can see for myself."

"I would do it again," she told him matter-of-factly. "Sir, I asked you to call because, first, I wished to thank you for the kindness and protection you have given me these last several weeks. Without your help, I would almost certainly be dead. But now, with the mission done, I must see about fending for myself."

"You cannot remain here indefinitely, it is true. Neither will we relinquish our obligations on your behalf. As it happens, Phoenix has been considering what should come next, and—"

"So have I," she said. "Don't think I intend to be careless. I'll not station myself on a corner at Piccadilly and wait to be cut down. But neither will I close myself off from life. I have decided, sir, to go abroad."

A wide smile stretched across his face. "Our very thought! Have you somewhere in mind?"

"To reside? No. I mean to visit Italy, and Switzerland, and every other place that catches my fancy. It is no hardship. I have always longed to travel, I can well afford to do so, and I know from my charity work several widowed ladies who have been many times to the Continent. I expect one of them will agree to come along as my companion." She frowned as a new thought entered her mind. "I suppose I'd have to tell her, though, about the dangers of being in my company."

"You must not consider doing without bodyguards, Lady Eve."

"I won't. Perhaps you will help me recruit a suitable array of servants."

"Then it's settled," he said. "I will get to work straightaway. When do you want to leave?"

"As soon as possible. If I may, I'll remain here until departure. Are my parents still in London?"

"No, indeed. They endured the scandal storm for no more than a week before fleeing back across the channel. You haven't asked about the end of your betrothal, my dear. Aren't you at all curious?"

A sharp pang, and Cordell's name had not even been spoken. "Not really. I feel something of a coward not to have been here to face it, but that couldn't be helped."

"It wasn't so bad. Your parents caught the worst of it. Their arrival coincided almost exactly with the news getting out, and everyone assumed Marbury had threatened or bribed Cordell to drop you back into the marriage pool and leave the country. Shortly after, the Season dwindled to its end and people straggled to Brighton or to their estates. Barely a nine-days' wonder, in fact."

"Did he?" she said, wishing she had the restraint not to ask. "Leave the country? I believe he planned to go out to India."

"That is his intention. But he's got only so far as Paris, at Wellington's request. Like you, the duke has—*had*—a friend, Madame de Staël, in the throes of her last illness. He asked Cordell to handle a few ambassadorial duties while he spent time at her bedside. But the need, alas, has ended. Wellington is due home shortly, and I imagine Cordell will head the other direction."

She had thought him far from reach, freeing her from an obligation that had sunk its claws into her when last they were together. But with him so near,

she had no excuse not to go to him. Perhaps if she
did, the heavy weight inside her chest would finally
dissolve and let her eat again. Sleep again. Breathe
again.

"I should like to see him," she said. "Is it possible
for me to arrive in Paris before he leaves?"

"He may already be gone. But if you set out immediately, you might catch him." Sir Peregrine was smiling again, and she could almost hear the wheels
turning in his head. "In fact, I've a hankering to visit
Paris myself. Will you mind if I tag along? We'll bring
Mrs. Kipper and Indigo and the others and make a
party of it. How's that?"

That was his way of taking the arrangements from
her hands and providing an escort. More than likely
he fancied himself a matchmaker as well, charged to
reunite a lovelorn lass with her handsome colonel.
Why else would she be seeking him out?

In fact, she dreaded the moment they would come
face-to-face. But if heaven granted her the chance, she
would offer Cordell the apology she desperately owed.
Make amends, if possible, for what she had said and
done to him. Only then would she be able to let go
of what she had already lost.

As so often happened of late, she felt an instant
and powerful need to cry. But of course, she did not.

The windows of the crowded reception rooms at
Tuileries, stifling in heat of a late July evening, had
been flung open to catch any breeze that might float
in from the Seine. Few did.

Cordell, in full medaled dress uniform, had found a
spot near the French window leading onto a terrace
and the gardens. His sole duty, so far as he could tell,

was to assert the British presence without being pushy about it. The occupation was not popular.

From where he stood, his back to a marble statue of Ares, he had a clear view of the main room and the large chair where the even larger King Louis sat, welcoming his guests. His gout-swollen legs rested on a stool, and the crutches without which he could not walk were propped against the wall behind him.

Cordell had made his bow, spoken briefly to those who would expect to be greeted, and considered his work done for the evening. When Wellington took his leave, he would be free to go as well. Meantime, he spoke to the people who stopped by with a piece of gossip or a political opinion to air, and only once had he withdrawn behind the statue to avoid unpleasantness. That was when Lord and Lady Marbury entered the smaller room where he was lurking, saw no one worthy of their attention, and wandered out again.

There had been a contentious scene at Carleton House a month earlier, when Marbury had learned of his daughter's betrothal and, an hour later, discovered the betrothal had been broken off. Given the awkwardness of the situation, Cordell had been inclined to let the earl rant at him, which he had done with gusto until his wife towed him away.

It was nearing midnight, and Cordell was thinking up an excuse to leave when he saw, coming his direction from the main room, a popinjay wearing lavender brocade and dripping with lace. Sir Peregrine Jones. He would have news of Lady Etheridge. And of Lady Eve, no doubt, but Cordell didn't want to hear it.

He hadn't noticed, until Sir Peregrine wove his way through the milling crowd and got clear of it near the door, that he was not alone.

The first sight of Lady Eve struck unexpectedly and hard, made worse because she was too thin, too pale, too uncertain. Wherever he went, whatever became of him, he'd wanted always to imagine her confident and happy. Not like this.

Not like this.

Sir Peregrine touched her arm, pointed to Cordell, and gave him a wave before vanishing into the crowd like a deserter.

For a few moments she stood alone in the doorway, her pale green gown threaded with gold, her hair caught up and let to fall in soft curls. She looked too fragile for this world. Finally she crossed with slow grace to where he was standing.

He put his hands behind his back so that she wouldn't know they were shaking. "Lady Eve," he said. "I had not expected to see you here. Are you traveling with your parents?"

"Oh, God." She looked around. "They're in Paris again?"

"They are here tonight. Lady Etheridge, I take it, is—"

"Yes. A few days ago. And Styles as well. Just before we left Dover, Sir Peregrine got word that she had hanged herself in prison." Her eyes kept searching his face. "I wanted to thank you for sending over the letters, sir. While I was with Lady Etheridge, I could not bring myself to read them. But after she was gone, they were a great comfort to me."

"They were yours," he said stupidly. His mind had stopped working in an orderly fashion. It kept hopping between questions he couldn't bring himself to ask and things about her he'd suddenly observed, such as the lack of bruises on her face. For most of the time

he'd spent with her, she had been a patchwork quilt
of colors. Now she'd no color at all on her face.

"Black Phoenix decided I should go abroad for a
time," she said after another troubled silence. "Sir
Peregrine brought me as far as Paris. He says Phoenix
will not stop until it uncovers the identity of my attacker, and that I can be of most use by keeping out
of their way."

"It is what you wanted. Travel."

"Yes." A flash of the mischievous smile that never
failed to enchant him. "For a change, I want to do
what I am supposed to do."

He had run out of words. Out of strength in his
knees. She had come to tell him something, he was
sure. His instincts were screaming as much in his ears.
Could she be . . . ? Surely not. He had been more
than careful. And had she not been punished enough?
It was too much to ask of her that she bear the child
of a man she hated.

"Eve!" The Earl of Marbury's voice cut across the
room like a whip. "Come to me this instant!"

He was standing at the door, the countess a little
behind him. "You!" He glared at Cordell. "Get out.
This is a family matter."

Cordell had already backed away, his presence certain to create more trouble than it prevented. But he
went only a short distance, to the side of the statue,
his gaze pinned on the choleric earl.

Lady Eve hadn't moved. Hadn't even turned to face
her parents. Cordell had thought her pale before, but
now every trace of color had drained from her face.
All the light in her eyes had been extinguished. She
was shivering.

Marbury stalked up to her, a head taller, every inch

of him frigid with disapproval. He took hold of Lady Eve's shoulder and spun her to face him. At his side, Lady Marbury regarded her daughter the way she might a spider that had crawled onto her tea table.

"You were not granted permission to come here," Marbury said. "How dare you arrive without invitation or notice, bringing with you the scandal that has all but driven us into exile?"

She didn't respond. Like a creature paralyzed, she looked helplessly up at her tormentor.

"Were you meaning to carry on your affair with this scoundrel here, at Tuileries Palace, in the presence of the great men of Europe?" The earl was at full gallop now. "You should be in sackcloth, exiled where females of low character can bring no further shame to their families."

The tight hold Cordell had twisted around his temper unraveled. He stepped into the confrontation, one hand on the hilt of his sword, the other gently moving Lady Eve to the side. Planting himself in front of her father, he looked directly into the disdainful blue eyes. "You have said quite enough, Marbury. Render your apologies to the lady and take yourself elsewhere."

"Who the devil do you think you are, talking to me like that? I may have a fool for a daughter, but you'll not find me so easy to meddle with. Seducing her has not secured you her fortune, Colonel. Her disgrace is her own. There will be no marriage."

"That is correct. Neither will you be permitted to speak again in such a manner to Lady Eve."

"I am her father. I can speak to her however I will. You think you can prevent me?"

"I am certain of it. In your life, Lord Marbury, you have accomplished one thing of value. You have provided to the world a remarkable young woman, brave and accomplished and wise. On that account, I refrain from calling you out."

"Ha!" The earl, a fit man about ten years Cordell's senior, looked as if a puppy had snapped at him. "You forget yourself, sir. The offense is to *my* honor. I would not demean myself by answering the challenge of a Norfolk ditchdigger."

"*Lord* Ditchdigger to you, sir. But these theatrics are growing tiresome. If ever again I hear you insult Lady Eve, if anyone reports a rumor of such an insult, if I wake up one morning and imagine you *might* have insulted her, I will hunt you down and beat you senseless. I hope that is perfectly clear."

He turned to Lady Marbury, who was quivering with outrage, gave her a curt bow, and took himself in the direction of the terrace before he could do something he probably wouldn't regret. He didn't look again at Lady Eve.

He must never again look on her. Whenever he did so, he felt sick with longing and hopelessness. He ought not have listened to Wellington. He could have been on his way to India by now, safe at sea, alone with his dark thoughts.

He was standing in the torchlit garden, his back to the palace, when a sense of her presence overwhelmed him. He turned to see her standing a little distance away, hands clasped loosely in front of her, her expression infinitely sad.

"I don't know," she said quietly, "why it is they still turn me to custard. Why I cannot stand up to them, or put my back to them and walk away."

"Nor do I. You have never lacked courage." The anger he still felt showed in his voice. Inside his white

gloves, sweat gathered at his palms. "You are dis-
obeying them now."

"Because nothing is more important to me than this.
I must finish, if you will permit me, what I have come
here to say."

Heart pounding with dread, he nodded.

Her gaze lifted to his. "I have done you a great
wrong, sir. I have not, until now, learned my own lesson, the one I thought to teach you with my petty
vengeance. We will never agree about Johnnie Branden and the judgment you passed on him, but people
of honor and goodwill can find themselves at odds.
My judgment of you was even more unfair than the
verdict you rendered on him. And I had far less evidence on which to build my hatred, which had sought
a target and fixed on you."

It wasn't what he had expected. His first reaction—
no child, thank God—sent relief flooding through him.
He scarcely heard the rest, except that he recognized
an apology she did not owe. He had condemned himself a thousand times for failing to uncover evidence
that would exonerate a young man he had come to
care for. He had worked tirelessly with the Duke of
Sarne to clear his brother's name. But there was nothing to be found. The difference was, he had resigned
himself to Branden's treason, and Sarne would never
give up trying to disprove it.

"Can you not forgive me?" she said, her voice and
her eyes pleading with him.

"There is no blame," he said. "If you need forgiveness, then you have it. But none is due. I can only
hope to one day merit a friend like you, one who will
find for me the passion and trust and generosity you
have given to the people you love."

Tears, until this moment welling in her eyes, overflowed them. "It is not true," she said. "I am not a good friend. Not to anyone. I am selfish and willful and greedy. It is true, I promise, that I am sorry for hurting you. But I am even more sorry for myself, because I have caused you to stop loving me."

"No." He laid his hands softly on her shoulders. "You have not done that. You *could* not."

"T-truly?" She lifted her face, shining with tears. Leaned into him, asking now for more than forgiveness.

He took her into his arms, not believing in this miracle, knowing it could not endure but clinging to it while he could. He lowered his head, brushed her weeping eyes with his lips, and when her lips sought his, he kissed her. Kissed her deeply, with all the fire of the love that had burned inside him for so long.

She was there for him, generous as he knew her to be, greedy as she said she was. Soon his cheeks, too, were wet, and not all the tears were hers.

Their solitude could not last. People were strolling in the gardens. The sound of voices grew more insistent.

Finally, with a little gurgle of laughter, Lady Eve put a fraction of an inch between them. "It appears, sir, that we have compromised ourselves once again."

He saw, through the expansive windows opening onto the terrace, half a hundred heads turning their direction. "Never mind. This is France. The French don't care what we do."

"But they're interested. I don't mind. And this time we will do the proper thing. Only my parents will find fault with our behavior."

"What proper thing? You don't mean another betrothal?"

"I'd rather bypass that stage." Another laugh. "You see how confident you have made me? One kiss, a very long one, to be sure, and I am now ready to conquer the world. Surely you don't mean to decline my offer of marriage, sir."

"You haven't made one."

When she started to protest, he set her at arms' distance. "Don't. I love you, and I will be yours to want, or not want, as it suits you. But nothing else has changed. Not my rank, my status, my lack of fortune, or my inability to provide you the life you have been preparing for yourself. Love will not suffice, Eve. For all the other reasons, we cannot marry."

"Pah!" She stood defiant before him, shoulders back, chin lifted. "There is no *other*. There is only you, and there is me, and there is love. Oh, yes, and your pride. Fortunately, I haven't any. Not where you are concerned."

She seized his right hand between her own hands, lowered herself to one knee, and gazed up at him from shining eyes. "I am proposing to you, sir. No. I am *begging* you to marry me. I will be a difficult wife, but you'll get used to me. And I may improve with age. Will you have me? Please?"

She had been wrong, he knew. *He* was the selfish one, the greedy one.

And he had been wrong. Love would suffice. She would teach him how to do it.

He dropped onto his knee, his hand still a prisoner of her hands, and said, "Will you be so foolish, Lady Eve Halliday, as to become my wife? I will be a diffi-

cult husband, but you can train me. I am older than
you and unlikely to improve, but I will love and protect you for so long as God grants me life and
strength."

They didn't, either of them, give a reply or need
one. In silence, promises were made with their eyes.

Then they rose, the applause of onlookers like
waves crashing on a distant shore, and set out hand
in hand to the river and the start of their journey
together.

Epilogue

On a cool October morning, Cordell and Eve guided their horses off a narrow road in the northern mountains of Spain and onto a path that required them to ride single file.

They had been married three months, and Cordell was fulfilling the promise he had made to her on their wedding night. When asked what gift she would like from him, she had said, "Take me to the Peninsula. I want to go on campaign with you. I want see where you lived and fought for all those years, and hear the stories from you, and ask the questions I have been storing up since I was fourteen. And when we are done, take me to Johnnie."

She had wanted to see the world, starting with Cordell's world, so he showed her the war though his eyes. The sun-baked country was hot and dry in late summer, but she hadn't minded. They cooled off in slow-moving rivers and ate bread, cheese, and fruit from local markets. He introduced her to a simple Portuguese priest, a dignified Spanish doctor, a knight of Malta, and scores of shepherds, farmers, soldiers, and spies.

She'd have been happy to spend more time in every place they visited, but as autumn began to whisper of winter, they had to reach their last destination before the snows cut it off. These were the mountains Johnnie had explored and mapped, watching out for the French, seeking a route both secret and traversable by a detachment transporting a heavy cargo of gold. They were on the first stage of that route, and a few hours of hard travel later, they arrived at the pass where the ambush had occurred.

She had expected ghosts to be hovering there, to hear sadness in the sounds of the wind. But the sun shone on the bleak, rocky landscape, the sky was blue overhead, and the stillness when they stopped near where Johnnie had been found dead was peaceful. Serene.

Cordell reached for her hand and held it for a few silent minutes. Then they dismounted, tethered their horses, and climbed a path that wound up one of the jagged, boulder-strewn hills.

As they came around to the eastern side, she saw a small patch of dry field grasses sheltered by two olive trees. On the grass, a mound of water-smoothed round stones was topped with two bars of iron bound together to form a cross.

She hadn't known, until Cordell told her during their climb, that he had carried Johnnie to this spot and dug the grave himself. Done it at night, in secret, so that the treatment accorded the body of a traitor would not be visited on him. It was Sarne, when Cordell brought him here, who planted the olive trees.

"From the time I was a child," she said, "my parents, who were desperate for an heir, told me to pray every day for a brother. And I did. But the prayer was never granted, not the way they wanted. And it wasn't until now that I realized it had been granted, after all, for me. Johnnie was the brother I had asked for. I could not have had a better one. I must try to make him proud of me."

Cordell wrapped an arm around her waist. "He would be glad to know, I think, that you are happy."

"Oh, yes." She looked up at his face, so strong and so dear to her. "When we were brought together for the Black Phoenix mission, I was sure Johnnie had something to do with it. He had chosen me to be the instrument of his revenge. As if Johnnie would even think of such a terrible thing. The hatred, the wickedness, were in my own head."

"Not for long," he said. "You should put all of that away now."

"I will. I am. It is one reason I asked you to bring me to him. I wished to say good-bye. But I'll not do that. The people we love do not vanish just because they have died. I can keep them with me. And perhaps their spirits have power to affect the living. At the least, I expect they pray for us and visit us in our thoughts. But you don't believe any of that, do you?"

"I am a dedicated skeptic," he said, "as you know. But in this one matter, I am not so sure of my convictions. It was, indeed, a strange coincidence that we met. I won't go so far as to charge Johnnie Branden with putting us together, but if he had anything to do with it, he gave me the greatest gift any man on the earth could receive."

She smiled. "I'm happy with my present, too. And I believe, with all my heart, that Johnnie is happy for us both."

It was time to go. From the oilcloth pouch at her waist she took a folded paper stamped with Cordell's seal on the wax. "One last letter, Johnnie," she said. Leaving down, she slipped it under the round gravestones. "With love from your Ensign."

The invitations have gone out,
offering a select few the chance to
live in Paradise...

Dangerous Deceptions
by Lynn Kerstan

0-451-21248-7

One invitation is accepted by Jarrett, Lord Dering,
a family outcast who lives by his own rules.
Another invitation is accepted by Kate Falshaw, a
hot-tempered actress on the run
from a scandalous past.

The exclusive resort they travel to promises to fulfill
every desire, but beneath the glittering facade,
deadly games are in play.

Available wherever books are sold or at
penguin.com

Lynn Kerstan

Love, intrigue, and
unforgettable adventure...

The Golden Leopard
0-451-41057-2

Heart of the Tiger
0-451-41085-8

The Silver Lion
0-451-41116-1

"EXQUISITELY WRITTEN...STUNNING SENSUALITY."
—LIBRARY JOURNAL

"LYNN KERSTAN REIGNS SUPREME."
—LITERARY TIMES

Available wherever books are sold or at
penguin.com

*The Greek goddesses have seduced
readers—and lovers—for centuries.*

*Now Signet Eclipse introduces a new series—
tales of love and seduction filled with
passions of mythic proportions.*

NOW AVAILABLE:
LOVE UNDERGROUND: PERSEPHONE'S TALE

COMING OCTOBER 2005:
FATAL ATTRACTION: APHRODITE'S TALE

COMING JANUARY 2006:
ALL'S FAIR IN LOVE AND WAR: ATHENA'S TALE

SIGNET ECLIPSE

Available wherever books are sold at penguin.com

"Wickedly, wonderfully sensual and gloriously romantic."
—Mary Balogh

"A delicious...sensual delight."
—Teresa Medeiros

"One of romance's brightest and most dazzling stars."
—*Affaire de Coeur*

New York Times Bestselling Author

Jo Beverley

SKYLARK	0-451-21183-9
WINTER FIRE	0-451-21065-4
SECRETS OF THE NIGHT	0-451-21158-8
DARK CHAMPION	0-451-20766-1
ST. RAVEN	0-451-20807-2
LORD OF MY HEART	0-451-20642-8
MY LADY NOTORIOUS	0-451-20644-4
HAZARD	0-451-20580-4
THE DEVIL'S HEIRESS	0-451-20254-6
THE DRAGON'S BRIDE	0-451-20358-5
DEVILISH	0-451-19997-9
SOMETHING WICKED	0-451-21378-5
LORD OF MIDNIGHT	0-451-40801-2
FORBIDDEN MAGIC	0-451-40802-0

Available wherever books are sold or at penguin.com

All your favorite romance writers are coming together.

SIGNET ECLIPSE

penguin.com